"I loved how *The Dog of Saint Petersburg* was written. Throughout this novel, the atmosphere of San Francisco was vividly and perfectly captured. The story flowed, not choppy or confusing. The plot was engaging and sets itself apart from other crime thrillers. Most times, you know who is who, but just when you were sure who the bad guys were, the next chapter proves you wrong. The action is lively, heart-pumping, and realistic, and picked up in the middle of the book."

—   OTrain M, Online Book Club

"Mystery lovers should enjoy *The Dog of Saint Petersburg* as the story moves along at an enjoyable pace. The descriptions pull you in and the dialogue is crisp and gets to the point. If the author writes more, I'd be interested."

—   F. J. Zukeb, Author

"I myself am not into the theatre scene, so I found this interesting and fascinating. Real, historical events, combined with international espionage, some stimulating twists and some faced-paced action made this a thriller I wanted to read until the end."

—   Fiona Perry, Marketing and PR

THE
Dog
OF
Saint Petersburg

KELLY LIBATIQUE

The Dog of Saint Petersburg

ISBN: 978-1-7375552-0-9

www.KLVoice.com

"Theatre is a sacred space for actors.
You are responsible;
you are in the driving-seat."

– Greta Scacchi

1 : Bad Day to Be a Hero

She shifted nervously as she felt the change. It had been more colorful just a short time ago, fuller of sound and life, even at night. But now it was different. It was darker and void of even some of the usual objects that had strewn the sidewalk, as if an unseen force had swept things aside. Even the moon, which normally cast a hard-white light in odd-shaped splotches along the sidewalk and large brick wall, was now a bit more obscured. A tension in the air produced a growing heaviness, like a quiet perhaps too quiet before *something* happens.

A faint trickle of water could be heard, and stabbing visually through the darkness, she could barely see the murky rectangular shape of a gutter opening along the crumbling face of the sidewalk. A light breeze sounded but could not felt. Small objects, like that of leaves and paper trash could be heard rustling on the ground.

Her eyes travelled up the brick wall to an old, rusted lamp that hung precariously from the end of a crooked wood-brown pipe, like an aged finger. The lampshade, a beat-up and weathered relic, still covered the dark yellow bulb that struggled to light a small section of sidewalk below. The weary but resilient filament inside the thick glass blared and sputtered defiantly from within the round, airless encasing. The illumination cast a dull triangular shape against the wall, the edges still sharp and straight, defining where light and shadow met.

The light revealed bricks that, perhaps at one point had been red and proud, but were now timeworn and cracked. Some original color remained, but only where the surface had dislodged and fell to the ground. So defined were the cracks, an agile individual with strong fingers could ascend the structure, if the blocks didn't surrender to the weight. The old mortar between the bricks still oozed out, but frozen in time, exactly as it had been left decades ago.

She heard the breeze again and felt the mounting apprehension.

And then from the stillness there was movement. From behind the wall a head slowly inched out. The silhouette hid details, but one could see cautious movements. It was unclear what sort of person it was, or what intentions the face communicated.

A hand snaked around the edge and slowly gripped the old bricks, one finger at a time. The individual appeared male, mid to late twenties and wearing a brown leather jacket. More of the upper body came into view as he eased out into the dim light. He had dark brown hair, an average but handsome face, and large eyes, alert and determined.

A sudden noise from down the shadows of the alleyway startled her and the figure whirled back behind the wall. Both heavy and light shoes thudded and tapped on the ground and voices could be heard. Whoever they were strode casually, their volume steadily increasing.

The talking was between two men. One was a little older, his voice possessing a deep roughness of a man in maybe his early forties.

"Over here," the voice was saying.

"He'd better hurry up," a younger voice said nervously but with a pretense of confidence. "I'm not waiting all night."

She could see three figures in the light now—two men and a woman. Right away it was obvious the woman was out of place. Her body was stiff and her motions irregular, her head down.

From somewhere a cat screamed causing everyone to freeze. A second cat shrieked followed by the sound of a metal garbage can lid bouncing and rattling loudly to a stop. The group remained motionless for a few moments listening, then continued.

"*That* scared the crap out of me," the younger man said in a harsh whisper.

The older man laughed.

The men moved the woman forward with jerking motions, one of them holding her arm near the shoulder, giving her tugs as they moved. She cooperated, but with defiant resistance. Although frightened and roughed up, she was attractive in professional attire with a skirt that fell modestly below her knees. Her hands were empty, no purse or bag. She looked as if she'd been snatched out of an office in the financial district far across town earlier that day.

The men, on the other hand, in black biker style leather jackets, faded jeans, and thick motorcycle riding boots, were right at home. The older man was bald, stocky with broad shoulders, and surrounding his mouth was a thick growth of hair. He strutted arrogantly, one hand securing the woman, the other loosely swinging at his side. His coarse and average face bore a permanent smirk.

The younger man was taller and much thinner. His jet-black hair combed back '50s style almost shimmered in the dim light. His hands were dug into jacket pockets, and he glanced about as he moved. In contrast to his young and handsome face, several red scars ran across his cheeks and forehead, presumably from fights. Although dressed for the part and making every effort to look tough, he appeared out of place.

As they neared the end of the wall, the bald man abruptly stopped. He continued to hold the woman as he peered around listening. The younger man hesitated and shuffled nervously.

"Alright, we wait here," the bald man said after a few moments. He backed the woman roughly up against the wall directly under the old lamp in the center of the triangular light.

Don't you hit her, you big brute, she thought.

The woman hit the bricks with a dull thud. He paused for a moment and glared at her, his chin slightly down and eyebrows raised in way to warn her against doing anything stupid. She watched him as he took the moment to let his eyes run up and down her body. She looked as if she were going to fight back, but then dropped her head. Her fingers came together and began wringing, her bright red nail polish visible even in the dim light. Caramel brown hair fell over her face. She scraped her feet on the concrete and whimpered faintly.

"Shut up," the man said.

The younger man turned and glanced at the woman. He shook his head and began scanning up and down the street.

The bald man pulled a package of cigarettes from his pocket and shook one out with two loud taps. Turning to the woman, he extended an arm. "Want one?" he asked mockingly.

Still looking down, she shook her head, her hair jiggling.

He laughed and stuck the cigarette in his mouth. In two quick, well-practiced set of motions, a shiny Zippo lighter was snapped open and lit. The silver casing gleamed in the light. As quickly as it came out, it was shut and back in his pocket.

He blew a big cloud of smoke up at the old light, the bluish gray whisps defining the shadows. He glanced at the younger man. "Relax, okay?"

"You relax." The younger man jammed his hands deeper into his pockets.

You don't want to be doing this, she thought at the tall, young man. *Do the right thing and help that woman.*

"What time you got?" the bigger man asked.

"About eleven thirty," the younger man said, pulling on the leather of his right sleeve, squinting closely at his wrist.

"Anytime now," he said, taking another pull on the cigarette. He glanced back at the woman and fell into a stare. She slowly looked up and met his eyes. The two faced off again for a few seconds. Reaching out, he began to move her hair aside and put his hand on her face. Her arm snapped up and bounced his wrist out of the way. He laughed, drew hard on his cigarette and blew smoke in her direction, making her cough and turn away.

"Knock it off," the tall man said, now beginning to pace. "I told you to relax."

"Just leave her alone," the younger man said as he took a few uneasy steps away. He breathed deeply and rocked slightly on his feet.

The bald man smirked. "Whatever."

A sudden noise came from down the alley making everyone turn and look. The three figures froze. The sound bounced, skipped, and tapped several times.

It was then that the silhouetted head reemerged from behind the wall, opposite to where the two men were looking.

Ah yes, a diversion! she thought.

This time the figure moved fast and within moments, had stepped out and was facing the three as they peered into the blackness of the alley. He hunched down and began moving stealthily toward the two men. But as he approached, the woman suddenly turned and saw him and in reflex, drew a quick breath in and clamped a hand over her mouth. The two men glanced at her, then spun around.

"Well, well," said the bald man, the muscles in his face forming a wide, menacing grin. The woman stiffened up and clung to the wall. "Don't you move!" he yelled at her. He tossed the cigarette to the side.

The younger man edged backward in a semi-circle to get behind the woman, his eyes riveted on the stranger with the brown jacket.

With the same quickness he had produced the lighter, the bald man whipped out a narrow black object. With show and drama, he held it for a moment, wiggling it slightly, then pressed an unseen button. With a loud snap, a knife blade appeared. Rotating his wrist, he turned the blade back and forth, letting the reflecting light dance up and down the steel.

"Eric!" the woman yelled. She leaned forward and tried to step away from the wall, but the tall man, now behind her, grabbed her arms securely and yanked her close.

The bald man grinned even more. "Eric, is it?"

Help her, Eric! she thought. *You can do it!*

No one moved.

"Well, *Eric,*" the knife-wielding man said. "Bad day to be a hero." Large beads of sweat began to form on his forehead.

With two quick steps he lunged at Eric, swiping the knife in a horizontal arc. The move would have gutted Eric clean open had he not quickly and smoothly leaped backward out of reach.

The bald man grunted angrily while taking another step forward and slashing again in the opposite direction. Eric dodged again, proving to be faster.

The bald man continued to smile but less now, a growing anger filling his eyes. He paused as if unsure of his next move, then took a step forward, slower this time.

Eric remained where he was, his feet spread a little wider than his shoulders, his knees bent, his torso slightly angled, and his hands open and ready—a perfect fighting stance.

The bald man lunged again, this time going for a stab to the chest. With lightening-quick reflexes, Eric turned and parried by planting a palm to the man's forearm, sending the large hand past him. He then caught the man's wrist, and with one sharp motion, twisted it up over his head and around to the other side. Now bent backward and off balance, the attacker yelped and twirled his arm trying to balance. But Eric continued the motion by grabbing the man's jacket collar and yanking downward. The assailant fell with a hard thud, first his back, followed by a hairless head which smacked the ground and bounced the way a bowling ball might. Groaning and cupping the back of his head, he rolled to his side.

Eric retrieved the knife, then looked up at the woman and the tall, slender man that held her, his eyes now wide and frightened.

With an angry roar, the big man suddenly twisted up to his knees and scrambled away, his face red from pain and fury. "I'll kill you!" he snarled.

Eric hunched down again, the knife now extending from his right hand.

The bald man glanced at the younger man. "You gonna help me or *what?*"

The younger man pulled the woman in tighter, his eyes darting.

She watched the woman's wide, frightened eyes and pleaded silently for her.

Looking down, the bald man spotted something on the ground, then quickly strode to the curb and picked up a piece of wood—a two by four, maybe three feet in length. Inching forward, he waved the board to one side half-whispering, "Come on. Come on, man."

Eric held back and waited.

The big man moved forward and swung hard, like a major league baseball player.

Eric easily ducked. The momentum of the swing kept the man turning, leaving his right side open and exposed. Eric took advantage, stepping up, and in one quick motion, put a hand on the big man's shoulder and yanking in a downward motion while bringing a right knee up and planting it hard into a wide ribcage.

The bald man yelled in pain and grabbed his side. Stepping in closer, Eric swung himself around and put his hips under the bigger man's. He then pulled the man's weight over him while straightening up, executing a flawless judo hip throw. The big man rolled over Eric's back and landed with a smash. This time, he didn't move.

Good! Stay there, she thought.

Breathing hard, Eric turned and looked at the tall, slender man who still held the woman. All at once and with panic in his eyes, he shoved the woman at Eric, fumbled frantically into a pocket, and with a snap, produced his own knife. The woman stumbled then scrambled along the wall until she was behind Eric.

Eric stood a little straighter and faced the tall, dark-haired man. He slowly lowered his arms, shook his head, and extended his palms outward in a gesture that asked, *do you really want to do this?*

The tall young man remained in a fight stance but shifted nervously, rubbing his nose and wiping his mouth. The black pupils in his eyes flitted back and forth. He suddenly yelled and lunged at Eric, but it was more of a leap to the side, and Eric easily stepped out of the knife's way. Now past Eric, the young man slashed threateningly once more in the air, but much too far away to inflict any damage, then turned and fled. As the sound of thumping boots faded away, Eric walked to middle of the street and watched him disappear. He then turned to the woman.

"Eric," she said again, running to him and flinging her arms around his neck, and kissing him firmly on the mouth. Pulling away, her sparkling, green eyes piercing his, she said, "I knew you would be here."

Eric dropped the knife and cupped her face in his hands. Then, looking quickly in both directions, he took her hand and said, "Let's get out of here."

"Not just yet," she said, reaching up to his face. She pulled him forward and they kissed again.

The light began to grow dimmer and from somewhere a soft music began, growing louder and more dramatically, until the place was filled with an unmistakable signal that this was the end, and all was well.

She realized she'd been gripping the ends of her armrests. She glanced at her friend beside her and they both grinned, stood, and began applauding.

2: An Elephant Sized Heart

From behind the far ends of the wings on either side of the scene, two stagehands, both donning large headphones, heard the cue from the stage manager and began tugging the long ropes that worked the grand drape. As the two ends of the long purple cloth began to converge, a generous and almost enthusiastic applause slowly gained momentum and peaked after a few seconds.

The moment the curtain edges met center stage and the narrow beam of light between them vanished, "the woman" abruptly pulled back, dropped her arms, turned, and strode decisively away without a word.

As much as he hated to, Dax Ribeiro simply could not help watching as Meygan Knight quickly created as much distance as possible between them. That was how the game had been played for every show.

The fact was, the actress was gorgeous, even in the '80s era business outfit she wore, which was anything but her normal attire. In this conservative set of clothes, more was left to the imagination. But she would be hopelessly appealing in any getup, and whether her character was frightened, sad, or in high spirits made no difference. It also didn't matter what makeup she had on, if any. Indeed, it had been utterly tantalizing throughout rehearsals and performances. Her curves showed just enough through the thick material of that white skirt, and her hips swayed ever so lightly with each step, not to swagger or tease, but because it was perfectly natural for her to stride that way. He had watched her walk away in the dim light of the curtained stage, at precisely this same angle many times, and could recognize that particular set of female parts just about anywhere, in just about anything.

"The bald man," an actor named Glenn Brock, grunted and sat up. The slick wooden platform that made up the stage had been dirtied and painted to look like asphalt, but still hurt to land hard on it. Rubbing the back of his head, he looked up at Dax. "You mad about something?" he asked, swabbing sweat from his face with the inner lining of his jacket.

"Sorry, man," Dax said, forcing his eyes off Meygan.

"Oh, no worries. Just making sure."

Dax turned and gave his full attention to Glenn. "You okay?"

"I'll know later tonight after a trip to the emergency room." Glenn paused, watching as Dax's gaze returned to Meygan.

Without missing a beat and fully aware of all the eyes on her, she stepped through the stage door and disappeared.

Glenn laughed. "Dude, why do you torment yourself?"

Dax sighed deeply. "I don't know, same reason you do." He stuck out a hand and helped Glenn to his feet, a task not easily performed on the 230-pound man.

Glenn began wiping dust off his jacket. "I first ran into her ... when was it, three years ago, in '93, at a party. She was as chilly then as she is now."

Dax raised his eyebrows. "Meygan goes to parties?"

Glenn shrugged. "Now and then, when it might help her career along, I guess." He glanced at the door Meygan had just walked through.

"She could be your daughter, Glenn." Dax smirked.

Glenn hunched down in a mock fighting stance. "Any time you wanna go at it for real, pal."

Dax smiled but took a step back. For the show, he'd gotten to kick Glenn's tail nightly, but in real life, the big man would be more than a formidable opponent.

From beyond the curtain the murmuring of the exiting audience was dying down.

"Knock it off you two," a voice said behind them. The "younger man," Dennis Sheridan, was returning to the scene from stage left where he had fled. Dennis wore a perpetual and genuine smile that made just about everyone like him. At six-foot three, with a twenty-eight-inch waist, he was admired for his looks as much as his personality. His thick jet-black hair and narrow, square face was a gift from his Irish roots and one that had already caught the attention of photographers. It had also landed him an internship at a local TV station who was now training him to be a field reporter. Next to Glenn's five-foot-ten frame, with a thirty-eight-inch waist and shoulders at least twice as spacious, the two made a wonderfully odd couple of bad guys, when Dennis managed to look mean enough.

Glenn took a fake swing at Dax. "You see what this guy did to me tonight?"

Dennis strode up with his arms akimbo. "Yeah, but I also heard what he just *said* to you." He turned to Dax. "He's just feeling the sadness of the show coming to an end. Right, lover boy?"

Dax shrugged to feign indifference.

"He should have enjoyed it while it lasted," Glenn said. "I mean, a few hundred people in this city think he could whip me." He paused. "Of course, that's because of *my* performance."

"I did enjoy it," Dax said quietly, then realized how unenthusiastic he sounded.

"Oh, *puleez*," Dennis said grinning. Then his expression turned puzzled. "You okay?"

Dax caught himself staring at the ground. "Sure," he said. "I'm A-plus."

Glenn smirked. "One more kiss from Princess Meggie then it's all over. That's his problem. Forget me throwing the fight."

Dennis rolled his eyes and shook his head. Dax only smiled and looked down again, his eyes betraying deep thought.

"See you ladies in the dressing room," Glenn said, turning to leave. "Hey, try not to kill me on the last show?"

Dennis clapped a hand on Dax's shoulder. "You're too serious, Dax."

"About what?" Dax asked.

"Everything. I've told you before. Come on."

"I'll be there in minute."

Dennis shrugged and headed for the door, leaving Dax in the middle of the lonely, faux street scene where the fight and rescue and been portrayed nine times now. This evening had been the last Saturday he got to be Eric, the hero, then one more performance tomorrow.

Ceiling lights behind the curtain suddenly turned up and killed the illusion, revealing a modest stage, which, between shows served as the theatre's scene shop. The old "bricks" now resembled the pipe sealant that was used to create them, and the color looked fake and spattered on. The surface of the "wall" was actually quite delicate and could be scraped off with a putty knife. After all the rehearsals and performances, there were real scuffs and chunks missing from where an actor or stagehand had inadvertently caused damage. Directly on the other side of the wall, amidst a tangle of electric wires and circuit breakers, several brace jacks held the main structure upright.

In the bright light, the ends of the bolts that held speakers in place from behind the wall were now obvious, the ones that produced the various sounds of the night—the breeze, the trickling water, the brawling cats. The illusion was effective. Suspension wires that held the taller props up were also visible and resembled the handiwork of a giant spider.

The sidewalk now looked like the painted plywood crisscrossed with gaffer tape that it was. The gutter now looked like a rectangular shape of black paint. The whole setup was an effective smoke and mirror job when the lighting and sound came together.

Dax smiled. He had to admit that despite the limited budget, the aesthetic and dramatic components of this show had been well conceived and implemented. He looked down and kicked a foot iron that was used to keep a small serving table in place in a different scene.

Aaron Tisdale, the stage manager, walked quickly around from the behind the wall bearing his usual shy and socially awkward expression. "Good show tonight, Dax." He said it in a way to convey enthusiasm but failed. He waited and stared at Dax for a response.

"Thanks," Dax said quietly.

Aaron's sad, droopy eyes shifted. The bags under them looked especially puffy and dark tonight. The thumb on his right hand scratched the index finger nervously. "Well," he said, looking around for something. "One more to go." He paused again, then strode away trying to look like he had something important to do.

Dax looked up at the ceiling that had years ago been converted into fly traps and a catwalk. The old Godwin Theatre had been around so long, it had acquired a life all to its own. Late at night after a performance, one could hear creeks and groans, like an old man turning in his sleep. The building gave refuge to odors as definitive as the colors of the faded paint that cracked and chipped on the rear interiors, an area the audience never saw.

No one knew what the property had been before its renovation to a place of performing arts just eleven years ago in 1985. Perhaps first-generation immigrants to San Francisco had lived here, frying calamari and baking sourdough bread. These timeworn smells, now mixed with chemicals, molds, and musty cement, greeted people who walked into the back of the building. A contracted company came in each week and emptied the mouse and rat traps that lay in the deep dusty corners.

The front of the building, the part patrons saw, was a different world, a gilded masterpiece of maroon-colored theme décor. Over aged walls had been glued beautiful modern wallpaper designed to resemble the original stenciled motifs. Ceramic figures, done up to pass as wood carvings, had been placed strategically along the walls. Between them, colorful playbills advertised upcoming shows and various sponsors. A coffered ceiling had been installed with 1920's designs of arches and rafters.

To mask the old odors, a dozen colorful, scented candles were always burning in and around the lobby before and during showtime. A thick burgundy carpet had been laid over an old wooden floor that had been replaced several times over the years. The original renovations had been paid for by a rich old widow, but she was long gone, and the place scraped by now with ticket sales and donations. Good shows and even better reviews meant the money kept the theatre's heart beating.

Patrons to the theatre were greeted by personnel who donned attire of a departed era. Women wore headbands with bright colored feathers, silk and mesh forearm covers over tight, colorful, one-piece dresses, that draped from the mid-torso to the mid-thighs. Legs were wrapped in black lace and feet were adorned in glittery pumps with three-inch heels.

The men wore black shiny dress shoes under drawstring pants that were loose around the legs, but tight on the hips. The upper half was a sharp, long-sleeved shirt with six buttons that fastened when the long flaps overlapped. The mostly solid burgundy outfit had a gold stripe that ran along the sides from hips to ankles, and shoulders to wrists. On their heads were round caps with a shiny black visor and a gold braded decorative rope that looped around the front and over the top.

It all created the desired visual effect.

"Nice show tonight, Dax!" a voice called from above. He watched as Elizabeth Brauner was slowly lowered to the floor by cable and pulley. She spent her evenings about sixty feet in the air on the upper corner of stage-left, suspended in a reasonably comfortable plastic chair, right next to a movable spotlight. Directly above her were thick booms where stationary lights hung. Several small C-clamps holding the lighting structures were the only things keeping hundreds of pounds of metal and glass crashing down on hers and the actor's heads. About twenty minutes before showtime, she was hoisted up into position and trapped there for the entirety of the performance. Spotlight operators learned to bring snacks and drinks with them as well as take care of any personal business beforehand.

Elizabeth hopped out of the swinging chair and bound at Dax with a high-five. Dax obliged and tried to look cheery. He always liked Elizabeth. At five-foot one, slightly chunky and with a less than average face, her theatrical role had long left her to behind-the-scenes duties, which she did with grace and enthusiasm. When she wasn't running a light or helping with props, she occasionally appeared on stage as Woman Number Three or some anonymous bystander, but it seemed to make her happy to do whatever was needed.

"I've never seen that end fight look so real," she was saying, her dark curls partly covering her eyes. The headset clamped on her for the last two and half hours had left an amusing imprint in her hair that ran ear to ear.

"Maybe it *was* real tonight," Dax said, deadpan.

"What?"

"Kidding. Hey, listen, you've done a bang-up job on this show. Must be smokin' up there next to that big bulb."

"Did you just say *bulb*?"

"Uhm, yeah. As in light bulb."

"*Lamp*. Don't ever say 'light bulb' to a theatre lighting technician." She looked away and swaggered her head as she said this.

"Sorry. Our in-house connoisseur of *lamps* and barn door technologist."

Elizabeth smiled admiringly. "You know what barn doors are. Impressive."

"Ha, ha. Really though, has anyone told you that you do an incredible job?"

Elizabeth looked away shyly while her hands moved behind her back. "Well, thank you. But the real talent is on the stage."

Dax waved it off. "Wouldn't be much of a scene without the lights."

"True." She smiled and shuffled her feet.

An amusing image flashed through Dax's mind. In college he had watched a show about the civil rights movement where three guys came out wearing Ku Klux Klan outfits. It was alarming at first, until one noticed underneath the white gowns three sets of regular athletic sneakers. This promptly destroyed the illusion and made the group look about as intimidating as three cream puffs.

"Hey, Dax," Elizabeth said, reaching into a pocket. "I wanted to give you this." She held out a small porcelain elephant attached to a tiny chain via a little loop on its back. She slowly lowered it into Dax's outstretched palm.

"What's this?"

"An elephant, silly."

"Well, yeah." A lot of thoughts flashed through his mind. He'd seen many elephants growing up, or images of them anyway. "You know why actors and elephants are always so broke?"

"Why?"

"We both work for peanuts."

She grinned and slapped his arm.

Dax held it up by the chain, admiring the intricate details as it slowly swiveled in the air. "What's the occasion?"

Elizabeth shuffled her feet. "Nothing. I just wanted you to have this because ... because you have a heart as big as an elephant's."

Dax looked at her and genuinely admired the gesture. He knew she wasn't flirting, just being kind. He had known Elizabeth for several years, his first encounter in college drama classes. Of all the women he'd ever met, he probably liked her the most, which was a strange feeling because he never had any attraction to her, *that* way. But that was good. It was precisely the allure to women like Meygan Knight that usually ended up ruining everything. He smiled at the thought that there actually were genuine friends in the world. Perhaps life wasn't all just a performance, as Shakespeare had put it.

"Thanks, Elizabeth. This is great."

Elizabeth smiled, paused for a moment, then tiptoed up and gave Dax a quick hug. "One more to go," she said, turning to go and heading toward the equipment closet. "See you tomorrow night!"

"Yes ... one more."

Dax stood for a moment and realized how much he would have wanted this show to continue on. Not because he got to kiss Meygan Knight, but because it really was a great moment in his life.

Cupping the little white elephant, he stuck it in his pocket as he headed for the stage exit.

3: Dreamers

The fluorescent ceiling fixture in the hallway flickered like a strobe light as Dax walked past the greenroom. Several of the lights had been this way during the whole run of rehearsals and performances, but the Godwin's owner was being Ebeneezer Scrooge and not doing anything about it.

Glancing in the greenroom, he saw that Meygan Knight had already changed and was reclining in one of the ancient and tattered Manhattan lounge chairs. She was talking quietly and seriously on her new Nokia cell phone and paying no attention to anything around her. Her costume had been swapped for stylish tight designer jeans that had bright white stitches on the side, which left far *less* to the imagination. Her hair had been brushed and now flowed uninhibited in all the right directions.

Dax smiled and shook his head in disgust at himself. Why couldn't he just look at her snobby and indifferent face and not bother with anything else?

Truth be told, he didn't want to think about the actress – it always ended up producing unhealthy feelings. But this show, he had to admit, had been killing him. Glenn was one of several guys that envied him. It was fun at first, but her genuine display of discarding him like a used contraceptive immediately afterwards stung and superseded the illusion.

It would be that feeling he would carry after all this was said and done.

He knew he needed to heed Dennis' advice and lighten up, stop taking himself and others so seriously. He smiled again. Dennis was another real friend, although he didn't know him too well. Maybe the two of them could hang out after this was over.

The light was brighter in the makeup room from extra fixtures as well as bulbs installed around the mirror frames. The popcorn had long been shaved off the ceiling and what was left was covered over in white paint. The malodor of hairspray and sweaty actors had taken permanent residence.

Many of the cast was still here, removing the layers of façade that had created the play's illusion. Dillon Christie's station was by the door. The thin and flamboyant actor was silent at the moment, roughly scrubbing his face and ignoring Dax. Dennis was directly opposite on the other side of the room. He made eye contact through the mirror and smiled and nodded.

Dax made his way past the utility table and seated himself before his mirror. In the hard, white light, the makeup-covered faces looked obscenely counterfeit. But for audience members in the far corner of the last row to see anything other than a white-flushed ghost, it was necessary. His olive complexion required a blush medium foundation, and by the end of a show it felt awful mixed with sweat.

Marcy Kotowski, the makeup lady, came along with her soft nylon cooler. "Been waiting for you," she said. "I have two left."

"I can always count on you."

Marcy unzipped the flap and removed two small face towels, moistened and microwaved hot.

Dax took one, unfolded it, and flapped it on his face like a pancake. "Oh, that feels good," he said leaning back.

Marcy smiled. "You men who know how to apply their own makeup are as rare as good husbands."

Dax laughed. Marcy had been married three times and meant every word. At fifty-two, she had a narrow and average face but with handsome features, large eyes, and a broad smile. She kept in good and energetic shape and if she wanted a fourth spouse, she could acquire one.

"You do better than some women I know," Marcy continued, watching Dax. She put her hands on her hips. "You will use the *face*, and not the hand wipes on your eyes, right?"

"For the hundredth time, yes."

"Just watching out for you."

"Thanks, mom."

She whipped him on the arm with a towel.

"Get him, Marcy," Glenn said from the other side of the room. "I owe him after tonight." His face was rubbed red and now missing the scars and rough lines he wore in the show, revealing more of a big baby face than a mean street brawler.

Marcy turned and sat on the edge of the table next to Dax. "What a week. Glad it's over."

Dax glanced at her.

"Not the show," Marcy said casually. "I'm not glad *that's* over."

Dax just smiled.

"I am," Glenn said. "Already gearing up for *Wild Hearts*." He spoke like he'd already been given a part.

"You got in that?" Marcy asked with genuine surprise. "What part? Do tell."

Glenn glared at her. "Auditions are next week. I'm trying out for Denny," he said nonchalantly.

Dax smirked loudly then turned to look at Glenn. For a brief moment, all the façade was gone. In the big man's eyes and slightly open mouth, Dax saw just another regular guy with an acting bug, hoping for the next part in a grander show.

"Jim Kirkland is directing. He only goes for *real* actors," Dax said with a wink.

"Means you won't be in it either," Dillon muttered just loud enough so that people around him maybe *thought* they'd heard the comment.

"You're mean, Dax," Marcy said, ignoring Dillon.

"Just you wait," Glenn said, giving Dax the evil eye, the actor in him snapping back.

"Marcy, twenty bucks he doesn't even make callbacks," Dax said.

"That's cold, Dax," Dennis said from his corner.

Glenn was pointing and wagging his finger at Dax but laughed and shook his head when he saw Dax grinning in the mirror.

"Just be nice," Marcy said.

"I won't need a callback. I'm gonna get casted right then and there," Glenn said.

"Dream on, big boy," said Dax.

"You'll be auditioning, right Dax?" Marcy asked.

Dennis turned and looked. Dillon stared straight into his mirror, listening intently, but pretending not to.

Dax had thought about auditioning for *Wild Hearts* but changed his mind. He wasn't sure why but knew a break from the theatre scene was in order.

"Dax?" Marcy asked.

"Oh, uhm, maybe."

"*Maybe?*" Glenn chided. "Listen to this guy. Maybe I'll saunter in and get a part. Maybe I won't."

"Yeah, right," Dax said.

Glenn just stared, the actor gone again, the regular, hopeful guy back. Dax watched Glenn for a moment through the mirror while rubbing the side of his face.

"So, what's next?" asked Marcy. "You gonna pack up and head across country for Broadway now?"

Dax laughed. "Uh oh, you found me out."

Glenn scoffed. "Now *you* dream on, boy."

Dax turned back to Glenn. "We're all just a bunch of silly dreamers, my friend."

Dillon finally shot Dax a contempt-filled look, but then quickly turned away. Glenn returned Dax's gaze for a moment, his eyes narrowed, his face serious. He then laughed, waved off Dax and returned to his mirror.

"You should go for it," Marcy said.

"For what, Broadway?"

"No. *Wild Hearts.*"

Dax shrugged. "We'll see."

Mary sighed loudly. "Well, one more," she said, turning to leave. Dax watched her for a moment through his mirror. Marcy was nice but sometimes overly serious, like himself. She helped with makeup and wigs for certain shows. She was tough and always spoke her mind. In the heat of the moment in the middle of shows, a certain austerity in her sometimes reared its head when her patience ran out with those who didn't take their makeup seriously. It always amazed Dax that when she saw *her* actors on stage done up correctly, it gave her the same satisfaction that performers felt when things went well.

Dax turned back to his mirror. Unlike most of the others who already more shows lined up, Dax wanted a sabbatical from theatre. He was sick of auditions. He was sick of rehearsal schedules. He was sick of the sinking low that came after the high of a performance.

Since the day he decided he loved the stage, he had lived for when the curtain opened and the energy from the audience hit him like a strong wind, jolting his body and giving him a rush. But getting to that moment was time consuming, and not always pleasant.

A coworker, Enrique, was a mountain climber—an expensive and even more time-consuming hobby. But when Enrique talked about the sport, he didn't just talk about getting to the top. He loved the whole process. He loved all the equipment and how it worked. He loved traveling to the climb sites and seeing them in the distance, anticipating as he approached. He loved the feeling of starting a climb, of being halfway up, and especially being on top. He loved each step of the way. Dax wanted to feel this way about theatre and perhaps he used to but didn't anymore. Maybe it was beginning to lose its purpose in him.

He looked down at his makeup kit and sighed. It needed a refreshing. The facial hair sponge was crumbling apart, there was only one decent blush brush left, the cake type foundation was almost empty, and the black eyeliner pencil was getting too short to hold comfortably. He couldn't remember the last time he had any translucent powder and when it wasn't convenient to borrow any, like tonight, he went without it which meant risking Marcy's wrath if she caught him looking "shiny" on stage after a good sweat. He grabbed a face wipe and began scrubbing around his eyes.

The loud voice of Dillon suddenly filled the room. He was on his cell phone and riled up about something as usual. "Oh—my—*gaaawd!* I so hate him," he was half-yelling. "What a prick. I've never had to deal with anyone so obnoxious." He paused and looked in Dax's direction. "Well, maybe not *quite* as obnoxious."

Dax ignored the bait and kept his eyes on the mirror.

Dillon continued as he flounced toward his chair. "Tell him that nothing is going to get accomplished if things continue this way." In his peripheral vision, Dax could see Dillon plop his skinny five-foot four frame into a chair and quickly cross a slender leg over the other. He began wiggling his ankle in a small kicking motion as he continued. "No, I mean it! I'm not taking any more of his BS." The room had gone relatively quiet; Dillon's volume was too loud to compete with. "Okay, nighty-night, sleep tight." He pulled the phone away from his ear, stared at the screen for a moment, then stabbed a key with curved wrist and a pointed index finger. Then, swiveling quickly around to his mirror, began singing loudly. "Every single day, I walk down the street! I hear people say *baaaaaaaby's* so sweet! …"

"Shut up, Dillon," Glenn said, picking up his bag to leave.

Dax smirked loudly which made Dillon turn slightly. Dennis ignored the scene and continued working at his eye liner. Dillon started to look in Dax's direction but changed his mind, swiveling quickly around to face Glenn.

Glenn paused near Dillon's station. Even though he and Dillon were dead opposites in just about every way imaginable, they had somehow developed a flippant but cordial friendship.

"We practically have *Rent* memorized by now, can I tell you that?" Glenn said staring down in a mock scolding way.

"Well then I'm doing you a favor," Dillon said winking.

"Hey, whatever."

"It's only like *the* greatest musical ever," Dillon said with a *duh* expression.

"You think so? Nice job tonight with the hat, by the way," Glenn said tapping on his hairless skull, referring to a little number Dillon did with a couple guys who swap hats by tossing them at each other's heads.

"Well thank you, at least one performance went without incident." Dillon glanced at Marcy in the corner putting away her things. "Hey Marcy, isn't *Rent* the greatest musical ever?"

"What if I said it wasn't?" Marcy asked.

"I would say you need to see it again, and then again, and again until you love it."

"Don't listen to him," Glenn said.

"I'm not," Marcy said putting her bags on the table. "It's a depressing show. Too many story lines to follow."

Dillon's ankle was wiggling faster. "It's real life. It takes us through times of friendship, struggle, and love."

Dax wanted to say, *yeah, and drug addiction*. But he thought the better of it, especially since he himself drank a tad too much now and then.

"I don't like depressing," Marcy continued.

"It's not! It's just life."

"Goodnight, all," Glenn said heading for the door.

"Goodnight," Dennis said, looking at Glenn from his mirror.

"What do you think, Dax?" Marcy asked.

"Hmmm?" Dax turned.

"Of *Rent*. What do you think?"

Darn it, Marcy. Inadvertently, Dax shifted his eyes to Dillon who promptly turned back to his mirror. Dax decided to be sarcastic. "I don't really think anything of it. I prefer shows like *Las Vegas Ladies*."

Dillon let out an audible scoff which made Dax grin to himself. Dennis shook his head silently.

"You're joking, right?" Marcy asked, one eyebrow arched.

Dax couldn't suppress a laugh now.

"Typical," Marcy said, snatching up a small hand mirror. "Women forced into revealing uniforms and Barbie doll makeup. Costumes with a miniskirt and a plunging cleavage over a corset so tight they probably bleed under their arms."

"Sounds good to me," said Dax.

"Exploitation," said Marcy.

"You're absolutely right," said Dax, "Sexist, terrible. But I'd see it again." He winked at Marcy.

"Pig." She waved him off. "Only because I know you're really a nice guy." She began walking around to gather the last of her towels.

Outside, a strong wind sent a rushing sound through the old vents making the building creak slightly.

Dax had managed to eradicate the eye liner under his right eye, which was now red and puffy from the assault. He stared at himself again and wondered for the hundredth time how he got this role. Les Abraham, the director, had always liked Dax as a person, but not so much as an actor. Dax had wondered throughout the show what divine intervention had given him the opportunity to play "Eric," and felt it probably wouldn't happen again.

On impulse, he leaned back and dug the little elephant out of his pocket and studied it in the palm of his hand. The small figurine was rearing its head up while the trunk curved back and over the forehead. The legs appeared to be in motion as if it were charging forward.

It reminded him of images he used to stare at as a child, and he was hit with a flood of memories.

4: Karma

Growing up, Dax's family lived near a Buddhist temple. He became good friends with one of the boys there, Typhoon.

Dax remembered long hours with Typhoon watching the adults. The place was always quiet and mysterious. And there was red everywhere. Several red columns covered in Chinese symbols rose from floor to ceiling. One of the main columns, front and center, had a large wooden lockbox with a sign on top in both English and Mandarin that said, "Give Generously!"

Red-painted tables in the middle of the room were covered in scrolls, small statues, and bowls, many adorned with sweet smelling burning incense. The permanent haze in the air, at certain times of the day, created long, angled beams of phantom timber from the window that went the length of the room. From the ceiling, there hung a multitude of hexagon shaped lamps, intricately decorated with hammered iron and tops that resembled the curvy rooftops of traditional pagodas, with bright red tassels hanging from each corner.

There were also elephants—big ones, small ones, paintings of them, precision-carved wooden ones, sculptures made from pieces of metals. One could stare at the décor for hours.

Dax came to know and like an old man at the temple named Zhao. The two boys spent time with the old monk listening to his teachings.

Zhao was always dressed in the traditional orange robe that draped over his body like a loose curtain leaving one shoulder exposed. While most of the monks bore a solemn face as they quietly shuffled along or sat meditating, Zhao smiled easily. Dax would stare at the old man's garment, its folds and creases and the small rope around the waist. He learned that the orange color held no significance other than tradition carried down, the dyes made from vegetable matter or spices like saffron. Sometimes the robe was red, and occasionally a monk donned yellow, a color considered to have healing qualities like that of the sun.

Zhao explained that the Kung Fu practiced by the monks went back over 4,000 years, and for most of that time, only by the military elite. It wasn't until almost the first century it was made available to everyone. Over time, Kung Fu meshed with philosophies like Confucianism and Taoism resulting in a fighting style that embraced mystical elements like comic energy as well as the practical applications of music and mathematics. Zhao assured the two fascinated young boys that despite his years of training and discipline, he could not scale walls, run straight up tall bamboo stalks, or bend steel with his bare hands.

Alongside the old teacher, the boys spent many hours performing the slow, methodical movements of yoga exercises, strengthening obscure muscles, and practicing the discipline of patience. They also sparred and repeated the quick motions of block and counterstrike movements that utilized almost every part of the body. They practiced breathing holding a pushup position, tightening up and enduring when getting kicked or punched in the belly, and balancing on one foot atop wooden posts.

Dax never fully appreciated or understood the spiritual aspects of this training, things he was repeatedly told were an integral part of it. He wasn't sure if Typhoon did either, although Typhoon seemed more receptive. Sitting motionless, his ankles crossed and his thumbs and middle fingers of each hand touching, Typhoon attempted to meditate a whole day once, but had to quit when hunger and thirst got the best of him. Supposedly, Zhao had once meditated for two weeks straight—no food, no water, no breaks. As the story went, he had wanted to go thirty days, but gave up exhausted and not at all happy with himself. Dax couldn't imagine sitting around doing nothing for even half a day.

One day when Dax was about twelve, they were all reclining in the garden. A warm pot of herbal tea sat nearby exhaling thin wisps of gray steam. Dax was watching the small tuft of white hair under Zhao's lip bob up and down as the old man spoke. Sunlight was pressing through the vine ceiling in spotty patches on the monk's shaved head, which, like the robe, symbolized both victory over vanity as well as the renunciation of worldly things.

By this time, Dax knew he did not embrace many of the philosophies of the temple. He was far more interested in learning Kung Fu. The teachings on reincarnation frightened him, as he could only image what sort of nasty creature he would be in the next life as retribution for his sins—a flea, a worm, perhaps a dung beetle. The part that confused Dax was, who made these decisions about everything that lived and died, and by what power was it performed?

It was impossible to believe that some power doled out all this justice but in return offered nothing of any real meaning. What was the purpose of coming back over and over again? Who or what decided between right and wrong or what deserved punishment or reward? He knew enough to know the concept of "sin" was largely understood to be ignorance and being out of balance. The whole business of Karma was action and response, rather than "right" or "wrong." Sow goodness, reap goodness; sow evil, reap evil. But this concept was strikingly similar to what he had learned on those rare occasions he found himself in Christian Sunday School.

"What is it that you want?" Zhao had asked out of the blue, perhaps sensing Dax's puzzlement.

Still dwelling on the thought of waking up one day with six legs and an appetite for animal feces, he replied, "I wish to live a thousand years!"

Typhoon laughed, but Zhao only frowned. After a moment he asked, "In the body you have *now*?"

Dax shrugged.

Zhao shook his head sadly and said something in Cantonese.

"He says your wish is foolish and narcissistic," said Typhoon.

Dax swallowed hard and felt his face flush hot, like the color of the tassels hanging above him. "Nar-si-*what?*"

"Nar-ci-ssi-stic," Typhoon said, spelling it out in the air with his finger. "It means you love yourself too much."

Dax's eyebrows crunched up. "But … I don't love myself."

Zhao spoke again. "Be careful that you do not spend your life in desire. Desire causes suffering and implies something is missing. All of us have everything we need, right now. You need not desire anything more."

Dax pondered this. The world was so full of desires. He understood the philosophy's teaching not to desire too much, but wearing a robe, shaving your head, and abandoning everything except basic needs was over the top. Plus, he was already at an age where he looked at females and someday, preferably sooner than later, wanted to get his hands on one.

He looked at the old man's skinny and shriveled body. Had he really lived all these years both denying himself and being totally content in doing so?

"A desire like to live a thousand years is simply not necessary," Zhao continued.

Well, that was true. At his young age, Dax had already lost two pets and had been to three funerals—two grandparents, and a forty-five-year-old aunt who died of cancer. He was familiar with death's certainty and finality.

"Is there something you need you do not have now, or could not have in one lifetime?" Zhao asked. "And were you to live a thousand years, would that be enough time to find it?"

Dax never forgot that question.

Several months later, Zhao was chanting in the temple when his eyes suddenly rolled up and he fell over, never to get back up. So, monks die just like regular people. That, despite the generous daily measure of green tea consumed, a habit Dax would later learn often helped protect a person from both Alzheimer's and cancer. Dax asked Typhoon what he thought Zhao would be reincarnated as, but Typhoon just shrugged and never tried to answer.

Another year later when high school began, Typhoon announced he was going to finish school in China. Dax saw him get into a car bound for the airport and never heard from him again.

The time Dax had spent in those growing up years around Typhoon had indeed shaped him in many ways. The lessons in Kung Fu and the physical exercises to maintain a body and mind, he would continue practicing on his own.

Aaron Tisdale suddenly appeared at the doorway of the makeup room jarring Dax from his reverie. "Great job everyone," he said looking around. The room remained silent, and he was ignored the way furniture is after it has occupied a certain space for a while. Even Marcy remained silent while placing towels into her bag. Only Dennis turned after a moment and gave Aaron a pleasant smile and a wave. But Aaron didn't see that. He was looking at Dax.

Dax noticed but kept pawing at the stubborn black lines under his eyes.

"Well, see you tomorrow night for the finale," Aaron said. He paused for a moment in quiet uncertainty then disappeared from the doorway. "Hi, Les," you could hear him say down the hallway.

Les Abraham strode in and stopped in the middle of the room. He moved quickly and energetically for a man his age. "Okay everyone, I'm here, you can shut up now," he said with a grin.

"Hi, Les," Marcy said.

"Heading home, Marcy?"

"I'm tired. Need to do some shopping, clean the house tomorrow. Blah, blah." She headed toward Dax and he tossed his towel in her bag.

"Take care," Les said.

"See you, Marcy," Dennis said.

Marcy stopped at the doorway and squinted at Dennis. "The *scars* were too thick on your face tonight, young man," she said, wagging a finger.

"Oh, now you tell me?"

"He looked beautiful!" said Les. He turned and looked at Dax, who was stuffing the little elephant back in his pocket. Les was probably in his early sixties, though no one was certain. With a balding head, a thin gray beard, and a protruding belly, he looked like everyone's eccentric uncle. Although he could shed a few pounds, he moved quickly when riled up and in director-mode and yelled a lot. During rehearsals he had more than his share of cussing out actors, particularly at those who didn't have their lines speedily memorized.

Les was actually nice and engaging most of the time but took theatre seriously. As a college acting teacher, he could be ruthless. He enjoyed taking newbie actors and shoving them through the wringer right away. He had a collection of scenes from plays that did just the trick, from erotic bedroom scenarios to improv exercises where a spouse or live-in partner suddenly breaks the news to the other that he or she has mysteriously acquired a venereal disease.

There was one class Dax had taken with Les years ago where Les had made a young actress allow the actor who was kissing her to caress her breast. The two performers cooperated, the young man readily, but afterwards she ended up crying and walking out of the small arena theatre where class was held.

Later, Dax impressed Les when talking to him about his teaching style. "I know why you kick new actors around so much."

"Oh?" Les said. "Why do you think?"

"Because you want to know who is serious about acting and who is there just to fulfill their liberal arts requirements."

"You nailed it!" Les had said. But there was more.

About twenty years before that, Les and a partner had finally given up on a dream to have their own production company. They had worked tirelessly in the background of several companies that produced mostly bad television and their plays never became Broadway hits. In resignation, Les became a full-time drama teacher and peddled books he authored that students had to purchase each semester. His first love was still the camera though and the more Stanislavsky System-bred teachers had no tolerance for his technical and blocked style. Dax's favorite class to date, however, was the acting-on-camera class he had taken from Les.

"Dax," Les said, putting his palms together. "I'm proud of you."

Dax turned and looked at him. He stole a quick glance at Dillon who had adjusted his mirror and was watching through the reflection.

"Why's that, Les?" Dax asked, feigning humility.

"I like the way the show's gone," Les said, picking up a chair and moving in Dax's direction. Of course, Les was lying. While he was somewhat satisfied with how things had gone, the play was probably half what it could have been. Fortunately, this was not all Dax's fault.

"You've shown real commitment," Les continued, sitting next to Dax. Now Dillon had turned and was watching. Even Dennis was looking while tossing a few things into his bag.

Les usually didn't hang out in the makeup room, but perhaps he was going to offer Dax a part in something upcoming. Les had his hands in his lap with his fingers intertwined. "You have been both truthful and consistent. During the first couple shows, I sensed the energy coming from your head, but it moved to your gut. I like that." He said this with absolute seriousness and no one in the room reacted. This was normal talk for Les. He was famous for telling his students that Al Pacino had thrown energy from his gut in *Dog Day Afternoon*, but Kirk Douglas had energized himself from the groin when he performed *Detective Story*. Dax understood most of what Les said in his classes but found this one concept a bit peculiar.

"So you believe me—*Eric?*" Dax asked.

"I believe *you* finally came to believe it."

Dax shifted uncomfortably at both the slap and compliment. "You wanna know the truth? I didn't think I'd still be acting by now." Dax started to chuckle at his own comment but stopped, realizing there was nothing amusing about it.

"I know," Les said, looking away thoughtfully. Then, after a pause, "I was glad to see you audition."

Dax had the feeling he was hearing half-truths. Even in college, he never got vibes that Les was all that impressed with his acting chops. As a hard-working and sincere human being, sure, he had Les' respect. But when it came to acting, Dax fell a little short in both looks and talent. He possessed sufficient aptitude to get smaller parts, but he'd always be overshadowed by those made for leads. The truth was, this was a small production, in one of the less prestigious houses, and Dax had heard there were a handful of other actors Les would have chosen to play Eric had they not been busy doing something else.

"So, what are your plans now?" Les asked in a tone of plain curiosity.

"I wasn't sure. Maybe take a break." He noticed Dillon, who had gone back to his mirror, give a quick sidewise glance.

"Well, listen," Les said putting a hand on Dax's knee. "Come on over to the office when you're done. I have a couple gentlemen for you to meet."

Dax turned and looked at Les.

"Talent scouts?" Dennis asked, but Les didn't respond.

"I'm not in trouble, am I?" Dax asked.

Les laughed. "No, no, nothing like that. Just come on by when you're ready." He smiled, then stood and turned to Dennis. "Trying to steal the show, were you, young man?"

"Who, me?" Dennis asked with exaggerated innocence, pointing both fingers at himself.

Les grinned. "I've not seen you so scared."

"Dax made me do it, practically broke Glenn's neck tonight."

"Yes, I know. Wonderful, wasn't it? That's what I like about Dax—persistence, until he gets it right."

Dax looked away. In class, Les talked about how creative ideas usually came frequently to the "reasonably talented actor" and how an attitude of persistence and imaginative exploration was important.

Dillon started to turn as if to jump into the conversation, but Les abruptly about-faced and marched out of the room.

"Hollywood agents? Talent scouts?" Dennis asked again.

A few years ago, an apprentice of Les, an actor with that athletic, rustic all-American look, got a spot in a national TV commercial. Les talked about it nonstop for months. But as time marched on, the luster of it all faded when it became clear it had been a one-time deal and not a stepping-stone to bigger opportunities. The actor had been, well, "reasonably talented," but a few big appearances in theatres in the area forever sealed his fate as one who would never move on to the big leagues.

"No idea," said Dax.

Dennis nodded. "Well, lemme know. It all sounds interesting." He picked up his things. "See you tomorrow night."

The last of the cast filed out and only Dillon was left who was now worked up and furiously scrubbing his face.

Dax leaned back and looked in the mirror again. He wished cameras were nicer to him. He was in pretty good shape, ran a couple miles most mornings before breakfast and did a little weightlifting at home, but knew it was time to pick up the pace. His face was a little better than average, but not considerably. On a stage he looked pretty decent, but through the lens of a camera, he was too round in the cheeks and waistline. It didn't help that his eyes were the garden variety dark brown of his hair, not green, gray, or baby blue. Since the first time he really started looking at certain actor's features, he wished badly he had those blue eyes, but by the time his embryo was developing, that choice had been made for him.

In the last several years Dax had been in a couple non-union commercials and had been an extra on a dozen films and television sets. A couple of those films were big. His claim to fame was appearing next to Robin Williams in a movie scene filmed in a U.C. Berkeley classroom. It all seemed so exciting at the time, causing him to dream of more opportunities, but they never came. He was just one of the endless and countless wannabes, and more importantly, he didn't have the networking and people skills required to really make it in the business.

San Francisco had had only two television shows regularly filmed on location in the last ten years, and both didn't last long. He knew SAG actors who still clung to the area but longed for the good ol' days in the '80s when there was more work. It had been going great until one fine day, the mayor at the time put an end to a lot of it. He had been in the pockets of some of the more wealthy and influential people in the city, who were upset at the traffic and other problems film companies made. Suddenly the permit rates tripled, the red tape became much thicker, and the bulk of the cameras and their crews disappeared for more fertile ground in LA.

Dax grabbed his things and headed for the door. As he passed Dillon's makeup station, he simply could not help but to turn and look at Dillon in the reflection of the mirror. Dillon silently stared straight ahead, his eyes riveted on himself. Dillon pursed his lips and utterly ignored the lead actor for this show he had been so jealous of. It was clear Dillon was dying to know who those two gentlemen were Les wanted Dax to meet, but in pride would not ask.

And so the game was played.

Dax smiled and walked out. He'd had his share of Dillon-types over the years. They used to bother him, but he'd grown indifferent. A thought struck him that he was becoming indifferent to a lot of things anymore.

Some real excitement of some kind was in order.

5: Old Ben's Secret

The office of the old theatre was located near the lobby. Dax skipped down a set of stairs and entered the side door of the main auditorium. The large room, strewn with maroon-colored rows of seats, was still warm and filled with the smells of the audience, but now quiet except for the sound of sweeping.

Dax glanced up at the stage and saw Old Ben, the theatre's long-time janitor, in his customary threadbare overalls and herringbone twill cap. Still healthy and alert, he'd probably live to see his 100th birthday. His wrinkled face was covered mostly by a thick white beard that curled off him in wisps, as if a cloud had been drifting by and became entangled on his face. Shadows from large bags under his eyes were outlined from the stage lights directly above.

Ben's trademark was the Briar tobacco pipe that seemed to be permanently protruding from somewhere inside his beard. The pipe curled out and down, starting with a small black end, then ballooning into a beautiful bell-bottomed, timber bowl, like a tiny rosewood saxophone. Smoking was forbidden in the auditorium, but in the dark, post-show hours, he'd gotten away with it for years.

Dax stared for a moment at the old man. He wondered where he'd be when he was that age, if he made it that far.

Old Ben glanced up and nodded.

Dax felt a little embarrassed and decided to make some small talk. "Say ... how long you been here, Ben? Just curious."

"Oh," Ben said, straightening up and tapping the brim of his hat a little further up his head. "Long time, almost a quarter-century now I imagine."

"Did you like theatre when you were a kid? You do any acting?"

Ben chuckled. "There wasn't a lot of acting opportunities for a young Black kid in Mississippi back then. Don't imagine there still is any. After my mother passed, my father told me to get out of that small town and never look back. So, I did. Got on a bus and came out here. Ended up delivering for a law firm. Later they taught me some paralegal stuff, got me a desk job. Paid me better than anything else someone with no college could get. The cool, ocean air and city life agreed with me, so I stayed. And the years passed." He paused and looked up in thought. "Ended up *seeing* a lot of theatre though. I loved to put myself in another place and time, feeling what the actors were feeling. So, when I retired, I started doing this. Get to see every show for free as much as I want." He grinned and winked.

Dax thought deeply about what Ben said, how quickly a person's life flew by in this world.

Ben looked around the stage. "I think I spend more time here than at home. I sometimes even come here on the weekends between shows and just relax in the one of those seats there. Someday they'll find me here dead enough to stick a fork into." He took a couple steps forward and motioned with his head for Dax to come closer. "There's an old door around back," he said in a lowered voice. "Not the main one next to the service entrance. But further down. Old one that was there before the conversion. Surrounded by ivy and a small gate that used to protect an old electric box. Hasn't been alarmed in years. Owners too lazy to spend money on it. So I come and go as I please." Ben grinned again, tipped his hat, and returned to his broom and dustpan.

Dax watched for a moment then headed up the center aisle, through the main doors, and then headed toward the will call windows. The weathered theatre office door had an Employees Only sign in imitation embossed gold. He paused and could hear muffled voices from within. He suddenly realized he was nervous. Taking a deep breath, he knocked twice.

"Come in!" he heard Les say from inside. The old doorknob looked and felt aged – faux copper and imprinted with intricate engravings, thick enough to feel on the palm. He turned it slowly and gave the creaky door a push. Les was reclining in the chair reserved for guests and visitors.

"There he is!" Les said.

As Dax entered, he saw two men dressed in almost identical dark gray cashmere suits. They both glanced him up and down quickly, the way cops do when sizing a person up.

The police?

Under the coats they both had starchy white shirts and black ties. The only thing missing were dark sunglasses, earpieces, and a lapel microphone.

The men stood and the older of the two extended his hand with a broad smile. "Hi Dax, I'm Jack Dauer."

Dax cautiously took the hand and felt a firm, strong grip.

The other man extended his hand as well, no smile. "Michael Staggs, good to meet you."

"Hi. Dax Ribeiro." He stood for a moment wondering what to say.

"Where does that name come from?" asked Jack.

"Brazil. In America, it's *reh-be-roe*, but in Brazil, it's *hee-beh-doe*, accent on the *eh.*"

"Ah," said Jack, smiling and nodding. After a moment, and seeing the look of intimidation on Dax's face, Jack said, "We're from the FBI, but no worries, Dax, it's all good."

Dax raised his eyebrows. He glanced at Agent Staggs who just stared back and nodded. "Really?" was all he could manage.

"We're just here to talk," said Jack.

Dax glanced at Les who sat smiling in an odd way.

Jack continued. "We're in need of the right man for a job."

"It's a matter of high importance," Staggs interjected, this time at least trying a casual but forced smile.

"Relax. Sit down," Jack said. "We've lots to talk about."

Dax shrugged and took a seat.

"Dax," said Les, "I want to you hear what these gentlemen have to say. You might even be intrigued." He patted Dax on the shoulder.

"Sure, okay," Dax said.

"You've never met real FBI agents, have you Dax?" Les said with a twinkle in his eyes. Dax felt as if he were getting setup for an improv scene. Was this an audition?

"Only in the movies," said Dax.

As if on cue, the two agents reached into their coat pockets and produced two badge wallets. The black folders, which flipped open horizontally, were identical. On the bottom flap on the right, a shiny gold eagle badge strutted its wings atop a bell-shaped plaque that proudly said FEDRAL BUREAU OF INVESTIGATION DEPARTMENT OF JUSTICE. To the left was a square piece of paper with a stone face and grim looking picture of Agent Staggs; Dauer's looked slightly more pleasant.

Dax looked at the signatures and blue watermarks. In his theatrical experience, he'd seen various police and other ID props and could not tell the difference.

Agent Staggs snapped his shut first and turned back to his seat. Jack watched Dax for a moment and then slowly tucked his away.

"Well, I'll leave the three of you alone," said Les. "Chin up Dax, you're far too serious." He winked and exited. The door creaked behind him as it slowly shut.

"Sit down Dax, please," said Agent Dauer, sitting down and crossing his legs. Agent Staggs sat a bit more rigid with his legs out straight and his palms planted firmly on his knees.

"Sorry for the unusual and unexpected visit," Agent Dauer began. "I assure you everything is fine."

"I'm not in any trouble?" asked Dax.

"Of course not."

"And no one I know or associated with is any trouble?"

"Absolutely not," Agent Dauer said, waving off the suggestion.

"None that we know of, anyway," Agent Staggs said with a sheepish smile, attempting humor.

"Figures," said Dax. "My life isn't that exciting."

Agent Dauer grinned and let out a knee-jerk laugh. Agent Staggs chuckled along, but a second too late, as if trying to follow suit, then shifted and rubbed his nose.

Agent Dauer leaned forward slightly. "Maybe that'll change soon," he said, his eyes smiling.

"Yeah?" Dax asked.

"We're just here to ask you something, that's all. Just hear us out. Afterwards, you can say yes, or you can say no. If you say no, we go away and no more surprise drop-ins. If you say yes, then a once-in-a-lifetime-opportunity may be in store for you."

Dax realized he had heard a faint accent just now, just a trace, but couldn't place it. He felt like he was about to hear a sales pitch. Additionally, Agent Staggs was beginning to make him nervous, but couldn't figure why.

Jack Dauer was maybe in his mid-fifties. His skin was olive and his receding grey hair thinly covered most of his head around the back. He tended to raise his chin when talking, exposing large nostrils at the end of a long narrow nose.

Agent Staggs was younger with a full head of light brown hair and a round face that would almost look pudgy were not for the stocky shoulders and beefy arms that filled in the suit coat. He wouldn't be a fun opponent in a wrestling match.

"Mr. Dauer ... uh, Agent Dauer—" Dax began.

"Call me Jack."

"Okay, Jack," Dax said, folding his arms. He waited a beat for Agent Staggs to make the same personable offer, but the man did not. "This isn't anything dangerous, is it? I might be a hero on a stage, but it's all smoke and mirrors, I assure you."

"No, no, nothing dangerous at all."

Dax paused, chiding himself for feeling nervous. He felt slightly out of control, opposite to being on stage where all his choices were predetermined. "Okay, I'm listening."

"Good," Jack said putting his palms together and rubbing them in a circular motion. Staggs sniffed loudly and leaned back, his eyes shifting on the floor.

"Dax," Jack began, "we work in a special division of the Justice Department. We help the international folks hunt some of the most wanted individuals in the world. We've had some run-ins with some pretty bad dudes as of late."

"Really?" Dax asked, raising his eyebrows, his interest piqued. "Are you part of INTERPOL?"

"Sort of," Jack said, folding his hands. "We work with groups closely tied to INTERPOL. But we stay pretty much local on our end."

"Local as in the city, the state?"

A shrug. "The United States."

Dax's nervousness began to make way for curiosity. "So if, say, a KGB spy was on the loose here, in San Francisco, they'd send you to nab him?"

For a split second the pleasant smile on Jack's face dropped. Staggs glanced up, but then returned his gaze to something on the floor. Staggs had a thick neck that bulged round when his head was down.

"Something like that," Jack said with a shrug of his hands. "If the KGB still existed. But it could be anyone."

"The KGB was dismantled five years ago with the breakup of the USSR," Agent Staggs suddenly interjected.

Dax shifted his glace back and forth between the two agents. "Right, just saying." He paused a beat then said, "I studied a little *pa-Russki* in college."

Agent Staggs leaned forward. "Yes, we know—" he began.

Jack cut him off. "That's partially why we're here, actually. Giving you this little surprise visit."

The room suddenly felt heavier as Dax realized they'd done homework on him. He imagined a dimly lit room full of file cabinets, a small round light hanging low over a desk. His file was occupying one of those cabinets. They knew all the places he'd lived, his job and salary, his friendship with Typhoon as a child, his grades. They might even know about Samantha ...

Ridiculous—he was no criminal, had no suspicious ties, and had never done anything very extraordinary. But then they must also know his name wasn't really Dax either.

"Uhm, I thought I wasn't under investigation," Dax said.

"You're not," Agent Staggs quickly interjected again. "Not really," he added with a phony smile.

"Dax," Jack said warmly and leaning back. "We had to do a little research, standard procedure background. After all, we couldn't make any offers or work with you if you were a wanted criminal, right? This is normal routine, nothing to worry about. We're here to ask you for a favor."

"A favor?"

"That's right. Think of it as favor for your country," Jack said, looking a bit more serious now.

Dax had heard that line before, probably in movies. "You must have the wrong guy. I am the most uninteresting person in all of the greater Bay Area. But then you already know that, of course."

Both agents chuckled.

"*Interesting* has nothing to do with it," Agent Staggs said, trying to sound reassuring, but failing.

Jack said, "I disagree, Dax. We saw the play. You're very talented."

"Well, thanks."

"Dax, really, we have a situation here, and we could use your help."

Dax realized he was beginning to feel a little more at ease. Although Agent Staggs struck him as a bit odd, these two seemed genuine enough. And it wasn't like they were trying to strongarm him.

"Okay," Dax said. "What does this favor involve? And why me of all people?"

A slight smile formed on Agent Staggs' mouth as he nodded and looked down again.

Jack leaned forward. "We've been on the tail of a couple individuals we think could be involved in some shady dealings. They're running a front business here in the city but using it to launder cash and smuggle certain items of interest out of the country."

"What's the front business?"

A pause. A shrug. "Business optimization, consulting."

"What are they smuggling?"

Agent Staggs' eyes went from the floor to Jack, then back down again.

Jack took a breath. "Mainly parts for high-tech weaponry."

"Weapons? I don't want to get mixed up with any kind of weapons."

"No worries, you won't be anywhere near any of that."

"Okay … but where do I come into play in all this?"

"Hang on," Jack said, holding up two hands, "I'm getting to that." He folded his hands and looked straight at Dax. "For months now we've been looking for a way to get the info we need to crack this case. If we move too quickly, there won't be enough evidence for a conviction, and everyone will disappear. Literally years of investigative work by several agencies around the world will have gone down the drain."

"Get in where?"

"Get in close to these guys, and gals."

"How?"

"By using an undercover, of course. A convincing one. One that has the looks and skills we need. We've been checking out the profiles of dozens of individuals who may fit the bill."

"Me?" Dax let out a genuine laugh. "You gotta be kidding. What if they've seen my shows?"

Agent Staggs suppressed a chuckle. Dax glanced at him.

"I seriously doubt they're the theatre type," Jack said. "We really don't anticipate that would be an issue. Besides, you're not really, uh, high-profile, if I may say so."

Dax smiled to himself. The man did have a point. "You mentioned this was partially for the Russian I studied in college. Let me be clear, I am in no way, shape or form fluent in Russian. I know a few greetings and phrases, maybe a couple cuss words, not a whole lot more. I found Russian to be just a small step or two below Mandarin Chinese in difficulty."

Dax expected Jack to take the comment with at least some humor, but the man only narrowed his eyes slightly. Agent Staggs was watching him again.

"We know you're not fluent," said Jack. "Well, we *assume* you're not. You got good grades, you learned a few things. But of course, it takes years and living with native speakers to get fluent at any language. We're not expecting you converse with anyone. But you may hear a few things around you that you recognize. It just helps that you've got some background, that's all. Your role is really more being a decoy than some infiltrator."

Dax drummed his fingers. They really had looked at his grades. He was feeling an odd sensation of excitement and something else.

Jack eyed him carefully with a slight smile. "Dax, let me give you the high-level perspective on this. The way we select an individual for an assignment is to first and foremost identify the type of behavior the person or persons being investigated are most likely to exhibit. In this case, we're looking for a particular action. Once this is established, we then select an undercover possessing characteristics and mannerisms most likely to draw that action out. There are many determining factors besides looks. There's your background, your work experience, whether you've been married, have kids, where you've traveled, et cetera. You're the best so far." He paused to let Dax process this.

"I think I'm getting more interested. But I still need to know what's expected of me," Dax said.

"Of course."

"I'm curious, why didn't you just put an ad out on *Backstage* or one of those? You'd have plenty of experienced actors to go though."

Jack shifted and crossed one leg over the other. His argyle socks were three shades of dark gray, a nice contrast to his shiny black dress shoes. "We considered all avenues of acquiring the right person for this job. But we didn't want to be so open and obvious. The quieter, the better."

"I guess that makes sense."

"Besides, we don't even necessarily *want* full-time actors. Sometimes a trained actor takes it too far, like trying to manipulate a scene from a show. We just need people who can follow strict instructions and protocol. In these situations, acting experience is often a plus, but not essential. Some of the best undercover decoys we've utilized never acted formally a day in their life."

Dax watched him for a moment. "I can back out and say no at any time, right?"

"Well, we'd appreciate a solid commitment. After all, we're investing some time and dollars into this. But of course, if you feel uncomfortable or threatened, sure, you can back out."

"But you won't want to," Agent Staggs suddenly said. "We think you'll like this. It's for a good cause. And you'll get paid." He raised his eyebrows and tilted his head on the word *paid*.

"Yes," Jack said, "there will be compensation."

Dax breathed deeply and caught himself from ogling at the ground. "Alright, tell me what's involved."

"Absolutely," Jack said. "We're going to prep you and dress you to make contact with an individual who we think will approach you."

"Will I have a microphone on me?"

"Yes. You'll be wearing a hidden camera and a body-wire system. Shouldn't be a problem with your experience on stage with costumes and wireless mics."

Dax took note that Jack was speaking as if he'd already said yes. His pulse was quickening again at the thought.

"Am I going to be alone in … there, wherever this is?"

"No. We're going to have at least two operatives very close by. As close as possible anyway. You'll never be left completely alone."

"And you said no danger."

"Dax," Jack said soothingly, "safety is paramount. We know you never trained to be a cop or soldier. We understand this isn't necessarily your thing. But there should be no danger at all, and if by some crazy chance something does happen, everything in our power will be done to protect you."

Dax shifted in his chair. "You said this was a favor for my country?"

"This potentially involves the security of United States citizens both here and abroad, yes."

"About when would this take place?"

"In the next ten days or so."

"And the compensation?"

Jack's eyes smiled. "The United States government will pay you $750 per day for your part. And that would include preparation and briefing time."

This made Dax pause. "That's not bad," he had to admit.

"We wanted our offer to be comparable to what a SAG principal performer might make in a day."

Dax knew some union people who were lucky enough to get commercial work now and then in the Bay Area. They made close to $2,500 per week, but only when they were actually working.

"Unfortunately though, there will be no residuals for this job," Jack added.

"Right," Dax said. With that kind of money, they would probably be expecting quite a bit out of him. Stuff they weren't telling him. "You're sure I'm the guy, huh."

"We're pretty sure. These things are never a hundred percent guarantee. We do the best we can."

"Do I have to give my answer right now?"

"No, but can you give us an answer by Monday?"

"Sure," Dax said, but without a lot of confidence. "How will I contact you?"

"Don't worry, we'll be in touch."

"For your country, Dax," Agent Staggs tossed in. He bore a smile thickly coated with cheap cheese.

Dax wanted to tell Staggs to shut up, instead, he pulled his cell phone out, flipped it open and held it up. "Do you have my phone—," he stopped and looked at the two agents. "Dumb question, huh."

Agents Jack Dauer and Michael Staggs of the Federal Bureau of Investigation smiled as they stood to shake hands and leave.

6: Desperado

Aaron Tisdale sat nervously in his red Ford Escort at the corner of Fifth and Hearst, one of his favorite fishing holes. He was gripping the steering wheel so tightly his knuckles were turning white. The odor from under his arms was unusually pungent this morning even though it was still early, not quite 8:30 a.m.

Monday morning, his scheduled appointment, and he was right on time. But things weren't looking so hot today, and it appeared the pickings were going to be slim. The coffee he had purchased a while ago was cold, but the two or three sips he'd taken earlier hadn't tasted that great anyway.

He sat back and sighed. Although not terribly unclean, the interior of his car housed a permanent aroma of fast-food and musty clothes. The windows seemed to always be dirty with smears even though he used a squeegee on them every time he filled up. It was a good thing he didn't smoke, considering the hours he spent here.

Sensing movement, his eyes moved to the side rearview mirror and saw the unmistakable markings of a police car as it made its way up the street. He watched to see if it would turn or start in his direction. Nope, it wasn't turning. He cursed under his breath.

Aaron reached for his cell phone lying on the passenger seat. Keeping his eyes on the mirror, he clicked the phone's contact menu button to bring up a list of numbers he had. He rarely called anyone, and no one ever called him, but he had a nice collection, as if he was someone important. If it was the same cop who had driven by earlier and bothered to stop and ask what he was doing, which was unlikely, Aaron would claim he was lost and trying to get hold of a friend nearby. The cop wouldn't buy that, of course. There was only one reason a sorry looking white boy like him was at this particular location in downtown Oakland at this time of day. But no matter, he hadn't been caught with his pants down, at least not yet. The explanation would be good enough to get him away without anything else happening. He smirked bitterly.

As the police car drew closer, he felt a sense of relief. Not only was it a different cop, but the officer was scanning up and down the sidewalk, paying little attention to the parked cars. It also looked like he was pecking away at his keyboard and trying to read something on his monitor. Through the small reflection, Aaron could see that the cop wore large dark sunglasses and donned the standard tough guy moustache.

As the black and white car passed, Aaron made a deliberate effort to sit up so he wouldn't appear to be ducking. But at the same time, he turned his head slightly down and away, just enough so that the policeman couldn't get a good look at his face, just in case.

Safely ahead now, the police cruiser slowed to almost a crawl at the corner, then turned and disappeared. Blood pressure up, then down again. Curse this little cat and mouse routine.

The stereo had been on but at an almost inaudible level. Aaron turned it up. The Eagles were performing a live version of *Desperado*, and Don Henley was moaning and wailing about how lonely it was to be all alone in the wintertime.

Aaron smacked the back of his hand against the volume knob to turn it off. Silence was usually better, and there wasn't much on the radio he enjoyed anyway.

About two blocks up he looked again at a woman who had been pacing for about the last twenty minutes near the overpass where she had stationed herself. She had disappeared around the corner when the police car had driven through but was now back. She wore a rumpled long, shiny black coat, the type that made a desperate attempt to look classy but had *well-wore cheap* written all over it. She looked troubled, and sad. Clearly, she needed quick money, probably for a drug fix, but didn't look mentally prepared to do what was necessary to acquire it.

Aaron didn't like the ones that appeared angry or otherwise disturbed in some way. They made him feel worse for the experience. He preferred ones that at least tried to smile and act seductive, as phony and deceptive a game as it was. Besides, he didn't find her all that attractive anyway.

He sat up and glanced at himself in the rearview mirror. His somewhat hollowed eyes stared back. He could see red veins branching out on a dirty white surface from the center of a plain, dark brown iris. He never could look at himself for very long. He sat back again and watched the woman.

She was typical white trash, maybe in her early thirties, but a hard life gave her an older and weather-beaten look. Her hair looked like it had been pulled back roughly and clipped behind. The only makeup on her face visible from this distance was bright, red lipstick. Under the coat her legs were bare, and she wore shoes that looked like cheap imitation black velvet Spanish style heels, the kind one picked up at a theatre prop store. She'd probably been a stripper a few years ago when the bloom was still on her flower.

Theatre—there was one thing Aaron was familiar with. And speaking of which, the last few weeks had been pure hell. He'd almost ran out the door last night after everything had been put away.

Never had he felt so alone, so isolated. There was something about the cast and crew of this latest gig. They had an energy and some kind of connection with each other, even the ones that didn't really get along. But as usual, Aaron felt none of it. Well, not quite true. He felt it, but as though through a transparent wall that kept him at bay. It had been one of those shows that made him feel once again like he should drop out of the theatre biz altogether. But he had nowhere else to go.

He'd often thought about his role in theatre during the many long, tiring hours behind the scenes with his oversized headphones wrapped around his head and the foam-padded microphone tickling his lips when he spoke. There was something about it that made him feel at least somewhat important, standing there with his cue sheet. Not *wanted*, but needed, nonetheless.

In reality, most of the cues and instructions he doled out to the actors were nothing they needed to hear, provided everything went according to plan. But there were those rare moments when something unexpected happened with a prop or an actor, and the director would start barking orders from the sound booth. At that point everyone needed him to know what was going on. Moments like those were just exhilarating—there in the dark, whispering as loudly as possible, eager eyes of attractive and talented performers looking to *him* for direction, the audience waiting just beyond the curtains and backdrops.

The other scenario where his skills came into play was when an actor or actress got sick or injured and someone else had to replace them last minute. This stand-in actor, having not been there during the rehearsals, was totally dependent on Aaron for direction. In those rare and fleeting windows of time, he felt like his life had purpose.

The thought made him smile to himself, but right away the smile dropped. After the show, when all was said and done, he would be put aside like one of the props. Ignored like one of the scuff marks on the faux wall. Discarded and forgotten like a soiled hand towel. They would all go out together while he would go out alone. Well not quite all, but the stuff he'd seen over the years made it seem that way. He saw more sex acts and other forms of hanky-panky in the changing rooms and even backstage during shows than he saw on television, not that he watched TV a whole lot.

And all that was why he felt the need for this Monday morning routine. It provided a little relief, short-lived though it was, from the world of loneliness he had long ago come believe was his permanent dwelling place.

Movement caught his eye, and he glanced up to see an old Volvo station wagon pulling to a slow stop by the woman in the black coat. Did she have a customer? It didn't look like it. She was looking strangely at the driver with a sad expression.

Abruptly, she turned and walked several steps up the sidewalk, her chin dropping with each step. A middle-aged Black woman dressed in jeans and a denim jacket got out of the Volvo. She walked to the woman in the black coat and put an arm on her back. It was a kind and gentle touch. The woman in the black coat kept her head down and appeared to maybe be crying, the Black woman gently patting her back and saying something to her.

Finally, the two slowly turned around, and went to the car. They sat in the Volvo for a minute or two talking, then the car started and eased away.

With mild but indifferent curiosity, Aaron wondered what the connection was between the two women and how often that little scene had taken place. Perhaps the Black woman worked for some shelter or program that helped get women off the streets. It didn't matter. But perhaps, just maybe, his story wasn't quite as tragic as the woman in the shiny, rumpled black coat.

More movement and voices caught his attention. Just across the corner from where he was parked, two young women strode down the sidewalk chatting away. One girl was white and slender, almost to the point of skinny, and was sucking hard on a cigarette. Her face was neither ugly or attractive, just sort of plain and uninteresting. She wore tight jeans and a long-sleeved black top. The other girl was Black, a little beefier but nicely curved, and wearing red shorts and white top. She had large and inviting eyes and her full lips were adorned with a dark, violet kind of color. The two of them were probably in their mid-twenties, but like the woman in the black coat, were already looking older than their years from the mileage of their street activities.

Aaron was immediately intrigued because had not seen either of them before; it paid to rotate locations now and then.

The two paused at the corner, exchanged a few lines, and then casually looked around. Aaron sat and watched but was already imagining himself with the Black girl – she had that erotic appeal that got his anticipation going.

A loud clanking engine could suddenly be heard up the street. Heads turned as an older, Datsun pickup drove up and stopped in front of the girls, breaks squeaking. Aaron was going to be mad if this guy took the Black girl. The driver leaned over and rolled down the passage window. Both girls watched but stayed where they were with wary expressions. The driver said something and the Black girl took three steps forward and bent down to listen, but kept her distance.

Aaron cursed loudly and smacked the steering wheel. He should have moved quicker while he had the chance.

Suddenly the girl stood straight, her eyes wide and her hands waving in front of her as she walked quickly back to the white girl. With head shaking no, she took the other girl's arm, and the two began hiking swiftly up the sidewalk.

The driver of the Datsun yelled something, but the girls kept walking. A loud clunk was heard as the car was put into reverse and began backing up to follow them.

Aaron folded his arms, sat back, and caught himself smirking as he watched. He was quite familiar with these streets and had seen a lot of things. Although it looked potentially dangerous, this little scenario wasn't going to escalate into anything. The "John" had either tried to offer too little money, or more likely, judging by the girl's reaction, was probably a strange or scary looking creep. No shortage of those types around here. Whatever the case, the girls were probably armed to some degree and were prepared to defend themselves if need be.

Aaron himself had a boot knife with a five-inch blade he kept covertly attached to his left leg under his pants, just in case. He knew he'd get into big trouble if he ever had to use it, but better to have and not need than to need and not have.

The trio went up the street, the girls walking and the car following in reverse. But after about thirty feet the pickup stopped. Another loud clunk was heard as the car was put into drive. With a slight screech of tires, it jerked forward and then squealed around the corner and was gone.

The two girls slowed their pace but continued to walk to the overpass where the woman in the black coat was earlier.

Aaron put his hand on the keys hanging from the ignition. It was time. He always kept his wallet locked in the glove compartment when he was doing this sort of thing. One of the biggest mistakes one could make was to let one of those girls see a wallet, let alone one with extra money in it. In the change drawer he kept a couple condoms, but never coins. When they saw coins, they always asked for them.

In two different pockets he kept a little cash. The first stash was the main offer for services, normally around forty dollars. He would claim he had no more. The second stash was in case the girl called his bluff and demanded more.

On these streets, with your average looking walker, one could get about anything for a fairly cheap price. The attractive ones usually asked for more, but it was easy to pretend he didn't have that much. It was an art form to know how to bargain with walkers, how to lie about how much you had and were willing to spend. And knowing where to start the bargaining was key. If you started too low, they got mad, and that ruined things. But if they were just plain unattractive and knew they weren't worth that much, they were grateful for what they got. For this girl with the red shorts, he could maybe start as low as forty and then play the game of having her implore for ten or twenty more for an "extra" good time.

Playing off other people's desperation ... he was going to Hell for this.

Breathing deeply, he started the car and edged off the curb. These moments of combined thrill, fear, and eager expectation were such a rush. Over time, he had managed to make the excitement of it all exceed the fear factor. He remembered the first time that had happened and considered it an important milestone.

A block away across the street and in the other direction, a man with a small furniture upholstery business was unlocking the door and going through a mental checklist of to-dos for the morning. He glanced up the street and saw a red Ford Escort pulling up to two prostitutes. He shook his head in disgust and watched for a moment. He'd been tempted dozens of times to call the police on these people, but since no one was getting hurt or killed, at least not in front of his shop, he didn't bother.

The girl in red shorts stepped up to the driver and leaned in. The other girl watched sullenly as she took a final drag on her smoke and flicked it aside. After a few moments, the girl strode quickly around to the passenger side, got in, and the car took off.

The white girl watched them drive away, then slowly looked around. She paused as her eyes locked on the man in front of the shop watching her. He pointed with his thumb up the street while jerking his head in a *get outta here* motion. She scowled back, her upper lip curling slightly, as her arm rose and extended a middle finger at him.

He snorted through his nose, shook his head again, and went into his shop.

7: Memories of Sam

The sun was bright and the temperature was rising fast on this Monday morning. It was only around 9:00 a.m. and already edging into the eighties. It was going to be a hot one, which meant another day working in the frigid cold of the air conditioners.

With a computer laptop bag hung around his shoulder, Dax made his way down the long hallway of the cube farm where he'd spent a good part of his life in the last four years.

The aging building was rented by a large telecom company and had a lot of mileage on it. The walls near the floor had a dark-colored trim that looked like mold, and the carpets had been shampooed so often the original designs could no longer be seen. The vents rattled all day and maintenance workers were constantly replacing the long fluorescent tubes that kept burning out in the old fixtures. In the building next to his, the tenants had been experiencing so many issues with the heating and air conditioning, they finally withheld their $12,000 monthly rent as ransom until something was done.

Dax had laughed to himself many times about the atmosphere in which he worked. He performed here as much as he did on stage, it was just a different kind of put on. People in the corporate world performed because they had to, they were wage-slaves just like himself and their goals were monetary based. The people who performed in theatre did so because they also felt they had to, but for reasons impossible to explain to non-actors.

But corporate workers and actors could behave quite the same when it came to competing for the good "roles." In both worlds, there was backstabbing, throat-cutting, political games, and closed-door deals. And in the end, it often mattered far more who you knew rather than how talented you were.

Uptown in the bigger and nicer theatres, a few of the leads were in unions and actually did get pretty decent pay, all things considered. But it lasted only as long as the show did. Those that got into the long running cash cow productions were fortunate indeed. But like everything else, there were only so many opportunities for a countless number of wannabes, the vast majority not talented or connected enough to ever get those parts.

Dax was in a strange mood. There were too many thoughts bouncing around in his head. He wondered if he would be able to get anything done at all today.

First off, there was last night, his final chance to be Eric, whip Glenn, and kiss Meygan. It would be the end of a lot of game playing and a big part of Dax was glad it was over. He strongly sensed Meygan's relief as she dropped her arms for the last time and turned and walked away.

It was great, Meygan, thanks. Hope to do it again. Ta-ta.
Whatever.

The final show had gone well enough, and Les Abraham was about as pleased as he could be, but Dax had been distracted. He'd almost missed a line or two. But at the same time, there'd been an exhilaration from within, and it couldn't be helped that some of that spilled over into his character. It'd made him more energetic, more enthusiastic, a more spontaneous, shoot-from-the-hip Eric.

The reason for this rush of energy was that he had made a decision—he was going to go for it. He was going to tell Agent Jack Dauer he was in.

Some of the other actors sensed this and had given him odd looks during the performance. Backstage in the sweaty, dark confines, waiting for queues and while fanning away the smoke from fog machines, people acted as if they wanted to ask him about this change they saw. But no one did. Maybe they didn't feel comfortable doing so, maybe they just didn't care. Glenn had given him curious glances. Dennis had smiled as if he was truly happy for him. Dillon had refused to even look in his direction.

Elizabeth had given him a big hug on her way out. Sweet Elizabeth. But even she pulled back and gave him a peculiar stare. "You were amazing tonight," she had told him. "You were really ... *into* it." Of all the people, she was perhaps the one he could trust to truly speak honestly. Well, Dennis too. He'd keep that little elephant she had given him and already thought about where he was going to hang it in his cube.

And then there was Les. The director had avoided Dax, either that or did a hell of a job pretending he was too busy to at least thank his lead man for a decent run. But then why should he? The show hadn't been a smashing success but hadn't been a flop either. In truth, Les was quietly as frustrated as the actors who wanted to be doing bigger things in bigger venues. He was probably not pleased with Dax for changing his style a bit on the final night and keeping everyone on edge wondering what was going to happen.

With regards to the FBI gig, Dax realized he should be happy about the potential money alone. He knew of a hundred actors that would kill for the opportunity both for the pay and the addition to the resume. He was just feeling a little apprehension. Sure, the two agents said it'd be risk free, but he didn't entirely trust them, especially Staggs. So why take the chance? It was the same question he'd asked himself several years before when he had gone skydiving. He smiled as he relished a feeling in his gut that he hadn't felt in a long time, perhaps since jumping out of an airplane. But even skydiving had ended up being disappointing in many ways when he discovered he'd never fit into the social circle that did that sort of thing regularly.

Dax glanced at his watch—9:12 a.m. Wait ... the symbol for new voicemail was flashing on his desk phone. When did it ring? Moving quickly, he auto dialed the voicemail number, then entered his password.

Hi Dax, Jim Kirkland here. I've noticed your name isn't on the audition list for Wild Hearts yet. This is the only week. Come on by, I might have a part for you. Talk to you soon.

Dax slowly hung up. Wow. Did one of the biggest directors in the area just give him a call? First a job offer from the FBI and now this. He started to dial back but stopped. Why hesitate? He'd be insane not to call Kirkland back. But did he not say to himself he was going to take a break from theatre for awhile? He'd think about it and call Jim back.

He realized he wanted Jack Dauer to call more than Jim Kirkland. When would they contact him? How would they contact him?

He left the cube to go to the kitchen for a cup of coffee. Shaheen, a software developer contractor from India, made her way toward him. She was studying some printouts, her thick eyebrows furrowed in deep thought. Taking advantage of the moment, Dax quickly moved his eyes up and down her. She had a cute but stern face and a petite figure, impossible to ignore as it swayed back and forth under lose clothing. Smooth waves of almost jet-black hair bobbed gently on her forehead as she walked. She always dressed conservatively which Dax appreciated. She never wore heals either, despite being just a couple inches over five feet.

When she first came onboard, Dax had attempted friendliness, but to no avail. He wasn't trying to be flirtatious, but she may have interpreted it that way. He even learned the Hindi word for hello—*namaste*—and tried it on her a couple times. But it never impressed her, and she always responded in English anyway.

She glanced up at him as they passed. The corners of her mouth formed a brief, unenthused smile and then dropped again before she was even past him. Typical. She was pleasant enough, but only because it was protocol. She was well aware of her high-caliber combination of brains and pretty, and if anything, was merely amused at being able to easily outclass the majority of people around her, male or female. But what Dax really noticed was the self-confidence. So much did she possess, there appeared to be no need to flaunt herself in any way. People were impressed with her exactly as she was. This caused her to treat almost everyone with the exact same level of unfussy indifference. How completely opposite this was to many theatre actors and actresses Dax encountered over the years who always had something to prove.

Dax shook his head and refocused. Returning with the coffee, he chuckled to himself as he rounded the corner of his cube and plopped down into his chair again. He pulled out the laptop and snapped it into the docking station. As it whirred and purred to life, the Mitsubishi twenty-one-inch monitor flickered to life and the Microsoft Windows 95 logo appeared.

He glanced at the time again. 9:15 a.m. He logged in and saw the new emails piling up quickly in the queue. It was going to be another typical Monday putting out fires and answering questions.

Hit with a sudden urge, he pulled out his wallet and began thumbing through some pictures he had stuck in one of the side pockets. In the back he had tucked a small photo away that was now a couple years old. And there she was—Samantha. It used to pain him too much to gaze into her eyes, but for whatever reason felt he could at the moment.

Sam smiled back. *Dear Lord, she was pretty.* Her shoulder-length, ash brown hair rolled gently and gracefully off her head. At the curves, it shimmered in the flash of the studio light, wherever the photograph had been taken. Her eyes didn't have much makeup, just a thin line of dark mascara, and they didn't need any. They carried themselves just fine, as he had often told her, not because of some unique color, but because of the way they smiled. In fact, they smiled bigger than her mouth. Come to think of it, Dax had never really considered what color exactly her eyes were, which in this picture appeared to be a light chestnut brown.

The photo might be getting old, but the memories were as fresh as yesterday. In the past, the tears would have immediately begun to well up just looking; perhaps time was doing some healing after all.

He held the image to his nose and inhaled deeply. They say of all the senses, smell is the most provocative. It must be true. The things we associate with scents—the memories, feelings, emotions—bring an instant response to the mind and body. As he breathed, he could imagine his nose buried in hair that was always so clean and fresh. He felt his body starting to become warm. He carefully slid the small picture back into his wallet.

The computer was fully booted now and on impulse, Dax opened his Netscape Navigator browser to Infoseek and did a search for the name, "Jack Dauer." The search came back with a few odd results, but no one remotely resembling the man he'd met on Saturday. He then did a search for "Agent Jack Dauer," and then "Jack Dauer of the FBI." Nothing. He did the same for "Michael Staggs" and found a lot more individuals with that name, but still nothing he was looking for.

Did FBI field agents normally carry pseudo identification as standard protocol? Wouldn't it be unethical to try to recruit someone to do a job while giving phony info about who they were or worse, what they really represent?

Still though, he couldn't shake the thought that he'd heard an accent. As an actor, he'd put on accents before, so his ears were always ready to pick up on things like that. Maybe Jack Dauer was a foreign agent in prior years that had moved here, attained citizenship, and was now working for American intelligence.

Dax sighed and drummed his fingers on the keyboard, his thoughts swimming. And then it came.

Beep-beep.

The high-pitched alert indicated he had received an email to his work address. He fumbled with his password and tapped the Enter key loudly. His spirit dropped when he read the subject line of the text: *Your account statement is available …* Frowning, he opened it anyway. Just a notification about a car insurance payment.

He minimized the window. Why was he so jumpy?

He opened his drawer and fished out a bag of green tea he kept stashed away. He sighed – coffee tasted so much better than this stuff. He had liked it for years, mainly for the health benefits, but as of late it was getting old. He put it back.

Music, that's what he needed. He found his headphones under a couple email printouts, plugged it into the laptop, and looked to see which CD he had in the CD ROM drive. He was about to listen to some Pink Floyd when it came again.

Beep-beep.

The new message had no subject line. His heart thumped a little heavier in anticipation as he read.

Dax, JD here. Starbucks on Locust at 11:30. See you then.

Dax reread the line three times and then realized he'd been holding his breath.

"You okay, Dax?" came a loud voice from above.

Startled, Dax quickly looked up at the large head hanging over his cube wall. Tom Kuka, the technical end user support guy for the campus, was staring with a puzzled expression.

"I'm fine. How about you?"

Tom laughed noisily. At six-foot four, he easily saw over all the cube walls and had an imposing and often intrusive personality to go with the large frame. Dax knew Tom had been in the military but didn't know much else.

"You were staring at your phone just now like you were looking at a ghost, dude," Tom said.

"Maybe I was."

"Heh … girlfriend dump you?"

"Maybe."

"Bad news from the doctor?"

"Maybe."

Tom grinned. "*Maybe*, you've finally gone off your rocker."

Dax leaned back. "What can I do for you, Tom?"

"Nothing. I just enjoy jerkin' with you."

"Don't I know."

"Well, take it easy." Tom saluted and strode away with heavy footsteps thumping, a large monitor box under his muscular arm.

Dax wasn't in the mood for any horsing around. His normally all-too-serious persona was currently on overdrive.

He looked back at the screen. Jack didn't say please respond if you can make it, it just said meet me.

Dax hit the reply symbol. The email address looked odd, just some numbers at a Yahoo address. Yahoo? Why would the FBI be using an address like that?

He glanced at his watch again. Oh, what the heck. He typed, "*Ok, see you there,*" and sent the reply.

8: Mr. Claiborne's Critique

Mario Silvestri sat watching his father, waiting for a response. He was trying not to look pushy or too eager, so he feigned indifference. But his fidgeting betrayed him. No matter what pretense he tried to put on, the decision his father was going to make in the next few minutes mattered greatly.

Rinaldo, Mario's aging father, sighed heavily and ran his thumbs along his thick red suspenders. His high-back leather executive Belgium chair squeaked a little as he leaned his large frame back. The sleeves on his white dress shirt were rolled halfway up his forearms exposing rough, spotted, hands and arms that had seen both poverty and luxury.

Where had he gone wrong with this son of his?

Mario, the second son of the family, had been properly named after his mother's father, according to old Italian naming traditions. Mario's older brother, Arturo, had been named after his father's father. Arturo was doing okay, soon to be graduating from UC with an MBA, and being groomed to run the family business.

Mario, on the hand, was a dreamer, a wannabe Hollywood actor. Not to mention a mob boss, whatever glamorous ideas he entertained about that. He had bumbled through a few theatre and film classes in the city a couple years ago and didn't do very well. Currently, he was taking a hiatus from higher education. When it came down to it, he was a spoiled kid who didn't appreciate what he had or where it came from.

Mario avoided his father's gaze and instead stared at the second hand on the old man's Cartier Santos wristwatch. The small dial clicked its way passed large Roman numeral symbols. The ticking was audible in the silence of the room, though just barely. The timepiece's thick, square 18-karat brushed gold case and brown leather strap looked good against the man's scarred, muscular arm. Mario remembered hearing it had cost almost twenty grand.

The Silvestris owned three thriving restaurants, one in the North Beach part of the city known as Little Italy, and the family was well known and respected in many circles. If you wanted fine authentic Italian dining with the best wine selections and the classiest service, you spent money at one of Rinaldo's joints.

Rinaldo's father, Arturo Sr., was part of the first settlement of Italian fishermen in the San Francisco Bay Area in the late 1800's and early 1900's. He and his immigrant friends had helped provide most of the fish consumed in the area at the time. It was a rough and competitive trade, but with hard work and some luck, had lucrative rewards.

Little Rinaldo was just a boy when he was already spending long hours in the boats with the cold, salty wind beating against his face, and on the slippery docks helping hack up piles of slimy, stinking fish. He had worked hard since he could crawl and had the scars to prove it. Some were from hooks and knives, some were from rope burns, some were from fights.

As he grew up, he saw the potential of the restaurant business. If businesses could pay that much for wholesale seafood, how much more were they charging for preparing and serving it? He began to make plans, and while doing so, more friends and relatives had arrived, and one of them brought a beautiful girl named Marinella. She had eyes as deep as the ocean waters they cast nets in. It was love at first sight, as well as some heavy encouragement by future mothers-in-law, and they were married before they were twenty.

By the time Rinaldo was twenty-six, he was running a little eatery in Oakland. The facility was part of a large storage building that had been partitioned out. It was the only location he could afford at the time. Nearby was a small fruits and vegetables stand that came in handy when the kitchen needed some quick supplies.

The quaint little establishment had one old fashioned wood burning stove and the rickety tables could seat about twelve at the most. It had one cook, himself, one waitress, his wife Marinella, and one busboy, the sixteen-year-old son of a friend who lived up the street. Baby Arturo was at home eating mashed carrots and bananas with his *nonna*, Marinella's mother.

They worked hard all day because the locals couldn't get enough of the fresh seafood and traditional Roman cuisine dishes that were served—dishes that came straight from the Lazio region peasant recipes. Nobody could take one's taste buds back home like Rinaldo. His cooking, by all accounts, was simply too good to describe in words. It didn't take long before there was a line at the door by eleven thirty, and extra tables had to be lined up outside to accommodate the traffic. They even shelled out for a part-time waitress to help work the peak hours.

But the big break came when a San Francisco food critic got wind of Rinaldo's growing reputation and decided to venture into Oakland. And one fine Tuesday at about a quarter to noon, the gentleman, Calvin Claiborne, walked casually passed about nine individuals who appeared to be loitering in front and strolled in like the alpha rooster.

Expecting to be gushed over like the celebrity he was, he instead was shocked when the very busy waitress rushed by while saying, "There's a line, sir. We don't take reservations, sorry." She wasn't rude, and in fact, had said this as pleasantly as possible. He took note of an authentic Italian accent. He also took note that she was quite lovely.

She left him standing by the small partition wall astonished, his coat and gloves hanging over one arm. Mr. Claiborne, though, was a reasonable man and promptly decided not to take it personally. It was a little insulting though, considering his picture had been in the newspaper for years. But this was, after all, a hole-in-the-wall in a city he normally didn't find himself.

He was about to turn and leave, never to revisit, when he suddenly stopped. The initial offense he had taken caused him not to notice the most amazingly delicious aroma his olfactory had ever encountered. It pushed its way out of the place like a thick wall. His well-trained nose did a quick analysis. The odor was not greasy or burned, nor a construed scent carried about by fans and manufactured with frying onions or garlic, a little trick he had encountered before. It was, rather, a perfectly homey blend of aromas that only the freshest and perfectly prepared food could create. He decided right then and there to do something he hadn't done in years—wait in line.

Within thirty or so minutes, he found himself welcomed in by the same waitress who had denied him entry earlier. As he followed, he had to make a conscious effort not to let his eyes drift down to the lower half of her body and legs, which showed nicely under her skirt. He was, after all, a suitably married, *older* gentleman, but still a man who, like any, would find it a challenge not to admire such natural beauty. Most of the rest of her was wrapped in a red-checkered apron.

He was seated at a petite round table barely big enough for one covered by a thick white tablecloth and a simple arrangement of salt and pepper shakers. A small dish with sugar and artificial sweetener packets rested by the edge along with a little glass vase that contained a single rose.

He looked around. The ambience was charming, with simple and tasteful décor that included paintings—real ones, mind you, oils and acrylics, not prints—and oversized, decorative wine bottles. Customers looked content and in no hurry to get through their meals. Soft, old-world European street-musician melodies sounded from invisible speakers.

The waitress, though hurried, moved with elegance and precision. The way she interacted with many of the patrons suggested she knew them in close and informal ways. She returned a minute later, gave Calvin a basket of warm bread and a menu which consisted of two folded pieces of thick stock paper, tea-stained in color. She also set down a small plate and two bottles of dipping oil, one a dark burgundy color, the other, the distinct green-yellow color of olive oil.

She paused, smiled, and said sincerely, "Sorry for the wait."

"Quite alright," he said moving the other chair around next to him and placing his belongs on it. He then put his hand out and said, "I am Calvin Claiborne. I've not been here before."

He saw right away that his name bore no recognition with her. No problem. Her large dark eyes made forgiving the offense easy. All bets would be off though, of course, should the food prove to be unsatisfactory.

She hesitated a moment, then gingerly took his hand and shook it. "Thank you for coming by Mr. Claiborne." She spoke with old-fashioned respect. She was probably quite used to the stares and advances of males and appeared to be skilled in the art of sizing people up.

"Marinella?" came a voice behind her. A man at a table was holding up a wine glass.

"Just for you," she said to the man. She turned back to Calvin, a wink still in her eyes.

"A pleasure to meet you," Calvin said. "May I call you Marinella?" He didn't wait for her consent. "Please, call me Calvin. May I inquire what sort of wine you serve here?"

She studied him for another moment and decided he was harmless, albeit a bit forthright as well as a little smug. Supremely confident, though. She was twenty-four and had been married since nineteen; men had ogled at her since she was fifteen and she took it all in stride and amusement. Italian men, at least where she grew up, could be far more macho behaving in general than Americans anyway. But this man was at least twice her age and had a wedding ring on, something she'd noticed, as all women do, the moment he walked in.

But Calvin had a professional flair about him, like he was there on business. He was also impeccably and stylishly dressed, but not to flaunt. Overall, he had several qualities that made him intriguing.

She smiled again and said, "I'll get you a list."

About ninety minutes later, and after a sapid meal of dishes with names most Americans couldn't pronounce, half a bottle of moderately priced but delectable Righetti Amarone, followed by a dessert of Crostata di Ricotta, he sat glowing. He simply could not remember feeling better about an eating experience. He sat back and breathed deeply. Using his finger, he carefully ran it around the inside edge of the plate, gathering the remains of some risotto sauce Marinella had said included a combination of cow, goat, and sheep milk and as many cheeses. He glanced around stealthily as he stuck his finger in his mouth and sucked it like a baby to a nipple.

He caught Marinella's attention and before he could stop himself, asked her to introduce him to the cook. "I would like a word with the chef of this delectable meal, please. Would you be so kind as to introduce me?"

She seemed amused by his use of the word "chef." She also gave him a puzzled look that asked, *just who are you?*

He smiled genuinely and pulled from under his coat a copy of the San Francisco Chronicle. It was already opened to the Food and Wine section, *his* section, and contained a review he had done three days ago. He held it up tapping near his picture.

She took the paper and peered closely at it. Several other patrons were now watching, wondering who this man was. "A food critic?" she asked, after reading a few lines. She asked in a way that implied she'd never heard of one.

He smiled and nodded, his eyes sleepy from the meal and wine.

She read a few more lines and cocked her head. She was interested, but not terribly impressed. But he didn't care, not at this point. He liked her and this lovely little place too much already. In fact, he just may have fallen in love with it.

After another few seconds of reading, she grinned, turned, and disappeared behind a small curtain. He could hear muffled words go back and forth in quick, organic Italian.

A tall, slender, handsome young man with jet black hair and eyes almost as dark emerged from the kitchen. His white uniform and apron were covered in various food and oil stains. His broad shoulders and long arms looked toned and full of muscle. He paused, quickly looked Calvin up and down, then strode confidently forward while wiping his hand on his apron.

"My name is Rinaldo Silvestri," he said, pronouncing his name with distinct subtleties that only native speakers of the language could produce. The young cook's voice was suave and poised.

Calvin stood and extended a hand. Calvin himself was a respectable six-foot-one, but he had to look up another two inches to meet the young man's eyes. He took the man's hand and said, "My name is Calvin Claiborne. May I call you Rinaldo?"

Chef Rinaldo smiled, but warily, and nodded. Calvin could see that he was a little suspicious. But there was something else in the young man's self-assured eyes, something … dangerous.

"Please call me Calvin."

Rinaldo nodded. "Okay, Mr. Calvin."

Although slightly embarrassed, Calvin spoke slowly and with as much sincerity as he could muster. So out of character was the act of complimenting the cook, he was almost unable to start. He sensed people in nearby seats watching and listening. "Rinaldo, I have not had a dining pleasure like this in years." He paused for a response, but Rinaldo only looked at him. "I do not say this lightly," Calvin continued, wiggling an index finger upward. "Or to most anyone, for that matter. You, my friend, are simply brilliant. I am wondering what other talents you may possess. I, I never go out of my way to say this …" He paused again, realizing he was repeating himself. The food and wine had clouded his senses. Clearly, he was better at writing reviews than giving improvised verbal ones. "Suffice to say," he continued, "I am deeply, *deeply* impressed with your modest establishment."

Rinaldo turned to look at his wife who stood a few feet away grinning. Looking back at Calvin he said, "*Grazie.* Thank you. I learned to cook from my grandmother. And my mother."

Calvin had to forcibly yank his stare away from Marinella's striking smile. "I don't care where you learned, young man, you are going places. And I'm going to help you get there, if I can."

Rinaldo was not at all sure how to respond. "I … well, I don't know what you mean, I –"

Claiborne held up a hand. "Your cooking speaks entirely for itself. But let *me* handle the words for those who've not yet had the pleasure."

Sensing something important happening, all eyes in the restaurant were now fixed on the two men.

"Marinella says you write about food?" Rinaldo finally asked.

"Yes," Calvin chucked. "I *write* about food, about service, about atmosphere—about the entire experience. You've not heard of me. Quite alright. Do you know this paper?" he asked pointing to the paper that Marinella still held.

"No," Rinaldo said. "I am sorry. I don't have time to read papers."

Calvin waved it off. "Quite alright. Listen, I want you to keep this one as a reminder, and I want you to buy a copy of it this Friday. In it, you will see that I am going to write about this place of yours. I don't know how I am going to give it the credit it deserves, but I will manage."

Rinaldo shifted his weight. "*Grazie mille.* Thank you very much."

Calvin waved it off again. "Oh, *prego*. And I will return. Take care." He extended a hand and the two men shook again. He then turned and gathered his belongings. He wanted to walk over and kiss Marinella's hand, an impulse partially encouraged by the wine, but he controlled himself. It wasn't some adulterous attraction, it was, rather, that he was simply in love with her presence, her qualities, and her natural beauty that blended so perfectly with the atmosphere of the place. If it were all one big flower arrangement, she was the principal and most alluring center of it.

With a final smile and nod, Calvin Claiborne exited, leaving the stunned young husband and wife team watching with jaws half-open. A moment later, the patrons in the restaurant began a modest applause, grinning and congratulating the couple.

That Friday, Rinaldo visited the newsstand down the street for the first time and picked up a copy of the San Francisco Chronicle. He thumbed through the pages until he came to the Food and Wine section. At once, he saw the unmistakable and dignified picture of Calvin Claiborne. In the photo, Claiborne held a fork and knife and bore a serious and almost challenging expression that said, *just try to impress me*. Above him was an article entitled, "Looking for the best place to eat in San Francisco? Try Oakland instead."

Rinaldo stood frozen holding his breath while he read, unaware of the sounds of the city around him. In the last couple days, he had asked around about Calvin Claiborne, and was assured the man had clout. His endorsement or jab, particularly to a new establishment, could mean success or failure.

In Rinaldo's case though, he had already been in business for almost two years, and had a good reputation, at least among the locals. Still though, after all the time, energy, and everything else he invested into his restaurant, this was an important moment.

Claiborne was true to his word. The article gushed, almost embarrassingly so. It described in exquisite detail the dimensions of the room, the furnishings, the music, the arrangement of the tables. It spoke of how walking through the door was akin to stepping through a time portal into the heart of rural old-world Roman Italy.

In words and in ways Rinaldo didn't even think was possible, the article meticulously described the smell, color, and texture of every item on the plate, all the way down to the consistency of the sauces and melted cheese.

Enchanting and enticing, it offers an unusually indulgent array of fish and meat, as well as an impressive wine selection ... the dishes spoke for themselves ... without a flurry of embellishments ... never mind the lunch time wait, the slightly cast-off furniture, or small interior, focus instead on what lands on the tables, and the lovely and charming server. And so on and so forth.

The results of the review came swiftly. In the first week, three more reviewers from two more newspapers and a local radio station came by for a visit. Two were drop-ins and were forced to wait almost forty-five minutes. One called in advance and although it broke protocol, a small table in the corner was held. In the week following, a nationally syndicated cuisine magazine sent scouts over to investigate, a couple who would later call Rinaldo's *the place* to eat when in the Bay Area.

The months that followed went by as colorful blurs and out of focus images, and a proud Rinaldo, along with his lovely wife Marinella, now bulging with their second unborn son, already named Mario, found themselves in a plush office inside one of North Beach's better eateries. They clinked fine crystal glassware in a toast to their success, Rinaldo sipping the contents of a $400 bottle of Giorgio Primo La Massa wine, and Marinella, a light zinfandel, as she patted her protruding belly.

"Papa?"

Rinaldo looked up at Mario, his eyes refocusing on the immediate surroundings. "Hmm?"

"What were you smiling about?"

Rinaldo had to look around to get his bearings back, so lost had he been in reverie. "Nothing," he said, sweeping his hand in front of him.

"Come on, pops." Mario leaned forward on his elbows, an eager look in his eyes.

It was moments like these that he forgave his wandering son with the impractical and idealistic dreams. And he knew why. Because those deep brown eyes were the eyes of his mother. She, too, was a dreamer in many ways, but she was also quite sensible. Too sensible, in fact, to have ever become a professional artist, although she probably could have. For years people told her she had the looks, the charisma, the charm, the whole package, but she brushed it aside. She chose instead a safer life of an anonymous wife and mother for her family. She would let others dream. Rinaldo would have supported her in every way. He would have done anything for her, without hesitating. But she was content to be who she was.

But not Mario. This kid's head was in the clouds since he could crawl. He also had that American independence and put his personal goals on par with family. Who knows, maybe even higher. But he couldn't be blamed too much for that after being born and raised in the San Francisco Bay Area.

Rinaldo steadied and looked at his son. "You remember the story I've told you over the years about that restaurant reviewer guy that came in one day and turned our world upside down?"

"Yeah sure, you told me. You still have the paper. You showed me."

Rinaldo folded his hands and looked up thoughtfully. "I always thought he was so impressed with the meal I gave him that day."

"He was. I read what he wrote."

"He loved your mother, I think," Rinaldo said, slowly looking down and lowering his chin exaggeratedly.

"Get outta here, pops."

Rinaldo smirked. "He did. I saw it. Had a hard time keeping his eyes off her."

"Can you blame him?"

"I guess I can't."

"And can you blame him for *not* wanting to look at *you?*" Mario grinned. His smile was his mother's too.

"Take it easy on your father, young man." He looked up again in thought.

How he had ended up with the two boys he did was beyond comprehension. The older Arturo was scrawny, homely, and with little personality. Thank God he was smart though and had goals. Mario was the looker, and his physique and appealing qualities had beguiled the girls, and a few boys, since he was sixteen. Yet one more thing that made him like his mother. As for smarts, well, he wasn't stupid, but he'd never be a college professor either.

Rinaldo sighed heavily. He loved both his sons deeply but in different ways and for different reasons.

Mario looked down and tapped lightly on the smooth dark surface of the mahogany desk where the old man spent a better part of the day anymore.

"Okay," Rinaldo said at last. "I will speak to them."

Mario slapped the desk. "Thanks, papa."

"You go on now, I have work to do."

Mario jumped up. "Love you, papa."

Rinaldo waved him off. He didn't like what he was going to do but would do it anyway. In the years he'd been travelling a very successful road in the restaurant business, he'd also gotten into other things, and had made friends in important circles. His trucking and distribution trade, which started humbly as a restaurant food and supplies delivery service, now brought items in and out of city from as close as the docks to the east coast. Not everything in those trucks was 100% kosher, but who could resist a little on the side, especially when it was far more than just a *little*. And besides, he was a good Catholic who routinely confessed everything.

But he had worked hard for everything he had. Nothing had been given to him for free and favors given always came with the price of returning favors. That was how the system worked.

Mario, on the other hand, had grown up privileged. He never experienced the eighteen-hour days and the hard, manual labor. He never spent time in the fishing boats or on the docks. Rinaldo had tried in every way to instill a work ethic. *Everything you have, I wanna see you perform for it*, he'd tell his boys. But in retrospect, the kid was always as different as north and south to his older brother Arturo. Marinella had understood this earlier and helped cultivate some of his more imaginative propensities. Perhaps she saw, in him, a way to live out some of her youthful dreams.

Whatever the case, Rinaldo was going to do Mario a big favor, and not for the first time. And it was imperative that Mario didn't take this one for granted. After this, it'd be up to the boy to do the rest. There'd be no handholding after that. The time was quickly approaching to where either the talent was going to speak for itself, or it'd be obvious that there wasn't enough of it.

Rinaldo glanced at his watch and then began rolling up his sleeves. In an hour he and Marinella were going to have coffee and then later, lunch. Perhaps today they would do something different.

Maybe they'd have Chinese.

9: Storytelling Savvy

Dax had to turn the music off as he drove—too much sensory input right now. Twice already he'd had a close call, glancing down at his phone while driving. He was usually a conservative driver and never pulled over for anything, but cops always took a second look at his navy blue 1989 Ford Mustang.

Turn left on Tenth Street, then on up to Locust. Relax.

The stern and guarded face of Agent Michael Staggs flashed in his mind, an image that furthered a feeling of discomfort. Hopefully he'd have little contact with the man. Even if he did, he was getting paid to do a job.

A horn next to him made him jump. A pedestrian had started crossing an intersection a little too soon and the driver screeched to a halt and yelled an obscenity. The person didn't even look at the car, just kept walking. As he waited and watched, Dax had to smile; he needed that kind of cool.

Turn right on Locust. Three blocks ahead on the right.

Dax parked in front of the Starbucks and instinctively glanced around like some fugitive on the lam. But the scene looked perfectly normal. People hustled up and down the sidewalks as the sounds of cars, horns and delivery trucks echoed around. An Asian girl sat directly in front of him at one of the outdoor tables, sipping something hot and donning headphones, listening to music on a Sony Discman. From where he was, he could see five or six people in the coffee house by the window tables.

He glanced at his watch – 11:27, swung the door open and hopped out. The warm, scrumptious smell of strong coffee and pastries hit Dax as he walked in. He glanced right and then swiveling his head, covered the entire place, briefly stopping on the face of each person as he went. No Jack Dauer or Michael Staggs, no men in black, no suspicious characters peering at him from over their newspaper. He turned around, no one on the sidewalk.

"You!" came a loud voice.

Dax gasped and looked up at the counter. A large man with a beard and a mohawk was pointing at him. The man was maybe in his late twenties and donning the standard issue green apron.

The man grinned. "Just kidding, bro. Step on up. What can I get you?"

Dax ordered a small coffee, no room for cream, thank you, and looked for a seat on the other side of the window where that Asian girl in front had been. But she was gone. Her cup remained on the table and now smiled at him with a rosy-red crescent-moon shaped lipstick smudge near the top.

Dax sat and took a sip of his coffee too quickly and burned his tongue good, causing a few hot driblets to roll down his chin. Swearing softly, he swiveled around to the serving table behind him to grab some napkins. With his back turned, he didn't notice the man wearing dark sunglasses who had quietly entered and was looking in Dax's direction.

The man stood for a moment and smirked as Dax wiped his face and dabbed a napkin at his shirt. The man wore a long gray coat over dress pants and casual dress shoes. On his head sat a saber-gray fedora-style hat with a leather band.

He waited quietly and then at the right moment, casually walked briskly toward Dax. As he passed, he said softly, "Hi, Dax."

Startled, Dax quickly looked up and saw the unmistakable long and narrow nose of Agent Jack Dauer. Dax started to say something, but Jack kept walking around the serving counter and to the door at the other side of the room.

Dax could only sit and watch in puzzlement. Jack paused at the doorway, turned, and then motioned with his head to follow.

"Oh, what is this now ..." Dax muttered to himself as he gathered his coffee and napkins and started after Jack like an obedient puppy.

The door looked like some sort of service entrance that led down a dim hallway. At the end of the hall Jack swung the door swung open and bright light flooded in. Jack continued walking out and let the door swing shut behind him.

Dax made his way to the door and pushed down on the release handlebar.

Behind the building was a smaller parking lot and a narrow road for delivery trucks. A black Lincoln Town Car sedan was waiting several feet up from the door, the engine idling, the back door open and inviting. Dax stood and stared for a moment. Jack stuck his head out the door and waved for Dax get in.

Dax approached the car and looked in. Jack now had his hat and sunglasses off and was smiling at him in an odd way. Next to him was a large man Dax had not seen before.

"Hop on in, Dax. Let's go for a ride," Jack said, patting the seat next to him.

Dax shrugged to feign cool confidence. He'd already decided he was going to go through with this, he just wished he felt a little better about it. He climbed in, shut the door, and the car jerked forward.

"How ya doin', Dax?" Jack said extending a hand.

"Great. How about yourself?"

"Excellent. Dax, I'd like you to meet Agent Kimball, Al Kimball."

"Hello, Dax," Agent Kimball said, breathing heavily and extending a chubby hand the size of a basketball.

Agent Kimball looked like he could barely fit into the brown sport jacket he was wearing. His body was thick, round, and muscular like a Samoan slap dancer, but his face, which had the circumference of a dinner plate, looked more European with maybe a mix of Spanish. Long sideburns of black mixed with gray jutted and rounded down the sides of his jaw. He was a contrast next to Jack's older and slender body whose clothing appeared to hang loosely on him.

Kimball's hand wrapped easily around Dax's and Dax could feel the strong muscles under the warm, pudgy, and slightly damp flesh. Dax guessed the man's weight was pushing three bills, if not more. The seam on the crotch of his light blue dress pants looked like it was about to split open. On his ankles and feet were white athletic socks and brown casual dress shoes.

Dax looked back and forth between the two men and then asked Jack, "Where are we going?"

"To a place where we can talk." Jack was still smiling.

"Why not back there?" Dax asked.

"You already have an idea of what we're dealing with here," Jack said, holding his palms open. "And you know we like to be cautious."

"Right," Dax said, glancing out the window. "Are we going far?"

"Not far. To the airport. Then we take a little trip out of the country," Jack said expressionless.

Dax jerked his head back at Jack, his eyes round with astonishment.

Jack laughed loudly and slapped his knee. Agent Kimball joined in shortly afterward.

"I'm kidding, my friend. We're just going down the street. You okay?"

Dax blew out a breath. "I'm fine. Where's Agent Staggs? Just curious."

"Oh, he's around," Jack said with a shrug.

Dax now had his hands folded in his lap and was twirling his thumbs.

Jack leaned forward a little. "Well?"

Agent Kimball watched curiously.

Dax tried to put on a big confident smile. "I'm going to go for it." He knew he didn't sound terribly enthusiastic.

Jack's expression turned warm and fatherly. "I knew it. I knew you were the man for this job."

"This is good news," Agent Kimball breathed, nodding.

"I hope so," Dax said. He stared at Jack for moment. "What if I change my mind after we talk?"

"Well," Jack said, his lips pressed back in a facial shrug. "We'd drop you back off by your car, and bid you farewell. Forever."

"After all that work digging up my not-so-exciting past?"

Jack chuckled. "It wasn't that much work, trust me."

"I suppose not." Dax stared out the window again.

"You're gonna like this, Dax. It's gonna be fun," Jack said. "You think you've done some acting before, well, get ready for the real stuff."

Dax smiled nervously and took note of Agent Dauer's lack of thespian lore. An actor with passion for their craft considers all performances the *real* stuff. But then this was real, right? Real scenario, real criminals. Real guns?

"You don't need to tell me I can't put this on my resume," Dax said.

"Actually, something might be able to be worked out. A lot of what's going to happen will be confidential, of course. And you'll need to sign some paperwork whereby you agree to a certain amount of secrecy. But for your resume we can give you the name of a private investigating company and good story."

"Really?"

"Trust me, we're good at stories."

Dax didn't like the way Jack said that.

The driver took a right on Sansome. The traffic was congested, and they were moving slowly, horns blaring on both sides.

A thought suddenly hit Dax. "Jack, you mentioned these … bad guys launder money. How exactly does that work?"

Agent Kimball glanced at Jack, smiled softly and looked out his window.

Jack said, "Why? You got some cash you wanna hide from Uncle Sam?"

"Yeah, right. I think you know the answer to that."

"Know someone who does?" Jack leaned forward, his hands clasped and his elbows on his knees. He stared at the floor for a moment as if gathering his thoughts.

"The movies make money laundering look simple. It's a simple concept, but never quite that simple to pull off without eventually ending up in prison. Depending on the amount of funds we're talking about, of course. Under ten grand, and you're probably not gonna be on the fed's radar. But over that, and eventually someone is going pay attention. There's two ways to launder money, and they work in kind of an opposite way. There's traditional or classic laundering, back when there was more cash floating around and less technology. And then there's the more modern take on it."

"Let's start with the modern," Dax said, grateful to have something for his brain to chew on.

"Okay," Jack said rubbing his hands together. "Let's say you have a big sum of cash you'd rather keep quiet about. People do this for all kinds of reasons. If the money's stolen, then it's obvious. If they want to avoid taxes on, say, skimmed cash, then that's also obvious."

"Skimmed cash?" Dax was somewhat familiar with the concept but wanted a more detailed take.

"Yeah. Cash skimmed off the top you don't report. You run a business and for every hundred dollars you take in, you only report ninety. Pretty soon you've got a pile you don't want the government to know about."

"Makes sense." Nothing new there.

"Also makes dollars. But sometimes a person wants to keep a stack of money from coming to the attention of, say, a creditor, a girlfriend, an ex-spouse, someone you own a favor to, et cetera. Someone who may claim entitlement to your cash. So, you wanna make the money disappear, right? Now all this isn't really laundering as we traditionally know it, mind you. But it's close. So, to make money go away, you can use a shell company, or a foreign bank, like those famous Swiss bank accounts."

"What are shell companies?"

"We have ourselves an eager student," Jack said to Agent Kimball, who just smiled and nodded.

"A shell company is a vehicle for business transactions. But in and of itself, there are no assets, nothing of value. They're not all illegal. You could buy some product at a huge bulk discount, and then immediately resell at a much higher price under a different name, the name of your shell company. And unless the buyers do research, they've no idea you're jacking up the prices. Perfectly legit. You've probably heard of *personal investment companies* or *international business corporations*. Those are usually shells."

"Interesting."

"But many of them are illegal," Jack continued. "Used primarily to defraud, hide, and transfer funds. I'll give you a simple example. For less than fifty bucks, anyone can go to the local county clerk's office and acquire a *doing business as* certificate which allows you to start and run a business under a fictitious name. You take the certificate to a bank and open a business account, and then you're in business. All that is still perfectly legal. But at this point, you can begin making up retailers, vendors, whoever, produce phony invoices, and start billing people. Often these kinds of things are inside jobs done by someone who works for a company or knows someone who works there. Say you work for some big corporation where purchase orders and invoices for thousands of dollars are going in and out all day. You slip your counterfeit invoices in under the radar, in the name of some fictitious counterfeit vendor, to be paid to your company. Then checks start getting written to you. If controls and accountability are lacking, and you possess the know-how, you can go completely unnoticed. Depending on the company, many invoices under a certain amount are hardly even flagged. Only the big ones."

"But you can get caught."

"Of course. A good auditor who knows what he or she is doing can find the anomalies in the books. The thing about these scams is that at first you're conservative and cautious. But once you've gotten away with it a few times, you start getting bolder. Or stupider. That's just one example."

"So now you've got money from the fake invoices, and you need to make it disappear," Dax said.

"Exactly. A person will usually spread it out over multiple bank accounts, safety deposit boxes, or investments. But then after doing that, you gradually make it reappear in some legitimate-looking fashion. In a way that doesn't draw anyone's attention. You can also start a shell import and export business so you can move the money out of the country easier."

"What can you invest in?"

"Whatever. But it's often best to go overseas. If you can stuff it in a carry-on bag, go on vacation. Visit your European roots and take a little excursion to Switzerland or Austria. Or in your case, Brazil. Put it in banks over there, out of your own country's jurisdiction. Or, if that's not an option, use your phony export business and have a trusted collaborator send you bills."

"These folks I'll be working with, are they doing this?"

Jack stared for a moment. "Let's just say they're into a little of everything."

Agent Kimball was staring again with his big, round, expressionless face. The car braked hard for a moment as several people crossed in front and the driver swore under his breath.

Dax was in deep thought. "How about, what did you call it, classic money laundering?"

"Well, it's kind of the opposite of modern laundering in that, instead of hiding the extra money, you fake a source for it. Say you're a drug dealer or an expensive hooker or a cat burglar who had extra money. If the government finds out about it because they caught you putting it in your bank or buying nice things, and they run an audit on you, you get busted for tax evasion. They may not be able to prove where you got the money, but they *can* prove you didn't report it. Tax evasion is how they got guys like Al Capone, and in part, the likes of John Gotti."

"How much extra income does one need to start thinking about doing something like this?"

Jack smirked. "If the illicit income is small and you have a legitimate job in some cube farm, like you, then there's little need. Just take a little less of the clean cash from the company paycheck and use the dirty money to makeup on the groceries, gas, and small toy shopping. They don't have the resources to go after the small fry anyway. If they did bother, they'd have a hard time proving anything anyway. And, since you also file your taxes regularly there's even more reason not to give you a second look."

Jack said that last line in a way that implied a lot of things. Dax wondered again just how deep they'd dug on him.

Jack continued. "But say a guy like you turns some good tricks and makes a bigger amount. Large bank deposits – over ten grand usually – get flagged, and then someone from the IRS may show up at your door asking where you got the new Beemer SUV and fur coat for the girlfriend. The classic money laundering way to avoid this is to create a cash-earning business that superficially earns the extra money. Any business that brings in a good deal of cash will do. But you'll want a business where it wouldn't be easy to compare your supplies in and out versus the receipts—like a commodity reselling business."

"Would a bar work?"

"Maybe. It could be proven that you purchase a grand a week in re-sellable booze but for some reason you're earning three grand. Coin operated arcades like in the old days were effective. You can still get away with it if you run, say, a car wash."

"Or a laundry mat."

"You've got the idea."

Dax's eyes were drifting in thought as he contemplated what it would be like to play a character who was skilled in money crimes.

"I'm glad you find all this fascinating, Dax," said Jack.

"It's interesting. As an actor it helps to learn new things about people, study their behavior and what motivates it. You never know when one day I'll play the part of a money launderer."

Jack stared at Dax for long, thoughtful moment then looked out the window. The car drove up another block, took a right, and came to a stop in front of a warehouse.

10: Dax the Axe

"We're here," Jack said.

The sign on top, in bold white all-capital letters on a forest green back said GENADY. Under it a rounded yellow awning with the same words hung over a burgundy red door. The building itself was a beige-white with green trim. It looked old but freshly painted.

Jack was watching Dax stare out the window. "We like to keep a low profile."

"Right," Dax said opening the door.

Somehow Agent Kimball managed to squeeze and grunt his way out of the car, making the vehicle's chassis bob and bounce. The three of them entered and walked past a small, clerk's desk that looked like it had been unoccupied for some time. The whole place smelled like disinfectant and fresh paint.

They mounted a staircase and began a creaky ascent on well-worn carpet. The carpet was frayed to where some of the old wood peeked out from the faded oval-shaped holes where many-a-shoe had stepped. Agent Kimball waited a moment as if psyching himself up, and then started up slowly, gripping the handrail tightly, his body taking up the entire width of the stairwell. Behind him, Dax could hear the man's huffing and puffing.

Down the hall and to a room, Jack slid a keycard through a device that looked like it had been mounted yesterday on a door that was at least twenty years old. The new paint looked like it had been done quickly and recently, the brush strokes and dried droplets of paint gleamed dimly from the ceiling fluorescent lights. The window at the end of the hallway looked like it had been painted shut and hadn't been opened in a long time. The whole place was dead quiet.

As Jack opened the door, a strong odor of food and tobacco smoke pushed its way out of the room.

"Me!" Jack said loudly as they made their way into the main room. Dax heard the faint sound of a radio with an unintelligible voice being clicked off.

The room they entered was large and somewhat disheveled. On a shabby green couch against the wall sat a man pecking away at a laptop that rested on a crowded coffee table. Next to the laptop was a full ashtray with a stack of cigarette butts, and one burning that was half smoked. Papers, wrappers, and an odd assortment of food items filled the rest of the table.

Dax looked at the snacks that included boxes of breads and crackers, as well as plates with pickles and onion stalks. On a side table by the television, which was turned off, he noticed a couple bottles of vodka, brands he didn't recognize.

"Dax," said Jack, gesturing to the man on the couch. "This is Leo."

Leo reached for the cigarette and stuck it in his mouth as he looked up at Dax and nodded once. Leo was a lanky man, maybe mid-forties, dark hair, and with a narrow, chiseled face that was two or three days unshaved. His mouth formed a half smile as he sucked smoke in, his eyes regarding Dax somewhat suspiciously.

Leo's a bit busy right now," Jack offered. "Let's go in here," he said, motioning to a smaller side room. "Sorry about the smoke, if that bothers you."

Leo was already tapping away again at the computer keys.

"I've spent years breathing in fake fog, hair spray, and makeup powder," Dax said. "Probably worse on the lungs."

"Could very well be. Have a seat." Jack pointed to a chair.

In the small room, there was a table and several folding chairs on either side. Another laptop sat on the table alongside manila folders and a couple small stacks of papers. Two Styrofoam cups with the remains of cold coffee rested near the edge.

"This isn't headquarters, is it?" Dax asked.

Jack smirked. "Like I said, we keep a low profile."

Dax sat facing the back of the laptop screen while Jack tapped at it and appeared to be logging into something. Heavy footsteps and shuffling could be heard and then Agent Kimball waddled through the doorway and sat heavily in a seat at the end of table. He was still breathing hard from the climb up the stairs.

"You ever smoke cigarettes, Dax?" Jack asked.

"I did in high school. Quit my second year of college."

"You're a smart man," Jack said.

"Not really. I'd have a better career by now. Or my own business or something." Dax had to laugh at himself. "You know how career counselors always ask the question, where do you see yourself in five years? I haven't been able to answer that question in the last fifteen years."

"Like what kind of career?" Jack asked.

Dax shrugged again. "FBI agent maybe."

Jack shook his head.

"Now that's not so smart," Agent Kimball said.

"No?"

"Nah," said Agent Kimball, his large face frowning. "Fourteen to sixteen-hour days, lots of boring surveillance or research. No life, little pay." He said this in a way that Dax couldn't tell if he was joking or not.

"He's right," said Jack. "Now your next question will be, then why do we do it?"

"I was curious, yes."

Jack sat back. "Lots of reasons. We come from all sorts of backgrounds and have all kinds of ideas about it. But in the end, the ones that stay are those that try to see the big picture and remember that we're a part of something much larger than ourselves. At the end of the day, the general public has no idea who all was involved in solving some big crime or thwarting a terrorist attempt or assassination. But we know, and that knowledge brings with it a certain amount of satisfaction. But don't get me wrong, a lot of people do drop out once they found out it's not all glam and action like in the movies." He paused for a moment. "I'm hoping you'll get something like that out of this, Dax. A sense of being a part of something big and important."

"I hope so too," said Dax. "But you're not saying anything about FBI agent pay."

"That's because there isn't much to talk about," said Jack. "For a long time, you don't even make fifty-k. More money comes with climbing the leadership ladder."

"No wonder you know so much about money laundering."

Jack raised his eyebrows. "Watch it, wise guy," he said with a smirk. "Feel free to apply. Heck, you'll have experience after this."

"Yeah? I'm qualified?"

"You might be. You need to be between twenty-three and thirty-seven, which you are, to apply as a Special Agent. You've got a four-year degree. You're in pretty good shape. You're right there. But there are plenty of other positions within the department where age and other things don't matter. Linguistics, forensics, training, research, and analysis."

"Don't do it," Agent Kimball said while he cracked open a can of soda he had produced from somewhere.

"My degree is in Psychology," said Dax.

"I know," said Jack. "You might be good in criminal profiling."

"And I suppose they'd do a full background check on me, even more thorough than what you've already done."

"Of course. Standard check goes back seven to ten years of your life, unless anything suspicious is discovered."

"Well, they won't find anything more interesting than what you have," said Dax.

Jack just eyed him for a moment. "Maybe. But there'd be a polygraph too. You want something to drink? Coffee, water, a soda?"

"No, I'm good." Dax looked at a round clock on the wall. He wondered if the small hole in the center had a camera like in the scene from *Scarface* when the undercover agents were setting up Tony Montana.

"Dax," Jack said, breaking the silence. "Do you have the ability to remain calm under duress?"

"Uh, well, that would depend on the level of duress. I guess.'"

"We're not talking wired-up-to-electrodes interrogation here. But sometimes a person gets spooked when strange people start asking questions. We're thinking you'd not do that."

"Why's that?"

"You're composed, even kinda serious. Maybe too serious."

Dax smirked. "I hear that a lot."

"And this is where your acting skills are going to come in handy," said Jack. "You know how to audition, right? You remember your first audition and how you got better and more confident after that? Think of this as one big audition."

"Okay," Dax said nodding.

"We also need people who possess the ability to act according to the assigned character profile. This is important. This is where you really fit the bill."

"Really?"

"Oh yes. Isn't that right, Al?"

Al nodded in agreement while taking a loud slurp from his soda can.

"Finally," Jack said leaning in, "we need someone with the ability to ask the relevant questions of the subjects." He paused and watched Dax think about this. "You think you can do all this?"

"Yeah, I think so."

"You're gonna *know* so by the time we're ready. But first things first. Al?"

Agent Kimball reached down and produced a small briefcase which thumped heavily on the table as he set it down. With two loud snaps the case opened. He took several sheets of paper out and began thumbing through them.

"We need you to sign some paperwork and wavers, Dax," said Jack.

"Wavers?"

"Standard protocol kind of stuff. Just like when you get hired by anyone." Jack saw the blank look on Dax's face. "You know, hired? You're going to be a temporary government employee. A contractor."

Dax nodded. "I guess you know my name isn't really Dax."

Jack tapped a couple keys on the laptop and then sat back again. "Yes, David, we know."

Dax cringed for a moment. He couldn't remember the last time anyone had called him that.

Jack folded his hands in his lap. "So now that the subject's on the table, just curious, but when and why did you acquire the name Dax?"

"You don't know?"

Jack chucked. "No. We didn't go all the way back to your childhood."

"When I was fifteen or sixteen. I was watching some movie and the bad guy was named, or nicknamed, *Dax the Axe*. It seemed cool next to my real name. The Dax part, not the axe."

"David's better than Al," Agent Kimball offered, still shuffling through his briefcase.

Dax smiled. "Maybe. But what can I say, I just liked the name Dax."

"Hmm," said Jack, nodding. "The bad guy, eh?"

"I guess it was going to be my stage name if I ever got famous."

"Was this *Dax the Axe* an assassin?" Jack had a wink in his eye.

"Nah—sophisticated cat burglar. Knew how to get in and out of places without being seen."

"Sounds like our kind of guy," said Jack looking back at his computer screen and then typing something. "But why the axe part?"

"He had tattoo of a bloodied axe on his forearm. Told someone he got it to look intimidating when he did time in the pen."

Agent Kimball slid some papers in front of Dax.

"You need to see my license or anything?" Dax asked.

"We already have a copy," Agent Kimball said. "Page four."

Dax stared at the document in front of him. At the top it read, *AGREEMENT, CONSENTS, DISCLOSURES AND WAIVER BY PARTICIPANT.*

The next paragraph said, *THIS AGREEMENT is made and entered into this date between the parties—The Federal Bureau of Investigation (a division of the Department of Justice of the United States Government) and (Full name(s) (no abbreviations): DAVID PAULO RIBEIRO, hereinafter singularly referred to simply as "Participant."*

ACTIVITY: Case 312A-C9451-03. Surveillance and Undercover Operations in the city of San Francisco, California ... It then had some dates and descriptions of the investigation.

Most of it didn't look worth reading, but Dax felt compelled to at least glance through it. The next paragraph was a confirmation that he wasn't acting as an agent for or on behalf of any third party, and is an adult over the age of twenty-one, blah, blah ...

A couple more paragraphs down, and something caught his eye because it talked about risks and injuries:

The Participant and The Federal Bureau of Investigation understand and agree that there are a number of various programs on and off various premises, involving activities and individuals that are often not under direct control or supervision of the Federal Bureau of Investigation, and that there is an overriding policy that each participant involved in these programs does so at their own risk of personal injury or damage to property. It went on to say that the FBI had no control over such things and cannot be held responsible.

Great.

Dax skipped down a few paragraphs to a non-disclosure agreement that had to do with the confidential treatment and protecting of sensitive information. After defining what "sensitive" is, it threatened legal action if the agreement was violated which could result in fines and prison sentences.

Ah, then the important part. *As compensation for the services provided, the Participant shall be paid a wage of $750.00 [per day] until completion of the position*, blah, blah. Sweet.

Then on the next page, there it was—a copy of his most current driver's license. It was blown up two and a half times or so, clearly showing the boredom and irritation he was feeling that day at the DMV office.

DAVID PAULO RIBEIRO; SEX:M; HAIR:BRN; HT:5-10; WT:180. This was followed by his promise to agree to all rules and regulations set by the FBI and if he doesn't, can be terminated without liability or cost to the FBI.

The last page had a few date and signature lines to complete. He signed and slid the papers back to Agent Kimball.

"So, if I learn any secrets and tell them to anyone, some men in black are going to come knocking at my door?"

Jack just smiled while looking at his computer screen. Agent Kimball was going over the last page.

Dax glanced back up at the clock on the wall again. "I need to get back eventually. Got a lot going on at the office."

"No problem," Jack said hitting the Enter key loudly. "We're just going to take a few minutes to over some preliminaries. Then we'll drive you back to your car."

"When does the, uh, *activity* begin?"

"We should be able to make first contact this Friday."

"*This* Friday?"

"Yeah. I told you we need to move kind of fast. That too soon? You got something going on?"

"No. Do I need to take any time off from work?"

"You shouldn't, no. Most of this is going to happen in the evening hours. I'm going to give you some basics here in the next few minutes, and then this Thursday we're going to fit you and give you more details."

"Fit me?"

"Yes. You're going to a nice party. We gotta dress you for the part."

"Black tie? James Bond style?" Dax put on his best Sean Connery impression. "Shaken, not stirred."

Agent Kimball laughed.

"Funny. And not bad," said Jack. "You oughta be on morning radio."

"What's the occasion?"

"A high-profile vendor is putting on a social for a few potential buyers. Ostensibly, they are an international trading company that does business with cheap product makers in China, Korea, Brazil, and other places. They bring back stuff like aluminum tubing, pet laminated steel, silicone electric wires and cables, et cetera."

"But that's not what they really deal in?"

"Oh they do, and maybe a few other things. But it's not them we're interested in. Your job is to be more like a decoy. We're hoping you're going to bring someone up to the surface that we highly suspect is going to be there."

"Why would this person be there?"

"To make contact. But not with you, not initially anyway."

"Will this person be wanting to kill whoever they think I am? Do I owe them money or something?" Dax was trying to sound cool but heard a little alarm in his own voice. "Absolutely not," Jack said reassuringly. "We just need to know who he is and record his face and voice. We'll fill you in on Thursday. For now, I need you to stand up. Please."

"What? You going to frisk me?"

"Relax, double-oh seven. Just need some measurements," said Jack reaching for a role of yellow cloth tape measure.

Dax stood clumsily and pushed the chair back with the crook of his knees. He watched Agent Kimball grunt himself up from his chair and shuffle heavily out of the room.

"Okay, relax your arm at your side and bend your elbow slightly."

Dax did as he was told. Jack measured from the center of his neck, over the point of his shoulder, and then down the outside of his arm past his elbow and to the wrist. He then jotted some numbers down on a form.

"They teach you this stuff at the FBI?" Dax asked.

"Oh, I have all sorts of skills you don't know about. Alright hold still."

Jack carefully wrapped the measuring tape around the largest part of Dax's neck, then under his arms, around his chest and across his shoulder blades and noted the numbers. "Looks like your blazer size is around a thirty-eight," said Jack, writing again on the form. "You work out a lot?"

"When I can."

Jack measured Dax's waist and inseam and wrote everything down.

"The rest we'll figure out and finish up on Thursday."

Agent Kimball appeared in the doorway again with a large and expensive-looking camera.

"Step over to this wall for me," Jack said, motioning to the wall behind Dax.

"What am I going to be wearing?" Dax asked standing straight against the wall as if getting his mug shot taken.

"A nice suit. Something expensive."

The camera snapped, temporarily filling the dim room with a bright flash.

"Do I get to keep it afterwards?"

"We'll see. Please turn to your right."

The camera clicked again and the bright light flashed.

"What is that?" Dax asked, nodding at the camera. Agent Kimball was staring into a small screen on the back of the camera looking at the pictures he had just taken.

"What do you think? A picture of you."

"Instant image? Like a polaroid?"

"It doesn't use film, it's digital."

Dax stared incredulously. "A *digital* camera?"

"Yeah. Only the military and certain branches of the government have them. In a few years they'll be available to the average consumer."

"Really …"

Kimball gave a thumbs-up and a nod.

"These are for our wardrobe person," Jack said. "To make sure we get the right color and style on you. And this is not going to be ordinary garments. You're going to have a body microphone and a camera, like I told you about. They have these cameras that go right through your shirt buttonholes. Practically invisible unless you look close."

Dax began staring at the ground, his mind racing.

"Come on," said Jack, taking a step closer. "Tell me this sounds like fun."

"Actually, it does. Will I have a gun?"

Agent Kimball chuckled as he turned and exited the room.

"Dax," said Jack, "we're going to have people right there. You're not going to be alone. What you're doing is important." He put a hand on Dax's shoulder. "We'll shore things up on Thursday and give you the rest of the details then. Okay?"

"Sure, no problem."

"Come on, let's get you back to your car." Jack turned, walked back to the table, and snapped the laptop shut.

The couch was empty in the main room. Dax noticed Agent Kimball downing a small glass with clear liquid and the way Kimball pulled his lips back when swallowing suggested it wasn't water. The quiet, muffled voice of who Dax guessed was Leo could be heard from the small bedroom down the hall, but Dax couldn't understand what he was saying.

"See you, Dax," Agent Kimball said with a small wave. Dax waved back and paused for a moment, listening to Leo.

"Let's go," said Jack, taking Dax's arm and leading him out the door.

The warehouse was still dead quiet as they descended the old stairs, past the small, dusty clerk's desk, and out onto the sidewalk.

11: Insider Info

Auditions for *Wild Hearts* were being held at the Treasure Box Theatre near Union Square close to where O'Farrell ran crosswise into Third and Fourth Streets. Although a small venue with less than 450 seats, it had a quaint old feel and proscenium-like stage left over from the renovated opera house it had once been. This type of stage was normally built for larger houses, but they had somehow made it work. There were two square sections of red folding seats on the main floor separated by a center aisle that led to the exit at the top. A little U-shaped balcony stretched its wings out along the walls and held several box seats. It was the kind of intimate place where every seat in the house had a good view of the stage and a person felt close to the actors.

The house lights were dimmed, but the stage was hotly illuminated. Hopefuls who stood on the platform overlooking the seats could barely make out the faces that gazed up at them. But once the eyes adjusted, actors were able to zero in on Jim Kirkland, the slender gray-haired gentleman with the thick glasses who sat in the center of the fifth row. As director of the show, he was the one they had to impress.

Les Abraham sat patiently in the seventh row a few seats down from Jim to keep a respectful distance. They watched as wannabes shuffled on and off the stage. A young female intern with fire-red hair that Les recognized as Sharon Toomey from one of his workshops sat next to Jim with a pile of folders full of headshots and resumes on her lap. Several other individuals associated with the theatre group were scattered around in the first several rows.

Les sighed at the weak lineup. It was rumored the actual showing of *Wild Hearts* was going to be at the legendary Grand Theatre, but it was still up in the air. Bids were being placed and negotiations made at levels beyond his reach or care. Personally, he'd like to see it shown at the Lamp Setter, but it wouldn't be his call. He was trying to be unconcerned, and more importantly, not bitter about being denied the job of directing this show.

Les turned to look at the wispy grey hair that was combed neatly back on Jim's head. Jim's skin was taunt around the temples and neck, slightly blotched and red-tinged from years of excessive drinking. He wore his customary casual dress pants and rumbled sport coat over a polo shirt. He sat a little less patiently, than Les, the edginess beginning to manifest itself in odd ways.

Jim wore thick, black-framed glasses that tended to slide down a narrow nose. As the morning grew longer, he began more and more to grab the side of his glasses with thumb and index finger and readjust them on his face.

In his younger years, Kirkland had been a devoted thespian student of one of Stanislavsky's mentees. Having had that third-generation line up to the master of method acting, he was passionate about the inner feelings and truthfulness that actors displayed. Whatever an actor did, it had to be genuine. In Les' opinion, Jim was a bit fanatical about it. Les' approach stressed more the visual impact to the audience rather than how the actor was actually feeling. A few years as a hopeful television producer had done that much to him.

A young actress was on stage now wringing her slender hands nervously and shifting her weight back and forth. A lone spotlight beamed down on her, both highlighting and isolating her. Jim was looking down jotting some notes on a pad in his lap. One could almost see the poor girl's anticipation dripping off and puddling around her feet. Les smirked silently and sat back. She had too much makeup on her eyes and lips for her small and milky-white face, making it look like a porcelain mask with brightly exaggerated paint. He could see right away she was wasting her time and would not get any part, not because of her looks primarily, but rather, lack of poise. Sad. She probably had not slept last night in anticipation and was prepared to give her whole heart to this moment.

The room ticked away in silence. Finally, Jim looked up. "Hello," he said. She just stared back. He had her resume in front him but asked anyway, "And what is your name?"

The girl looked out into the mostly empty theatre and did her best to put on a genuine smile while introducing her monolog. "My name is Donna. I'm going to do the part of Mary from the play *Fortune and Men's Eyes* by Josephine Preston Peabody."

Jim nodded and adjusted his glasses. Good, something different. He sat back to listen. He thought he'd maybe heard this monolog once before but couldn't remember it. "Please, proceed," he said, taking a quick breath that sounded more like a sigh.

Les paid little attention as Donna went through her lines, and he was pretty sure Jim didn't either. Nothing about her stood out—her appearance, confidence, or believability. That made her garden-variety, something that would haunt her attempt at an acting career until she finally gave up. And to make matters worse, despite all her efforts, it was obvious she was making the classic blunder of focusing on getting every word correct, to the point of sacrificing character.

Jim turned slightly to see if Les was still behind him. He didn't hate Les but didn't like him either. He wished Les had something more important to be doing right now. Les had some good merits, and students that came through his classes and workshops before going on to Jim's normally had many of the assertive and purpose of character concepts drilled into them that directors looked for. But truth be told, Les' technical style of directing was enough to drive Jim quite mad, to the point where he had long given up watching any of Les' plays. Les would begin the process of blocking, even on the first rehearsal. That was a serious taboo to a Stanislavski Method loyal. Let the actors move how their hearts told them to; block only after that process had run its course.

Another thing Les would do is cast a person almost solely, it seemed, on looks and appearance. Les preferred handsome, young men in particular, this was no secret, but come on. This was no doubt a carry-over of his commercial camera days, an arena that far more stressed an actor's outer shell than inner talent.

The girl finished her monolog then clasped her hands in front and waited, her weight shifting again. Les looked a Jim, who had been staring at the floor lost in thought. The intern was looking at Jim as well.

"Oh, yes," Jim said, glancing up with a forced smile. "Thank you, uh …" He looked down at his notes, "Donna." He then said his usual line. "That will be fine for today. We'll give you a call if we need to see more."

Donna smiled pleasantly then turned to go, her mannerism showing the enthusiastic albeit futile hope she still clung to.

Les shook his head. Over the years he had seen countless hopefuls who would never come anywhere near the big leagues of either theatre or camera work. He had long reached a point to where he would be bluntly honest during auditions, far more than Jim. If a person would not be getting a part, he would tell him or her right then and there. And he would probably tell them why, in precise terms. This could, at times, make actors, especially actresses, shed tears, but it was better, in his opinion, than giving a person false hope. Yes, it was a cruel world where losers sorely outnumbered winners – no point in pretending otherwise. When these moments came, he did not do this in a rude or sarcastic way, or so he thought, he just told it for what it was.

A young man appeared and strode cocksure up to the center of the stage, looked back and forth between Jim and Les, and decided correctly that Jim was in charge. Then, in a volume of almost yelling, said to Jim, "Good morning!"

Jim had been taking a resume from his intern and looked up almost startled. The young man smiled broadly and gave a small wave. Jim chuckled and looked down at the resume.

"My name's Adrian!" the young man said, or rather, yelled again.

Jim adjusted his glasses, set the folder on the seat next to him, and with a palms up gesture, gave the young man the signal to proceed.

"Adrian Stares!"

Les glanced the young actor up and down. Adrian was slender, maybe twenty-four, but with a boyish face. His messy hair was dark and thick, and appeared to be a big part of his personal character. He donned faded blue jeans and a gray t-shirt. His eyes were bright and mischievous. He was a guy ready and willing to do probably anything.

With excited eyebrows up, he nodded and began. One foot crossed over the other as his arms came up and bent, as if he were trying to mime a tree. Making a strange falsetto *whoop*, he turned his head and looked up. He then whistled and looked down. One arm dropped as he began tiptoeing to the right, his body beginning to twist.

Some of the actors began giggling. Others stared with puzzled expressions. Sharon sat back and smiled in amusement. Back and forth the young actor moved, making odd sounds and even odder gestures. Les laughed loud enough to make Sharon turn around. She was grinning. Adrian continued, and this went on long enough to where it was obvious there were no words to this little act.

Jim interrupted. "Uh, excuse me. Do you have a monolog I could see?"

Adrian froze and looked up, one elbow still pointing toward the ceiling. "No," he said with a sheepish smile.

Jim breathed quickly, shifted, and adjusted his glasses. "Well, I need to see a monolog. You know, with words."

Adrian's arms dropped, but he looked straight up with that boldness in his eyes, shrugged and said, "Sorry, I don't have one."

Jim regarded him for a moment. "Paul," he said loudly. A big, broad-shouldered man in a long-sleeved plaid shirt and dirty blond hair walked out from behind the curtain. "Please get me the small table we were using yesterday."

Paul nodded and ducked behind the curtain. A moment later he returned with a small candle stand style table and set it in the middle of the stage. It looked like a well-used prop that had seen many performances, mostly period pieces from the 18th century or earlier. He held up a piece of paper and looked at Jim. Jim nodded and Paul placed the paper on the table.

"Okay, Adrian," Jim said. "Please do something for me. Go to the far end of stage left," he said, then waited. After a moment, he pointed and Adrian followed the direction, puzzled, but obedient.

"Now," said Jim, "walk across the stage and around the table. You make up the reason why you're here. As you pass the table, stop and look at the paper. Then react to it. Give me something to believe what you just saw and then give me a reaction, both physically and verbally."

Adrian's eyes moved back and forth while he considered the instructions.

Les frowned. This was a basic acting 101 exercise in character building and commitment.

"Please proceed," Jim said, waving him on with his hands.

Adrian propped his shoulders up, and with an almost arrogant smirk, strode confidently across the stage to the table. As he passed the table, he looked down exaggeratedly and froze with one leg still in the air, cartoon style. Several people smirked loudly. Then leaping to the table with wide-eyed panic, he grabbed the paper and quickly held it up to his face. After a few seconds of pretending to read, his head rapidly turning back and forth, he suddenly began jumping in the air. Without words but with plenty of groaning and wild animal like sounds, Adrian bounded up and down, back and forth across the stage, before finally picking up the table and throwing it several feet in the air. It crashed down with several loud thuds as it bounced on the hard wooden stage.

Everyone was laughing now, and most eyes turned to Jim, who was not amused. Shaking his head, his hand came up under his glasses as he massaged his nose with thumb and forefinger. He was reaching threshold for the morning.

Les sat back grinning, genuinely enjoying it all. The morning hadn't turned out to be so dull after all.

"Okay, okay," said Jim.

Adrian either ignored Jim or did not hear and was now running back and forth, leaping like a pursued gazelle.

"ENOUGH!" Jim roared.

Now all eyes were on Jim. It was out of character for him to yell like that.

Adrian stopped at the front stage right and was looking at Jim with those overly confident eyes again. It was impossible to tell if he was even remotely aware of what a ridiculous scene he had just made.

"That'll be enough for now. Thank you," said Jim, composing himself.

Sharon tucked Adrian's folder away at the bottom of the pile. The young actor would not be getting a call-back.

"Everyone take fifteen," Jim said, reaching into his coat pocket and producing a cell phone. He looked up at the control booth and gave a thumbs up. A couple seconds later the lights in the house came on. People began standing and milling around. Some were still laughing.

Les glanced at his watch. He'd probably spent enough time here and didn't have a lot of desire to see much more anyway. He'd been curious about who was going to audition. He knew Glenn Brock would be here and was pretty sure Jim would give him one of the minor roles. Dillon Christie would get one of the majors.

Jim slowly stood to stretch his legs and put the phone to his ear.

Les took the opportunity to walk over and tap Sharon's shoulder. The girl's freckled face turned to look at him.

"How are you, Sharon?" Les said with a beaming smile.

"Hi Les. I'm great. How are you?"

"Couldn't be finer. How's it going so far today?"

"Well, as you've seen, an unusual mix of maybes and no-ways."

Les smiled sympathetically. "Jim may need a drink after that last one."

Sharon smiled mischievously. "He *was* kinda cute though."

"Hmmm?"

Sharon blushed. "That Adrian guy that just auditioned. Had a face like Elvis."

Les smiled. "You don't say? I knew you've always admired singers."

"Oh yeah. He could be in *Bye Bye Birdie*, if he really could sing."

Les laughed. "Now, you know that musical isn't really about Elvis."

"It isn't?"

"Conway Twitty, my dear. Well it sort of is, it's a parody."

"Oh."

Les chuckled, then shifted in his seat. "Say," he said casually. "Mind if I see whose here today?" he asked, pointing down at the stack of folders in Sharon's lap.

"Sure!" Sharon said, as if she were still in class trying to please the teacher.

Les began thumbing through the folders, glancing mostly at the headshots. "So how are you, Sharon?" he asked while browsing. "I haven't seen you in anything lately." He remembered her as nothing out of the ordinary in terms of acting but recalled she could carry a tune pretty well in musicals.

Sharon sighed. "I've been real busy. I'm almost done with my music degree. Three more semesters."

"Really," Les said glancing at her. "That's fantastic."

"Yeah. I'm excited."

"You should be. Go where your *real* talents take you."

Sharon smiled and then frowned at the comment. "Yeah, I guess."

Les kept thumbing. Although hoping, he didn't think he'd find Dax Ribeiro here. The young man had matured tremendously in his growth as an actor, in ways Dax himself wasn't even yet aware of. Now that Dax had lead roles on his resume, he may be able to start getting bigger parts. The big problem was that Dax didn't believe much in himself, and even appeared lately to be losing some interest in theatre. That would be a shame.

"So, what do you think, Les?" came Jim's voice. He stood at the end of the row watching, one hand in his pocket.

"I wish I had this much talent to choose from," Les said waving a couple folders.

Jim smiled knowingly; Les always had ulterior motives.

"Have anyone in mind yet for callbacks?" Les asked.

Same smile. "Not yet."

"I have some folks in mind," Les said with an impish smile.

"I'm sure you do," Jim said with sardonic gratitude.

"Jim?" came a voice from the back row near the exit door. Cheryl Bronson, one of the play's producers, gave Jim a quick wave. "Do you have a moment?"

"Impeccable timing," Jim said, taking his glasses off and starting up the aisle. He turned and looked at his intern. "Don't show Les our *secret* auditionees," he said with a wink.

Les turned and looked up at Cheryl. She was a handsome, middle-aged woman who maintained a healthy, vibrant figure. Her manner reflected her always professional attire. Behind her through the door stood a man wearing slacks and a white shirt with red suspenders, a man Les immediately recognized.

"Now what could *he* be doing here?" Les muttered.

Sharon turned. "What?"

"Nothing," Les said, handing a few folders back to her.

"Looking for anyone in particular?" Sharon asked.

"Oh, just wasting a few minutes. Say, give me a call and let me know who gets the good parts, will you?"

"Sure, no problem."

Les leaned in, thumbed behind him and whispered, "Don't tell the big boss man you're giving me *insider* info, okay?"

Sharon giggled.

"Take care," said Les standing to go. "And congratulations in advance on the completion of your degree."

12: Who Are You, Mario?

The two men stood at the entrance to the unoccupied hotel suite and looked around. One lit a cigarette and pulled on it while they both studied the layout. Both wore latex gloves with rubber fingertips. One gave a small snort of amusement. This was going to be an easy job. Still though, caution had to be exercised.

The spacious room had a dark interior, making it appear bigger than it really was. Burgundy drapes, currently closed, covered the windows, and matching sofas lined the walls. The chairs around the main table were skinned with dark leather, almost black, and cabinets and furniture of dark mahogany color ornamented the floor space.

Immediately to the right of the entrance was a long granite counter which made up a wet bar. Around a dozen various bottles of different shapes and sizes cluttered the center. Above the bottles hung a thick framed, blown up black and white photo of Humphrey Bogart flanked by Lauren Bacall and a giddy Marilyn Monroe, a famous image found in many places. Under the counter, a small refrigerator and icemaker with a shiny black swing door rested snugly between cabinets and drawers.

One of the men walked to the counter and snuffed out his cigarette in the smooth, round, stainless steel ashtray, adding to the dozen or so other butts – it wouldn't be noticed. Near the microwave oven in the corner was an electrical outlet. He looked at the other man, nodded, then reached into a pocket and produced a small case. Inside was array of different screwdrivers, including a small cordless electric one, as well as several lock picking apparatuses.

He unscrewed the wall socket cover, a black plastic face with a brushed steel frame. Removing a pen flashlight from another pocket, he snapped it on and shined it inside. Two more small screws were undone and he had the socket itself out, dangling by the white, black, and ground wires. He set everything down and produced a leather pouch. Inside were a handful of small metallic looking boxes that were no more than an inch and half tall and half an inch wide.

To an untrained eye, the objects would appear to be little more than components of a larger electronic contraption, perhaps the innards of a computer. But the object was quite self-contained and packed a substantial quantity of sophisticated micro technology. Weighing about four grams and with a battery life of about thirty days, the little box was a voice-activated digital recording and storage device. The built-in microphone it carried had a sensitivity of up to twenty-seven feet and the audio was amazingly clear. But the range could be adjusted to suit. This particular one had been programmed to listen for up to ten feet in any direction.

The recorder could sample at a rate of 5 to 22 kHZ and hold more than 150 hours of compressed voice recording. It would sit here for a few days in the room collecting all nearby conversations, recording only when voices were present. Later, it would be retrieved, and the voice files uploaded to a computer. A bit more cumbersome than a broadcasting device where audio was collected remotely and in real-time, but such a system could be easily detected with a radiofrequency sniffer.

The audio files were password protected and military-grade encrypted should the device get discovered or stolen.

Using the tip of a pen, he activated it by flipping a tiny switch at the top. A small green dot glowed momentarily then dimmed, indicating the gadget was ready and on standby. The man softly hummed a song for a couple seconds, causing the green light to glow again. He grunted in satisfaction.

The pouch also contained a sheet of wax paper with little, round double-sided stickers. Removing one, he stuck it on the center of the device, careful to use the side opposite of the microphone and above the battery compartment. He then removed the cover of the sticker. Using index and middle fingers, he cradled the device as he reached up into the wall socket hole and pressed it against the inside of the sheetrock. He pressed twice then tried to wiggle it. Satisfied it was securely in place, he began the process of reinstalling the socket.

The other man had gone further into the room, around a corner, and was already lying on his back under the meeting desk. The desk had room for six chairs and one recording device concealed in the lip in the center would suffice for documenting all that was said here.

The two men worked in silence and had not spoken a word. In all, it took about thirty minutes to cover the key areas. The sofa across the room from the table had a device stuck to the backside of the center support leg. The phone on the wall in the kitchen area had one on the inside the phone's cover. The side table in the corner had one resting in the base of the lamp on it. The tall two-door armoire next to the bedroom divider curtain had one stuck to the bottom of a drawer. In the bathroom, one was fixed to the inside of the sink cabinet behind the door divider. And of course, the bedroom was bugged, one clinging nicely to the underside of the box spring.

They stood again at the entrance to the suite and took a final look around. One pulled a cigarette out and offered it to the other. They stood in silence smoking, each considering anything that may have been missed. The job on the other side of the city in that old warehouse had been less intricate, as the place was a mess. This one was more demanding. In a few days they'd get instructions and be back here to collect the recordings.

***

Aaron Tisdale entered the Treasure Box Theatre and was planning to waste an hour or so watching auditions while munching a cheeseburger lunch.

He suddenly thought of a card his mother had given him on his eighteenth birthday. It said he'd been on earth for 6,570 days and that going forward he needed to utilize every remaining moment of his life to work toward goals and achieve.

Whatever. He was going to waste an hour of his precious time here anyway.

In the past, he'd read and listened to some of those motivation authors, those guys that became millionaires and owned yachts and islands before they were thirty. And he had even tried to take some of their advice. He wrote down goals. He imagined negative thoughts as pieces of paper in his mind he could wad up and toss in the fireplace. He said positive things about himself. He made a conscious effort to smile at people. He even got a cool haircut and wasted money on a few nice clothes.

But in the end, he discovered a commonality among those motivation folks. They loved people. They loved being around people, and people loved being around them. When you've got this going for yourself, the right individuals will come along and help you get to where you want to go in life. The rest—the undesirables, the unwanted, the unloved—get left behind to fend for themselves. Plain and simply, that is how this wretched world worked.

And this is where Aaron flopped, like a beached whale. No matter what he ever did, no matter what he ever tried, he could not get people to like him. It was apparent that certain types of flaws were hardwired into a person. Like a wannabe comedian that just wasn't funny, the harder he tried, the more he put others off. Long ago he'd conceded defeat and fell into a behavior of indifferent but professional mannerisms around others. This he could be consistent on for the most part. It was enough to get by and allow him to function enough to do something he somewhat enjoyed—being a theatre stage manager.

In the end, the motivation books and tapes went into the garbage as well as any remaining desire to change himself. He decided that going forward, if he never tried anything new, he'd only miss out on life's many great disappointments. Sorry, but not all pain was gain. Besides, there was no need to worry about a long-term future – his little escapades were probably going to cut his years short anyway.

Aaron strode into the theatre lobby, greasy bag and drink in hand, ice cubes rattling inside the tall, lidded paper cup. Several people were standing around the lobby, chitchatting. He kept his eyes on the floor. To his right a woman with blonde hair was standing by the counter reading something. He glanced at her feet and saw black dress boots with a large, flat heel. Peripheral vision saw attractive legs in gray dress pants held up by a thick belt. She might have glanced at him, but he wouldn't bother to look up or say hello. She wasn't anyone he knew anyway. He could recognize almost anyone familiar with his eyes fixed downward. She smelled good as he passed by though, a heady aroma he associated with various high-end female beauty products. Goodness knows, she smelled better than he did at the moment.

As Aaron made his way across, he noticed the doors to the house were open indicating they might be on a break. As he walked past the will call booth, he suddenly paused. He thought he recognized a voice coming from behind the closed theatre office door. The voice sounded riled and angry. He leaned closer to the door.

"This is completely unacceptable!" the voice roared.

"It's not entirely unreasonable," a woman's voice said.

"It is to me," the voice said.

"Now Jim, just listen to me, please," a man's voice said.

Jim ... was that Jim Kirkland? Aaron leaned in to where his ear was almost touching the door.

"You want me to ruin this show because—" Jim was saying.

"I would appreciate it if you would not disrespect my son," a man's voice said. He had a commanding tone, but Jim didn't sound intimidated.

"You would *appreciate* it?"

"Yes."

"Well, I would *appreciate* it if you wouldn't come in here flexing your muscles and pulling strings—"

"Jim," the woman's voice was a little louder now. "Try to see the big picture."

Was that Cheryl Bronson?

"I'm *trying* to see my show a success."

"*Our* show, Jim," the woman's voice said. "Please help us out here. Help *me* out."

A pause, then Jim's voice again. "Tell me this is about more than just money."

"Jim! I resent that."

Another pause. "This is outrageous. I won't accept it."

"Mr. Kirkland," the man's voice said. "All I am asking is that you give him a chance."

"This is *not* giving him a chance. This is going against my will and better judgment. Whatever jobbery is really going on around here is going to come to light."

The woman's voice sounded angry now. "Jim, you're crossing lines."

"You want to discuss boundaries? In all my years, this is one of the most blatant examples of line crossing I've ever experienced."

"This isn't the Curran or the Golden Gate here, Jim."

"And what if it was?"

"Then there'd be even more things to comply with, potentially things you just might have to live with, like it or not."

"Cheryl –"

Ah, it was Cheryl Bronson.

"I deeply respect your work, Mr. Kirkland," the man's voice said calmly, but with enough sternness and volume to interrupt everyone else. "I am sorry you feel this way. I would hate to see another less talented director do this show."

The room behind the door went silent for several long seconds. Aaron realized he was holding his breath. His eye caught something and he glanced up. The blonde girl at the counter was glaring at his obvious eavesdropping. She had a cute face and thick eye makeup. Aaron stared back indifferently for a moment then went back to the door.

"Understudy," Jim's voice finally said.

"He gets the part of *Cash*, Mr. Kirkland," the man's voice said.

"Let's give it a try, Jim" Cheryl's voice said.

"A *try* … So if he can't do it, which he can't, he doesn't do it. Is that what you mean by try?"

"He gets a shot at the part," the man's voice said.

"A hundred actors with more talent and experience get a *shot* at the part," Jim's voice said. "One of them gets it. The best one for the part. His age, his appearance, his talent, his ability to handle the lines, everything is considered."

"And?"

"*And*, no disrespect, but Mario is not the right actor for this."

Aaron stood straight for a moment, his eyes bouncing in thought. *Mario … who was Mario?* The blonde girl was still staring, but this time she looked away and pretended to read whatever it was in front of her.

"So put on the right makeup. Taylor the right suit for him," the man's voice was saying.

"Are you joking Mr. Silvestri?"

Mr. Silvestri …

"I never joke, Mr. Kirkland, not when I'm doing business."

"So this *is* all about money."

Cheryl's voice came in again, a bit calmer now. "Jim, it really doesn't matter. The decision has been made."

"And I comply, or you fire me?"

"Jim … I don't want anything like that to happen."

"But it *would* happen?" Silence. Five seconds. Almost ten. "Cheryl—"

"Jim, I need to know you're going to cooperate," Cheryl's voice said.

"If I feel he's going to wreck the show, which I do right now, I walk."

"There's no need to threaten, Jim."

"Not a threat, simply a statement. I – oh, forget it."

The sudden sound of a chair bumping and scraping from behind the door made Aaron stand rigid and whirl around so quickly he almost dropped his drink. He took a quick step back just as the office door flew open. He looked up at a sign pointing to where the restrooms were as Jim Kirkland walked quickly out, the sides of his sport coat flailing in the wind.

Aaron turned, "Hi, Jim."

Jim ignored him and hurried by, one hand roughly adjusting the thick black frames of his glasses.

Aaron now stood a few feet away from the open office door. He brought the drink straw to his mouth and looked in at Cheryl Bronson sitting behind her desk rubbing her temples. She looked attractive for her age in her nicely tailored business getup. He didn't really know Cheryl but had seen her around. Her achievements and standing in the Bay Area theatre community were admirable. She was a confident administrator who was past the age where females had to battle the dualistic experience of being both business-like and sexy, something only females had to deal with. Not that he cared. At least in the world of live theatre it wasn't as bad— talent was actually respected here, and there remained a deep reverence for art. A person didn't have to have a model's image to get good parts.

Partially visible in the doorway was an older man with thick, gray hair. His left shoulder and part of his back, adorned with the strap of a thick red suspender could be seen in the light. Cheryl looked up and made eye contact with Aaron. Without expression and eyes dropping to the floor, she stood, walked around her desk, and calmly but firmly shut the door.

Aaron smirked and looked into the auditorium.

Jim settled back into his seat and yelled, "Okay everyone, let's go!"

Aaron waited for the house lights to dim and then stole in, choosing the third row from the back and easing into the center seat. Besides bottled water, food and drink were normally forbidden, but on most audition and rehearsal days, he got away with it.

Who are you, Mario?

A woman in her early thirties walked on to the stage and stepped up to the front center. She began her introduction, but Aaron wasn't paying attention. He was smiling and his thoughts were turning. From somewhere near Jim, he saw Les Abraham stand and make his way to the aisle. Les paused for a moment and watched the back of Jim's head. He then turned and began to slowly make his way up and out, a curious expression of unpleasantry on his face.

When he was near Aaron's row, Aaron whispered loudly, "Hey, Les!"

Les stopped and peered into the darkness. "Who is that?"

"Aaron." Aaron leaned forward and gave a little wave.

"Oh … hi Aaron," Les said. For a brief unresponsive moment, his eyes narrowed. He then turned and exited.

Aaron smirked bitterly and stuffed an onion ring in his mouth. It tasted good.

13: Knuckle Dusters

Dax leaned on his desk drumming his fingers and staring at the screen. The morning had started so nicely, full of promise and excitement. But it had gone downhill from there.

The secure access login and password fields were flashing and beckoning him to enter something. He glanced at the Pepto-Bismol bottle on his desk. Should he take another swig? His stomach was seriously aching.

He was already behind in the network interfacing class he had been taking in the last several weeks. Truth be told, it was starting to bore him to tears. The thought of going through another round of research questions made his stomach all the worse. He'd been in and out of certificate and degree classes for several years now and it hadn't done anything noticeable for his career. But then, he never had much of a career path to begin with.

He reached for the pink bottle and glanced at his watch. A few more hours and he'd be on his way to some hotel room to get suited up for the gig. Hey, a *real* gig, right? Part of his problem was having the jitters about what was going to happen. The feeling was very similar to the preshow anxiety all actors feel. Well, it was a big show, wasn't it? Only this time he was getting paid. He tipped the bottle and took a swallow.

"Freeze!"

The booming voice above Dax made him jerk the bottle resulting in a thick pink ooze that poured out and began to drip off his chin and on to his shirt. He slammed the bottle on his desk and scrambled for a pile of napkins he kept near the phone.

Tom Kuka was standing over the cube wall in his usual invasive fashion, laughing, but stopped when he saw the mess and the look on Dax's face.

"Sorry, dude."

Dax roughly wiped his chin then began scrubbing the pink stain on his shirt. "What do you want, Tom?"

Tom held up his hands. "Whoa, whoa, hang on now. Just making my usual rounds."

"Do your rounds have to include me?"

"*Oh yeah*. Makes my day a little more complete." Tom rested a big elbow on the top of the cube wall and winked.

"Get a life, man."

Tom laughed then paused. "You've sure been acting weird this week."

Dax pretended to look at something important on his desk. "Oh? How so?"

Tom shrugged. "I don't know. But you know when someone's acting different. And you've been acting different. At first I thought it was girly troubles, but I don't know."

"Just been a little busy, that's all."

"We've all been busy. And we're getting busier. Work harder *and* smarter—that's the motto now." Tom continued to stare and then cocked his head slightly.

Dax tapped a few keys and breathed deeply.

"Saw you at the Starbucks the other day," Tom suddenly said.

Dax continued to peck at the keyboard and didn't respond. He finally looked up. "And?"

Tom was smirking. "And nothing. Just saw you there. I was sitting in traffic. I turned, and there you were by the window."

Dax kept a deadpan look on his face. It hadn't occurred to him that people he knew from work or wherever might have been around.

"Okay, I do a coffee break now and then, so?"

"Sure. Only I never see you drinking coffee past mid-morning." Tom continued to stare and smirk.

Dax sat back. "So, what other observations have you made about me, Tom?"

Tom looked up thoughtfully. "Well, since you asked, I've noticed that while generally you're a recluse with a solemn look on your face, you're actually a pretty agreeable guy if one takes the time to get to know you."

Dax managed a smile. "Gee thanks, Tom. Or was that even a compliment?"

"It was, trust me."

"What else?"

"Well, like I said, you've looked different in the last few days. And when I saw you, you looked, well, I dunno, scared or something. Maybe just nervous."

"How so?"

"Your eyes were wide. You were looking around, back and forth."

Dax waved it off. "I've no idea what you're talking about."

Tom stared for another couple seconds, his smile melting into something more serious. "Hey." He leaned in closer and lowered his voice. "You in trouble or something?"

Dax looked up nonchalantly. "No. Why do you ask?"

Tom regarded him for a moment. "I dunno. Military training. Listen," he said, digging into a pocket. "You ever see a pair of these?" He held his palm out flat, and in his hand were thick, shiny brass knuckles.

Dax stared, wide-eyed. "You bring those in here? You'd get fired if you're caught."

Tom grinned. "I carry them everywhere. Cuz you never know when you might need a fist-load. Feel them. They're the real deal."

Dax held them for a moment. They indeed had a heavy, solid quality.

"Try 'em on," Tom said.

"These aren't wanted in some assault case, are they?"

Tom laughed. "Yeah, right."

Dax slowly slid the object around his fingers. The thick rings felt cool but started warming quickly. He made a fist and lightly punched his other hand. He looked up at Tom. "These things could get a person in trouble."

"They could also get a person *out* of trouble. You keep 'em."

"Nah, not my thing."

"I got others. You know some Bruce Lee moves anyway, right? You never know when some good knuckle dusters will come in handy." He glanced at his watch. "Gotta go, sport."

"Oh, so soon?" Dax said with sarcasm.

"Don't worry, I'll be back." Tom waved and walked away.

Dax balled his hand into a fist again and gently but firmly hit his desk. The brass around his fingers made a loud whack. He slipped the knuckles off and put them in a small desk drawer, then looked at the Pepto-Bismol bottle again. He was beginning to get sick of the thick, sweet taste.

He had yet to hear from Agent Jack Dauer. He didn't like the fact that things were so mysterious. But the FBI had their reasons, right?

His cell phone suddenly chirped. He didn't recognize the number. "Hello?"

"Hi, Dax," said a female voice.

"Hi, uh—"

"Lourdes," the voice said with annoyance.

"Oh, Lourdes. Hi." Lourdes Binaoro was a Filipina who had started hanging around the theatre scene a couple years ago. A very talented singer, she'd been called back twice for Beach Blanket Babylon auditions, but never got in. She was friendly, gregarious, and although in her early forties, remained as cute and energetic as a twenty-five-year-old. She did have the tendency to dress a bit gaudy though.

Dax wracked his memory. "Uh, *kamusta ka na?*"

"I'm fine, thank you."

"Gee, uh, *sa*-lamat."

"You're welcome. But it's sa-*la*-mat. Accent on the second syllable. I should teach you Cebuano, I'm better at that than Tagalog."

Dax smiled. He recalled an older Filipino guy he knew who spoke the Cebuano dialect and he always messed up English words with more than two syllables. Words like register, came out as reh-g*ee*-stair.

"I've no more room in my brain. What can I do for you, *maganda?*"

"*Maganda?* I'm going to slap you, Dax. No wait, better not, you might like that."

"Ha, ha."

"First, you were great in the show."

"Sal-*aaa*mat."

"I've never seen Eric look so …"

"Sexy?"

She giggled. "A little."

"Realistic then."

"Hmmm, maybe."

"Well, what then?" Dax was genuinely grateful to be having this conversation; it was a great distraction.

"Confident. Eric was confident. And passionate about his character."

"Really. I put on a good act then." Dax smiled to himself and felt a moment of pride. "What show did you see?"

"Does it matter?"

"Maybe."

"The closing night last Sunday."

"Ah, makes sense then."

"That was your best night?"

"Might have been. I don't know. I was just really into it. And enjoying smacking Glenn around."

Lourdes laughed. "You'll need to tell me more."

"Anytime."

"Good, tonight then."

"Tonight?"

"Yes, I'm inviting you to a party for Gene Palmer's retirement farewell."

"Uhm—"

"Of course you wouldn't remember, that's why I'm calling."

Gene Palmer, wow. Gene had been a theatre teacher for decades. Many of the actors who had trained around the Bay Area could tell stories about the astute and sometimes eccentric professor of thespian arts. He could be stern when he had to but was a caring and respected teacher and director.

Dax rubbed his temples. "Right, right. But I can't go."

"Why not?"

"I have something to do."

"Sure you do. Bring your date."

"It's not a date, well it is a date. It's kind of date." Dax quietly put a hand over his mouth and shook his head.

"What are you talking about? You sound strange, Dax."

"I'm fine."

"If it's a date with another guy just bring him."

"Right. Okay."

"Seriously, you should be there."

"I know. There's just something I need to do."

"You used to talk about him a lot."

"Who?"

"Gene Palmer. What's the matter with you?"

"Right."

"Fine, don't tell me. But you can drop by at least. What time is your appointment or whatever it is?"

Lourdes could be a pushy, but she meant well.

"I'm not sure. I'm waiting for a phone call." He clamped a hand over his mouth again.

"Now you're really sounding strange. Listen, it's at Bob and Carol's, remember where they are?"

"Yeah."

"It's from six to whenever. Stop by. A few of us want to congratulate you."

"For what?"

"For a good show!"

"Okay. Thanks."

"See you tonight then, okay? Bring your boyfriend."

"Bye Lourdes. *Sige na.*"

She laughed and hung up.

Dax set his phone down and drummed his fingers some more. He sighed, put the mouse arrow on the login field and got ready to view the latest pile of emails and trouble ticket notifications.

14: And So the Game Is Played

The blue Mustang rumbled nicely as Dax cruised north along highway 580 toward Berkeley. His thoughts were bouncing between memories of the past and anticipation of what was going to happen in the next couple days.

He was irritated at Jack. Special Agent Dauer never called him today about where and when he was supposed to hook up to get fitted for the job. At that warehouse? Somewhere in the city. But here he was driving north to Berkeley.

As Dax drove, his mind wandered. His memories of Gene Palmer went back a long way. Dax had taken a handful of acting classes at City College of San Francisco. Gene was a part-time teacher at the time, overseeing makeup and props and various aspects of the college's Theatre Arts program. Dax had landed a part in a show, *A. Ratt*, the loan shark from Tennessee Williams' *Camino Real*. The part called for a big gaudy moustache. *Go talk to Gene Palmer*, he'd been told.

Dax had waited patiently outside the college greenroom next to the main theatre house. The Theatre Arts faculty offices were located behind the greenroom, and everyone walked through there at one point. He was looking forward to meeting the teacher and director he had heard so much about.

Professor Palmer finally ambled in, his chin down and his eyebrows furrowed in deep thought. As Gene walked by, Dax got up and began following him to his office.

"Mr. Palmer?" Dax said.

Gene slowly turned and stared but with no recognition.

"I was told to ask you about making a custom moustache." Dax took a couple steps forward. "Sorry, I'm Dax Ribeiro, a student here."

Gene smiled. "Of course you're a student. And call me Gene. Come with me."

Dax followed Gene up one flight of stairs, a task Gene performed slowly and a bit laboriously.

Gene's office was small and quaint—a writing desk, a chair, a bookcase. The furniture was sparse to create more room, or so it appeared. Maybe he went over scenes with students against the far wall where there was ample floor space.

The writing desk was solid wood, traditional style, warm dark brown and shiny on top, with framed side panels covered in cherry veneers. The lamp, which rested on a couple books with worn covers, appeared to be an old-fashioned milk jug that had been painted brown and fixed up to be an office lamp, complete with a smooth dull yellow shade.

Gene's chair matched the desk perfectly in color and style. He eased into the thickly padded soft brown leather and Dax could hear the air whooshing out as the man's weight settled in.

Gene motioned Dax to sit down. Dax glanced up at the solid wood bookcase behind Gene and took note of the variety, from old theatre picture books to modern collections of monologs. He saw a couple Stanislavski books, including one he'd read, *The Stanislavski System*. He saw a few others on cinema, scriptwriting, and makeup. He also saw novels by Charles Dickens, Mark Twain, and James Boswell. On the far right of the middle shelf was a large black leather-bound Bible.

On the other side of the wall hung framed certificates and degrees. The collection included a Bachelor's in English and a Master of Arts in Theatre Studies from Ohio State University. He also noticed a Master of Arts in Theology from the University of Notre Dame.

"Dax, is it?" Gene said.

Dax pulled his eyes from the wall and looked at Gene. "Uhm, yes."

"So, you need a moustache?"

"Yes, Sir."

"For what production?"

"*Camino Real.*"

"Ah," said Gene, leaning back. "A very misunderstood play."

"I can imagine."

"Do you find it confusing?"

"A little."

"It makes a big difference how it's presented."

Dax wondered if the man was making a statement about the director, Rob Crouch. Rob was new, young, and already had a reputation for putting modern spins on classic plays, choices that were sometimes frowned upon.

Gene reached for a pencil and a piece of paper in desk drawer. "What part will you be playing?" He paused and held up a hand. "Wait, let me guess." He stared at Dax.

Dax returned the gaze for a few seconds then looked down.

"Ah," Gene said wagging a finger. "A. Ratt, the avaricious businessman," he said nodding. "Am I correct?"

Dax smiled and patted the desktop. "Yep, that's me. Good guess."

Gene continued staring and then nodded again. "Good. I think that will be good for you."

"Yeah? I look the part?"

Gene shook his head. "No, not really. You're a tad too innocent looking. But the right moustache and outfit would give you a start. The rest will be up to you."

Dax asked, "How would it be good for me, playing the loan shark?"

Gene leaned forward a little. "It will be good for you as an actor. To gain skills. Some … confidence."

Dax furrowed his eyebrows. "You know what I think got me the part?" he suddenly asked. "My laugh."

"Oh? Show me, please."

Dax stood, the student of acting eager to show off, and put a hand to his chest. Then looking up wide eyed and grinning, he let out the most animated *bwah-ha-ha-ha!* laugh he could muster. He then looked around the empty office and quickly sat back down, feeling somewhat foolish.

Gene cocked his head slightly and went back to his soft and warm smile. "That's very nice, Dax."

"But not, confident?"

Gene waved it off. "Dax, do you feel *bad* when you play this part? Bad as in evil, bad."

Dax shrugged. "Not really."

Gene raised his eyebrows. "Because this character is a real slimeball."

"I know. I try to feel evil."

"You take advantage of people. You manipulate. You're entertained by their desperation and helplessness."

"I know. Guess I'm not that *bad*."

Gene chuckled. "And *that's* why you lack confidence. If you felt like a dirty, rotten scoundrel, you'd not just be pretending to be dirty, you'd actually *be* dirty."

Dax sighed softly to himself. He had heard many lectures on the sort of Stanislavsky method acting concept Gene was talking about.

"Don't get me wrong," Gene continued. "You can do this. You just need to believe in yourself more."

Dax was beginning to think the man was reading too much into him for having only met for the first time. But what the professor was saying was spot on. Truth be told, Dax had always had a hard time believing in himself. Gene probably sensed Dax's insecurity the moment he laid eyes on him.

Gene watched Dax for a moment. "Step up your pace more, mentally that is. Keep your eyes fixated on what that character is really after."

Dax nodded.

"And when you're off stage, fixate on what *you* really want. That'll be good practice."

"What I want?"

"Yes," Gene said, pointing. "What Dax wants."

Dax looked up and met eyes again with Gene. The man had a fatherly caring about him. He wished his own father had supported his dreams of being an actor.

Sliding the paper forward and picking up the pencil Gene said, "Now then, let's see about this moustache."

Dax had made a friend that day in the mild-mannered theatre teacher. But in the next two years he would be sorely disappointed he was never able to get into any of Gene's classes or partake in any of his shows. Timing was always everything.

The two of them ran into each other frequently around campus and Gene was always interested in how things were going, and in what direction acting was taking Dax. They would talk about the shows Dax was in or auditioning for and Gene would give advice on things to practice or what monologs to use. Unlike teachers like Les who could cuss like a marine drill sergeant, Gene never used course language or blew his top. That in and of itself made an impression. By the end of his stay at the college, Dax had been quite influenced by the man.

Dax was now driving north on Highway 24. He would exit on Claremont and make his way to Ashby. Bob and Carol Grayson lived in a neighborhood between Ashby and College Avenue, close to the renowned campus. He glanced at his watch and cursed Jack. It was a little after seven.

The narrow street was packed with cars as Dax rumbled in. He was thinking less about Jack and more about a nice glass of red wine and some appetizers. He cruised slowly down the street staring at the houses. He thought it would be easier to recognize, but the light was getting dimmer and the large, boxy two-story houses with old paint and large trees started looking the same. Berkeley ordinances didn't distinguish between a property line fence or hedge, and it was difficult, particularly at night, to see where one property ended and another started. He stopped at the house that was the most brightly lit and welcome looking.

Bob and Carol Grayson were pillars in the Bay Area theatre scene. If you were a Who's Who in theatre, you knew Bob and Carol and they knew you. For years they had run an outdoor theatre in the Berkeley Hills and were known for helping up and coming actors get seen by those who mattered. In addition to attending every major theatre event, they were also known as charitable givers to art schools, children's theatres, women's shelters, and various other philanthropic endeavors.

Dax checked his watch again as he made his way across the street. His breath was beginning to show in the cooling air, which would probably drop to the low forties tonight.

Carol Grayson answered the door. "Hello. Good evening." She stared for a moment, a look of half-recognition on her face. She wore a brown eighties-style hippie sweater jacket and jeans. Although she was in the latter end of middle-age, she had an animated and healthy appearance.

"Hi. Dax Ribeiro," he said extending a hand. "I was a student of Gene's. Or rather, he was a mentor of mine."

"Oh yes, come in, please. Didn't we just see you recently?"

"Les Abraham's latest show, yes, at the Godwin Theatre."

"Of course. Come in. Welcome."

Obviously, she thought I was fantastic.

Inside, it was warm, and the air was filled with the delicious aroma of assorted hors d'oeuvres. Modern jazz music softly floated through the air. He immediately recognized a few of the mingling faces that had come to felicitate Gene Palmer.

"You weren't one of Gene's students?" Carol asked.

"Unfortunately, no. Well, in a way I was. I knew him pretty well. He helped me on a number of things."

"I see. Well thank you for coming. Can I get you something to drink?"

"Sure. What do you have?"

"Coffee, soda, white wine."

"Do you have a good cab by any chance?"

"Will merlot suffice?"

"It will, thanks."

"Be right back." Carol turned to go leaving a lingering scent of perfume, her dirty blonde hair with greying sides swirling in the air.

Dax stood for a moment looking around. There was a time he found himself at about a dozen of these kinds of events a year, but as things went on, there were less people he really wanted to spend time with.

"There he is!" a bubbly female voice said. Lourdes quickly sauntered up, her feet shuffling softly on the carpet, and threw her arms around his neck.

Dax bent down to match her five-foot-one frame and returned the hug.

"So, where's your date? Was *he* not able to make it?"

"You're hysterical."

She stepped back and looked him up and down.

"What?" Dax asked.

"Okay, you look fine I guess," she said grinning.

Dax rolled his eyes.

"From hero back to homeboy. Must be rough."

Dax smirked and looked at her for a moment. She had the kind of eyes that were always mischievously grinning. It gave him the urge to kiss her on the cheek just for being so friendly. Her lips were painted much too bright though, an effort, perhaps, to match the loud, red polo racing shirt she had on. It was stretched a little too tight on her, but she still looked pretty good in it.

"So did you organize this?" Dax asked nodding toward the center of the room.

"I helped. I also brought some homemade lumpia."

"Nice. That's what I smelled."

"What are you drinking?" she asked.

"Red wine."

"I'll get you a glass."

"*Sa-lamat*, but Carol is already getting me one."

A big, heavy hand slapped Dax's shoulder making him wince and start to duck. An arm slid over his other shoulder, and he felt something jab his back. He turned and sighed. Glenn Brock.

"Relax, *Eric*," Glenn said in a sinister tone, mimicking the character he'd played with Dax.

"Why Glenn, the man, the myth, the legend in his own mind."

"Wow, that's original, Dax."

"Did you steal the prop knife, or is that a pencil you've got stuck in my back?" Dax asked.

Glenn winked, held up a small, bright orange nibbler carrot, then plopped it in his mouth.

"Nice. So, did you get a callback from Jim?" asked Dax.

"You'd just love to hear me say no, wouldn't you?"

"Just asking."

Glenn shrugged exaggeratedly, then asked, "Did *you* get a callback?"

"I didn't audition."

"Why not?"

"Didn't feel like it."

"What? Are *they* calling *you* now and offering parts? No more groveling on the stage floor like the rest of us?"

For a brief moment, Dax toyed with the idea of telling Glenn that Jim Kirkland had actually called, but Glenn wouldn't believe it. "Not in this lifetime," Dax said, shaking his head.

Glenn stepped back and took a big swig from the Corona beer bottle in his hand. "Well, the answer to your question is, not yet."

"You'll be fine, big guy." Dax punched Glenn lightly on the shoulder.

"Gee, thanks. I'm all reassured now. I'm gonna sleep good tonight."

"So where's the man of the hour?" Dax asked looking around the room.

Glenn spread his arms wide at Dax. "Looks like he just arrived."

Lourdes laughed. "Just follow the crowds to the main room. And follow your nose to the food," she said.

"Oh I won't have any trouble finding that."

Carol walked up behind them. "Here you go, Dax," she said, handing Dax a wine glass filled with burgundy colored liquid.

"You see that, Lourdes?" Glenn said pointing at the glass. "Wine. The man's getting all sophisticated on us now. A real aristocrat."

"I'm all smoke and mirrors, just like you," Dax said walking away. "If you'll excuse me."

Glenn cupped his hands to his mouth. "Everyone clear the way. The man who doesn't need to audition anymore coming through."

Dax thought about flipping Glenn the birdie behind his back but didn't know who might be looking. Several heads turned as he walked through to the kitchen to get to the other room.

In the kitchen the smell of food was stronger, and he suddenly felt hungry. Wine on an empty stomach was an invitation for a headache. He would have to track down some of that lumpia.

By the sink two men were having a quiet conversation. Dax right away recognized the one facing him, Steven Kensley, a director with a caustic reputation. Dressed impeccably as always, he wore a tan camel hair sport coat over a black turtleneck sweater. The man easily wore multiple layers over his thin frame.

Dax neither liked nor trusted Kensley. Dax had briefly worked with a talented actor named Derrick Guzman who was gay, but very closeted about it. During a show some time back, Steven, who was openly gay, became attracted to Derrick's medium athletic build and made moves on him. Derrick turned him down. A few months later, Steven would get a bit of revenge. When *The Boys in the Band* was being produced, Steven got the job directing it at the Lampost. Derrick auditioned, and being the talented singer and actor he was, would have been a good fit for a couple different roles. But when the callbacks came, he was called back for the part of "Cowboy Tex," the one role the dark-haired, Polynesian blended Derrick was absolutely not suited for in appearance or mannerisms.

But Derrick, everyone had told him, *you're no skinny, Texas whiteboy. How come you're not Emory or Michael?*

Derrick went back anyway, fully aware of Kensley's ruse. He smiled as he was humiliated throughout the entire process and then "rejected" for the part.

And so the nasty game was played.

As Dax passed the two in the kitchen, Kensley started to look up, but Dax dropped his eyes before making contact. The other man, Carl Sadler, turned to look at Dax. Dax knew Carl better, but didn't care much for him either, for different reasons.

"Carl," Dax said quietly with a small nod.

Carl nodded back without expression.

Dax kept walking while their classified discourse continued.

Stopping at the doorway to the next room, he took a sip from his wineglass. The robust flavor of fermented grape juice hit his tongue pleasantly. Dax pulled back and sniffed the glass. It had been probably two months since he had a nice glass of red wine. Maybe he'd stay for a second glass. But food first. He glanced around and spotted his target.

15: The Real Stuff

The assortment at the hors d'oeuvres table didn't disappoint. In the center was a large platter stacked with light brown, deep fried, finger sized lumpia – the Filipino version of an eggroll. Next to that was a dish with goopy, red, sweet chili dipping sauce.

He was stuffing one in his mouth when he heard Gene's voice. Against the wall by the couch, the aging professor was chatting, flanked by several former students and a couple colleagues. Gene spoke calmly and with authority, all eyes on him and all ears attentive to whatever wise and encouraging words the man was saying. One of the folks listening was Dennis Sheridan, looking as tall, dark, and handsome as ever in a button sweater and jeans. Dax helped himself to a few more of the appetizers while watching and taking in the scene.

Although the house had a bit of mileage on the outside, the interior had been renovated and was more modern. The room was spacious and homey, but with a contemporary black and gray theme, and scattered conservatively about were stylish wooden furniture pieces with rich, dark mahogany and cherry finishes. The fire crackled away and gave off a pleasant aroma of natural wood burning.

"Hey, Dax!" a voice said making him turn. Elizabeth Brauner was approaching with a tall gray-haired gentleman. Dax recognized the man as Bob Grayson.

"What's up?" Elizabeth said holding up a high-five.

Dax gave her hand a light smack. "Not much. How are you?"

"Superb, thank you. You know Bob?"

Bob reached out his hand. "Hi, Dax. Carol mentioned you were here. We enjoyed your performance last week."

"Thank you. Did you notice how great the lighting was too?"

Elizabeth slapped his shoulder.

Bob was tall, at least six-two, with a thick full head of grey-white hair. He looked down at Dax through stylish, rimless regatta eyeglasses.

"Nice place you have here," Dax said looking around.

"Thank you. Getting ready for your next show?"

Dax shrugged. "Not yet. I've not decided what I want to do." He looked at Elizabeth. He had not seen her before in a formal black dress. "You look smashing, Liz."

She grinned up at him. "You oughta party with me more often."

"Can you I get you another, Dax?" Bob asked.

"I'm sorry?"

"Your glass." Bob nodded down at Dax's empty glass.

"Oh. Yes, please. Thank you." Dax hadn't realized he'd already drained it. He handed it to Bob, who turned to leave.

"Having a good time?" Elizabeth asked.

"Indeed. Been a week. Have you tried some of this lumpia? It's fantastic. Lourdes made it."

"I know, but I can't eat that deep-fried stuff. I have a hard enough time fitting into the clothes I've got."

Dax laughed. "Come on."

"If I really want to fit into a nice dress, I just eat Taco Bell for a couple days."

Dax paused for a moment until the full meaning of the comment struck him. Then he started laughing a little too hard, his face turning red. He needed a nice alcohol-enhanced laugh.

Elizabeth was laughing too, not at her own comment, but at Dax's reaction. "Have you talked to Gene yet?" she asked after Dax stopped, nodding at the crowd.

"No, not yet." Dax caught his breath. "I'm sorry to see him officially leaving even though I've not had a lot of contact in the last several years."

Elizabeth grabbed a cucumber slice and dipped the end of it in a bowl of ranch dressing. "Same with most of us, probably. But he's a guy you don't forget."

"For sure."

Elizabeth crunched on the cucumber. "He was one of your instructors at City?"

"No, unfortunately. I would have loved the opportunity. But he helped me on a few things. Represents a sort of turning point in my acting career. A career that never became a career."

"Career? How many of us have a career doing this?"

"Exactly." Dax smiled and looked at her. "Hey, you really look good."

"You think? Then do me a favor." She pointed at the platter of lumpia. "Don't offer me *that* kind of food." She looked hard at Dax for a moment and then asked, "Why don't you have a girlfriend, Dax?"

His smile vanished and his eyes quickly found the floor. "I did ..."

Elizabeth suddenly regretted asking. "Come on," she said, taking him by the arm. "Let's go say hi."

Glancing around the room, Dax asked, "Is Les here?"

"I think he should be, haven't seen him yet. Why?"

"Just wondering. Need to ask him something."

Gene glanced up as they approached. "There he is," he said with a warm smile and an outstretched hand.

Dax took the man's hand with both of his and shook it slowly and respectfully.

Gene turned to Elizabeth. "Elizabeth. Nice to see you again." He bent down to kiss her on the cheek.

Dax glanced up at Dennis, who'd been standing next to Gene. "Hey, Dennis."

"Hi, Dax," said Dennis, smiling warmly. He held a Diet Coke in his hand.

Gene glanced around at the crowd. Raising his voice, he said, "Did all of you have the privilege of seeing this young man's most recent performance?"

Dax felt his face get hot.

"I saw it," Dennis said, raising a hand. "And *felt* it too." A couple people chuckled.

Gene looked Dax in the eye and said, "Now that was a *confident* performance." He then winked ever so slightly.

Dax felt a warm wave of feel-good wash over him.

"I'm proud of you, Dax," Gene said stepping forward and taking Dax by the arm. He glanced around at everyone. "Will you excuse us for a moment?" He pointed at the appetizer table and said, "Recommend something for me, will you? I have yet to try any of this stuff."

"Well, there's nothing too unusual here."

Gene paused at the table then finally picked up a small celery stick. "So how have you been, my friend?"

"Taking a breather right now."

"From performing?"

"Yes."

"Really? A young, healthy man like you?"

"Just feels good to pause, and, well ..." Dax shrugged.

Gene faced Dax. "And consider where you're at?"

"I guess that's a good way of putting it."

Gene smiled. "You have gifts, options. You're quite blessed."

"Thanks. Hey, you still have your scarf on."

"It's a tad brumal out there," Gene said, nodding at the window and taking a bite of his celery. "Takes me awhile to warm back up. The blood doesn't circulate as fast anymore. The two things I don't like most about getting older is that I can't eat what I used to and I'm cold more often than not." He paused. "While you're young, remember to stretch and take care of your body. And remember to take care of the people in your life. The people you love and your heath, that's the *real* stuff."

Dax stared for a moment then looked off in thought. Images of Sam swept passed his vision. He also thought of his widowed father.

Gene was watching him. "Do you know how old I am, Dax?"

Dax looked up. "Not a day past fifty?"

Gene smiled.

Bob walked over with a fresh glass of red wine. "Here you are, Dax. How's everything, Gene?" Bob asked.

"It simply could not be better. May I retire here again next year?"

Bob gave a small bow. "By all means. It would be our pleasure."

"I shall hold you to that."

"Of course. Excuse me." Bob turned to leave.

Gene turned to Dax. "By the graces of powers beyond mine, I've lived seventy-two good years so far."

"Wow."

Gene laughed. "It's not much of an achievement, I assure you. But I shall dodge death as long as God permits," He pointed at Dax's glass. "A little of that now and then helps."

"So I've heard."

"A *little*," Gene continued. "Everything in moderation. The average human heart beats 100,000 times per day I'm told." He tapped his chest lightly with a fist. "Do the math on my ticker. But worry not, I am in fine fettle and plan to be for some time."

Dax raised his glass. "I plan to have mine beat as many times or more. What advice can you give me?'

"Count your age by the number of friends you have, not how many birthdays," Gene said, pointing at Dax. "Friends are more valuable than gold. *Real* friends."

Dax looked away in thought. He had a lot of acquaintances but often wondered how many real friends he actually had.

Gene continued. "As far as actual physical health, well I've done all the usual. I've maintained a reasonably healthy weight, attempted to engage in regular physical activity, eat reasonably healthy, et cetera, et cetera." He took a small step forward and tapped his head with a finger. "But really, it's what's up here that counts. It's your attitude. Your happiness."

Dax listened thoughtfully, nodding, then impulsively asked, "What's a real friend anyway?"

Gene chuckled. "A real friend," he leaned in to emphasize, "doesn't abandon you when it costs something to be your friend. I'll let you in on a secret. *Old* to me was always a few years ahead. When I was sixteen, thirty seemed old. When I was forty, sixty seemed old. Now that I am seventy-two, an old man to me is someone who made it to ninety."

Dax laughed.

"There is a natural curiosity in all of us. To meet new people, to learn new things. We lose that as we get older. But don't ever lose your innate curiosity. When that happens, then you'll really start aging."

"I hear you," Dax said nodding.

Gene looked down thoughtfully. "In the end, it's the people you love and your health. That's the real stuff. Oh, but I said that already didn't I. And where you're going to spend eternity, of course. Nothing else really amounts to much more." He looked up. "Sorry, this retirement stuff makes an old man say these things, not to mention repeat himself."

Dax smiled. "No problem."

Gene stood a little straighter and shifted mental gears. "Your folks aren't in the area, is that right?"

"My father is in New Mexico. My mother passed away several years ago. Cancer."

Gene looked thoughtfully at Dax. "Make sure you see him personally while you can. Don't just use these Star Trek gadgets." He held up a hand and tapped his palm, like there was a cell phone in it. "Us old folks aren't around forever."

"I will," Dax said, genuinely meaning it. "I plan to."

Gene looked around at the party scene then back at Dax. "I am looking forward to your next performance. Have you any plans after your break?"

Dax wondered for a moment if he should hint about the undercover gig but decided not to get into it. "No, not at the moment."

"Really ... a young man with your talent. And one on the verge of getting where he needs to be."

Dax stared, curious and puzzled. "What do you mean?"

Gene gently took him by the arm and led him toward the window. "Your performance last week was wonderful. I very much enjoyed it. But I was still waiting for you to take that one final step into your characterization."

"How so?"

"The proper level of maturity and experience is already there, in here," Gene said tapping gently on Dax's heart. "But I still sense a raw inner you trying to work his way out of a shell."

Dax felt a little hurt. "Did it look shallow to you? Insincere?"

Gene waved it off. "No, no, not shallow. You're an intense actor. You're passionate with your character. But what you could be is a bit more ..." Gene looked up and thought for a moment and then said, "*dangerous,*" with mischief in his eyes.

Dax took a big pull on his wine and realized he was feeling the alcohol strongly. His senses were being enhanced, and the whole room—the music, the fire, the mingling people, the black and gray carpet—was becoming almost surreal.

Gene put a hand on Dax's shoulder. "Dax, the next time you perform, be dangerous, be cunning, even shocking. Take a few more risks. Do exactly, precisely, what your instincts tell you to do. Don't hesitate, hold nothing back." He held up a thumb and index finger. "You're so close."

Dax stared thoughtfully into his wine glass and digested the words. His imagination was taking him back to the street scene and his fight with Glenn and Dennis. That whole event, although played out many times, felt as though it never happened.

Dax took a gulp from his glass and realized it was almost empty again. He let out a feigned chuckle. "My father wanted me to be a lawyer or engineer or something, like him. I suppose if I went to Hollywood and started making a million a movie he'd change his mind. I don't know ..."

Gene put a gentle hand on Dax's shoulder. "Follow your heart. We were all made for something. You were made for the thespian arts. But only you know if you'd be happier doing anything else. Take it from an old man. Life is going to fly by at appalling speed. They say youth is a slave to passion, and the old is a servant to regrets. Don't be like that. When your hairs are grey, know with satisfaction you did what you were made to do."

Dax looked at Gene and almost felt his eyes begin to water. But he held back.

"Hi, Gene!" came a voice. Two middle-aged women decked out in casual winter party outfits were approaching.

"Barbara!" Gene said. He turned to Dax. "Excuse me, I have to return to my shindig."

Dax smiled and nodded. His cheeks felt hot, but he felt good. He hadn't been this relaxed in a while and was thoroughly enjoying the moment. He watched Gene give a quick hug and peck on the cheek to the two ladies and begin talking.

Searching the hors d'oeuvres table, his eyes landed on a tray with crackers and cheese. Gathering up a couple in a napkin and draining the last of his glass he casually walked to the far wall and hoped Bob or Carol would come offer him another. He'd stop at three, really.

He heard laughter from a group that had gathered near the fireplace.

"How long were you there?" a woman's voice asked.

"Fifteen hours at least," Glenn's voice replied. Dax could see the back of Glenn's large bald head.

"You sat in a seat at the Oakland Coliseum all night for fifteen hours?"

"You must have been freezing," someone else said.

"Not with *his* thick hide," said Dennis. "Ask me how I know."

Several people laughed.

"They herded us around like cattle," Glenn said. "They'd sit us all down, shoot a scene, then stand us up and move us to another section of the place. They tried to mix it up each time. Get us to change coats or hats or something between shots."

"Did they say it would last that long?" another asked.

Glenn laughed loudly. He had put away several beers by now. "They never tell us little extras how long. You just show up and take orders."

"Been there, done that too many times," said Dennis. "Not worth the money. Minimum wage. Then time and a half past the eight-hour mark. But it's still not worth it."

"You've been an extra in movies a few times, right Dennis?"

"Yep. And each time it was the same thing. Hurry up and wait for everything to get setup between shots. Then they do the same scene over and over, each time taking an hour or two to re-do all the equipment. By the end of the day, you're exhausted, and the next day is ruined. Often the shoots require the extras to be there for two or three days in a row. Later you get this measly paycheck after Uncle Sam takes his cut. Then in a few months the movie comes out and you rush to go see it. You wait for the scene you're in and it blurs by so quick you can't believe it took them three days. You might, if you're lucky, catch a tiny glimpse of yourself, but more likely you ended up on the cutting room floor." He took a sip from his Diet Coke then shook his head. "I'm done doing that stuff."

"Oh sure," said Glenn at Dennis. "Just because you're the bigshot TV reporter now."

"Glenn needs the extra work money to update his headshot," Elizabeth smirked.

"Every six months," Glenn said, shrugging.

"In Glenn's case, he oughta be updating every week," Dennis said.

"Keep it up," Glenn said wagging a finger.

Elizabeth noticed Dax by the wall watching. "I remember when Dax was in a movie with Robin Williams," she said looking at him.

Several heads turned in his direction. The room was swirling slightly, and he squinted and blinked stupidly.

"You lucky dog," Dennis said. "I had been in like three movies up to that point and hardly saw my face once. This guy goes in, sits next to the star, and has the biggest extra role I'd ever seen anyone I know get."

"Tell us what happened!" Elizabeth said.

Dax shrugged. "Well, I sorta sat right behind him." "How'd you manage that?" Glenn asked. "You're not pretty enough to sleep with the director."

Elizabeth slapped Glenn's arm.

Dax took a deep breath. "Well, they needed a bunch of extras that looked like nerdy college kids to play med school students in the early '70s. Set in Virginia, but filmed the scene in a UC Berkeley classroom. So I go down there and they put me in this disgusting plaid shirt and do my hair up all Robert Redford style—"

"Ooow," Elizabeth cooed.

"We're killing time in the main theatre at UC Berkeley. I get bored and walk outside to hang out with the smokers. All of the sudden this guy, one of the crew, runs up and points at us and says, 'All of you, follow me.' So we followed him past a bunch of cables and equipment into this classroom. We sit down in this cluster of seats. They had the place all rigged so that the lights and screens and cameras were behind us."

Dax paused and looked around. Steven and Carl had made their way out of the kitchen and were approaching the group.

Dax continued. "Anyway, I notice this guy in the seat in front of me. Sideways he was just a guy that was there, maybe one of the students but a little older. But then I noticed that the back of his head and his chin, even his nose, looked just like Robin Williams. Turns out this guy had been the star's double for years. He starts telling us all these stories of movies he's been in and big co-stars he's met."

"What a job," said Elizabeth.

"We spend two days there with the camera behind us while the actor playing the head doctor is up front giving a speech to the med students. I figure if the star's double is sitting right here, I just may get lucky enough to be here when the cameras are in front."

"Did you?" someone asked.

"So yeah, we come in on day three, and now all the cameras and lights and screens are in front. We're told to take the exact same seat we had before. Then one of the crew comes up and tells us that Robin is on his way in. We were not to touch him, bother him, ask for his autograph or any of that. And finally, a few minutes later, the man himself walks in and everyone starts cheering and applauding. He gives us that famous smile and bows. They point him in my direction, and he walks up and stands right in front of me. Looking around he says, 'Gentlemen,' then has a seat. I'm thinking, well this is cool. Spent two days on the set with him right there."

"What's he like?" Elizabeth asked.

"He's like a fidgety kid, high on sugar. Or in his case, maybe high on Peruvian marching power."

A few people chuckled.

"He can't sit still. Always cracking jokes. There's rarely a dull or quiet moment around him."

"God gave you a blessing. Good for you," said Dennis, smiling with his Coke raised in salute.

Dax shrugged. "Nothing like that has happened since."

"Oh? What do you mean, *Eric?*" said Elizabeth.

Dax smirked. "Our little show had a slightly smaller audience."

The crowd shifted and groups of two or three began to talk. Dax heard Steven Kinsley ask Dennis, "Must you invoke your imaginary deities?"

"Not imaginary to me," Dennis replied.

Elizabeth took Dax's arm and they walked away. As he went, his attention abruptly shifted to a woman with mocha brown skin in a red sweater who had entered the room. He had seen her before but could not associate a name with her. Elizabeth saw him staring.

"Vitoria," she said with a knowing smile.

"Oh," Dax said without moving his eyes. Vitoria's near flawless figure nicely filled her knitted drawstring pants and sweater. Her face beamed with a bright smile as she was talking to someone nearby.

"I know her somewhere," Dax said. "Some class, I guess."

"Well, how could you forget? She's from Brazil, isn't she? You've got Brazilian blood in you, I thought."

"Yes. My grandfather. My dad is half and I'm one-fourth."

Elizabeth sighed heavily. "Funny how a person always wonders about a beautiful woman. Stories are written about women like that. If she were ugly, no one would care where she was from or who she was."

Dax came out of a semi-trance and looked at her. "How do you mean?"

"I mean, a good tale always calls for a beautiful woman. The man who wins her, rescues her, *gets* her, is usually handsome, but that's not as crucial. As long as he can fight the good fight and have the courage to face evil, it's okay if he's been scarred or ugly. But the woman," she nodded at Vitoria. "She must be beautiful. That makes the fight worth the effort."

Dax smiled. "Well, I recall in *The Hunchback of Notre Dame*, the handsome dude still got the beautiful girl in the end. The ugly guy, and the real hero, lost. That always bothered me. Of course, they depicted him as thrilled for the two lovebirds."

"It would have made you wonder though if the girl had been ugly. Then there would have been nothing to fight for," Elizabeth said. "But ugly girls still have their place. They make great witches or evil stepmothers. They might even make great theatre lighting techs."

"Liz ..." Dax started to say, but then realized he wasn't sure what to say. He thought of his scene with Meygan Knight. Much of what Elizabeth was saying was accurate – Meygan was far more attractive as a female than he was a male and the audience didn't seem to mind.

Elizabeth laughed. "I'm just venting."

Dax felt relieved. He didn't want to say something stupid like, *oh, don't worry, you're pretty, Elizabeth*. Nor did he want to feel sorry for a genuine friend who had always come across as one of the most agreeable people he'd ever known.

He glanced at the kitchen door. "Hey," he said, "come with me to the kitchen. I need one more drink."

She looked at his glass. "Careful, you're driving."

"I'll be fine, come on." He took her arm. A vibration in his pocket grabbed his attention. He stopped and fumbled for his cell phone. He looked at the small screen and saw the strange number – Jack. It was almost 8:00 and he was in a good enough mood to stick around the party for a while. "Sorry, gotta take this."

"Big shot," Elizabeth said, grinning, then turned back to the main room.

"Good evening, Dax. How's it going?" said Jack cheerfully.

"I was waiting all day for your call," said Dax.

"And I came through, didn't I?"

Dax was rubbing the bridge of his nose. "Jack, it's getting a little late. You know where I am?"

"Sure. In Berkeley, somewhat near the campus. And it's not late – barely eight."

"How did you—" Dax started to ask but stopped. These guys could be tracking him any way they wanted. "You want me to drive back into the city, don't you."

"We had an appointment, right? And eventually you'd be coming back up this way anyway."

Dax sighed. "Okay, where to? That warehouse again?"

"No, no, not that," Jack said quickly. "Sutter Hotel. Twenty-five hundred block of Sutter Street. Close to Union Square. Can you come by in about forty minutes? I've some people here I need you to meet."

"Okay."

"You sound tired. You okay?"

"I'll be fine. See you in a few."

Dax stuffed the phone back into his pocket and returned his glass to the kitchen. The air was much cooler as Dax stepped out into the night. His breath showed in thick white mist, dimly lit by the streetlights which were mostly obscured by thick foliage.

I'll be a better actor after this, he thought to himself. *I'll be more … confident. Maybe even dangerous.*

16: Tasha's Touch

Traffic moved along nicely as Dax made his way across the Bay Bridge and into downtown. He took 4th Street to Market, then headed up Taylor, to Sutter. The night was clear and crisp, a typical fall evening in the city. Around Post and Geary, he saw the usual streetwalkers, both female and transvestite.

Along Sutter Street, the night life bustled about. People wandering in and out of bars and cafes, flashing neon signs beckoning. A lone panhandler with a thick, dirty grey beard made his way slowly up the sidewalk soliciting to those who passed.

The wine had settled in and was slowly leaving his bloodstream, leaving him sleepy. He thought about getting a coffee but didn't want to lie awake all night.

He knew approximately where the Sutter Hotel was and parked several blocks away. The walk in the cool night air would be refreshing.

A few minutes later, Dax glanced at his watch as he stood before the hotel's entrance. He strolled into the lobby looking at the reception desk which was manned by a middle-aged Chinese man who briefly glanced up and then went back to whatever he was doing. The place was quiet except for the bubbling of a large aquarium inside the door next where three sizable orange and white koi swam lazily about. He turned toward the seating area by a small fireplace. A young man was reclining in one of the lounge chairs reading a magazine. He suddenly looked up, glanced at his watch, then stood.

"You must be Dax," he said with a smile that was a little too big as he approached.

Dax sized him up and figured he was maybe twenty-two or twenty-three. He was thin framed with sandy blond hair, slightly thicker on top but cropped short on the sides. He fit nicely in his suit jacket and the solid shoulders and arms underneath suggested regular workouts.

He held out his hand to Dax. "I'm Agent Forrester. But call me Jeremy. How are you doing?"

"Doing okay," Dax said looking Jeremy up and down. "Am I early?"

Jeremy pursed his lips and shook his head exaggeratedly. "A little – always better than late. You must be cold, yes?" he asked with raised eyebrows, staring inquisitively at Dax.

Dax smiled and used a word he'd heard Gene Palmer say earlier. "It's a tad brumal out there."

Jeremy frowned, perplexed, then caught himself and nodded in agreement. He gestured toward the elevators. "Shall we?"

"Is Jack up there?" Dax asked.

"Jack? Oh yes, Jack is here. Follow me please."

Dax stared at the back of Jeremy's head as they made their way toward the elevator, the agent's dress shoes clicking and clacking on the tile floor. For some odd reason, Dax felt as if he were on a stage with this Agent Forrester performing a scene.

In the elevator, Dax asked, "Is Agent Staggs here?"

Jeremy turned, eyebrows raised. "Hmm?"

"Michael Staggs. Just curious."

Another quick frown and Jeremy glanced down at the ground in thought for a moment, then started shaking his head. "No, he's not here."

As the elevator slowed to a stop, Dax looked up at the numbers – fifth floor.

Jeremy exited and turned right. "Please follow me," he said over his shoulder. He walked briskly down the hall and stopped at room 509 where he inserted a door key.

Upon entering, Dax was hit with stale cigarette smell. Naturally, these guys would be smoking up the whole floor. The light above him was off and the atmosphere shadowy.

Jeremy closed the door and walked past. In a room further down Dax heard voices and some laughter. One of them sounded like Jack. Another voice was female. Dax heard Jeremy say something to the others who all at once became quiet.

The sound of a chair rolling on plastic could be heard and then Jack came around the corner with a big smile. "Hi Dax. Just on time."

Jack was looking more casual tonight in tan khakis and a dark brown sport coat, no tie.

"I thought I was early," said Dax.

"The only holdup is you."

Dax glanced at a cluster of bottles in the dim light on the countertop next to him.

"You found us okay, no problems?" asked Jack.

"Easy peasy. But the guy tailing me probably already told you that."

"Funny," Jack said with a smirk. "Come this way," he said turning. "By the way, you're already on the clock."

"I'm getting paid for being here?"

"Of course."

Walking past the small entranceway, he looked to his right where he'd heard voices. A table with about seven empty chairs sat unoccupied in front of a window with the burgundy-colored drapes closed. Papers and folders were strewn about. Three cigarettes were still burning in ashtrays, sending little swirls of gray smoke up toward the ceiling light. Coffee cups and drinking glasses rested in front of the chairs. Whoever was here had scrammed at his arrival.

Jack entered a small hallway, also dimly lit. He paused at a closed door. "Need to use the restroom?" He thumbed over his shoulder.

"I'm okay," said Dax.

"In here," Jack said, opening a door which led into a room with a small table, some electronic equipment, and a white screen against the wall.

Jack walked to the table, turned around and rubbed his hands together. "Okay, almost showtime. You ready?"

The effects of the wine were wearing off and Dax was able to think clearer. "I guess, but I still don't know what exactly I'm doing."

Jack smiled. "Better to keep it that way for now. Just do what we tell you, and everything will be fine."

"Are we still a go for tomorrow night?"

"Yep. Got the green light a couple hours ago."

Dax looked at the table. "What are those?"

"Expensive toys, some of which you're going to get to play with." Jack walked past Dax and grabbed a chair by the door and moved it to the center of the room. "Have a seat."

Dax sat and took a big breath. The door squeaked and he turned to see Agent Jeremy Forrester sticking his head in.

"You want a water or something?" Jack asked Dax.

"Sure."

Jack nodded at Jeremy and the young agent disappeared.

"New guy?" Dax asked.

"Sorta."

"Where's he from?"

Jack paused and looked at Dax for a moment. "Why do you ask?"

"Just curious."

"He's from the east coast. His father was a military career officer, so he grew up in several places around the world. He's good in linguistics and familiar with different cultures."

"So now you're teaching him all about the west coast and California."

"Something like that. It's a whole different world out here. In the Bay Area you have no culture, just a lot of people dressing up to play whatever part they feel like."

Dax had to agree.

Jack stood and stared for a moment in thought, then said, "So here's the scoop, we're sending you to a party."

"Great, I was just at one."

"That's what you were doing in Berkeley tonight?"

"Yeah, an old drama teacher who influenced me. Retired after a long career. So what's this party, someone's birthday?"

Jack sat down. "It's the sort of party I don't think you've ever been to."

"You told me a few days ago you were looking for a couple of people."

"Yes," Jack said while rubbing his hands together in a circular motion. "We have a pretty good idea who they are. But they aren't the main target. Not at the moment anyway. We're hoping you'll get approached by someone who thinks you're someone he recognizes."

"Who is this person I'm supposed to be?"

"Let's just say he's a supplier. A big one."

"You have a name?"

"We have lots of names, and all of them phony."

"Who will he think I am?"

"A man whose real name is *Gavreel*, uh, Gavril, but goes by the street name, *Собака*. He's from Saint Petersburg."

"Soh-ba, what?"

"*Soh-BAH-ka*. Accent on the second syllable. A nickname."

Dax repeated it slowly while Jack looked on with both seriousness and amusement.

"Go easy on the *ah* sound," Jack said. "Gavril and his family are from Saint Petersburg and have softer *ahs,* whereas people from Moscow will have harder ones. From Siberia, they would say *O*, as in *oh*."

Dax stared dumbly. "They don't teach this stuff in college."

"Nope. Eighty percent of what you get in college is useless on the street."

Dax thought for a moment. "So if I was actually *from* Moscow, I'd say *M-ah-scow*, but if I was from Siberia, I'd say *M-OH-scow*."

"I knew there was a reason we picked you."

"So what does ... *soh-ba-ka* mean?"

"It means dog."

"Dog?"

"Yep. Dog, hound, pooch. Generic word; can mean any kind of dog." Jack brought his hands together. "Could mean a small lap dog." He opened his hands wide. "Or a big, scary one. But if you wanted to specify a small dog or puppy, you say *sobashka*."

Dax shook his head. "Whoa."

"Relax," said Jack. "You don't need to remember that. You'd normally never call anyone that, but in this case, it's a nickname he's proud of."

"Why's that?"

Jack shrugged. "Maybe he's good at fetching certain goods for the right price."

"Or maybe he has a reputation for attacking and biting."

"There's an old Russian expression," Jack said like a teacher. "*Собака на сене*, which literally translates to, 'dog in the manger.' It refers to someone who doesn't allow others to have or enjoy something useful, like a resource, while at the same time, he doesn't use himself. *Dog In the Manger* was the title of a Russian comedy-musical in the late '70s."

"All fascinating, but it doesn't help me if I get in trouble."

"You won't."

Dax took a deep breath. "Your accent sounds perfect. You've spent some time in Russia."

"I have, yes," said Jack.

Dax waited for further explanation, but Jack turned back to the table. "Okay, so I am Gavril, otherwise known as *The Dog*. I'm at this party because ..."

"Because you were invited," Jack said turning around. "But no one will know or expect that. Chances are there will be some individuals who may be surprised to see you. That's what we're hoping for."

"But what if they start talking in Russian to me?"

"Doubtful." Jack looked at the ground and shrugged with his head. "We're guessing most of the players there won't even be Russian. They're from all over and need English to communicate. The person we're looking for may speak Ukrainian to you."

"I don't know a single word in Ukrainian."

Jacked waved it off. "No worries."

"Does Gavril have an accent when he speaks English?"

"Maybe, slightly. But he's educated and been here a long time. Did some schooling in England. He's interacted with many Western Europeans, as well as those from the Middle East. They all have their own accents. The nice thing is that the common language they do most of their business in is English. For now anyway. Could be Mandarin in a few years."

Dax took a big breath and thought about Jack's last comment. "But I'm not going to know what to say."

"Just be polite. Be charming. Pretend you're a Russian James Bond who's there to enjoy a drink and flirt with the women. You can be a player, right?"

Dax scoffed. "I was never great at that game."

"Not part of the plan anyway."

"Good. Because if you want me to seduce the beautiful spy and steal stuff out of her purse the next morning while she slept, I'm afraid I'm not at that level."

Jack smirked. "You're watching too many movies. Look, your job comes down to this. You go in, you say hi to a few folks, but only if they approach you. You're there, but not parading the fact. We wait for a certain person to approach you. Once this happens, you're done. We'll give you a signal and then you scram."

Jeremy stepped partially into the room with a water bottle in his hand. He extended it to Dax.

Dax turned, took the bottle and said, "*Spacibo, torvarich.*"

For a split second, Jeremy's eyes widened, but then he smiled. He thought for a moment as if mulling over the appropriate reply and then said, "You're welcome." He then disappeared out the door.

Dax turned back to Jack, who was watching the doorway.

"How will you signal me?"

Jack turned, gathering his thoughts. "We'll have people there. Someone will approach and say you have a private phone call and motion you toward the exit."

Dax paused for a moment, thinking. "What if someone from Собака's past walks up and starts talking to me like old friends?"

"Pretend you can't talk there. Make like you can't be heard discussing anything about yourself."

"But what if they ask innocent questions like about my family or something? How's your sister Ivanna doing?"

"Make like you're pretending to be someone else. We'll be listening. If you get into a bind, we'll have one of our people step in."

"An imposter pretending to be another imposter. Nice. How will you know it's the person you're looking for?" Dax slowly opened his bottle, the plastic seal cracking softly a couple times.

"We've got a few faces and names we're on the lookout for. It's not the kind of party for small talk. Everything that's going to happen will happen for a purpose."

Dax took a slow drink from the bottle. "So you don't even know what he'll say to me or what he wants?"

"Not at this point. But pretend to recognize him. Play the game of, *we can't talk business here.*"

Dax pondered this. "Do I like him, hate him?" He took another long drink from the water bottle. It was cold and felt good in his mouth and throat.

"You've done business with him before. But we're not sure where you stand right now."

Dax stared at the wall and tried to envision all this. He turned back to Jack. "What if he pulls a gun on me?"

Jack laughed.

"Not funny. You're not giving me much here."

Jack held up his hands. "Sorry. Look, we don't believe you'll be any kind of danger like that. None of these people do that kind of stuff in a public setting like this."

"What if I get kidnapped and hauled away?"

"Won't happen, but the device you'll be wearing has GPS and we can track you."

"G, P *what?*"

"Global Positioning System," Jack said. "Started with NAVSTAR back in the late '70s. Today, the planned twenty-four satellite system is almost done. When enough satellites can see a device simultaneously, they can triangulate to find the exact position of the user."

"So anyone, any place on earth can be tracked?"

"Any coordinate, if they have a GPS device. And with it, any broadcasting cell phone. Soon, data will be collected on everyone – where you've driven and when, all your patterns. Eventually it's going to be a gold mine for retail marketers so they know where you shop and what kind of stuff you buy."

"That's a little unnerving."

There was a light knock on the door. Jack looked up and waved someone in.

Dax was staring at the floor, his thoughts bouncing around, when the distinct smell of perfume made him look up. When he did, his heart skipped a beat, and he involuntarily drew a big breath. He thought he heard Jack chuckle but didn't care. Standing in front of him was a woman who almost defied all description, at least at first glance. He gawked at her stunning beauty for a moment until he caught himself and looked away.

"Dax," Jack said slowly, as if it were a sacred moment. "This is Tasha, your tailor." He gestured at the woman, his face tightening to suppress a grin.

Tasha studied Dax for a moment. Her lips were full but subtle and painted in a warm, pink, glossy, flower petal hue. While her mouth was expressionless, her eyes, which fell between a soft shade of blue and gray, bore into him, and laughed knowingly.

Dax tried to smile politely. There seemed to be two versions of her, one that a person could take in at a single glance, and another that required careful inspection. An ample but shapely nose separated large eyes that were a bit far apart, but perfectly defined. She wasn't heavily decorated with makeup and didn't appear to need it. Her skin was creamy smooth and perfectly complimented her voluminous champagne-blonde waves which fell gently on her right shoulder over a stylish silver and black suit jacket. In her left hand was a yellow cloth measuring tape.

She took two steps forward while her eyes searched him up and down. Finally, her mouth formed a gracious smile as she held out her hand. "Hello, Dax. Nice to meet you."

Her smooth accent was distinctly Slavic.

Dax wondered if her name was really Natasha. It was hard to imagine she worked for the United States FBI. Maybe she was a contractor or consultant. Heck, maybe on the side she was one of those $500 per hour catwalk models.

Dax reached out his hand clumsily, like a sixth grader taking a girl's hand for the first time to the dance floor. Her skin was warm, and her thumbnail gently scratched the side of his hand, maybe deliberately, maybe not.

All at once he realized he was still sitting. He rose a little too quickly and the back of his knees pushed the chair, making it scrape backwards. He glanced at Jack who was now silently chuckling, his shoulders bouncing.

"Nice to meet you," said Dax. He vaguely remembered the phrase in Russian but decided not to try.

Standing eye to eye with Tasha, he saw she was tall, just a tad under him in height. He could smell her perfume again, a faint rosy-citrus scent that lingered for just a moment and then receded—obvious, but not overbearing. Like everything else about her, it grabbed one's attention, then left one strangely perplexed.

It was difficult not to stare at her, like admiring a both beautiful and fascinating piece of art. And it was impossible to tell her age. Depending on how she dressed and behaved, she could be twenty-five or forty-five.

Dax didn't care that he stood stupidly before her speechless. A woman like this had been ogled at her entire life. He was just one more chump she had to do a job for. Better not take all this too seriously.

"I am going to enjoy dressing you up, I think," she said at last.

Dax didn't know what to say, so he said nothing.

"Good," said Jack, clapping his hands together softly. "Like I said, this is going to be *fun*."

17: Too Much Freedom

"Take off your jacket?" Tasha said. It wasn't really a request.

Dax complied and draped it over the chair.

She then gently took Dax's right wrist and lifted it. "If you please."

He allowed her to raise his arm and hold it out straight as she placed the end of the measure tape on his wrist. Using her thumb, she flattened the tape slowly up his arm and to his lower shoulder.

"Hey, you know," Dax started to say. Tasha looked up and met his eyes. Dax nodded at Jack. "He already took my measurements."

She subtly smiled. "I know." She glanced sideways as if to tell a big secret. Then leaning in, said in almost a whisper, "But I don't trust him. I need to see for myself. You don't mind, do you?" She held his gaze, waiting for a response.

He felt her warm breath. She had a way of being both quiet and forceful at the same time. A puppy's innocence, and a wolf's cunning.

Stepping closer, she brought both hands around his bicep. Dax wanted badly to make small talk, ask a couple questions, anything, but his mind was blank. He heard a light buzzing sound and looked at Jack.

Jack reached into his pocket and produced a phone. He put it to his ear for a moment and then began walking to the door. "Excuse me," he said, exiting. He left the door partially open, and Dax could hear a couple voices out in the main room.

Tasha stepped back and slowly stroked the yellow measuring tape between her thumb and index, her eyes shifting in thought.

Dax thought of something brilliant to ask. "So … was Jack's measurements accurate?"

She looked up and met his eyes. "They are not bad," she said, stepping forward again, eyes still locked. "But I like to be perfect. Don't you?" It was a rhetorical question. She reached up around Dax's neck with the tape measure, then glided the edges of her thumbs ever so gently against his skin.

Dax felt a tingle dance up his spine and tried to suppress any involuntarily fidgeting. He was also hoping his deodorant was still effective.

She brought the end of the tape together at the front of his neck and pulled just a little bit too tightly. Dax met her eyes and saw that smile again. She lowered the tape but did not step back.

"It's remarkable," she purred.

"What is?" Dax felt crowded and wanted to back up but didn't.

"The … likeness," she said thoughtfully, her eyes drifting momentarily around his face. She refocused and studied his eyes. Reaching up and running a finger along his left eyebrow she asked, "Are you afraid?"

The question caught him off guard. Throwing on his actor's hat he stood a little taller and asked, "Do I have something to be afraid of?"

Her eyes drifted up and down his body. "Not yet."

Was she trying to freak him out? If so, it was working. He wondered how many unwary men she'd put under a spell. It struck him that he could spend a lot of time with this woman and know nothing about her or what her real endgame was.

Dax gave a casual shrug. "Jack said his people would be there."

"Yes. Of course." Her tone shifted to slightly more impersonal. With upturned palms, she gestured for him to lift both his arms. "Please," she said.

As he complied, she stepped right up to him. Her hair smelled delicious as her hands snaked around his waist. He could feel warm air from her nose, her body pressed slightly against his. He prayed a silent prayer he'd not respond in an embarrassing way.

The tape measure came together again just below his belly, and he felt the back of her fingers pressing against him.

"I think that will be good," she said. One edge of her mouth ever so delicately curled. She then added, "You will be good."

Tasha's face had such dramatic attractiveness, one had to gawk. Dax searched her countenance for something to tell him what impression she was trying to make but could find nothing. She wasn't flirting, scorning, teasing, tempting, or offering anything. She could probably hate a man or love him and the poor bastard would have no idea. She might prefer other women. Her subtleties could be saying, *I am going to seduce you*, or, *I am going to kill you*. If she approached you with her hands behind her back, you wouldn't know if she were holding a rose or a gun. She would make the perfect female spider, who, after mating, will often murder and consume her partner.

When she stepped back, Dax felt somewhat relieved. She casually wrapped the measuring tape around her hand and strolled toward the door.

"I need to make a couple minor adjustments, then I will be back. You will wait here, yes?" And then she was gone.

Dax stood where he was like a compliant child. From beyond the door, he heard more talking and smelled fresh cigarette smoke making its way down the hall. He heard heavy footsteps approaching. It didn't sound like Jack.

The large round face of Agent Al Kimball appeared and seemed to take up the entire doorway. "Hello again, Dax," he said.

"Hey. How's it going?"

Kimball smiled, his round cheeks ballooning, his breathing loud. "They getting you suited up?"

"Almost. Just got *examined* by Tasha."

Kimball gave Dax a knowing smile. "She's good at that."

"You could say that. She isn't FBI, right?"

Kimball looked at him for a moment but then shrugged and said, "She does jobs here and there."

Dax realized he wasn't going to get a lot of information from anyone here.

Kimball was looking at the screen on the wall. He pulled a handkerchief from a coat pocket and wiped sweat off his forehead. "I'm going to take some photos of you once they get you decked out. See you in a bit." He then waddled out the door.

Dax sat on the chair. He wanted to wander out into the other room, pour a drink, chitchat with the other agents, or whoever they were, but didn't feel comfortable doing that. He unscrewed the cap on his water bottle and took another gulp.

He heard more thumping of footsteps in the hall, this time faster. Walking briskly, Jack came back through the doorway. "How'd it go?" he asked.

"She didn't trust your measurements."

"She doesn't trust anything. That's why we like her."

"Oh, *that's* the reason."

"Funny."

Dax paused but then decided to ask. "Is she Russian?"

Jack took a slow pull from a drink glass he was holding. The ice cubes clinked softly as they slid forward, then back. "Something like that," he finally said.

Dax laughed and waved him off. "Okay, okay. I was just thinking maybe I could practice with her. Refresh some of my *pa-Russki.*"

Jack eyed him. "Private lessons, eh?"

Dax smirked back. "Something like that."

Jack set his glass down. "She's way out of your league, my young friend."

"I can learn from her."

Jack folded his hands in front of him. "You could indeed. But you couldn't afford her."

"That's probably true. But in the interests of national security, maybe Uncle Sam could foot the bill."

Jack laughed. "That's good, Dax. I like that."

Dax held up the water bottle. "I wouldn't be able to get a *real* drink around here, would I?"

Jack waved it off. "Not now. And by the way, no booze tomorrow night. I need you in full capacity."

"What do I order at the bar?"

"Tonic water. Add a lime if you want."

"Nice. What if someone offers me an actual drink?"

"Take it but sip real slow."

Dax nodded toward the door. "Tasha or any of them do undercover work?"

"Some have. Field agents and actors have a few things in common. The best investigators think like criminals. You catch a bad guy because you know what he's going to do or where he's going to show up next."

"Is that how one rises in ranks with the FBI? The number of bad guys you grab?"

"Not necessarily. A high-profile case may launch your career, but if you want to climb upwards the old-fashioned way it's all politics. Most people don't have the stomach for it. As the saying goes, if you wanna get to the top, there's a lot of bottom you'll have to kiss."

"Not your game, eh?"

"Nah. I'm a lifer in the field. The guys out here that slap the cuffs on the perps would rather be on the street playing bloodhound. It's in their DNA. Not sitting behind a desk playing bureaucrat. Most of the folks I work with are lifers out here too. But that's because they're mostly intel. People from intel never rise too far in the ranks."

"Interesting."

"And save for a collapse in the American economy, I'll always be employed. One out of every four adults in the United States have some kind of criminal record."

"You're joking."

"I joke not. That's what too much freedom does in a country."

Dax did a double-take and looked at Jack.

Jack looked down and continued as if talking to himself. "The FBI only wants former cops, detectives, unless you're young and eager and fresh out of college. And you need to know how to handle firearms. We're a gun culture."

Dax looked down at his bottle and swirled the water around, lost in thought.

Jack was watching him. "You ever fire a gun, Dax?"

"Yeah. My dad has an old .45 Colt semi-auto. Fired that a few times. A friend I grew up with has some shotguns I've fired."

"You and your dad haven't spoken much lately. Is that right?"

Dax paused. "Please don't go there."

"Alright. You like it?"

"Do I like it?"

"Shooting. The feel of a powerful weapon in your hand."

"It has a certain thrill I guess. But I never got into it. I guess you already know I don't own any guns."

"If you'd legally bought any handguns in the last few years. Auto-registration many don't know about. But there's plenty of ways to get hold of whatever you want, especially in this city."

"I imagine so. But I don't hang with those kinds of crowds." Jack smiled. "We know you don't."

A faint hint of that rosy-citrus fragrance hit Dax's nose again. He turned and saw Tasha standing behind him holding a black suit jacket. The coat had a white shirt underneath on the hanger. She'd done it again—snuck up like a stalking cat.

Dax looked at the flawlessly smooth, shiny black material of the coat.

"You're gonna look beautiful," said Jack. He picked up his glass again. "You don't mind we have you put on the shirt here, do you? We need to try on the body mic. You can put the pants on in the bathroom."

Tasha took a step around him. "Take off your shirt?"

Standing in the middle of the room bare chested, Dax self-consciously sucked his stomach in a little. His struggles with belly fat had started in the last two or three years.

Tasha stood and stared. Dax couldn't tell if she liked what she saw or was merely observing the way a researcher might look at a lab rat.

Jack busied himself grabbing at things on the table, then approached with a roll of cloth medical tape and a small black object in his hand. "Okay," he said, "let's attach this to you and see how it feels."

"What is that?"

"It's the transmitter for the camera." Jack held it up for Dax to see. The object was about the size of an extra-wide cell phone, but thinner. On the top corner was what looked like a tiny version of a standard three-prong microphone jack.

"Where does it go?" asked Dax.

"Probably best on your back. The jacket will cover it up. Here, turn around."

Dax felt the cool material but his skin warmed it up quickly. He heard the crackling sound of tape getting pulled out and then the rip.

"That should do it," Jack said.

"Where's the camera?"

Jack grabbed an object from the table and held it up. It appeared to be a small box with a little round hole in the center, no bigger than the fingerprint area on a man's pinky.

"We're going to hide this dead center in your bowtie. It'll be perfect."

Dax eyed the little piece of electronics. "That's small."

"They make 'em even smaller. But our system is not only a camera, but a mic, and it broadcasts live. Amazing sound and picture. We'll be recording the whole thing remotely. Nothing will get missed. Well, nothing *you* miss will get missed."

Tasha held up the white dress shirt. "Put this on, please."

Jack held up a small wire.

"Let me," said Tasha, taking it from Jack. She stepped up close to Dax and maneuvered her hands around his bare torso. Her hands skillfully felt for the microphone input and then snapped the cord into place. As her hands came back out of his shirt, her fingertips rubbed the flesh next to his ribs with a little too much pressure. She then began buttoning the shirt, her hands working quickly and adeptly. When the top button was secured, she picked up a bowtie. Stepping around Dax, she stood behind and reached around his neck, holding the bowtie in place while Jack pushed the camera through a custom hole in the middle of the tie's knot.

Dax felt Tasha's hand slide up his back. Despite the coolness of the air, he found himself suddenly trying to control a small sweat that was threatening to breakout.

Tasha's fingers brushed his back until they got to the top of the transmitter. She then took the cord and pulled it back, reeling in extra cable.

Dax felt two or three fingernails gently tease his skin, then felt her pull his collar down and straighten it. He was beginning to think he was reading too much into her touches.

Tasha stepped back around and stood next to Jack. They both stared at the bowtie. Jack nodded in satisfaction. She then held up the jacket and offered a sleeve. Dax slid his arm into the cool material and heard the faint swishing of sleek fabric. When the jacket was on, she and Jack stepped back again and stared.

Jack's mouth curved up into a wry smile. "It's perfect."

"What is your shoe size?" Tasha asked, looking his feet.

Dax thought for a moment. "Last time I bought—"

"Ten," she interrupted, "And a half. Wide?"

"*Da*," Dax heard himself say softly.

Tasha's slight smirk deepened as she turned away.

Jack was pecking the keypad on a small phone. He put it to his ear and waited a moment. "Stay there but turn your body to follow me," he said to Dax.

Jack walked around the table to the far wall. He stood with the phone to his ear, then covered it with his hand. In almost a whisper, he said, "Testing, one two three. Testing." He then walked across the room near the screen. Dax turned and kept the bowtie pointing at Jack. Jack whispered again, "Testing, one, two, three."

Tasha stood watching, her eyes running up and down Dax.

"How's that?" Jack asked into the phone. "Perfect." He pocketed the phone and rubbed his hands together.

"Is someone watching and listening right now?"

"Yep. Three blocks from here."

Dax was intrigued. "Lemme guess. From the outside, a common delivery truck— flowers? And on in the inside three or four people with headsets around glowing computer screens?"

Jack just smiled.

"What if I need to use the restroom with this thing?" His question was ignored.

"Now the pants," Tasha abruptly said. She held out a hand. "The jacket, please."

Dax was handed a pair of black dress pants of the same quality and material.

"We'll step out for a minute," Jack said and headed for the door. He winked. "The folks watching will politely look away."

The pants felt almost perfect, although a bit too long. A couple minutes later there was a knock on the door.

"All set, Dax?" said Jack from behind the door, tapping it lightly. He entered the room alone.

"The pants are a little long."

"No sweat. We'll fix that. Hey, look at you, a regular double-oh seven. We'll even get a matching hanky for the pocket." Jack paused and eyed Dax closely. "One last thing," he said, reaching for something on the table. He turned and held out a round plastic container with a clear top. In it were two objects that looked like little globs of flesh-colored playdough. "Mouth inserts to puff up your jowls."

"My jowls? You guys are into details."

"You betcha."

Dax took the container and removed the top with a small twist.

"Stick them here and here, next to your gums," said Jack, using his fingers to point at his mouth on either side of his lower jaw. "They're soft, you'll hardly notice."

Dax pushed one down between his gums and cheek. It felt smooth and spongy, like ear plugs. He used his tongue to push them as low as possible. "This feels a little weird," he said.

"You'll get used to it. Just don't swallow them."

"It wouldn't kill me if I accidently did, would it?"

"No, but you'll not want to stick them in your mouth again when you get 'em back."

"Funny, Jack."

Jack headed for the door. "Alright follow me."

In the main room, Al Kimball and Tasha were at the table, her pulling on a cigarette.

Jack turned on a CD player. The soft sounds of jazz-rock started playing. He turned it up louder. "Okay," he said, "Now walk to the other side of the room."

Dax complied.

"Now turn around. Al, say something."

Kimball waved at Dax. "Testing. Hello."

"Softer, Al," Jack said.

Kimball repeated in a lower volume.

Jack was on his phone, nodding. "Good," he said. Then to Dax, "Now walk toward the table and say something."

Dax approached the table, looking at Tasha. She casually blew smoke in the air, her lips puckered in a seductive kiss. "My pants are a little too long," he said to her.

"Keep talking," said Jack.

"This is a nice suit," Dax said. "Can I keep it?" He glanced at Jack who waved circles with his fingers to say, *keep talking*. He looked back at Tasha. "I'm not a photographer, but I can picture us together."

Kimball laughed. Tasha raised her chin slightly and smirked.

The implements in his mouth almost hindered his speech, but he could adjust with practice. Suddenly feeling emboldened, he leaned a little closer to Tasha and said, "Say, do you live around here, often?"

Tasha didn't flinch. Her eyes ran nonchalantly down Dax's body to his feet, lingered for a moment, then went back up. "Very nice," she purred. "I'll fix the pants."

Jack was talking on the cell. "Now come this way," said Jack motioning to Dax, his ear still pressed to the phone. He turned the music up a little louder.

Dax made his way toward Jack waving and saying, "Testing, testing, can you hear *and* see me now?"

Jack was listening to his phone, nodding. After a moment he ended the call. "Okay we're good to go. Let's get some pictures." He shut off the music and headed back to the hallway.

Kimball pushed himself up from the table with a grunt and waddled after them. He broke out his fancy digital camera and started snapping. He took about twenty photos while having Dax stand in various mugshot-like poses in front of the small screen.

After Dax had changed back into his own clothes, he'd been ushered out rather quickly. He reminded himself that these people were in another world and would never be his friends. They would never trust him, and he wasn't sure he could trust them. They would remain mysterious, aloof, cordial for the most part, but only because of professionalism.

As he approached the exit, he glanced up at the wall and looked at a black and white photo he'd seen before of Marilyn Monroe laughing away at something Humphrey Bogart was saying. A smiling Lauren Bacall sat watching. A unique blip of time documented. Instead of Monroe, he imagined Tasha there.

"Here's lookin' at *you* kid."

18: Private Auditions

The temperature was uncomfortably hot. People had already removed as many layers as possible, which didn't help much since everyone was dressed for the frigid city weather in the first place.

The heat was making everyone edgy. This wasn't good because Jim Kirkland had already been edgy from the moment he walked in. All sorts of rumors were swirling around as to why he was acting strange.

There was another element that made this morning's situation abrasive. Today was the last day of callbacks for *Wild Hearts,* the last chance many had to make their impression and hope they got the part they shot for.

It only meant one thing for a director to have this many callbacks—he wasn't satisfied with who he'd seen yet. This wasn't a good feeling for the hopefuls sitting around waiting for their turn. Most of the key parts were clearly already cast, the rest were just the leftovers. The question was, who would get the better of the scraps?

Jim was massaging his nose with thumb and forefinger. He hadn't felt this level of despondence about a production in years and rehearsals hadn't even started. "Has anyone figured out how to get the heat down?" he called over his shoulder to no one in particular.

Jim glanced at his watch – 11:40 a.m. At the beginning of the week, he'd made a decision he hoped he wouldn't regret—he'd taken some advice from Les Abraham. Jim could never admit this to anyone, of course. Not in his prayers, not to his deceased mother. Jim wanted a certain kind of actor for this one role, and Les had just the suggestion.

I understand Dax Ribeiro hasn't signed up to audition, Les had said.

Oh? How have you come to understand that?

A wink, a pat on the shoulder. *Call Dax.*

Les wasn't that bad a guy and did care about actors he thought had potential. If Jim truly respected the man's teaching and directing style, it'd be a different story.

So far it had been odd, though. Dax had just given a tremendous performance and should be capitalizing on that. The young actor should be excited about what was happening and what the next steps might be. To reach a level where directors or producers were calling *you* is a place many never got to.

But Jim had called. A well-known and respected director, and one in charge of a highly coveted show, gives an actor a ring and says, *hey, I might have part for you.* In a game of phone tag, he'd left voicemail, and at some point in the middle of the night when his phone was powered off, Dax had returned a casual message that he might stop by. *Might?* Wouldn't most actors behave like they'd gotten a call from the local lottery office?

Well, Jim wasn't offering Dax a lead role, but it was a significant one. It'd be wonderful exposure and a way to keep the momentum going. There was a lot of talk and anticipation about *Wild Hearts,* and all connected local actors who weren't already committed to something else wanted a piece of it.

Jim resumed fanning his face with a notepad. His underarms were already moist and he was getting uncomfortable. He turned and peered up the aisle toward the exit doors. Dax had agreed to stop by and chat, during lunch. Or he *might*, anyway. From what Jim understood, Dax worked not too far from The Treasure Box. Maybe they'd take a break and go to a coffee shop or something. He wanted an excuse to get out right now. Truth be told, he wanted an excuse to cancel the rest of the day.

"Jim?" a voice said.

Jim readjusted his thick, black-framed glasses and looked at his assistant, Sharon Toomey. She gazed back apprehensively, so he decided to smile and try to be more pleasant.

"Did you want to see Dillon Christie again?" she asked.

Jim started to reach up to massage the bridge of his nose again but stopped himself. "No, that's okay. Put him down for Jake."

"Oh, good," she said smiling, and started to take notes.

Jim frowned and watched her for a moment. Was he the only one frustrated with how things were going? If only he could divulge certain secrets. If only everyone knew just how close he'd come to walking out of this production already.

Part of theatre was forever ruined when it was turned into more business than art. How long ago that had happened was perhaps before even his time. He wished he could go back to another era, maybe all the way to the ancient Greeks. He'd studied Greek theatre in his time and found it fascinating. Sure, there'd be no lights, microphones, sound effects, nothing fancy. But it would be pure and raw theatre. His mind drifted to memories of him standing at the top row of crumbling seats overlooking the Hellenic theatre at Epidaurus. It was over twenty years ago when he'd taken that trip. Who knows what the full impact of plays written and performed in Athens between 500 and 200 BC have had on Western theatre and culture? He could only imagine being there when *Oedipus* or *Antigone* was first introduced, a time when writers like

Aristophanes did what they did to teach morality and dignity. A far cry from today where a play's success is measured purely in dollars collected both at the box office, behind closed doors, and the sale of t-shirts and coffee mugs.

Jim scoffed in disgust.

"What?" asked Sharon with that hesitant look again.

Jim feigned a chuckle. "Oh, nothing. Who are we waiting for?"

"Adrian called, twice now."

"Who?"

"Adrian Stares, the guy who was throwing the table around the other day." Sharon suppressed a laugh.

"Oh ..." Jim started to massage his nose again.

"I'm sure he'll call again."

Jim sighed. "If he calls again, tell him you heard a rumor that Les Abraham is looking for him. But that didn't come from me."

Sharon let out a laugh. "Les probably thought he was cute." She thumbed through some pages. "Have you made a decision about *Hank* yet?"

"No. I think though we need to break for lunch."

"You said lunch would be around 12:30."

"I know. But a serious intermission is in order here." *Not to mention about three stiff drinks.*

Jim began fanning himself while his thoughts once again drifted. It was starting to bother him that he wasn't enjoying this production. For years he'd savored all the hard work of a show – planning it out, auditioning, doing the callbacks, rehearsing. But as of late, he wasn't so sure. Especially after seeing his longtime colleague Cheryl Bronson sell out like she obviously did. Any more situations like this would be intolerable and maybe even call for retirement.

He should be so lucky to be chosen to direct this show. But at his age, he didn't need luck anymore. His resume and credits had ceased mattering years ago. His legacy as a writer and director of theatre was set in stone before a lot of the actors in the room presently were even born.

Jim glanced up and saw Sharon looking up over his head. He turned and saw the handsome and haughty face of Mario Silvestri strolling down the aisle.

Mario walked up to Jim and stood, shifting his weight back and forth. "Hi, Mr. Kirkland. I'm Mario." He said this with a little wave of his hand but made no effort to shake. He stood staring down at Jim, waiting for a response.

Jim regarded the dark-haired boy for a moment through his thick glasses. Despite himself, he allowed a pleasant and even partially sincere smile to come over his face. He turned to Sharon. "Sharon, this is Mario. Mario, Sharon."

"Hi Mario," said Sharon. She gazed at him the way most females probably had to upon first meeting the pretty boy. Mario's dark round eyes turned and confidently stared back into hers. When he gave her a smile and that same little wave, she dropped her stare in embarrassment and went back to her pile of papers.

"Mario is going to play Cash Giles," Jim said.

Sharon looked back up startled and almost dropped her pen. "Really?"

Jim held his smile and nodded. "Yes, really."

Sharon paused for a moment at the tone of Jim's voice, but then said, "Wow, congratulations, Mario!" She looked at Jim with subtle questioning in her eyes. The whole scene was feeling strange—Jim's odd smile, this Mario guy she never saw audition or play a lead character. Something was wrong with this picture.

Jim couldn't tell if the kid was being smug or aloof. Mario was wearing designer jeans and what looked like pricy dress shoes. Above that he had a dark suede sport jacket over a blue dress shirt that had the top three buttons open. If his hair was slicked back anymore, and if he wore a thick gold chain and maybe some big shiny rings, he'd be a character straight out of a mob movie.

Jim looked at his watch even though he knew the time. "You're a little late."

Mario shrugged and tried to look nonchalant. "Yeah, sorry about that. Had to take care of a few things."

Jim just nodded.

"So, what now?" Mario asked.

Jim leaned back. "I want to see you bounce some lines back and forth with the other actors."

Mario glanced at the stage, scanned a few rows, then went back to Jim. A couple of the other actors had turned and were watching.

Somehow, Jim kept his smile as he sized the kid up. Time was the downfall to those who are given freely what they didn't earn, he'd seen it before. There would only be so many doors like this kicked open. If he couldn't carry his own weight, he wouldn't last. But in the interim, Jim had to be part of the experiment. That meant possibly ruining his show and people wondering about his judgement as a director.

"We're about to break for lunch," Jim said.

Mario waved it off. "I've had lunch," he said glancing back to the stage.

Jim felt his neck get warm. "Well," he glanced at Sharon who quickly looked down at her papers. Jim spoke slowly. "I'm glad to hear that you have had your lunch. I, however, have not. So, I think we'll break now."

Mario shrugged. "Okay, I'll take a walk."

Jim's smile broadened. "You do that."

"Hi, Dax!" said Sharon, leaping to her feet.

Jim turned around and saw Dax Ribeiro walking down the aisle.

Mario gave Dax a quick glance then looked away.

Sharon edged around Jim's knees, stepped out and gave Dax a hug. As she did, Dax glanced toward the front of the theatre. In the second row, Dillon Christie and two others were turned around and watching. Dillon had a look in his eyes that suggested he wished he had superpower abilities to destroy with just a stare.

"You're looking good, Sharon," Dax said.

"Thanks."

"Dax," said Jim standing and extending a hand. "How are you, my friend?"

"I'm okay." Dax glanced across the aisle and up the opposite row. Aaron Tisdale sat staring, a curious expression on his face. He had a several food wrappers next to him. He smiled and waved at Dax, who nodded back.

"I was wondering if you were going to be here," said Sharon with a beaming smile.

"Well, I wasn't actually—"

"Dax," Jim interrupted, "this is Mario. Mario, Dax."

Mario put out his hand but stayed where he was. Dax took two steps forward and shook.

"Nice to meet you," said Dax.

"You too," Mario said with a nod while glancing at Jim.

"Hot in here," Dax said.

"Right," said Jim. "Why don't we get out of here for awhile," he said, adjusting his glasses. "Have you had lunch yet? My dollar."

"No, not yet."

"Sharon, please let everyone know we'll resume in an hour." Jim paused and thought for a moment. "Better yet," he said, "I'll do it. Mario, come with me." He started down the aisle to the front of the house.

Mario stood for a moment, as if deciding how quickly he'd jump when given orders. But with a *yeah, okay* shrug to himself, he shuffled down the aisle after Jim.

Dax looked at Sharon who returned the look, rolled her eyes, and shrugged. She leaned close and whispered, "That guy's going to play Cash. I thought for sure Derrick Guzman would get it."

Jim stood facing everyone at the front of the house by the orchestra pit. Mario plopped himself down in the front row almost directly in front of Jim. Jim's smile had returned as he looked at Mario, on whom every eye now rested. All talking ceased as everyone wondered at this handsome and sharply dressed person, clearly the object of Jim's immediate attention.

"Everyone," Jim said loudly, "I'd like you to meet Mario Silvestri. He's going to be playing Cash."

From down the second row, someone started to say, "Who …" but went silent. On the other side of the house, a girl snickered. Dillon stared in bewilderment, his eyes running up and down Mario.

Jim continued looking at Mario who sat silent, looking as casual as possible. Jim decided to milk the moment. "Why don't you stand up Mario, make sure everyone knows who you are."

Mario looked at Jim with raised eyebrows and hesitated. He then slowly stood and pulling on the ends of his coat, looked around and nodded.

Jim wondered what the kid would expect. He was sure few would recognize him. Mario had been in and out of college class productions in the last several years playing parts that didn't even have names, never landing anything significant. And now suddenly, here he was stepping into a major role of a show that people were already buzzing about. Did he think he'd get happily welcomed in? Jim didn't have to wait long.

Derrick Guzman, who sat several seats down on the first row, asked in a voice loud enough to be heard by all, "So, Mario, haven't seen you around. When did you audition?"

Mario looked at Jim.

Jim sighed. He not only had to deal with this humiliation but was going to have to hold this kid's hand. "Last week, actually," Jim lied, referring to the little chat he had in the theatre office with Cheryl.

"Really," Derrick continued. He looked at Jim knowingly, then looked back at Mario. "You must have been good."

Mario gave a nod and a tiny shrug as if to say, *of course.*

Dennis Sheridan, with an uncharacteristically serious look on his face, folded his arms as his eyes went back and forth between Jim and Mario.

Dillon Christie stared at Mario's shoes, then his eyes slowly worked their way up to Mario's face. Then, in a voice louder than Derrick's, and one thickly coated in sarcasm, said, "Can I be invited to the private auditions next time too, Jim?"

Several people laughed quietly.

Jim held his smile and remained steady. "Sure, Dillon." He waved around the room. "All of you can." He decided he didn't want to continue this. "Lunch break everyone, see you in an hour." He looked at Mario. "Mario, why don't you stay and chat a bit. Get to know the others." He started back up the aisle.

"What is going on?" Dax half-whispered to Sharon as Jim made his way back.

"Not sure," said Sharon. "But Jim's been acting odd."

"This Mario, is Cash?" Dax asked.

"Looks that way."

"Who is he?"

Sharon shrugged.

"Well," said Jim stepping up to Dax. "Shall we? Sharon, I'll see you in about an hour."

"Okay, see you later, Dax," said Sharon trotting off.

Jim started up toward the auditorium exit, eager to leave. "Sorry about the heat in here," he said to Dax. "Can't get anyone to fix it."

Dax felt oddly at ease and even amused as he followed Jim. Glancing behind, he locked eyes with Dillon who stared back for a moment, wickedness in his glare. Dillon swore under his breath, loud enough to hear even from up here.

Aaron was staring as well, but in an entirely different way. He had wonder in his eyes; he was wondering what it was like to be someone like Dax Ribeiro. But Dax didn't notice.

The air was crisp, clear, and cool as Dax and Jim walked leisurely down the sidewalk. Dax mused how it must have looked for him to just waltz in like that after several days of auditions and callbacks, then to stroll out the door with the director. He didn't care what people like Dillon thought though. A part of him was feeling as if he was growing out of the whole theatre scene, scrounging for parts, competing with others. It was a game he wasn't in the mood to play anymore, or at least for a while. Maybe he'd feel different after a break.

Dax and Jim had a light lunch at a small soup, salad, and sandwich bar. They sat outside and enjoyed the fresh air. Both wore coats, and Jim had a gray scarf wrapped around his neck.

Jim dived straight to the topic of offering Dax a very decent supporting role in the show. Dax listened, letting Jim do most of the talking. Dax asked about Mario and Cash Giles, but Jim was evasive and refused to give details. What Jim had been transparent about though was his frustration with either a lack of talent or "talent" he didn't want. The latter did make Dax wonder; unwanted talent was easily discarded all the time in theatre, like uneaten food left on plates.

As the lunch drew to a close, Dax considered a couple things. His thoughts had been completely wrapped up in this little job from the FBI, but that gig would be here and gone before he knew it. For all he knew, the meeting tonight would be the first and last of his part to play in it. In such a case, he'd be free going forward and probably bored afterward. As much as he'd told himself after the last show he was going to take a break, he also knew there wasn't a whole lot else for him to do right now. He didn't have a bunch of time and money to go traveling. He wasn't considering any other offers. Jim's offer was not only generous and flattering, but convenient. He didn't have to fight for this one by getting in line to audition. It came to him on a silver platter.

The conversation ended with Dax saying he had to wait a couple days until he could finish something. He had been as evasive with Jim as Jim had been about his own struggles with the production. Dax explained he wasn't sure how things would turn out, but if they didn't, he'd accept the part.

Jim wondered what offers Dax had gotten. How could Dax tell the renowned Jim Kirkland to sit and wait? The young actor wasn't at that level. At the same time though, he was proud of Dax in a way teachers and directors of theatre are for talent that may be going places.

They walked back to the theatre and stood at the entrance for a moment. Jim offered to have Dax sit in for a while and hang out, but Dax had to get back to work.

"I hope circumstances allow you to participate," Jim had said. "I'll need an answer soon because we're starting rehearsals."

"I do too," Dax had replied. And he meant it. "I really appreciate your offer. I'll let you know *A-SAP.*"

They shook hands and parted ways, Jim to the overly heated and tension-filled theatre, and Dax back to the cube farm.

19: Call Her

Dax yawned and gazed sleepily at the computer monitor. Between the regular daily workload and class studies, the afternoon had flown by.

He looked at his watch and sighed. A few people around the office spent company time surfing around or shopping for books on Amazon, but he never did. People weren't supposed to, and the network police had established rules that blocked a lot of outside sites, but if you knew how to tweak the browser settings, you could bypass the proxy servers and go wherever you wanted.

Dax's thoughts drifted to the strange scene at the theatre. He had known Jim Kirkland off and on for years. The man was a legend. His personal ties to Stanislavsky alone made him folkloric. But even one with no appreciation for the history of theatre would still admire the accomplishments a man like Kirkland had made. It couldn't be counted the number of shows he'd directed over the years. It *could* be counted the number he'd written, a dozen or so, but Dax didn't know for sure.

But Jim had looked like a man who'd been caught off-guard somehow, a feeling Dax had become quite familiar with in the last few days. Something was in the air about this production.

Dax shook his head and leaned back. He was trying to distract himself from the thought of what was going to happen tonight. Yes, this very night. It had finally come, his chance to do something not just different, but so much bigger than some local theatre show.

At four o'clock it came, his phone began ringing, the work phone, not his personal cell.

"Hello?"

An unfamiliar voice said, "Agent Dauer says we're a go for tonight. Be at the same hotel again at six, same room."

Dax almost asked, *who is this?* but did not.

"Are your instructions clear?" the voice asked.

"Yes."

The phone clicked and the called ended.

So, it was a go. After all the talking and brooding and decision making, he was going to do it. He was going to play secret agent, or at least secret decoy. Whatever the outcome, save for bodily injury, he made the firm decision he was going to have some fun with this.

When the timestamp in the lower right of the monitor said four-thirty, Dax decided to leave early. It was Friday anyway.

Grabbing his laptop bag and sunglasses, he headed for the door.

Tom Kuka was on his way in. "Big plans for the weekend?" Tom asked with a grin.

"*Privet, Gospadin. Dobryi den. Kak dela?*" Dax said with a wink in his eyes.

Tom's large frame stopped cold. "Cock de-*what?*"

Dax shrugged coyly. "*Nichevo.*"

Tom placed his hands on his hips. "Don't mess with me, Dax."

"*Ty govoriš' po-Russki?*"

Tom's eyes squinted then searched the floor. "Roosky!" he said looking up. "Russian!" Tom pointed his index with his thumb cocked like a pistol.

Dax smiled and nodded.

"No, I don't speak," Tom said. He looked up in thought. "I mean … *nee-yet*."

"*O-chyen harasho!*" Dax said with a thumbs-up.

"Dude—" Tom started to say.

Dax clapped Tom on the shoulder and began to walk away. "*Paka*," Dax said with a wave, leaving a big, stunned desktop support tech standing with his mouth gaping.

Dax strode out of the building feeling genuinely elated. His mood was akin to the unique sensation of being behind the curtain on opening night five minutes before showtime, listening to the murmur of the crowd.

The smile on his face dropped when the thought struck him again that he really didn't know what he was supposed to do tonight. Surely Jack would give him a little more to go on. He'd have to bank on Jack's promise there'd be people there watching, waiting to help if something happened.

A sight suddenly made Dax stop and gasp. A blonde woman with an alluring body in a pants suit was standing near the curb reading a magazine, her back turned. Dax gawked.

It couldn't be.

The woman, sensing his stare, slowly swiveled her head with an expression of both uneasiness and suspicion.

Oh … it wasn't Tasha, not even close. What was he thinking?

Dax laughed to himself and continued walking. "Sorry," he muttered on the way by. The woman's eyes followed him, squinting for a moment and then looking away with a shrug. It was the city, after all.

Dax looked up and around. The sky was quickly darkening and the wind was picking up, getting cooler. His eyes rested on several windows above, vantage points for an observer, or a sniper. He turned around and looked behind him. No one following; no one watching. Jack was right—he watched too many movies.

He stopped for a quick, light dinner at a corner café, but hardly tasted it. He knew he was at that turning point, a gut feeling he'd learned to fight off a few years ago behind the stage curtains. It was the difference between a positive feeling of excitement and an anxious feeling of trepidation. With practice, he'd learned to stay on the positive side of the fence, enjoying the moment, relishing the adrenalin rush. In that state, which was both mental and physiological, the exhausting act of performing was indescribably fun. But it had taken considerable practice to master the art. Once the line was crossed and the energy fed on fear, it was almost impossible to stave off. And that fear was also both mental and physiological, but with the opposite effect. It ruined everything, made everything stressful.

Dax tossed the napkin on the plate and punched the table. He was tired of this dueling battle inside himself.

"You okay, honey?" a voice said next to him.

He looked up at his waitress, a middle-aged woman with short, dark hair and mileage on her stern but pleasant face. She wore a thick wrap around a wrist, like a brace, as if it had been sprained, yet bustled back and forth between tables with more plates on her arms than a lot of guys twice her size would try. A career waitress.

"I'm good, thanks," Dax said with an embarrassed smile.

"Date stand you up?" she asked smiling. "Handsome guy like you?"

Why did everyone always assume he had girl issues? Well, because he kind of did, to be perfectly honest, but not the way people presupposed. "No," Dax said, shaking his head. "Nothing like that."

She winked and continued on.

Dax leaned back and looked out the window. There were over 800,000 in this city, he read somewhere. Out of all those people, he was the one chosen for this mysterious assignment. Thus far, it'd been an out of the ordinary kind of experience, to say the least. He'd also met some interesting characters. It was like being in a movie. He'd always fantasized about his debut on the big screen, but since he wasn't going to take that trek to LA any time soon, that would probably never happen.

"Call her," the waitress said.

"Huh?" Dax looked up. The waitress was back and setting the bill down on the table. An image of Sam flashed in his mind. "Oh, I will."

The waitress smiled and turned to leave.

That wasn't a bad idea. Enough time had passed, maybe he would call.

He glanced at his watch—5:45—time to go. Tonight, he was on the payroll of the U.S. government, so maybe he'd take a cab. It'd be better to leave his car parked uptown near his workplace anyway.

He paid the cab driver and stepped out into the cooling night air in front of the Sutter Hotel. He glanced at his watch – 6:05. He briskly mounted the stairs and entered the mostly empty lobby. He took a quick look around expecting Agent Jeremy Forrester to approach with a beaming smile and an outstretched hand, but there was no one.

Dax headed for the same elevator he had ridden up the other night. He punched the number five and waited while the aging machinery creaked and grinded its way up to the fifth floor.

When the doors opened, a tall, slender man in a dark suit stood directly across against the wall. He was staring down in thought and looked up as Dax stepped out.

"Hi," said Dax.

Without a word, the man nodded and motioned with his hand to proceed down the hall.

"How are you doing? I'm Dax," he said.

The man glanced at him with suspicion, no smile.

"Room five-oh-nine, right?" Dax asked, just to see if he could get the guy to talk. But the man only nodded again.

The room bore the same familiar tobacco smell.

Jack was standing in the main room. "You're a little late," he said, tapping his watch. He looked uncharacteristically serious.

"Sorry," said Dax with a slight shrug.

Jack waved him forward. "Come on in, let's get you ready."

He looked around the suite *half*-hoping he'd see Tasha.

"This way," Jack was saying, heading toward the same room Dax had been in the other night.

"How did work go today?" Jack asked picking up a coffee cup. "Just another Friday."

Jack took a sip then nodded at the wall behind the door. "Your glamour boy suit is ready."

Dax swung the door in and saw what looked like the same coat and pants he had tried on the other night on a large hanger. "Tailored just for me?"

Jack winked. "By the best. Go on into the bathroom and get changed. I need to brief you on a few things. Leave the coat here for now."

The pants fit perfectly, no surprise. The white dress shirt felt different, a little smaller, and also fit perfectly. Even the cuffs fit. Tasha had summed up his measurements with precise accuracy, the parts she'd measured as well as those she hadn't. He laughed out loud. A minute later he came back to the room with his street clothes draped about his arms.

"Something funny in there?" Jack asked.

"Sort of, yeah. Do I leave my stuff here?"

"Yeah. Don't take anything personal, especially your phone. Just toss them in the corner. We'll come back here after it's over and get everything off you."

Dax toyed with the idea of taking his personal stuff anyway; he'd feel strange without them. But it was only for a couple hours. He powered off his phone then slid it in the front pocket of his pants. After rolling everything up, he placed them against the wall near the door. "Do I have shoes tonight?"

"No, we're gonna send you to a black-tie party in your socks. Over there, Mr. Bond," Jack said pointing at the floor by the table.

Dax picked up a gold box with the letters GUCCI on the top. Next to the box was a new pair of black dress socks with the label still attached.

Opening the box, Dax looked at the nicest and probably most expensive shiny black leather loafers he'd ever seen. He pulled one out from the wrapper paper and slowly turned it. On the side of the front strap was a polished interlocking ornament in the shape of the letter "G."

"You pick these?" Dax asked.

"I got good taste, don't I," said Jack. He was busy tinkering with what looked like the bow tie camera they'd played with the other night.

Dax sat down and pulled the smooth black dress socks on. The material was thin and felt cool and tingly. He took one of the loafers and slid it over the sock. It felt snug. He stood up and wiggled his ankle until his heel slid into place. A perfect fit in both width and length.

Standing now with both shoes on, Dax realized that some of the nervousness he'd been fighting all day was beginning to wane and get replaced with an excitement. *Good.* A little excitement was what he'd signed up for.

He looked in the mirror and tugged at his coat. Just another costume and character, right? He cocked his head and smirked arrogantly at his reflection. Putting on his best Sean Connery again, he said, "World domination. The same old dream. Our asylums are full of people who think they're Napoleon. Or God."

"Dr. No," said Jack behind him.

"You got it."

After a pause, "And who is Dax right now?"

Dax turned to look at Jack. Feigning his best Slavic accent he said, "I am *Собака!*, the great dog of Saint Petersburg, da?" He rolled the "r" on the word *great* and pronounced *dog* with a hard "oh."

Jack frowned. "Don't bother with a phony accent. No trained ear would buy that."

Dax laughed. "I'm just playin' around."

Jack pointed. "This is serious business. Put on your serious cap."

"Sure, boss."

Jack stood for a moment looking Dax up and down, then finally nodded. "Okay, off with the jacket and shirt so we can do you up with this bowtie cam like before."

Dax glanced around. Tasha's absence had almost left a void in the room. He wanted to ask where she was but knew Jack wouldn't give him a straight answer.

About fifteen minutes later, Dax was fully dressed and wired up. He stood before the mirror and liked what he saw.

"Alright, let's go out to the main room," said Jack, walking to the door.

As Dax approached the table, he immediately recognized a man he'd seen at the warehouse that had been introduced to him as "Leo."

Leo had the same length of stubble growth on his chin. He was pulling on a cigarette and staring at a laptop on the table. As Dax approached, he turned and gave Dax a slight smile and a nod.

"Hi, Leo." Dax offered a hand. Leo glanced at Dax's hand and then slowly reached over to shake it.

"It's Leo, right?" Dax asked. And then on impulse, "*Privyet!*"

Leo's smile dropped and his eyes darted to Jack, who promptly chuckled. "Dax is practicing so he can make like he's from Saint Petersburg."

Leo looked away and grabbed a cup on the table to take a drink of something.

"Leo's going to put some of the finishing touches on you," said Jack. "We're gonna wet your hair down a little." He walked around behind Leo. "What have you got there, Leo?"

Leo pointed at the screen.

"There we go," said Jack. "Have a seat here, Dax," he said, pointing at the center chair. He turned the laptop so Dax could see the screen. On it was a picture of young man. The man's hair was flat and combed back on the sides. The top was also flat but not quite a much, with a little fullness in the front. Dax stared at the face.

"His hair is longer than mine," Dax remarked.

"Doesn't matter," said Jack.

"Wait … is that the *real* Dog of Saint Petersburg?" Dax asked.

"No," Jack said quickly, waving it off. "Just a likeness."

Leo stood and walked to the kitchen sink. It occurred to Dax he'd not even heard the man's voice yet.

"Now Dax," Jack started. "Let's go over a few things."

"I am Gavril, but I go by the name of *Собака*," said Dax. He emphasized the *aaahh*.

"Good," said Jack.

"You never told me his last name."

"Well," said Jack thoughtfully, "he has several names. We're not entirely sure what it might really be. But on a few legal documents we've seen Novikov."

"That sounds nice: *Gavril Novikov.*"

"It's a common name. Doesn't mean anything. If anyone there does call you anything but *Собака*, it'll just be Gavril. But it's doubtful. There won't be any Mr. So and So or anything like that."

"Okay."

"You're twenty-six, twenty-seven-ish years old, and you've done well for yourself. You're a bit arrogant, but not obnoxiously so. You have manners, class. You know how to play political and power games."

"But I don't know how to play political or power games."

Leo returned to the table with a bowl in one hand and a couple items in the other. He was eyeing Jack.

"Phony it up," said Jack. "That's what actors do."

"Well yeah, but—"

"What if I were a movie director and was telling you to be a mob boss running a casino or something?"

"I guess I'd do my best to act like Robert DeNiro or Joe Pesci."

"Exactly. Well, not Pesci. His characters are over the top."

Dax laughed. "But this is different. I don't know anything about Russian culture or what a guy who grew up in Saint

Petersburg would act like. You haven't given me much to prepare with."

"Like what?"

"I don't know, some Russian spy movies to watch or something?"

"You've already seen enough movies to give you the *wrong* ideas."

Dax heard the sloshing of water as Leo dipped a small towel into the bowl of water.

"Seriously." Dax was feeling nervous again.

"Dax," Jack said, putting a hand on Dax's shoulder. "Remember what we talked about. Your job is going to be very simple. You're bait, that's it. You're not there to make a lot of conversation or tell your life's story to anyone. There shouldn't be anyone there who really knows Собака anyway, not on a personal level. He's a mysterious character. A shadowy figure who has a reputation that precedes him. At a young age, he's already been a mover and shaker in the underground world, and all people really know about him is that he makes things happen."

Leo wrapped the small towel around the sides of Dax's head and gently pulled back. The liquid on the towel had an odd smell.

"We're going to make your hair nice and shiny tonight," said Jack. "A tad darker too. Who knows, some lady you meet there may want to run her fingers through it later."

Dax smirked. "Yeah, well, I've played a lot of characters dressed up in all sorts of ways with my hair done this or that way and it never made a lot of women real friendly towards me. At least not the women I actually *wanted* to be friendly."

Jack chuckled.

Dax turned to look at him. "Are you saying that Gavril Novikov is a ladies' man? An international playboy?'"

"Nah, not like that. No doubt he's had his share, but from what we know about him, that's not a preoccupation. He's never been married or had a long-term relationship, that we know of. Probably prefers an occasional high-end hooker. But a lot of women would gravitate toward a guy like him by virtue of the fact that he has influence and knows people in high places." Dax snorted in disgust. Then he thought for a moment. "So, some high-profile vendor, who's legit on the surface but shady behind closed doors, is throwing this shindig and some buyers of his goods and services—high tech weaponry—are invited."

"For your purposes, that's the gist of it."

"And the *Dog of Saint Petersburg* is one of those potential buyers?"

"Sort of. He makes the buy possible. Handles the logistics. We're hoping some folks there will be surprised to see you."

"Does Gavril have a middle name?"

"It's not important, although in formal situations, Russians will sometimes use all three names, the first name, middle and last. The middle name is usually a patronymic of the father's first name formed by adding *vich* or *ovich* for a male and *avna* or *ovna* for a female."

"So, if my father's name was Ivan, my middle name might be Ivanovich."

"That's good Dax. That's why we picked you. But no one is going to be formal to you at that level. Not at this place."

"Okay so I'm hanging around like I've been invited to this event though I've no idea what it is or who I'm looking for, but there I am anyway at the bar nursing a tonic water. How long is this supposed to last, say, if nothing happens?"

"We'll play it by ear. We should know fairly quickly if the person we're looking for is there or not."

"Then my job would be over?"

"Not necessarily. If someone makes contact, you'll need to follow instructions explicitly. You could have been marked by someone who is now curious and tailing you."

Dax let out a big sigh. "This just keeps getting better."

"It'll be fun."

Dax felt Leo's hands steady his head and begin doing something to his hair on top.

Jack stood and paced around Dax's chair. "Now, if you meet anyone, you need to know a little etiquette. When Russian men meet women, they shake hands gently but firmly. A typical greeting between men is a solid handshake while maintaining direct eye contact and giving the appropriate greeting for the time of day. You won't need to worry about that because you'll be speaking in English."

"What do women do when they meet each other? Just curious."

"They'll often kiss on the cheek three times, starting with the left and then alternating. I doubt you'll see any of that. When males meet who are friends, they may pat each other on the back and hug. But if we're right and the people we're looking for are there, it will be a formal business kind of thing wrought with secrecy and plastic-coated game playing. Russians tend to be business-only anyway and don't need to establish long-standing personal relationships before doing business with people. Opposite of say, South American culture. And that's what we're going to exploit here. Often though, an indication you've successfully developed a personal relationship is being asked for a favor by that person."

Dax felt Leo's hands disappear and heard the man walk away.

"What else can you tell me about Saint Petersburg?" asked Dax.

"What do you want to know?"

"I don't know, general info I guess."

Jack shrugged. "Well, it's the former capitol of Russia. In fact, it's the second largest city to Moscow. Russian authors, when referring to it, typically drop the 'Saint' and even the 'burg' and just say Peter. It's probably the most Westernized of all cities over there."

"Interesting." Dax took note of how Jack sounded when he pronounced *Moscow*. "I've never traveled anywhere around that part of the world. I'd like to."

"Saint Petersburg is a historic place. The Russian Revolution began there when the Bolsheviks stormed the Winter Palace."

"I've seen some good movies about that."

Jack chuckled. "I'll bet you have. A lot of people died. Bad time in Russian history. But all that's changed. Today there's a huge brewery and distillery industry there that has made it known as the beer capital of Russia."

"Oh now I'm definitely going."

"Good. Okay, stand up pretty boy."

Dax eased up and turned around and Jack handed him the same round plastic container he saw the other night containing his jowl enhancers.

While Jack eyed him up and down, Leo joined and the two men watched as Dax eased the objects into his mouth and shoved them inside his gums.

Leo gave a big nod, still no talking.

Jack smiled and gave Dax a big thumbs up and then looked at his watch.

Dax felt his pulse quicken. It was almost showtime.

20: The Woman in the Red Dress

The large government-issued sedan eased into the evening traffic on Sutter Street.

"Where are we going?" asked Dax.

Jack was staring out the window, looking tense. "The Omni."

"That big, old looking hotel off California?"

"That's the one—built not too long after the Russian Revolution, actually. Speaking of which."

"Really ... I've never been inside."

"You will tonight. They've got the best room all decked out. Open bar. But remember what I told you about booze."

"I remember. How should I walk in?"

"Cool but confident. Look around and get a mental note of the people you see, then head straight for the bar. Make sure to move your body so we can see as much of the crowd as possible through the bowtie. Hang on a second." Jack leaned forward and cupped his hands to talk to the driver. "Right here."

The car pulled over and a man in a long coat stepped up to the vehicle. The locks popped up, the door opened and in hopped Agent Michael Staggs. He plopped down opposite of Dax and Jack on the seat facing them and shut the door.

"Dax," said Jack, "you remember Agent Staggs."

"Sure do."

Staggs gave Dax a wry smile and then leaned forward offering his hand. "How are you, Dax?"

"A-plus." Dax shook the man's hand. "How about yourself?"

Staggs shrugged coyly, the smile dissolving.

"Doesn't he look pretty?" said Jack, nodding at Dax.

Agent Staggs studied Dax's face for a few seconds then ran his eyes down to the shoes. "It looks good," he finally said.

"It looks *great*," said Jack. "You notice his face?"

Staggs nodded. "Nice touch."

Dax turned to Jack. "How will I know who your people are?"

"You won't. And hopefully you'll never have to."

"Why not?"

"If you knew who they were, you'd instinctively look at them in some way that might tip someone off."

"You don't trust me," Dax said, trying to be sarcastically funny. He glanced at Staggs who was looking at the floormats.

"I don't trust anyone who's going to be there," Jack said. "They have trained eyes and a twenty-four-seven wariness about them."

"Where will you be?"

"Close by."

The car made a sharp right and the driver honked at a taxi that had cut them off. The three stared out the windows for a few seconds.

"I still feel like I'm going into this blind," said Dax. "I am used to a director and a script."

"I'm sure it feels strange. But for your sake we need to keep it this way. Like I've been saying, we're utilizing several things to our advantage. One, Собака isn't expected here. Most, we're guessing, wouldn't even recognize him unless they'd actually met him before. Or knew him personally, which is unlikely."

Dax thought for a moment. "Just curious, but where is the real *Собака* right now?" He glanced up at Agent Staggs who was looking at Jack.

Jack shrugged exaggeratedly and said, "We're not certain."

Dax got the feeling Jack was trying too hard to sound offhanded in that remark. He felt a little alarm go off in the form of a hotness and swirl in his gut. "Then what if the real Gavril Novikov shows up here tonight?"

Jack waved the question off. "Not a chance."

There was so much Dax was not being told. But to stay calm, he had to convince himself everything was fine and the FBI was in control.

The three remained silent for the next five minutes, watching the city's nightlife go by through the windows. The car then pulled over to the side of the road.

Jack turned his body to Dax. "Okay, we're at the corner of Sansome and California. The Omni is about two and half blocks west down California."

Dax peered out the window. Pedestrian traffic was light on what was otherwise a normal looking Friday night in this section of the city. "Yeah, I know where I am. Is the camera and mic working?"

"Oh yeah. Triple checked."

Dax took a big breath. Both agents were watching him closely.

"Take this," said Jack, extending an envelope.

Dax took it and turned it over. It was made of thick paper, light turquoise in color, sealed with a round gold sticker bearing a symbol that looked like two swords crisscrossing.

"Your invitation to the party," said Jack. "Go up the stairs to the Babylon Ballroom. Should be easy to find."

Dax tucked the envelope into his jacket.

Jack looked at his watch. "Alright, this is it," he said, clapping his hands lightly and rubbing them together. "Showtime. Just remember all the things we talked about. Easy in and easy out."

Dax looked at Jack. "*Hopefully*, easy out. The *in* part I'm not too worried about."

"Your country is depending on you," Agent Staggs suddenly said.

"Go get 'em kid, we're right with you," said Jack quickly.

Dax closed his eyes and did a final mental prep, same thing he did right before the first act. The car door clicked loudly as he pulled the handle and felt the rush of the cool city night air. He stepped out, shut the door, then started down the sidewalk without a backward glance.

The Gucci loafers felt good. The suit felt cool and slick to the skin on his arms and legs. It was an outfit that demanded respect, and it made him strut a little. At this moment, he was not the little wannabe local actor who still had yet to find himself on the stage. He was *Собака*, the Dog of Saint Petersburg, and he was on a mission. He was contributing to causes far bigger than himself and getting paid at the same time. It felt mighty fine.

***

When the car door shut, Dauer and Staggs looked at each other. Staggs raised his eyebrows in question. Dauer grunted a response that Dax would not have understood if he were still in the vehicle.

All at once Staggs leaned toward the window and peered out. A red Ford Escort heading up the street had stopped across from them, its driver staring. Both agents looked carefully at the person behind the wheel and whatever else they could see inside the car. The homely and pale face of the driver remained facing them for several seconds, puffy eyes blinking several times.

Staggs looked at Dauer who nodded. Reaching into his coat, Staggs slid his fingers around the handle of a Beretta 92 9mm pistol that was harnessed to his side. Yanking the door handle, he quickly stepped out and strode purposefully toward the Escort, his eyes locking on the Escort's driver.

The driver's blank face sprang into alarm as the droopy eyes grew wide and the mouth dropped. Staggs partially pulled the gun, keeping it mostly hidden inside his coat flaps. When he was about six feet from the Escort, the driver must have panicked for the little car jerked forward and sped away as quickly as it could.

Staggs continued several steps before stopping and leaning in, trying to see the license plate. The Escort made a sharp right and with a small squeal of tires, disappeared. Staggs waited a moment and then made his way back to the sedan. Once inside, the car pulled away from the curb, drove down one block, then turned left and stopped by a large vehicle. The vehicle, to any bystander, would look like nothing more than an innocuous medium sized moving truck.

***

Several people bustled by Dax as he made his way down the sidewalk, but they didn't ogle as he might have expected. Some gave him a lingering glance but that was about it. Here in this part of town, especially near the Omni on a Friday night, his appearance wasn't necessarily that unusual. He strode forward confidently.

The entrance to the Omni loomed up ahead. The yellow gold-colored bricks that made up the front were cast in a hard white light that didn't diminish the unique fan-shaped structure strewn with fluorescent lights that jutted out from atop the door. He approached the large glass doors with the shiny polished brass frames and stood for a moment looking at his translucent reflection. He raised his chin a little and turned slightly to the side. His hair looked wonderful, a little James Dean, a little early Robert Redford, and somewhere between gangster and spy. With the hair, extended jowls, and attire, he almost believed it himself. No, he *did* believe it. He had to. Suddenly remembering there were others watching everything through a little camera in his bowtie, he quickly opened the door and entered.

The swoosh of air ushered in a calmer and warmer temperature. The interior of the lobby didn't disappoint. The mahogany-colored wood in intricate Florentine Renaissance designs offered something interesting to look at wherever one's eye might wander. Real miniature palm trees in designer pots filled in areas in front of columns or next to staircases. Lit exclusively with extravagant and expensive looking chandeliers, candlestick style lamps and bronze finished wall sconces, the place held just enough luminance to see details, but not enough to spoil the surreal effect. It was the kind of skilled stagecraft Dax was accustomed to performing on.

He headed for the stairs that wound up and over the long and wide reception desk. At the top of the stairs, a hotel worker, adorned in a full suit with a gold name plate pinned to his lapel that read "Anton Stark," bowed his head and asked how he was doing this evening. Mimicking his FBI handlers, Dax merely smiled softly and nodded.

Signs directed him down the hall to the grand Babylon Ballroom. A small table was positioned near the ballroom's large double doors where a man and woman stood chatting.

When they saw him approach, they stopped talking and turned to him with courteous, professional smiles.

"Welcome," said the woman. She had a masculine voice and wore a dark navy pants suit with a yellow collar shirt and a beige tie. The man's suit matched, though his tie was a pale green.

Dax did his slight smile and nod routine and then waited.

"Do you have your invitation, Sir?" the man asked, his eyes narrowing ever so slightly.

With a poise and coolness that almost surprised himself, Dax kept his eyes steadily on the man as he reached into his jacked and produced the envelope. The actor in him took charge and created a look in his eyes that asked, *do you know who I am?*

Unfazed, the man took the envelope while returning the stare. The woman's smile drew back, but her expression remained pleasant. She moved her eyes up and down Dax and then to the envelope as the man carefully worked his finger under the sticker.

Dax felt his pulse suddenly quicken. If Jack didn't get this part right, who knew what might happen.

As the man studied the invitation, the seconds trudged on with agonizing sluggishness. The woman leaned slightly over to get a better look. Dax kept his cool and even stole a glance further down the hallway. A man stood looking at his cell phone. He glanced up and made hard eye contact with Dax, held it for a couple seconds, then looked away.

"Very good, Sir," Dax heard.

As Dax tucked the envelope into his jacket, the woman opened one of the doors.

Nodding once more, Dax strode past the two and entered the Babylon Ballroom for the first time in his life.

Okay, so how does James Bond enter the poker room? With confidence, of course. And a touch of arrogance.

Inside, the Babylon's entrance was a small set of shallow steps designed to look like ancient marble. On either side of the steps was a railing of shiny black vertical bars covered by a glistening gold handrail. Between the black bars were swirling golden designs that resembled hieroglyphics. At the end of the rails were two large round columns, highly decorated, that seated an arch that completed the entrance, the top of which was at least ten feet high.

Dax looked up. The height of the vaulted ceiling, mostly a smooth cream color, grew deeper in levels, pulling itself higher and teasing the eyes. At the highest point, the center of the ballroom's massive ceiling, was a golden dome in which a shimmering chandelier hung—an object as big as a mid-sized car. It made *The Phantom of the Opera's* famous light fixture seem miniscule. The edges of the walls were lined with huge golden columns adorned with Corinthian capitals sitting on square bases.

Dax stood staring around in wonder, until he realized someone might be watching the strange guy gawking by the stairs. His eyes jerked down to the scene on the floor and he scanned for anyone who may be looking his way. The place wasn't very crowded. Several small clusters of individuals milled about, their voices a jumbled and blurred murmur. Soft modern jazz music filled the air.

"Good evening, Sir," a voice said to Dax's right, causing him to jump slightly and spin quickly toward the source. A man in black dress pants, a black vest, and a long-sleeved white shirt with a bowtie stood staring.

"I am sorry if I startled you, Sir," said the man bringing his hands together. He had a hint of an accent Dax couldn't pinpoint.

Dax held up a hand. "No problem."

"May I offer you something to drink?"

"Why don't you show me to the bar so I can decide."

"Certainly," the server said.

As Dax followed the man toward the crowd, he wasn't sure how to carry himself. He thought he had it down mentally, but as he came near the people and heard the noises, he didn't know whether to confidently look people in the eye or keep his gaze down. Referring to the general game plan, he decided to keep the *here but not here* composure going and casually keep his eyes forward.

As he walked by groups of chatting individuals, he turned his body slightly toward them so the camera could pick up as much as possible. No one seemed to be giving him any special notice.

The server led him around several columns as they worked their way to the other side of the room. They had probably passed around thirty individuals. Most of the men wore formal dark colored suits, and the women, knee to floor length evening gowns of various shapes, patterns, and colors. One man, who appeared Arab, donned a dark red velvet Kurta with intricate designs sewn into the sleeves.

Dax had the uncomfortable feeling he was being led further into a confine of sorts, as if deeper into a spider's lair, and would rather have remained near the door where he could make a run for it if necessary. But he was being paid to do a job, and an important one. The thought made his chin lift a little in confidence. He breathed through his nose and didn't lose pace.

The bar was a gorgeous structure of smooth agate stone. The wall behind the bar displayed an assortment of rough, stony colors and patterns, illuminated like a stage at the front of a luxurious theatre auditorium. Lining the bar top were a neat row of art deco bar stools that looked more like fancy chairs in a pricey art gallery. A middle-aged gentleman with a neatly trimmed white beard, dressed similarly to the waiter, was behind the counter wiping down a glass.

"Sir," the waiter said, gesturing toward the bar. He turned to leave.

Dax stood and gazed up at the wall behind the bar. Stretching at least twelve feet in the air and lined with glass shelves brightly lit by lights somewhere behind them, Dax observed a dazzling collection of alcohol. The shelves hosted an array of all manner of various shapes, colors, and sizes of bottles of what had to be every type of high-end distilled drink invented.

"What will you have, Sir?" the bartender asked.

Dax drummed his fingers for a moment and seriously considered ordering a Bourbon Slush or a Long Island Iced Tea. They probably made stuff like that really good here, not to mention it would help him relax. But Jack and the gang were watching and listening. He sighed and said, "Tonic water with a lime."

The bartender paused for a moment, then turned, his eyebrows shrugging. Dax watched the man's back and heard a crack and hiss as he twisted the cap on a small, chilled bottle. He then scooped a small handful of ice into a drink tumbler and poured. It fizzled and foamed over the ice. He carefully wedged quarter cut of a lime into the side of the glass and handed it to Dax.

Dax stared at the drink for a moment. The tumbler was heavy and made of thick glass with a bottom that must have been an inch high. A real drink would taste so good in it right now. Between this bar, the dim lights, and the soft music, he could seriously hang out here for a while. But he had a job to do. Actually, his job *was* to just sort of hang out, until something happened.

Holding his drink up to his lips but trying to keep his wrist from blocking the bowtie, he slowly turned his body to face the scene behind him. The murmur of voices steadily continued with the occasional laughter from someone. No one that he could see was paying any attention to him. He looked back at the bartender who was going about his business and wondered how long he'd have to wait around, like a worm on the end of hook. He took a sip of his drink. It tasted refreshing to his hot and dry mouth.

"Ridiculous," a man's voice said in a quiet but agitated tone.

Dax eased his body a quarter turn to face the bar again so he could get a glimpse through the mirror at the person who had spoken.

A man and a woman approached the bar and sat down a couple seats away. The man, who had a light brown beard and a dark splotch that looked like a birthmark near his right eye, looked troubled. The woman's medium-length hair was about the same color brown and her lipstick was a bright and glossy rose color. They were both in their mid-thirties and nicely dressed.

The bartender approached the two. "Scotch, lots of rocks," the man said. The bartender looked at the woman who waved and shook her head no.

"He's getting greedy," the man said, this time a little louder. He shook his head in disgust while the woman put her hand on his shoulder. Suddenly, he looked into the mirror's reflection and saw Dax watching them. Their eyes locked. The woman turned and looked at Dax. Dax gave a polite nod and looked away.

Careful …

Dax pretended to become interested in something else. He took another slow sip of his tonic water and stared off in the other direction at nothing in particular. The couple next to him remained silent until the bartender brought the man his drink. Through his peripheral vision, Dax saw the man still eyeing him through the mirror as they got up to walk away.

Dax turned casually at them. The man gave him one final stare, his eyes asking who Dax was and then turned, the woman on his arm.

A new surge of stimulation flowed through Dax's veins as he realized he was enjoying this. Here he was amid real-life criminals and all he had to do was sit back and watch.

But the warm, pleasant thoughts he was feeling came to a sudden, cold stop. What was it that just caught his eye? He'd been scanning the clusters of people when he'd hit upon something that caused instant recognition.

There it was – the back of a woman. Roving from shoes to legs in high-cut dresses, he'd stopped on the nicely shaped rear end of a woman he suddenly realized he was familiar with. His gaze darted up to her smooth light brown hair that draped several inches over bare shoulders. The dress she wore was fantastically sexy—two lanky strands of red material crossed her back creating a thin "X" on what would otherwise be naked skin. Below, the dress came back together in a V-shape connected where the curve of her lower side started to bulge. While the red and shiny material went all the way to the floor, just covering matching pumps, a split on the side revealed a nicely shaped left leg all the way to her upper thigh.

Although he could mostly just see her back, it only took about three seconds to figure out who she was.

Meygan Knight!

21: Vadim's Resurrection

The ride up to the fifth floor was delayed by not just one, but two interruptions. There must have been some casual gathering somewhere above the fifth floor. It didn't anger the three men, but it was somewhat annoying. With each delay, they had to quickly move into a defensive position, if necessary. At the same time, they had to appear as if they were not the weapon-toting professional killers they were. All three were highly specialized and trained, working in synch, and prepared for just about any situation that may arise.

The first interruption was on the second floor. Two giggling women stepped quickly into the elevator, discussing some inane, verbal altercation at their office with another female coworker. One held a wine glass that almost spilled as she laughed. But the chatting abruptly stopped as the two suddenly noticed the emotionless stares of the three large men with long coats they now shared the small enclosure with. The men had glanced their way for a couple seconds and then, as if on cue, looked away indifferently. The man in the center, the tallest, bore a large, distinctive scar that ran from his right temple all the down to his chin, a dark pink fissure with permanently scar-swollen tissue on the edges. The odd behavior of the men as well as a sense of some unseen danger caused the two women to briefly look at each other then turn to the door. The five occupants of the elevator remained silent as the machine creaked upward.

The second interruption happened on the fourth floor. The doors opened and a middle-aged couple stepped in. They recognized one of the women and said hello. The woman quietly said hello back. The man glanced up at the three men at the back of the elevator.

"Are you with Tysco Systems?" the man asked. He directed the question at the tall man with the scar, sensing him to be the alpha of the three.

"Uh," the scarred man started to say after a pause, then remembered to put on a smile. "No, we are not." His accent was thickly eastern European of some sort.

"Oh," the middle-aged man said with a nervous chuckle and then looked at the woman he was with. The couple eyed the three men once more, then quickly turned around. The party of now seven stood in awkward silence as they moved another floor up.

The doors opened on the fifth floor and the people parted quickly to make room. The three men strode past silently and entered the hallway, two of them looking in one direction, the third in the other. As the elevator doors shut, the four party goers watched the men's backs with tense curiosity, relieved and looking at each other in wonderment.

The three men stood in the hall for a few seconds in total silence doing nothing but listening. The hallway was still and smelled faintly of cigarette smoke. They then pulled thin gloves out and worked their hands into them.

In unison, the three reached into their coats and produced large semi-automatic pistols. From coat pockets, they produced silencers and began attaching them to the ends of the weapons. The lead man motioned with his head to follow. They walked stealthily as one, like a giant cat inching up on its prey, one facing backward and scanning for any movement, their fingers on the triggers. As they approached the target door, the sound of shuffling feet from inside the room made all three stop. One of the men stepped past the door and waited.

The doors shut solidly and there were no cracks above or below so no shadows could be seen. The three waited silently and motionless. Their training enabled them to wait for hours without moving or making a sound if needed.

Suddenly there was a click as the door's lock disengaged. One of men nodded at another who slipped his gun back under his coat and produced a thin cable. The cable was about two feet in length and had small handles on each end that the man gripped tightly.

Another click and the door started to open. The three men flattened themselves against the wall. A tall, thin man with dark hair started to walk out and stumbled. In his hand was a plastic cup from which half the contents sloshed to the floor. In his other hand was an empty ice bucket.

"*Suka blyat,*" the man muttered to himself. The liquid smelled like vodka.

Good, the man was perhaps drunk.

He looked at the spill on the floor, shrugged, lifted the cup, and swallowed what was left in two quick gulps. He then turned to enter the hallway and froze, his eyes round with terror. A scream was just starting to come up from his throat but was abruptly stopped by a cable that quickly snapped around his neck and began to crush his larynx. Instinctively, he kicked backward like a mule, his heal grazing off the knee of his attacker. There was a loud grunt of pain, but the strong hands of the killer never wavered and continued to tighten the steel wire. The victim was already losing consciousness. He continued to thrash but felt his body going weak and the world around him getting dimmer. As he sank to the floor, he felt his hands getting heavy, then fall limply. The last thing his fading eyes saw were two other men watching him die as one gently shut the door to a crack.

The man with the cable continued to strangle his victim for another full thirty seconds. The other two waited patiently, scanning up and down the hallway and listening. When the cable was removed, it left a deeply indented red and purple line that ran neatly around the center of Leo's neck. His lifeless eyes stared up at the round hallway ceiling light directly above him.

The killer quickly wound the cable around handles and dropped it a coat pocket. He rubbed his knee where he'd been kicked, swore softly, and then a moment later, the pistol was out again.

The lead man put his ear to the door and listened intently for several seconds. Then, nodding at the other two, he slid his fingers around the edge of the cracked door and hunched down. The other men positioned themselves behind. In one swift motion, the door was open and three guns at three levels of height were pointing into the hotel room.

There was no movement, no sound. Two of the three men started slowly down the entryway past the wet bar and toward the main room. The third quickly pulled Leo's body into the room and quietly shut the door.

A clinking of glasses made them freeze. As they waited, they heard what may have been a microwave oven door shutting and the kitchen sink faucet.

As soon as the water was turned on, they quickly moved forward, using the sound as cover. One rounded the corner toward the kitchen while the other two kept a sharp eye on the rest of the room and down the hallway.

In the kitchen in front of the sink stood a young man in a white shirt and dark suit pants. Hanging on the back of one of the chairs was the matching suit coat. There was no one else in the kitchen. The young man at the sink continued to rinse a glass as the killer silently watched the back of his blond hair-covered head. The pistol raised into killing position. The faucet stopped and the young man turned around. But before he could react, the silencer coughed. About a fourth of his head exploded, sending fragments of skin, bone, and hair into the wall behind him. What was left of his head snapped back as if whiplashed, and his body bent backward over the sink as his legs gave way beneath him. The glass he was holding dropped to the floor with a thud. As his body relaxed, gravity pulled him off the sink. He landed on his knees and then fell forward, the remainder of his face hitting the floor with a wet, smacking sound. A dark red pool quickly began to form and spread under his head.

The other two gunmen were already in motion. One ran down the hall kicking in doors while the other dashed into the bedroom. The bathroom was empty. The room across from it was empty. One more door at the end of the hall was shut and locked. Without a pause, the man stepped back then lunged forward, his shoe striking just beside the knob. With a crack and snap the door flew open, the gunman on one knee aiming into the dark room. But it was empty.

The gunman in the kitchen turned and ran back to the entrance. No one was there except for the dead, strangled body. The door was still shut. The men met up again in the main room by the table. They nodded at each other.

At once, all three holstered their weapons and pulled small cases out of their pockets. They separated into different parts of the suite, each looking in the designated places where the recording devices had been hidden.

***

Dax stared at Meygan for a few more seconds then leaned back on the bar stool, his heart racing. What was he supposed to do now? He glanced at the bartender and caught the man watching him curiously, who then nodded and went about his business. But the actor in Dax raised a sudden red flag—the bartender's curiosity was beyond casual.

Dax let out a nervous chuckle. "This is crazy," he muttered to himself, and then remembered that Jack and the boys were out there somewhere listening. Should he tell them? A feeling of rising fear made the decision for him.

He turned his body at the crowd of people in front of him. Cupping his hand over the bowtie, he whispered, "Guys, you see that woman in the red dress?" He lifted his hand, clearing the view for the camera, hoping the people watching could see. "I know her! She was in the show I just did. What am I supposed to do now? What if she sees me?" He was tempted to say Meygan's name, but for some reason refrained.

Although knowing they couldn't talk back to him immediately, he paused as if waiting for an answer. Cupping his hand over the bowtie again, he whispered, "Waiting for instructions."

He looked again toward the bartender. The man's back was to him, but his head was partially turned as if trying to listen. Maybe Dax should get away from the bar, at least out of sight of Meygan until he received instructions.

Come on, Jack.

He looked at his glass and saw it was nearly empty. Bringing the glass up to his lips, he drained the rest. "Excuse me," he said to the bartender.

The man turned around slowly, almost cautiously.

"May I have another?" Dax asked, tapping the glass lightly. He tried to put on his hard, authoritative stare, but realized he was losing his nerve. He quickly glanced back at Meygan. He almost couldn't believe how fabulous she looked. From head to toe, she had both eloquent beauty and perfect sex appeal at the same time. And it looked like she was playing up some kind of role herself, laughing a little too hard at whatever was being said. The man on whose arm she had hers was decked out in an expensive looking Italian suit; his back was to the bar, but appeared to be about Dax's height, slender and with almost jet-black hair. Meygan Knight wasn't this friendly or outgoing when not in character. What the *hell* was she doing here?

The bartender slid the drink next to Dax's hand. Dax glanced up and saw the man watching his eyes. Dax nodded, looked away and swiped the drink off the bar top. The bartender was probably working for the hosts of this little get together and was there to watch and listen, especially to those quiet conversations people engage in at the bar when they assume they're alone.

Dax made a decision, he'd take his drink and nonchalantly work his way around the crowd, keeping on the edge and next to the columns. He'd get as far from Meygan as possible but without looking like he was avoiding anyone. He had no idea what would happen if she saw him—would she call him out? He chided himself for his reaction just now. If she, like him, was here doing some undercover work and made contact, hopefully she'd be professional enough not to do anything obvious.

Another thought hit Dax—maybe she was one of them. Maybe she had a boyfriend who was one of the buyers of high-tech weaponry, or whatever was being peddled here. He shook his head. No, not her, playing in second and third tier theatre shows like him.

The drink was cold and wet in his hand. He took a sip then eased off the bar stool. He heard Meygan let out a loud laugh and failed resisting the urge to look in her direction again. She was throwing her head back, mouth open and eyes shut in laughter while placing a hand on the shoulder of the man next to her for balance. She was playing her part well. The two men next to her stole a quick glance at her chest as she leaned back. Dax smirked bitterly at himself—he would have done the same thing.

Looking away, Dax turned and had taken about three steps when a woman's voice behind him made him halt.

"I don't believe it," the voice said.

Although he hadn't seen who'd spoken, Dax knew the comment had been directed at him. He slowly turned, making every attempt to feign unconcerned confidence.

Before him stood a petite woman in her mid-thirties with mahogany brown hair pulled back tight around her head and over her ears. Her slender face with neatly trimmed eyebrows was a smooth oval shape from her hairline to around her chin. Her skin was cream white which made her dark red lipstick and black highlighted eyes stand out. She was looking deeply into Dax's eyes.

"How? *What* are you doing here?" she asked, one hand now resting on her hip, a puzzled expression on her face. She paused, then added, "I thought you were ..." Her voice faded off.

She apparently knew, or thought she knew, who he was. He was probably supposed to recognize her. If she was the contact that Jack and the boys were looking for, or at least associated with this contact, the bowtie camera was getting a good look at her.

She continued to stare, waiting for some response. Dax felt his actor's instincts kick in which gave him a boost. He took two casual strides forward, smiled and nodded. This caused the woman to lean back just slightly and cock her head. Dax could see she knew something was wrong. She eyed him from head to toe. His movements, his mannerisms, something, everything, wasn't right to her. And as soon as he opened his mouth, there would be no doubt he wasn't the person she thought he was. But maybe, just maybe, the secret life of *Собака* could work to his advantage.

"Good evening," he finally said with a casual smile and held out his hand. Reluctantly, she gave him hers and watched carefully as he gave the back of her hand a small kiss. Her eyebrows began to furrow in confusion.

Come on, come on, improvise …

With pursed lips, he brought a finger to his mouth and tapped it lightly in a *ssshhh* gesture while using his eyes to glance at the crowd.

This seemed to make her relax a little, as if she understood. But she continued to stare, her expression quickly turning from uncertainty to outright suspicion. He glanced at the bartender who was wiping a glass but looking hard at him. Dax felt he should probably ask her if she wanted a drink, but he had to get away from that bar.

Turning, he took the woman gently by the elbow and motioned with his head to follow. She took two steps with him but then abruptly stopped and pulled her arm away. He felt his pulse quicken.

"I don't understand," she said, looking him up and down again. Her voice was a little louder.

"I can explain everything," he said on impulse, trying feebly to sound confident and even reassuring. He glanced around, hoping to make eye contact with someone who might be with Jack, but saw no one.

Dax smiled, motioned with his head again to follow, and then turned and began walking away. He kept walking, slowly. Not knowing where to go, he headed in the general direction of the door. If things got too heated, he wanted to be closer to the exit. After ten paces or so he took a sip from his drink and casually looked behind him.

The woman was gone.

He felt his heartbeat in his temple. Okay, just keep walking toward the door. He pretended to rub under his nose while cupping his hand over the bowtie. "Jack, who was that?" he whispered. "What's her name? Give me some direction here." He brought his hand down and glanced around again. Still, no one was watching. He cupped his hand again. "She seemed *very* surprised to see me, or *Собака*, or whoever." He wished badly he had a *real* secret agent getup complete with an earpiece whereby he could speak back and forth with Jack and the other agents.

"*Vadim*," a deep, male voice said, making him jump.

Dax whirled around and saw the woman again. This time she had a companion—a tall, huge man with dark, cold eyes who stared unwavering at Dax.

Dax stood dumbfounded and helpless. The fear he was feeling was beginning to betray him, and knew it was showing in his face. Any prospect of this assignment being fun or exciting was going out the window fast. Despite himself, he made the mental note that he'd been called Vadim just now.

The man was at least six inches taller than Dax. His light brown hair was short, almost shaved around an enormous head, revealing a low forehead that jetted out over sunken eyes. His facial features were hard and distinct, like he'd been chiseled out of granite. Buried in the mass of flesh and bone, the almost black pupils penetrated Dax. The big man had a day or two of stubble on his cheeks and square jaw. Under his suit jacket, a muscular body twitched slightly as one hand repeatedly flexed into a fist then relaxed again. He leaned in, his face a dangerous grimace, and growled something in what sounded like Russian slang.

Dax felt his heart thud so hard it shook his whole ribcage. Whatever the man just said, it didn't sound friendly. All he could do was stare back, his eyes giving away alarm and confusion.

The man looked at the woman, gave a knowing smirk, then back to Dax, this time with sarcasm said, "What is this, a resurrection? Perhaps a ghost." His Slavic accent, though not heavy, was noticeable.

Heat waves pulsed up Dax's neck and through his head. Everything felt wrong. Damn Jack Dauer for being so mysterious and not giving him enough to go on before walking into this mess.

Throwing on what little was left of his actor's impulse, he grinned and took a long sip from his drink. "Surprise, surprise," he said, shrugging. It was time to get out of here. "Excuse me," he said, turning quickly in the direction of the door.

He had taken about three steps when a large hand clamped down on his shoulder, stopping him instantly. Long fingers burrowed into his flesh in a painful, vise-like grip. His martial arts instincts sprang into action, and before putting any thought into it, he'd whirled around, the upper part of his arm coming up over the wrist of the offending hand and in a twisting, downward motion, forced it free.

But the man's other long, muscular arm moved with deadly speed and caught the edge of Dax's coat. He felt his body yanked forward and was suddenly looking up and close at a large and menacing face. The man had moved him a little too easily, like a rag doll, as the expression goes. Dax's drink, most of which had splashed on his attacker, slipped out of his hand and thudded heavily on the thick carpet. He looked around for help, but the little scuffle had happened so quickly, no one seemed to notice.

Except the bartender, who had now walked to the edge of the bar and was looking on with intense interest.

22: Strength at the Expense of Energy

Should he call out for help? Would that do any good here?

Holding Dax close, the big man's eyes wandered around Dax's face and then up and down his clothing. "We need to talk, I think, yes?" he finally said quietly.

Dax glanced at the woman. She stared back with wide eyes that conveyed mostly confusion. Stepping behind him, she quickly and casually slid her hands up and down the sides of his coat, probably checking for weapons. Amazingly, she missed the contraption taped to his back.

She nodded at her companion.

The man shoved Dax backward. "Move," he growled.

Suddenly feeling much too victimized, Dax made the firm decision to fight and make a run for it. He had a couple options. The way he was positioned, it would be easy to bring a swift knee into the man's groin. At the same time, his left arm was completely free, enabling him to deliver a simultaneous eye gouge. He could also jump and deliver a nasty head butt to the man's nose. He felt the heat and adrenaline start to rise in anticipation.

Go!

But his plans all at once ceased when he felt the painful thrust of something hard against his ribs. He looked down and although he'd never seen one in person, knew he was looking at the end of a silencer. The cylinder-shaped object was charcoal black steel and about eight inches long, smooth except for machined dimples. The end of it was digging angrily into his ribs.

"Make a move or sound, and the sound from *this* will be the last thing you hear." On the word *this,* he shoved the end of the silencer deeper into Dax's ribs, making him wince.

Dax believed him. He looked down again at the gun and saw that the man was carefully using his own coat flap to hide the weapon from the view of the mingling crowd that was just several feet away.

But the bartender could see it. Dax jerked his head toward the bar, pleading for help with his eyes. The bartender made no move. The situation had now taken a potentially deadly spin, and the thought hit Dax that he may not make it out of this alive. His mind began to whirl in panic and he had no idea what to do next.

The man jerked his head to the right. "This way," he said, taking Dax by the shoulder and turning him around.

"The gun isn't necessary," Dax said, so Jack would hear.

"Shut up," the man hissed.

"I can explain everything—"

"Move!"

Dax felt the powerful grip of the man's hand again, this time on his upper arm, as he felt himself get shoved forward. The woman led the way as the trio headed back toward the bar then made a sharp right. Surely Jack was on the radio calling in the cavalry. Surely he was going to get rescued any minute now. He glanced back at the crowd in the room. Where were Jack's people? Even the detached face of Agent Michael Staggs would be a pleasant sight right now. But still, no one was watching, except … there! His eyes locked with Meygan's! She had turned and was watching intently, alarm and recognition on her face. He stared back as he was being led away, trying to communicate with his eyes. Then a column came between him and the crowd and he lost sight of her.

"Keep moving!" the man snarled quietly through clenched teeth, repositioning the gun to the small of Dax's back.

Dax looked forward and saw he was being led around the other side of the bar where the restrooms were. Was he really about to get killed?

The man said something to the woman who walked ahead down a hallway and to the women's door. She held it open and stepped aside as the man shoved Dax in so hard, he stumbled and almost fell forward on the tiled floor.

Dax braced himself against the sink counter, stood, and turned around. The large luxurious restroom had four oversized mirrors in wooden frames with lamps that hung over the tops. Under each mirror was a sparkling white sink embedded in a long smooth marble top. Dax backed up against the sink's edge, looking around frantically. He felt cold sweat popping out of his forehead. The woman stayed by the door with it cracked open while the man stood before him, the gun now out in the open and pointed at Dax's face.

"*Kto ty?*" the man sneered, a cold killer's expression on his face.

Dax stared back stupidly.

The big man shook his head in disgust. "Who. Are. You?" he asked slowly.

Dax raised both hands. "Not who you think," was all he could say, his voice shaking.

"That much is obvious," the man said, adjusting his wrist so that the gun's line of sight aimed directly between Dax's eyes.

"This is just a big misunderstanding," Dax stammered. He could feel the heat and sweat of his body beneath his shirt.

A large drop of sweat ran down his right cheek. How could he stall for time until help arrived? *Would* help arrive?

"Is it now?" the man asked sarcastically. His eyes narrowed. "Who are you and why you are here."

"It's just a joke," Dax said impulsively, and lamely.

The man took a quick step forward causing Dax to jerk backward and hit the edge of the sink. "If this is a joke, then the joke is on you," he said, his finger tightening around the trigger.

Dax put his hands in front of him, palms forward. He was beginning to feel frantic. "Look, just let me go and you'll never see me again."

"Who are you!" the man yelled, his voice booming and echoing slightly on the restroom walls. "I won't ask again!"

Dax shook his head, scrambling for an answer. "Eh, m-m-my name is John," he started to say, then cursed himself. Every scared idiot trying to conceal his identity thinks of the name, John Smith.

"John …" The man's head cocked. "John who? Who do you work for and what are you doing here looking like *this*?"

Dax's hands were shaking, his thoughts spun. "I-I'm here representing a buyer. But I'm not really the buyer. I just know him. I-I don't actually buy …" Dax realized he was rambling. His improv skills were gone. He just wanted to get out of this alive.

The man's narrowed eyes drilled Dax. "Representing, *who?*" he asked slowly.

Dax's mind scrambled for a Russian name he knew. He thought of an actor and song writer he'd heard of. "M-M-Malikov. Dmitry Malikov," he managed to say.

For a split second, a smirk formed on the man's mouth, but quickly dropped back to a scowl. "Dmitry Malikov," he said in a disbelieving tone.

"*Da.* I-I mean yes," Dax stammered.

"You are correct about one thing. This is a joke." The man twisted the gun sideways and with a quick flick of his large forearm, smashed the pistol butt into Dax's left cheekbone.

Dax yelped in pain and grabbed his face as his head swiveled and snapped back.

The big man took a step back and watched Dax for several seconds. "And you just happen to show up here looking like this, *John?*"

Dax straightened up and shrugged helplessly. "Looking like what?" His face throbbed and he could feel a burning and swelling start.

"Am I a fool!" the man yelled. Turning his wrist ever so slightly, he aimed the gun somewhere to Dax's left and squeezed the trigger.

The next few moments passed in staggered slow motion. First there was a loud compressed thud, thunderous enough to rattle the mirrors behind him. He could feel the concussion of it over every square inch of his body. Never would he have thought a silencer would be that loud; in movies they were much quieter. Then there was a flash. He'd never had a gun fired at him and the flash from the end of the barrel spewed like fiery vomit. In that moment he instinctively began to turn and duck, but at such a close range it did little to help. A searing, hot pain tore through his upper left arm near the shoulder while the impact of the projectile caused his upper torso to spin sideways.

Clutching his arm, Dax screamed and fell against the sink. Glancing up at the mirrors, he saw they were splattered with blood. *His* blood. The mirror behind him now bore a large hole with wide cracks protruding from it.

"Just let me go. Please," Dax gasped, raising his right hand. The pain throbbed and burned in pulsating waves.

The man said something to the woman who was still at the door. She shook her head, waved him back hurriedly and said something in return. "Not yet!" he yelled back at her, in English.

"Please," said Dax, standing up, clutching himself. He looked at his arm and saw red oozing out from between his fingers.

The man took another step forward and was within arm's length. Aiming the gun at Dax's right kneecap, he said, "I am going to ask you one more time, who are you and what are you doing here." His tone was alarmingly calm, as if watching other human beings bleed was something he did every day.

Dax removed his hand and placed it on the sink top to steady himself, blood making the grip slippery. If he told the truth, this man would kill him. If he continued to stall, this man would kill him anyway, after torturing him a little more. He had no way out. He took a deep breath, the pain now turning into a steady, fiery burn. "I work for some competitors," he blurted, not knowing where it would go.

The man leaned in. "What competitors? Who?"

"Him," Dax said, nodding toward the door. "The man with the mark on his face," he said, pointing under his eye. It was nothing more than a desperate ploy. He looked down, breathing deeply and trying to steady himself, his heart racing with unstoppable fury.

"Oleg?" The Russian's eyes narrowed. "No …You are here spying."

Dax looked around, his eyes resting on a lotion bottle on the sink. It looked heavy and made of thick, orange-colored glass. He quickly looked away.

"The truth!" the man's voice boomed off the walls again.

The woman said something, her tone sounding anxious.

"*Zatknis!*" the man said to her over his shoulder.

Dax looked up and said a silent prayer—*God help me, please.*

"If you were spying you would not come here looking like *Собака*," the man growled.

There it was.

"I-I don't know any *Собака*," said Dax waving it off and looking away at the sink again.

"Oh? You just come walking in here, a near perfect replica of that dead dog. And you even pronounce it right, for a *pindosi*." Twisting in a windup, the man suddenly and swiftly brought the back of his hand up and smashed it into Dax's face, left side again, sending Dax across the sink.

Dax groaned as he hit the marble top in a lying position, his face grimaced in pain. For a few seconds his vision spun and his eyes couldn't focus. Lying sideways made trying to orient himself worse. The floor, ceiling, and stall doors moved and wobbled. He felt the end of the gun jab into his belly.

"One more time," the man said, sounding like it was difficult for him to control himself. "Who do you work for?"

Dax lay for a moment, a big part of him believing this was probably his last moment on earth. His shoulder pounded, the side of his face ached, and for an irrational second, he wanted to laugh. Screw it, nothing to lose now.

He looked the man straight in the eye and with as much threat in his voice as he could muster, said, "I work for your worst enemy – the United States government. And I've got a camera and microphone on me that's been recording everything."

The woman near the door stood straight, alarm in her eyes. "*Vassi!*" she said.

"Quiet!"

"In fact," Dax continued, "there's agents on their way here as we speak."

Stepping forward, the man quickly patted the front of Dax's sweat-soaked, blood-spattered shirt, then checked the inside of his jacket. "You lie to me!" he yelled, bringing his hand up again as if to strike.

Dax smiled and tapped his bowtie. "Smile," he said.

The man's eyes became wide and for the first time a wave of alarm swept over his large face. Leaning in, he peered at the center of the bowtie. His free hand came up and grabbed the tie, violently yanking it back, jerking Dax's head. Then, reaching into Dax's collar, he found the small black wire. Tugging it partly out, he twisted the wire in his fingers. Then reaching around, felt the lump in the middle Dax's back. His eyes moved up and locked on Dax and the two stared. "Now you die," he whispered menacingly.

The woman said something again, but the man ignored her, his face a grimace of rage. The woman called out again. Finally, in English, she said, "*Vassi*, people are coming!"

The man turned to look at her.

Years ago, Dax was taught in his Kung Fu lessons to never develop strength at the expense of energy or energy at the expense of self-defense. He realized the mistake he'd made in the last few minutes of draining away all his power through fear, ineffective resistance, and pleading for his life. He only had a little left. It was now or never.

Craning his head from his lying position, Dax locked on the orange lotion bottle. Thank God his right arm was still good. As smoothly and quickly as he could, his hand shot out and grasped the glass bottle. Then, using the momentum of sitting up, he swung like a man swinging for his very life at the head of the large man. The bottle made contact just as the man was turning back around, the thick glass bouncing violently off the thin skin of his temple next to his right eye.

Roaring like a beast, the man's head dropped, and his free hand came up, as if to block another blow. Then the gun went off and the silencer resonated again in the small confines of the restroom walls. Fortunately, the barrel was now pointed at the ground.

Before the bullet was finished ricocheting off the floor and under the counter, Dax was already leaping off the sink. The room spun, but there was no pain to be felt. There was not even any more fear. There was only savage instinct, the kind where adrenaline takes command of every cell of every muscle and the brain is acting on impulses that require little conscious effort.

Launching himself forward, Dax took advantage of the bigger man's hunched position and exposed ribs. With toes up and heel extended, he delivered a kicking blow with such force to the man's lower ribcage, it produced an audible cracking noise.

This time the large man went down, his knee hitting the floor first and then his head smashing into a stall door post, twisting his neck sideways.

Dax took the brief moment to glance up at the woman. The door was cracked open, and she was talking in urgent tones to someone on the other side.

The man on the floor grunted loudly and shook his head. The gun was still in his hand. Springing forward, Dax lifted a leg high and brought the full weight of his body down as hard as he could on the man's hand.

The man screamed, let go of the gun, and tried to pull his arm back. Then with speed and strength, raised a long and powerful leg up that hit Dax square in the back. The blow sent Dax forward in a backward arch position, throwing his body into a stall door, slamming it hard and causing the whole stall to shake. He could hear the woman at the door scream something.

Grunting in pain, the big man on the floor began reaching for the gun.

Dax turned and decided it was time to run. Leaping over the man still sprawled on the floor, he suddenly felt himself yanked backward. The man had somehow grabbed his leg. Dax looked at his own hand and realized he was still gripping the orange lotion bottle.

Standing over the man on the ground, Dax had the advantage. Using the full length his body and arm, he brought the bottle down on the man's forehead. The bottle still did not break, but bounced back again, and immediately there was broken skin and blood. The man grunted and mumbled in Russian. Dax raised the bottle and brought it down again, producing more blood. But still, neither the glass nor the man's head yielded. The big man, now looking disoriented, weakly raised his arm to block the blows, a thickening stream of blood trickling into his eye. Dax thought he heard himself scream as he raised and smashed the bottle down a third time. The room twirled even more as sweat poured into his eyes. He raised to strike a fourth time, but suddenly felt his groin getting crushed and his body propelled backward into the air. The Russian had worked a leg in and was now using it to shove Dax.

Dax flew airborne two or three feet before touching the floor again. Momentum sent him stumbling backward, his body angling at the sink counter. The room toppled as his upper back made hard contact with the marble top's edge, but instead of feeling it cut into his spine, he felt the square shape of the electronic device that was still taped to his body. The device crunched and snapped under his weight as it pressed into him.

Sinking to a knee to regain balance, Dax saw the man turning and fumbling to get hold of the gun. Ignoring pain, Dax found himself diving this time, both hands outstretched. He made contact with the gun just when the large man did, but the man grabbed first, and Dax could sense right away the superior strength. Laying his body across the man's arm, Dax clawed and tugged furiously at the man's fingers, but to no avail. The gun went off again, the flash and explosion acting as a stun grenade would, temporarily freezing Dax's senses. He heard startled yells outside the door as a bullet blew a hole in the wall near the floor sending bits of tile and drywall everywhere.

Despite the blood trickling all over his face, the big Russian immediately began hoisting himself up from the floor. Dax felt the movement under him and for a quick moment his clarity snapped back. Rolling toward the big man, Dax used his weakened and bleeding arm to bring an elbow into the man's temple with more strength than he knew he still possessed. The man grunted and hit the floor again. Dax screamed and began hurling blow after blow with his elbow. Facing downward with his arm pinned under Dax's weight, the man had no way to block the repeating strikes. But still he moved, moaned, and struggled to free himself.

After what had to have been at least a dozen elbow smashes to the side and back of the man's head, Dax rolled off. The gun had slipped from the large hand. Dax snatched the gun and continued rolling until his back was against the wall.

Both men, lying on their side, bleeding and sweating, stared at each other. The man looked at Dax's shaking hands, and a smile formed on the edge of his lips. Mockery flooded into his eyes as he silently challenged Dax to shoot.

Despite himself and the circumstances, Dax didn't want to shoot. He just wanted to get out. But if getting out alive meant pulling the trigger, he would. Easing himself up on one elbow while keeping the gun trained on the large face before him, he managed to say, with a quivering and breathy voice, "I'm going to leave now. Just stay where you are, okay?"

The large man kept his smirk and watched while Dax struggled to his feet, leaving a bloody streak on the wall. Dax looked at his left shoulder, then back at the man. Trying to steady his breathing and keep his balance, he moved cautiously around the enormous body stretched out on the floor in front of him.

"You have no idea what you're doing, do you?" the man said with heavy breathing, his eyes dead locked on Dax's.

Dax shook his head. "No, actually. I don't."

The expression on the man's face softened, his breathing still hard. "Are you going to shoot me?"

Dax paused. "I'd rather not."

The man struggled and sat up, causing Dax to step back. He wiped blood off his face then held out a large hand, palm up. "Give me the camera," he said calmly.

Dax hesitated.

The man's cold, dark eyes remained steady. "You have no idea the questions you have raised tonight. You will be found. Give me the camera and I will forget you and you can disappear."

The offer sounded reasonable. Too bad it wasn't the truth. Dax began to shake his head. "*Nee-yet*. It is *you* who will be found. In fact, you've already been found."

The man extended his hand further. "Give it to me."

"Too late. It's a broadcasting camera, not a recording one."

The man's eyebrows came together in a glare while he growled in rage and frustration. He then suddenly said something in Russian in a loud voice.

Dax glanced up at the door just in time to see the woman's arm swinging down in a chopping motion. Impulse once again took over as his eye caught the shimmer of a flash of steel as it spun through the air in his direction. Sidestepping and leaning back, he heard a whirling sound and felt a rush of air brush past the bottom of his chin. The mirror behind him cracked, then the lower half shattered as a razor-sharp looking throwing dagger bounced and clanged in the sink.

The man on the floor suddenly sprang like giant bullfrog and tackled Dax's legs. As Dax was thrown backwards against the wall, the hand holding the gun came down, pointing at the middle of the man's massive back. Dax squeezed the trigger, heard the *thwack* and felt the gun's handle shove hard against his palm from the recoil. A small hole exploded in the man's back causing a splash of dark red to erupt from the opening. He screamed and let go of Dax's legs. The woman at the door also screamed.

Dax stared in horror, but just for a moment. Losing all thought again, he turned, dropped the bottle, and sprinted for the door. In the five or six leg strides, he brought the gun up, preparing to shoot the woman. But she held no other weapon and only raised her hands and screamed. Instead of firing, he turned his good shoulder at her, leaned in and charged like a football linebacker. She started to duck, but Dax was moving too fast. He hit her dead center in the chest and his body mass, almost twice hers, smashed her violently. The door flew open with a loud bang as Dax and the woman spilled out on the floor. Dax heard a couple more screams and looked up. Three women were standing in the corridor, their mouths wide open at the wild and bloody man with a gun in front of them.

The woman underneath Dax gasped for breath, her face twisted in pain. Dax scrambled to his feet as quickly as he could. Dizzy and disoriented, he stumbled and hit the wall. Two of the women ducked and hit the floor, the other turned and fled. Shouting could be heard around the corner.

Without hesitating another moment, Dax ran down the hall and took a sharp left for the main door. The atmosphere of the Babylon Ballroom had changed. About half the crowd that had been in the vicinity of the restrooms were closer now and looking in his direction. Dax shoved past several people, including one man who may have been the bartender and sprinted for exit door. As he ran, a man dressed like a waiter mounted the stairs about midway up and held out his hands in a *stop!* gesture. Dax saw him reach behind and produce a snub-nose revolver.

Dax held up his gun with both hands, arms extended straight out and yelled, "Drop it!"

The "waiter" complied, dropping the revolver, his eyes never leaving Dax's. Dax stormed past him, grabbed the large handle of the ballroom doors, and yanked hard. As they opened, he impulsively turned and scanned for pursuers. His eyes locked on Meygan Knight's red dress, then up to her eyes, which were wide with fright and confusion.

Outside the ballroom entrance, the man and woman who had checked his invitation saw the gun and raised their hands. They stared but remained calm. Professionals. Dax sprinted at full speed toward the large staircase leading back to the lobby.

Leaping down four or five steps at time, he lost his grip on the railing and almost fell. His banging caused several individuals in the lobby to look up at the commotion. As he neared the bottom, he made eye contact with a man behind the counter who was on the phone and staring at him. The man hung up quickly, turned and ran to the side. Dax had the feeling the guy was coming to intercept him.

Where the hell were Jack's people!

As Dax hit the bottom of the stairs, people saw the gun and started yelling and scattering. One lady froze in her tracks and began screaming. Another couple turned and started to run, the woman tripping on her long dress sending them both tumbling to the floor. Dax didn't stop. Looking around and getting his bearings, he ignored everything else and bolted for the front door. As he neared the hotel's large glass doors, he saw in the reflection the man from the behind the counter coming in full pursuit, his arms raised in a shooting position.

Running faster, Dax rammed his shoulder into the door. The heavy door moved slowly despite the impact of Dax's body. As the cool air swooshed in, Dax ducked and wiggled out into the night and began running down the sidewalk with everything his remaining adrenaline could muster.

23: Who's Telling the Truth?

Dax ran as fast he could down the streetlight-lit sidewalk, the hard soles of his shoes clacking. His senses were returning. The pain in his shoulder was beginning to burn, the aches were making their presence known in his joints, the left side of his face felt hot and swollen. Adrenaline was receding and the night air began to feel cool and then soon after, cold against his sweat. But he ran on, his mind and body still in fight or flight mode.

Suddenly recognizing where he was, he stopped. This was the corner where he'd been dropped off less than an hour ago. "Jack!" he yelled into the night. "Where are you?"

The sound of quick footsteps behind made him turn. Two men were running down the sidewalk straight at him.

Dax cursed and started running again. He felt a weight in his hand. Looking down he saw the big Russian's gun. Should he turn and fire? There may not be many bullets left in the magazine. What to do? If they fired at him, he'd return it.

He made a sharp left and continued up a smaller and darker street. Keeping his pace, he looked frantically back and forth for a place to hide. A garbage bin, a large plant pot, anything. Somewhere behind him he heard the squealing of tires. Was that Jack finally coming to his rescue? Some rescue.

The pursing footsteps turned the corner. Dax ran even faster, his breathing beginning to get laborious. On one side of him a brick wall, straight ahead, blackness. The scene was eerily familiar to the ending scene of the last show he'd just been in. Up on the right, a dark and deep doorway.

Stooping low while running, and trying to keep his shoes quiet, Dax darted into the doorway. It was so dark he could hardly see more than a few inches in front, so he held his hands out. His palms hit damp wood and a cold metal object, probably an old service door. Turing around, he pressed his back against the inside of the door frame as much as he could. He could feel the pieces of what was left of the camera device taped to his back.

The tapping of pursuing footsteps got louder and then slowed to a stop. He heard one of them make a *shhhh!* sound.

Dax's heart hammered in his chest and boomed in his ears. He could feel the cold metal of the gun in his hand which now felt heavy.

Did you really shoot a man back there? Yes, you did.

The thought hit him so hard he almost gasped. But he had to, didn't he? That big Russian was going to kill him.

The sound of a shoe scraping asphalt made him stop breathing. They were close. In the distant, several police sirens were wailing away and steadily getting louder. Soon, the cops would be combing the surrounding blocks and streets. What would happen if they found him out here covered in blood and bruises *and* with the weapon that just shot someone at the Omni Hotel? What had Jack gotten him into?

A paper cup rolled just feet away making him jump.

Suddenly a whisper from someone nearby. They were very close now, maybe just several feet away and creeping up on the doorway. Dax held his breath again and tightened the grip on the gun. He was going to have to do it. He was going to have to shoot at another human being, or two. His jaw clenched and he peered into the darkened street, straining his eyes for any sign of movement. A slight shuffle and scrape. Closer now, five or six feet away. How did they know he was in the doorway? They must have heard his breathing. Silently he cursed and started to raise the gun.

A loud squeal of tires broke the silence and light suddenly flooded the narrow street. The sound of a car engine roaring and tires crunching the rough asphalt in their direction was all that could be heard. Dax pressed himself even harder against the door. The car moved quickly, the bouncing headlight beams getting wider and brighter.

A man just around the doorway suddenly cursed loudly and ran past Dax, right in front of him. A second man quickly followed. The car, hopefully a police car, would see them running and chase them, then Dax could ditch this gun somewhere and get out of here.

The headlights continued bouncing past Dax as a midsized sedan drove by. Dax prepared to run back up the street, but the car suddenly stopped, its brakes squealing. The little reverse lights came on and the car moved backward until it stopped right in front of the doorway.

"You gotta be kidding me," Dax muttered to himself. In the back window of the car, he saw what looked like a man with large goggles peering at him. Night vision?

The front passenger door flew open and a man in a long gray trench coat stepped out. He flicked on a powerful flashlight and the doorway Dax was hiding in was suddenly bathed in hard light. Quickly, the man reached into his coat and produced a revolver.

"Drop that gun right now!" he yelled. "Drop it or I drop you!"

The driver's door opened and a second man stood quickly, produced a weapon, and aimed it over the roof of the car.

Dax looked down and realized he was gripping the handle of the Russian's gun, tightly. He had to will his hand to let go. His fingers finally gave way and the gun clattered to the ground.

"Hands up!"

Dax obeyed.

"Step forward, nice and slow."

Dax took several steps forward, the light in his face blinding him. He found himself looking at a man that was maybe in his late forties, medium athletic build, clean shaven face. The man stood staring, gun raised, while the driver came around and picked up the silencer-equipped weapon from the ground. He held it up in the light.

"Nice gun," he said. "High-end. Where-ja get it?"

Dax stood with his hands still raised. "From the guy who tried to kill me with it," was all he could say.

"Who was that?" the man asked.

Dax shrugged. "I've no idea. I heard a woman call him Vassi. Big, scary Russian dude. He tried to kill me."

"Vassi?"

"Yes."

"Vassi who?"

"I told you, I've no idea."

"How do you know he was Russian?"

"I heard him speak it."

"You understand Russian?"

"Yeah, a little. I guess." Dax suddenly realized how frightened he was and wanted to cry. His hands were shaking and his left shoulder hurt. He started to lower them.

"Ah-ah! Keep 'em up," the man said, motioning with his gun.

"I got shot, man." Dax kept his hands raised as best he could, his left shoulder now a searing pain.

The driver gave Vassi's gun to someone in the back seat and then returned to Dax and began patting him down. Dax's shirt was completely soaked in sweat mixed with blood.

"Lemme guess. You came from the Omni Hotel."

Dax nodded. "Yeah."

"You use that gun to shoot him? This Vassi?" the man asked.

"Yes, I had to."

"And you say you got shot?"

"Left shoulder." Dax's voice was sounding weary.

"What's your name?"

"Dax. Dax Ribeiro. R, i, b, e, i, r, o." He sighed. "My first name is actually David."

"You got ID, David?"

"Yes," said Dax.

The man frisking him looked up at his partner. "No wallet."

"Really. Running around a party dressed like that and no wallet."

"My wallet is at the Sutter."

"The Sutter Hotel?"

"Yes."

"Why is it there?"

A thought suddenly hit Dax and frightened him. "Are you cops?" he asked.

The man eyed him. "Something like that."

Dax shook his head. "Come on, man. No more bullshit."

"Got something here," the man frisking Dax suddenly said. His hand was in the middle of Dax's back. "Hold still," the man said.

Dax closed his eyes and felt his body being tugged as the man pulled his shirt out of his belt and reached up his cold, sweaty back. The man looked at his partner. "Something taped here."

"What's on your back?" the man with the gun asked.

"What's left of some kind of transmitting device. I have a camera and microphone in my bowtie."

"Really. Now this is getting interesting. Is he clean?"

"Yeah," the man behind Dax said. "Looks like he took one in the left shoulder though. Just a graze it looks like."

Stepping forward, the man lowered his gun and put it back in his coat. "So you did get shot."

Dax shrugged. "I guess so, yeah."

The man reached up and took hold of Dax's bowtie and shined his flashlight into it. "Well, look at that."

The man behind Dax was still feeling around the device on his back. "Feels cracked. All banged up."

"How'd that happen?" asked the man in front of him.

"When I fell against the sink."

"The sink?"

Dax felt dizzy. "During-during the fight. In the bathroom."

"Where did you get it and why are you wearing it?"

Dax stared incredulously. "You're asking me?"

The man stared back hard but didn't answer.

"Seriously," said Dax. "Who are you?"

The man stepped back and eyed Dax. He then pulled a long wallet out of his coat and snapped it open. Dax saw a familiar emblem. "Agent Tommy Hicks, FBI. This is my partner, Roy Parker."

An odd feeling of both relief and confusion flooded over Dax. "Well, good. Then you should know who I am and what I'm doing here."

Agent Hicks stared at Dax for a moment. "I've no idea who you are or what you're doing here."

Dax laughed. "Really? Ask Jack Dauer."

Hicks looked at Parker. "Who?"

"Agent Jack Dauer. FBI. What, you guys don't know each other?"

Hicks shook his head. "I don't know any Jack Dauer. Not in any of the field offices out here anyway. You can lower your hands now."

Dax let his arms fall heavily to his side. "Is this a joke?" He looked at his hands and saw them shaking badly. A line of red was dripping out of his left sleeve and over the back of his hand.

Hicks' voice took on a rough edge. "You call shooting people a joke? You're in a lot of trouble."

Dax shook his head. A sick feeling was coming over him fast. His knees suddenly felt weak. Several more police sirens could be heard down the street.

"Cuff him?" Parker asked.

The feeling hit Dax like a swift fist to his gut. As the searing pain cramped up his stomach muscles he involuntarily leaned forward and vomited hard. He felt Parker's hand grab his arm. Hicks took a quick step backward to avoid the splatter.

When the heaving stopped, Dax gasped for air and swallowed thickly, feeling the acidic burn in his esophagus.

Hicks looked Dax up and down for a moment. The radio crackled and Parker turned away and said something quietly into it.

Parker released Dax's arm as Hicks looked him over and nodded. "Put 'em on loose, in the front," Hicks finally said. "Lemme see that shoulder."

Dax turned and Hicks shined the light at the wound as Parker gently snapped the cuffs around Dax's wrists.

"Looks like you got grazed. Bullet passed through," said Hicks. He then gently but firmly took Dax by the arm. "Let's get to the car, David. Or is it Dax? We have a lot to talk about."

"If I still have a choice, Dax will do."

Hicks led Dax around the car and opened the back door. Dax wearily got in, his head spinning, his hands still shaking. Beside him was a man dressed in jeans and a pullover sweater. On the seat was a steel box he was snapping shut as Dax sat down.

Hicks put the car in gear and began slowly moving forward. "This is Sergeant Donnelly," Hicks said, referring to the guy next to Dax. Sergeant Donnelly put a protective hand on the box and watched Dax closely.

The car radio chirped and a voice droned. Hicks picked up the microphone and said something back. Dax stared out the window and watched the streetlights go by. He felt so lightheaded, he wanted to pass out.

"Tell me again why your wallet and ID is at the Sutter Hotel," said Hicks.

Dax breathed deeply. "And my keys and my cellphone. That's where I was prepped for this job."

"What job?"

Dax thought for a moment. Either Jack Dauer had lied about everything—who he was and what this was all about— or this guy Hicks was lying. But a gut feeling was telling him he'd just now met the real FBI for the first time in his life. He chuckled in bitter disbelief. "The job of going undercover at this little party at the Omni."

Parker turned around and looked at Dax. Dax stared back indifferently.

"What room?" asked Hicks.

"The Babylon Ballroom."

"No, the room at the Sutter."

Dax closed his eyes, images flashing through them. "Five. Oh. Nine."

Parker whipped out a radio and said something quickly into it, but Dax paid no attention. He was envisioning the events of this evening. He saw the big Russian on the floor in the restroom, he heard the piercing thud of the silencer, the man's screams, the splattering blood. He again felt the urge to cry like a baby.

The car made a sharp right and sped up. They must have turned on a main street because traffic was heavier. On the sidewalk Dax saw people, mostly couples or groups, heading somewhere. They were having a good time, going out to dinner and entertainment. He was in the back of a car after having killed a man. Was life as he knew it over?

"What about Michael Staggs, or uh … Kimball, Al Kimball?" Dax suddenly asked. "And Tasha, Tasha someone. Oh, I don't know." He glanced at Sergeant Donnelly who calmly watched him, listening.

The car droned on for several seconds in silence. Parker glanced over at Hicks. "Those names don't mean anything to us," Hicks finally said. "Not yet, anyway. But you're going to need to remember them, every one of them."

Dax felt a despairing feeling. "What happened tonight? What happened to me?"

"That's what we're going to find out," said Hicks.

"Were you guys there? Did you have people there?"

Parker glanced at Hicks again.

"Where?" Hicks asked.

"The Omni—the ballroom!" Dax yelled, leaning forward. He felt Sergeant Donnelly put a retraining hand on his shoulder.

Hicks was watching Dax through the rearview mirror. "Calm down, Dax. We're going to sort this all out."

Dax breathed deeply. "Where are we going?"

"Headquarters. We need to talk while the events are fresh in your mind."

"Where's that?" Dax asked.

Parker turned around again and looked at him. "Golden Gate Avenue," he said. "Never been there?" His voice dripped with sarcasm.

Dax chortled bitterly. "No." He leaned back and closed his eyes, trying to relax under the movement of the car.

24: Nurse Amy

Dax felt his heartbeat and breathing slowing, the sweat all over him feeling cold and clammy. Every few seconds the radio would chirp, something would be said, and either Hicks or Parker would reply. It was mostly talk in codes, but it was obvious they were talking about the night's events.

Dax must have dozed off or passed out for a few minutes. He felt the car tip downward. Opening his eyes, he saw they were heading down into what looked like an underground parking garage. He leaned forward and peered out the window. The building they were going under looked vaguely familiar. He'd been up Golden Gate Avenue many times and had seen the gray-white structure with the neat rows of dark rectangular slots that made up the windows. It all disappeared from view as the sedan went below ground under the building.

The tires squealed lightly on the smooth cement of the garage. Long yellow-white fluorescent bulbs illuminated the area. There were a variety of vehicles scattered about: sedans, delivery trucks, at least one limousine, and a couple dual-sport motorcycles. Dax glanced at Sergeant Donnelly who caught his eye and glanced back. The car pulled into a stall and stopped.

Hicks put the car in park. "Let's go," he said turning off the engine and opening his door.

Dax fumbled for the door handle. His arms felt heavy. Parker opened the door and Dax stumbled out, his body aching and the throb in his left shoulder worsening. Hicks nodded with his head to follow. Parker fell in behind and Sergeant Donnelly stayed with the car.

In the hard garage light, he finally got a good look at Agent Tommy Hicks. The man was close to his height, early-fifties, balding, with light brown hair that stretched like a fence around the back of his head. His face was chiseled and featured with high cheek bones, a square jaw and deep-set eyes that appeared light blue in color. He was thin and in good shape.

Roy Parker was a few years younger than Hicks, but already graying on the sides over dark brown hair. He was heavier and had a beefier face, wide-set charcoal-gray eyes and a large dimple on his chin.

Both men wore long, dark coats, almost trench coat length that covered most of what they were wearing underneath. It occurred to Dax that the two carried themselves differently than Dauer and Staggs, a more serious air about them, less mysterious acting.

The three made their way to a wide door where a guard was seated behind a desk—a husky man with hard, suspicious eyes.

"Mr. Luciano," Hicks said.

The guard locked eyes on Dax then looked him up and down. They entered a hallway with four elevator doors. Hicks walked to the last one and inserted a key in a small keyhole next to the Up arrow. A light blinked and Hicks hit one of the buttons. A small hum and whir from elevator motors could be heard. Dax turned around and looked at Parker who casually stared back. The doors opened with a clack.

They rode in silence as the elevator creaked and groaned to the thirteenth floor, then exited. As they walked, Dax saw what looked like any professional work environment, cubes and desks on one side, office windows and doors on the other, men in dress pants, shirts and ties, and one or two women in business attire. The place looked about half full.

"We came in the back entrance," Hicks offered over his shoulder.

Dax glanced back and forth, feeling woozy. Most around the place ignored the three as they strode through, but when someone did make eye contact, they immediately looked Dax up and down with intense curiosity. This reminded Dax of how awful he must look after getting beat up, shot, and thrown around a restroom by a big Russian gorilla who was probably seventy-five pounds heavier.

Hicks stopped by a door and pulled out some keys. Twisting the knob, he turned to Dax and said, "In here."

They entered a modest but spacious office. Against the wall was a small couch and matching side chair with a coffee table in front of it. Against the other wall was a round table with four chairs. In the center was a U-shaped computer desk with shelves full of books and a few small decorations.

"Let's get these off," said Hicks, pulling out some keys and unlocking the handcuffs. "Nice suit, by the way. This Jack fellow give it to you?"

"Yeah, courtesy of the FBI. So I was told."

"We're gonna get to all that. How you feeling?"

"Been better," said Dax as he struggled with the coat. His shoulder was really starting to hurt. Parker stepped up behind to assist.

Hicks got on the phone. "Hey, get Amy up here, will you?" he was saying. "Yes please, my office. *A-SAP.*" He hung up and looked at Dax. "We're going to get that shoulder looked at. Hopefully a trip to the hospital won't be necessary."

Dax looked and felt a little astonished. Hadn't he just been shot? Or maybe Agent Hicks here had seen enough gunshot wounds to be able to make judgment calls on that sort of thing.

Hicks and Parker removed their long coats and blazers and slung them over the back of chairs. Tan brown leather shoulder holsters with pistols were strapped to each of them. Parker began untying the bowtie on Dax, carefully wiggling the small camera and cord out of it.

"Can you get your shirt off too?" Hicks asked. "I wanna see that thing on your back." Hicks opened a small cabinet and produced a bottle of water which he handed to Dax.

Dax suddenly realized how thirsty he was. He cracked open the bottle and drank about half it in several big gulps.

"Take it easy with that or you'll throw up again," said Hicks.

Dax ignored him. After the shirt was off, he looked down at the wound and saw it was only bleeding slightly, but it was swollen and ugly. He felt Parker peeling away the strips of tape on his back. The device came off and Parker walked over to Hicks and the two began examining it.

There was a knock on the door. "Come on in, Amy," said Hicks.

A tall woman, mid-thirties, with medium-length deep auburn hair, almost a dark velvet red and tied in a ponytail, entered the office. Her face bore a youthful energy and had simple, smart features. She wore plain gray dress pants and a long-sleeved yellow button shirt. Like Hicks, she looked physical fit. In her right hand was what looked like a medical kit.

Hicks thumbed at Dax. "Left shoulder. Dax, Amy. Amy, Dax."

"Hi," said Amy pleasantly as she sat on the small table in front of Dax. "I'm Amy."

Dax turned his shoulder to her. He watched as she examined his injury. "You're a nurse?"

Amy smiled. "An RN, yes, part-time. Also a field agent, part-time." She touched the edge of the wound causing Dax to wince. "Sorry."

Dax held his breath.

"Looks like the bullet passed through the first couple layers of skin. Probably won't even need stitches. You're very fortunate."

"I don't feel so fortunate," said Dax. A pause. "So, what's more exciting?"

Amy looked up. "Hmm?"

"Nurse or field agent?"

"Most of the time, nurse." She worked her fingers into some latex gloves.

Dax watched her. He was feeling dizzy. "You must come in handy around here."

Amy reached for a small bottle and shook it. "They bring worse in here, believe me." She and Hicks exchanged glances and he gave her a dirty look. "This is going to sting a little," she said.

"What is it?"

"Saline solution." She pressed a square cloth to the bottle opening and turned it upside down. Dax closed his eyes and gritted his teeth as the solution bit into open nerves. Amy gently wiped at the wound, making it burn hotly and cause a little bleeding. "Sorry, but this needs to get thoroughly cleaned." She grabbed a tube from her kit and squeezed a blob of beige-colored cream on her finger. "Topical anesthetic," she said, gently smearing the cream against the open skin. It felt cool and refreshing, the numbing effect immediate. She then resumed cleaning.

Dax breathed deeply and tried to relax.

"If an infection gets into your bloodstream, you'll be making a trip to the hospital," Amy said.

"You ever had to treat anyone you, yourself shot?" Dax asked, feeling lightheaded and not sure what he was asking.

Amy chuckled. "No, I don't go around shooting. I investigate; spend a lot of time examining bills and records. Occasionally I get to follow someone."

"Stakeout?"

"Not really. Not the all-nighters like you see in the movies."

Dax nodded and closed his eyes.

Someone wrapped on the window. A man was looking at Hicks and motioned with his head to come out. Hicks and Parker exited.

Amy put her hand to Dax's forehead. "Feeling any fever?"

"No. Have they told you anything about tonight?" Dax asked.

Amy shook her head. "No."

"Do you know anything about a Jack Dauer or a Michael Staggs?"

"No, I don't."

"Has the FBI been following some of the people that were there tonight?"

Amy met his eyes. "Where?"

"The Omni Hotel. The fun little party I was at tonight."

Amy studied his eyes for a moment, then said, "Not my case."

"But do you know anything about it? Has the FBI been involved? The real FBI, that is. You are a *real* FBI agent, right?"

Amy smiled. "Yes, I am. And regarding tonight, the FBI is obviously involved, but again, I myself am not."

"So you don't know anything then?"

"Dax, you just shot a man, remember? Even if I did, I can't talk to suspects about these things."

"Good point." He looked out the office window. A woman had joined Hicks, Parker, and the third man. Hicks nodded with his head toward the office and all four turned at once and looked straight at Dax. Dax looked away, suddenly feeling self-conscious.

Amy was watching. "You'll tell me if you get dizzy or cold or feel like you're going to pass out, okay?"

Dax gave a weak thumbs-up.

"Here, let's see again," said Amy. After studying the wound for a moment, she took the cloth she had soaked with water and began gently wiping around the bloodied area. She peered closely at it, then reached into her kit for another tube and blobbed something else on her finger. Dax was staring dumbly at her hand. "Antiseptic," she said with a smile. "Try to relax."

Dax let himself slump against the back of the couch. The antiseptic stung a little, but the numbing was still working. Forcing his eyes to stay open, he watched Amy put the tube away and then pull a small box out of her kit. He gazed sleepily as Amy skillfully applied small strips of odd-looking bandages.

She glanced at him. "Retention tape. Don't want this wound opening back up." After that she retrieved a roll of gauze and unraveled about two feet worth. She gently wrapped his upper arm with just enough pressure so that it didn't hurt.

"This will need to be changed in twelve hours or so," she said.

"I'll be fast asleep in bed," said Dax.

"We'll have someone wake you and take care of it."

"What, here?" Dax looked around.

Amy snapped her kit shut. "Hold out your hand, your good one."

Dax watched her retrieve a bottle, then tap out four cream-colored capsules in his hand.

"Antibiotics. Just in case. Take all four, please."

He tipped his head and let the pills slide into his mouth, then quickly took a couple gulps of water.

Amy then put a small packet with the word Ibuprofen on it in his hand. "I think you should expect to remain here for the next few hours." She watched his face. "I need you to tell someone right away if you get a fever, see any swelling, or feel tenderness or inflammation. Especially if you see any red streaks or feel numbness around the wound."

Dax just smiled weakly and nodded.

Amy turned to leave.

"Hey ... thanks," said Dax.

"Get some rest. And drink lots of water."

Dax looked longingly at Amy and suddenly didn't want her to leave. What he really wanted right now was a shoulder to cry on. "Hey, Amy. I didn't do anything. I thought I was doing something for my country. I don't even know what happened. Someone tried to kill me. I never wanted to hurt anyone." Dax felt his eyes begin to water.

Amy held up a hand. "It'll be okay, Dax. Just relax and answer all their questions." She gave him a sympathetic smile, then turned and walked out, leaving the door open.

Dax looked at his water bottle, then using his teeth, ripped the little packet open, spit out the paper, and dropped the tablets into his mouth, then tipped the water bottle up and drained the rest of it.

A moment later, Hicks, Parker, and a woman entered. The woman was smartly dressed in a dark, gray business suit. Her medium brown shoulder-length hair was almost straight, but with a slight and natural wave. She was maybe in her mid-forties and bore an austere expression with piercing and acute eyes. She approached Dax, her eyes stopping at the bandage on his shoulder, then up to his face.

"Dax," said Hicks, "this is Special Agent in Charge, Sharon Decker."

Dax and Agent Decker looked at each other. Decker regarded him with a mixture of curiosity and suspicion.

"You've had quite an evening," Decker finally said. "I am really interested in knowing why you were at the Omni Hotel tonight."

"To tell you the truth, I kinda wanna know myself," Dax said with no attempt at humor.

Decker continued to regard him for a few more seconds, gauging his sincerity. "We'll make you as comfortable as possible and then we have a lot to talk about. How are you feeling?"

Dax lightly tapped the bandage on his shoulder. "I guess I'll live."

Someone rapped on the door frame.

"Come in," said Hicks.

A man entered with a square, leather carrycase.

Hicks nodded at Dax. "Dax, this is Agent Lamison."

Lamison was Black with very dark skin, early forties, bald and clean-shaven except for a thin line of graying hair on his upper lip. Without a word, he crossed the floor, put the case on the table and snapped it open, then pulled out a rectangular device that almost resembled a tiny copy machine. Part of the top was glass and around the glass were several buttons.

"What's this?" asked Dax.

"Portable live scan," Lamison said without looking up.

"Elimination prints," said Hicks.

Dax watched lazily as Lamison tinkered with the contraption. Behind the glass, a small screen rose up and then a moment later, a soft green glow of light appeared under the glass.

Lamison turned to Dax. "Okay, I'll need you to stand up."

Hicks gently took Dax by the right shoulder and helped him to his feet.

"First, I need both your thumbs. Place them flat on the scanner glass." Lamison said as he demonstrated in the air.

Dax weakly stuck his thumbs out and pressed them on the glass, using his weight.

"Not too hard," Lamison said, watching the screen closely. "Relax your hands."

After a couple seconds, the machine beeped.

"Alright, now your right four fingers," Lamison said, again demonstrating the movement. The machine beeped again. They repeated the process with the left four fingers. After that, Lamison scanned all ten of Dax's fingers individually, helping him role each one across the glass.

When the process was finished, Lamison nodded at Hicks who helped Dax back to his chair. As wordlessly as he had entered, Lamison snapped the case shut, stood, and walked out.

Dax slowly looked up and met eyes with Decker.

She regarded him for a few more seconds then turned to Hicks. "Twenty minutes, okay?" She then turned and exited.

25: Clandestine Activity

Dax sat in a comfortable leather chair at the end of a large conference room table. The table was thick and heavy, a fake cherry wood with beige trim and a smooth, shiny surface. The room itself was sophisticated. Against the wall were four large flat-screen monitors, powered off at the moment. Dax stared at them in wonder, the way he'd stared at Al Kimball's digital camera. At his workplace, their Sun computer monitors were bulky, thick, and heavy. Mounted directly above was an LCD projector that pointed to an area on the wall where it looked like a screen rolled down from a rectangular slot in the ceiling. Around the edge of the ceiling were neat rows of fluorescent bulbs covered by the lip of an edge so what illuminated the room was light reflecting off the surrounding cover.

In front of Dax was an empty, crumpled sandwich wrapper, two empty water bottles, and a half-full coffee mug. Around the table sat Sharon Decker, Tommy Hicks, Roy Parker, a stern-looking woman introduced as Agent Michelle Milevoi, and Sergeant Donnelly. Donnelly pecked away at a laptop computer in front of him.

Although Dax had been exhausted, he now felt the blend of a caffeine-induced buzz and the rush of retelling his experience with the characters he'd met in the last few days.

Believing more than not he was now in the hands of the *real* United States Federal Bureau of Investigation, he held nothing back. He started with the first encounter at the theatre and how Les Abraham had introduced him. The old guy will probably freak out when real agents pay him a visit.

They asked many questions and took many notes. Parker was investigating calls to and from Dax's cell number. Dax did his best to recall every detail. He couldn't remember the Yahoo email address Jack had used to contact him at work, but he'd retrieve it as soon as he got back into his work account.

At one point Decker and Hicks left the room for a few minutes. When they returned, Hicks told Dax that a team of agents had gone to the Sutter Hotel and in room 509, they had found not only his clothes and ID, but two bodies. They watched his reaction carefully at this news. Hearing it put a serious lump in Dax's throat. They'd been reluctant at first to tell Dax, but Decker made the decision to show Dax pictures of the dead men in the hope Dax could identify them.

The first body had been found near the entrance to the hotel suite. "He was introduced to me as Leo, that's all I know," Dax said. He had a hard time looking at the image. He'd never seen a victim of strangulation before. "Leo" had a dark and almost bronze skin, but it was significantly paler now, especially his lips, which were an ashen gray. Both eyes were not quite closed and gave the false appearance of being sleepy. One eye bulged and was open slightly more than the other, both lifelessly staring up at nothing. Dax told them everything he knew, which wasn't much, only that the man appeared not only to be a techie but a makeup guy of sorts as he had done up Dax's hair this evening.

The next image was even harder to look at, but Dax did recognize what was left of "Agent Jeremy Forrester." They had found the young man slumped on his side in the hotel suite's kitchen with the upper third of his head missing. They'd rolled him on his back for the picture. One of Jeremy's eyes was still intact, making him recognizable, but the rest of the gruesome picture was now burned into Dax's memory. Dax thought he was going to throw up again. Just who was Jack Dauer and his creepy sidekick Michael Staggs? These were real bodies. A dark and dreadful feeling swept over him.

Dax heard a voice and looked up, almost startled. "What?"

"Any idea who may have done this?" Hicks asked again.

Dax shook his head. "No idea." His voice was shaky.

Decker asked, "Did this Jack Dauer mention anyone they were either working with or anyone they had to be careful of?"

Dax was staring at the sandwich wrapper. "No. Look, I'm thinking they're you guys, okay? They didn't tell me anything. They were always acting, I don't know, secretive. Clandestine."

"I think we're well past the fact that you were easily deceived by individuals claiming to be United States government agents," Agent Milevoi piped in.

Dax glared at her.

"What do you mean they were always acting secretive?" Parker asked.

"Oh, I don't know. They were good at giving information they thought you needed, but if you tried to ask any questions, they were elusive. The excuse was always that it was for my safety or security reasons and this and that. All info was on a need-to-know basis. Blah, blah."

"And you weren't suspicious?" Milevoi asked, with a condescending tone.

"Hey, gimme a break!" Dax almost shouted.

Agent Milevoi stared back, unfazed.

"Take it easy, Dax," said Hicks. He gave Milevoi a *back off* look.

Dax noticed Decker's eyes flick in Milevoi's direction for just a split second, a moment of "nonverbal leakage," as it's called in psychology vernacular, suggesting there were a few negative things between the two women.

Decker shifted in her seat and with a calm voice asked, "We're just trying to gather facts here, Dax. Did they do anything or say anything that caused you to be suspicious of *anything*?"

Dax stared up for a moment. A hundred images were whirling through his mind. "The ones that spoke English to me did so just fine. Like native Americans. Except one."

"This Tasha," said Hicks.

"Yes. Her accent was thick. Not hugely thick, but noticeable. Dauer would say certain words that maybe had a tiny accent of sorts, but nothing to make anyone suspect anything out of the ordinary. Kimball, the fat guy, and Michael Staggs, they both talked like they were born here. Oh, and what's his name ... Jeremy, the dude on the kitchen floor, he sounded pretty normal. There were other characters I saw here and there but I never heard them talk."

"Like the one they called Leo," said Hicks.

"That's right. Never heard his voice."

"And you saw them all at the Sutter Hotel?" Decker asked.

"Yeah. Hey, speaking of which, my car is still parked near my work."

"You took a cab to the Sutter?"

"Yeah."

Hicks jotted some notes down. "Where'd you park your car and what does it look like?"

Dax gave him the make, model, year, and plates.

"We'll check it," said Hicks. "So, then the cabby drove you to the Sutter? No stops?"

"No stops. Dropped me off down the street. I had a light dinner first nearby." He described the place and the waitress with the arm band.

"Okay." Hicks studied his notes. "After prepping you, they drove you to the Omni?"

"Yes. Dropped me off two and a half blocks or so from it."

"Can you show us where exactly that was?"

Dax closed his eyes. "I could show you if we were there."

"Who drove you?"

"Well, Jack was there, of course. Then Michael Staggs joined."

"You were all in the back seat?"

"Yeah. Didn't see the driver."

"Can you give us as much detail as you can about the vehicle?"

Dax did his best to describe the large, dark, government-style sedan. Then a thought suddenly hit him. "Oh my gosh!" He slapped his forehead.

They all looked up. "Yes?" said Decker.

"This warehouse." Dax snapped his fingers several times. "That's where I had my first meeting with them."

Parker began scribbling on the pad in front of him.

"Okay. Where was this warehouse? Do you remember a name or what it looked like?" asked Decker.

Dax closed his eyes again. He was tired. "Uhm … it had the name, Genady. I don't know how it's pronounced – g, e, n, a, d, y."

"*Gn-ah-jie,*" Milevoi said, with correct pronunciation.

"Do you remember where, what street it was on?" Hicks asked.

Dax shook his head.

Hicks looked at Decker, then at Parker. Parker shrugged.

Sergeant Donnelly clicked at his keyboard for a few seconds then looked up and shook his head. "No warehouse with that registered name around here."

Milevoi looked up from her notes. "Unbelievable," she muttered. Dax ignored her, so did everyone else.

"Try to remember, take your time," said Decker.

Dax plowed through his mushy thoughts. "I-I don't know."

Hicks tapped the table impatiently. It had been a long night and he knew they were pushing the tired and wounded Dax about as much as possible. They all waited silently, even Milevoi.

After a few moments Dax said, "It was the first real meeting I had with him since the initial one at the theatre."

"This Jack Dauer," said Hicks.

"Yes. I met him at a Starbucks and then we drove there. He drove me there. He and Al Kimball."

"Sounds like a lot of *clandestine* activity," said Milevoi, putting her pencil down. "Meetings in coffee shops, going off to warehouses that don't exist."

Dax opened his eyes but looked at Hicks. "You think? Check this out—we had a code when we met in public places. He would wear a Groucho Marx disguise and say, '*the eagle flies at midnight*.'"

"Come on, Dax," said Hicks.

Dax swore he saw Decker suppress a quick smile, but otherwise she remained serious. Milevoi glared like she wanted to be the next person this evening to point a gun at Dax.

Hicks tapped his pencil again. "We need to check this place out," he said. "We need to at least find the building."

"I know, I know," said Dax.

"Just focus," Hicks said in a calm voice. "Imagine yourself in the car and on your way over there."

Dax leaned back. After a few seconds, "Sansome. It was near Sansome, north end out of the business district. Not actually on it, but off it."

Sergeant Donnelly was pecking away again at his laptop.

Parker leaned forward. "Closer to the piers?"

Dax shook his head. "I'm really not sure."

They exchanged glances.

"There are a few places around there," said Hicks. "Some small warehouses off Clay near Sansome."

"And more off Battery," said Parker.

"How many blocks off Sansome?"

Dax shook his head. "One, I think. But I'm not positive."

"But you know for sure it wasn't actually on Sansome?" asked Decker.

Dax felt a serious headache coming on. "Yes. Well, no, I'm not completely sure of anything at this point. I remember glancing out the window and seeing we were on Sansome and then I remember the car turning."

"But you don't know what direction you were going?" asked Parker.

"Uh … north maybe."

"Right turn or left?"

Dax laughed and threw his hands up. "I really don't know."

Sergeant Donnelly looked up. "There's nothing resembling the name *Genady* in that area, or in the whole city for that matter. Businesses I mean. But there's a few Gennady's, with two n's, that live in the city. Seems to be a fairly common name."

"Do a check on Gennady's with either one or two n's that own businesses. Any kind of business," Decker said. She looked at Dax. "Would you remember what the place looked like?"

Dax closed his eyes again. "I think so. Like I said, there was a sign with big white letters in all caps that said the name of the place. I remember it looked kind of old, not that great a place. But freshly painted."

"Freshly painted," Milevoi said slowly, as if this were a huge and obvious clue.

"Yeah," Dax continued. "Smelled like fresh paint once we were inside. Had a yellow cover thing over the doorway, what do you call it."

"An awning," Milevoi said.

"Right. Yeah, that."

"Dax," said Hicks, "if we were to take you around that area, could you recognize the building again?"

Dax nodded. "Yeah, shouldn't be too hard. If it's still there."

"If the building is still there?" asked Milevoi.

Dax ignored her. His shoulder was throbbing again. "Could I get an aspirin or something?"

"Sure, Dax," said Hicks.

"I'm not sure Amy would approve of aspirin," said Decker.

"Aleve then?" asked Dax.

"Sorry, no blood thinners right now."

"Heroin?" Dax suggested. They all ignored the quip.

Decker set her pen down and turned to Agent Milevoi. "Michelle, would you please get Dax some Tylenol?" Her voice carried the tone of a schoolteacher.

Milevoi's eyes searched the area of the table immediately in front of her. Finding nothing, she slowly pushed her chair back, stood, and strode out of the room.

"I'm not spending the night here, right?" Dax asked. He glanced up at the clock on the wall. It was 11:48 p.m.

"Yes. We need you for the investigation," said Decker bluntly.

Dax's eyes widened. "Am I under arrest? You should have told me to call my attorney or something."

"Do you have an attorney?" Decker asked.

Dax snorted tiredly. "No."

Hicks placed his hands on the table. "Dax, we've got notes from the events of tonight. We believe what you did was in self-defense."

Dax waved his good arm. "Well there's a start. Do you know who this guy was, this *Vassi* who tried to kill me?"

Hicks looked down. Dax glanced around and sensed they had a whole lot of information they weren't about to divulge.

Decker smiled, it was actually a warm smile. "You'll be filled in on certain things as we go along."

"Great. Now you sound like Jack Dauer. How about my car?" he asked. "What if it gets stolen?"

Hicks looked back up. "Let's not worry about that right now. You're parked on a busy street, should be okay. Like I said, we'll check it out." A pause. "Dax, how well can you remember faces?"

"Jack's face? I've seen quite a lot of it."

"Yeah, and Michael Staggs and Tasha and some of those other characters."

Dax sighed. "Pretty good, I guess. I don't know."

"Tomorrow we're going to have you sit down with a sketch artist."

Dax shrugged. "I can try."

"Just do the best you can."

Milevoi returned with a bottle of Tylenol and placed it in front of Dax without a word. The headache was pounding now, and his shoulder was burning. Fumbling with the bottle, he poured four, then a fifth small white cylinder-shaped tablet in his hand. He plopped all five in his mouth and swallowed hard with a gulp from his water bottle.

He wasn't completely aware of everything that happened in the next few minutes. His mind was receding quickly into that corner where the brain goes to escape and shut down. He was asked a few more questions but his answers, apparently not satisfying anymore, caused the meeting to end.

Hicks and Parker helped Dax to his feet and escorted him out. As they walked, the floor and cube walls blurred by in slow motion. The whole place was darker and quieter now. He was led down two hallways and into an elevator. They existed down another hallway to a room with a thick and heavy door. The room was sparse and had just a small desk bolted to the wall, a metal frame bed, and a light on the ceiling encased in a thick, glass dome. He was shown a small metal plate mounted on the wall next to the door, an intercom with small holes in the shape of a circle for a speaker. If he needed anything, just press the button and someone would be there to talk to.

Dax looked around. This was a holding cell. The reality that he'd killed a man swept over him once more and made him shutter.

Someone asked him to remove his belt. He thought he heard Hicks tell him to get some sleep and everything was going to be okay. He mumbled something and nodded. A minute or so later the light was off, he was under the blanket, and his head was sinking into the pillow. He was vaguely aware of someone standing in the doorway observing him. His body became heavier and his mind was sinking into darkness when he heard the loud click of the door locking. It actually made him feel safer. Blackness closed in on his thoughts as he succumbed to sleep.

26: Everyone Has a Price

A noise made his eyes pop open. Dax found himself staring sideways at a wall and the edge of a table he didn't recognize. His mind struggled to piece things together. Another thump and then a buzzer, a rattle of keys and a loud click.

Dax sat up and instantly felt his shoulder burn. So intense was the pain that he could only groan and slump back down. There were also new, searing pains swirling about his body, places on his ribs and back, the side of his face.

The room was lit with a warm grayish light that looked natural. Craning his head up, he saw a small window near the ceiling with crisscrossing bars. A rush of thoughts and memories of yesterday filled his mind. He was in a detention cell of some kind at the San Francisco FBI building.

I killed a man last night.

With a crack and a small thud, the door opened. Dax made a second effort to sit up, but then slouched against the wall. In the doorway stood a tall woman he recognized as Amy, the part-time nurse and part-time field agent. Behind her, an older man peered in at him.

Amy smiled warmly at Dax. "How are you feeling, Dax?"

Dax ran a dry tongue around the inside of his mouth. He had to pee. He started to speak and was surprised at how horse he sounded. "I've felt better."

Amy turned around and nodded to the man behind her. He stared at Dax for another second or two then disappeared.

Amy approached the bed. "Can you sit up? I need to have a look."

Dax ran a palm over his face. "How long have I been out?"

"About ten hours maybe. I don't know exactly what time they put you in here. It was after midnight I'm told." She took him by the shoulders, careful to avoid the wound, and eased him up with smooth, graceful strength.

Dax groaned as he twisted to point his bad shoulder at her. He closed his eyes as he felt Amy gently remove the wrapping. The cloth nearest to his skin was soaked with blood and ointments and made a sound like saran wrap as it peeled off.

As Amy recleaned and dressed his shoulder, he sipped from a water bottle and stared about the room trying to ignore the pain. In the corner above the door was a small dark colored half-dome mounted to the wall. A security camera.

"What time is it?"

Amy glanced at her watch. "Going on a quarter to eleven." She snugly completed the wrapping. "No infection. Healing nicely. You're very fortunate."

"Well *doctor* Hicks said I wouldn't be needing a hospital."

"Well, I said you might." She touched his forehead. "No fever." She pulled a small bottle out of her kit and snapped the lid open.

Dax held his hand open and Amy tapped two tablets out.

"Mind if I take three or four? Both my head and shoulder are killing me. Maybe something stronger?"

"I don't want you to have anything right now that depends on a full stomach." She tapped a third pill into his hand. "The headache is from dehydration. That'll go away soon. But let's leave it at three for now."

"Yes, Ma'am."

"Give it another twelve hours. If there's no pain or symptoms of infection, you can remove the bandage yourself. If an infection does crop up, you'll need to get checked in to a real hospital. And don't take a shower until that gets removed, okay? You don't want the bandage wet."

"Yes, Ma'am."

She stood to go, then paused by the door. "You okay?"

Dax smiled again. "For now. Thanks for everything." He could really fall for a girl like her. She was a lovely, simple combination of so many positive things but without anything exaggerated or over the top.

Dax was still wearing the suit pants and dress socks but had slept shirtless. The room temperature had been kept reasonably warm and he'd been fine under the blankets, but now a dull chill was creeping in.

The door was ajar but there were individuals loitering about. A few minutes later the same older man returned and introduced himself as Agent Farley. Farley was maybe in his early-sixties and his nearly shaved head was covered in a paper-thin mat of gray hair. He had a hard stare and serious expression. His maroon-colored tie was knotted in a neat Full Windsor and pulled snug to the neck. He held a bulging plastic bag.

Dax looked around on the ground for his shoes but didn't see them.

Farley was watching him. "Don't worry about your shoes," he said. "You'll get 'em back."

"Those were kinda pricey, I was hoping I could keep them."

Farley watched with little expression.

"To impress my next date. Hopeful Nurse Amy."

Farley continued to stare, no hint of humor. He then motioned with head to say, *let's go.*

As they walked down the hall, Dax said, "I need to use the bathroom."

"That's where we're going," was all Farley would say.

They entered an elevator—Dax shuffling along in his dress socks and Farley in his shiny, leather flat-toe cap shoes. The elevator took them down to the basement level. There, Dax was shown a large restroom. On one side were at least ten stalls and on the other, a doorway that led to a shower room. One shower could be heard running. Next to the doorway, a large rolling stainless steel basket was filled with freshly washed and folded towels.

Farley handed him the bag, nodded toward the stalls, then took a seat near the door while unfolding a newspaper. Inside the bag was a traveler's toothbrush and toothpaste, a small deodorant, a shaving razor and can of shaving cream, a comb, and a new jogging suit.

It took Dax all of about twenty minutes to take advantage of the toilet facilities. He put his head under the faucet and scrubbed at his hair. Using a small towel, he wiped his body down with hot water, carefully avoiding the bandage. It felt good. It also felt good to shave. At one point he stopped and stared in the mirror. The swelling and bruises on the left side of his face looked awful. The jogging outfit was bright blue with white stripes; a little large, but otherwise comfortable. It had no logos of any kind, but Dax noticed the "Made in the USA" tag on the inside of the jacket.

Agent Farley handed Dax a pair of running shoes and white athletic socks. He made sure Dax put the remaining clothes he'd been given the night before in the plastic bag.

They rode the elevator to the third floor and when the door opened the smell of food and coffee hit Dax's nose deliciously strong. Down the hall and to the right, they entered a cafeteria, and a hunger pang punched Dax in the gut.

Spacious and bright, one wall was a row of large windows that provided a nice midmorning view of Golden Gate Avenue. Traffic was light and a dull overcast shed a gray but vivid, diffused light over everything. The floor space was strewn with round tables and chairs.

Farley told Dax he could order whatever he wanted, standard breakfast stuff, and ten minutes later Dax was looking at two plates with a stack of three pancakes, two scrambled eggs, five slices of bacon, and two English muffins. Farley casually read a newspaper nearby while Dax greedily gobbled it down. Afterwards, he asked for a coffee to-go and was given one.

Back in the elevator, they now stopped at the tenth floor and exited. Dax was ushered into a small conference room with a simple table that could comfortably fit five or six chairs. The walls of the room were a plain, beige color, no pictures or monitors. At the far end was a large window that was currently covered by closed, vertical blinds that shown a pale-yellow color as they blocked the sunlight.

A moment later a figure appeared in doorway; he held what looked like a small metal box with a clip mechanism on one end holding a couple sheets of paper.

"This is Jones," Farley said. "Jones, Dax Ribeiro. I'll be back in a bit." And with that, Farley was gone.

Jones stepped into the room and took a seat across from Dax. "Mr. Ribeiro," he said with professional courtesy while putting some things on the table.

Jones was in his early forties and wore a plain, off-white dress shirt and a light blue tie with black stripes. He had a nerdy, pudgy face and donned round, thin wire glasses over small eyes that appeared to be disproportionately too close to the sides of his nose. His hair was a dark brown with corkscrew curls.

"Are you the sketch artist?" Dax asked.

"I am," Jones said, looking up and pushing his glasses a little further up the bridge of his nose. "There are three individuals we're going to focus on this morning. Let's start with the woman you say was called Tasha." He leaned back in his chair and put the metal box on his lap.

Dax also leaned back, holding his coffee.

"Okay," Jones said, getting his pencil and paper positioned. "Let's start with the general shape of the head and hair style. Does she have a long head, a round head, a heart-shaped face? What is the length of her hair – is it straight, wavy, curly?"

For the next few minutes, Dax did the best he could to describe from memory things like "how tall" her forehead was, the color of her hair and where it was parted. He then described the eyebrows; how thick, how they arch, how close together. And then on to the eyes; are they wide-set, close-set, clear, dark, what color and shade. Then the nose, the bone, bridge; does the bone start thick and go to thin, how long. Then to the mouth, how full are the lips, how wide. How about the chin, is it pointed, round and so on and so forth.

Dax found the whole process more difficult than he would have imagined. In retrospect, it was Tasha's eyes that had kept his attention, so he remembered the most about them. Jones told him most of facial recognition comes from the areas of the face right around the eyes. The other parts of Tasha's body that he'd stolen glances at were indeed somewhere in the memory cells, but not at all as clear. After a while, and with some post-tweaks, Jones had a decent facsimile of her.

They repeated the same process with the men called Jack Dauer and Michael Staggs and by the time it was over, Dax was tired of trying to recall details of people's appearances.

After a restroom break and back on the thirteen floor, Dax found himself in the same conference room he'd spent the better part of last night. This time one of the wall monitors was on and a local San Francisco news station was broadcasting the headlines. He sipped his coffee and watched for a few minutes waiting for the story of last night's events at the Omni Hotel.

The door opened and Agent Tommy Hicks and Special Agent in Charge, Sharon Decker, entered. Today Hicks sported navy blue slacks and a white shirt. Decker wore an attractive, dark colored, almost black pinstriped skirt and jacket.

"How are you feeling this morning, Dax?" asked Hicks.

"Been better."

"Amy take good care of you?" asked Decker.

"She did," Dax said, his voice betraying an intrigue he felt for the in-house nurse.

Decker gave him a knowing smile. "You look rested," she said, picking up a small remote on the table, aiming it at the monitor and clicking it off.

"I am, somewhat. Thanks for breakfast and the new outfit."

"You can keep it," Hicks said.

"How about my James Bond gig?"

"We're still looking at it, but you'll put putting it back on shortly."

Dax looked at them, eyebrows raised. "I will be?"

Hicks sat and sipped from a tall Styrofoam cup, eyeing Dax.

Dax smirked but stopped when it made his ribs ache. "This secret agent stuff isn't what it's cracked up to be. Glad I won't be doing that again, unless I get the women and the Aston Martin with all the cool gadgets."

"You watch too many movies, Dax," said Hicks.

"So I've been told."

Decker looked up from some notes she had in a folder. "Actually, Dax, that's what we're here to talk about."

"About what?"

"About you *doing this* again." She and Hicks stared at Dax in a way that instantly made him uncomfortable.

Dax shook his head. "No, I'm done."

"Maybe not," said Decker.

"Not even if you offered twice the money Jack Dauer did, which wasn't bad, by the way."

Hicks smiled. "Yeah? How much more would it take?"

Dax paused for a moment, but knew Hicks and Decker were not offering him money. "Not interested."

"Everyone has a price, Dax."

"What price is that?"

"Your life," Decker said, and leaned back, swiftly folding a leg over the other.

Dax held up his hands. "Okay. First off, am I still under arrest?"

Hicks watched Dax for a moment, then asked, "Aren't you curious about the man you shot last night?"

Dax looked at him for a moment. He'd been trying not to think about that. "Is he dead?"

Hicks nodded.

"Who is he, or was he?"

"We haven't ID-ed him yet," Hicks said shrugging.

"Why not?"

"A couple individuals claiming to be SFPD forensic investigators hurried into the hospital right after the man you say was called Vassi was declared dead. Said they needed the body *A-SAP*. Put it in a wagon and took off. When our people got there and names and descriptions were given, SFPD said they'd never heard of them."

Dax just stared, his eyebrows furrowed. "So I'm not the only one getting conned around here," he said. "Well, good luck figuring it all out. I've done all I can. I'll be going now if we're done."

Hicks leaned back and looked at Decker.

After a pause, she said, "Technically, you were never under arrest. You're being detained pending the investigation. But getting arrested depends on you."

Dax looked back and forth between the two agents at the other end of the table. "I don't like the sound of that. If I'm not under arrest, then thanks again for breakfast and I'm outta here."

Hicks held out a hand, palm up. "Actually, we are kinda holding you here."

"Come on, guys. Why exactly can't I leave? I've told you absolutely everything I can possibly remember. I've held back nothing. If we go out there, I can show you where I was dropped by the Omni. Then maybe I can find where this Genady or *ge-nah-jie* warehouse is. Then that's it."

Decker folded her hands in front of her. She deliberately sounded very calm. "For starters, it can't be known you were *here* at all."

27: Double Agent

Dax sighed deeply. He was tired of this kind of talk. "Well, if I'm not officially under arrest, then I'll just bid you two *adieu*. Or should I say, *do svidaniya*." He started to stand.

"Sit down, Dax," said Hicks. Then after a pause added, "*Please.*"

Decker was staring hard.

"Tell you what," said Dax, "if there's anything else I could have possibly missed from last night, I'm happy to spill now. I *knowingly* committed no crime. I think you guys know that or I'd be in cuffs right now."

"Relax, Dax," said Hicks. He pushed his coffee aside and opened a folder on the table. "Let me spill a little to you now, for your information. Your suspicions were correct; we did have a … *presence* there last night. At the Omni." He paused and looked back up at Dax. "We pretty much know everything that happened last night, at least in terms of the events that went down."

"So you know who those people are then."

Hicks nodded. "We know who some of them are."

"Like this is all part of some on-going investigation then?"

Hicks looked at Decker who said, "Something like that."

"Well good then," said Dax. "I've done my part. You're welcome. Look, I don't want to know any more about these people. I don't care anymore who Jack Dauer or Michael Staggs are." He paused, suddenly thinking of Meygan Knight. He felt his face flush a little with warmth. He'd been so focused on the fear and pain, he'd totally forgotten mentioning seeing her last night, and still didn't think he should. He first wanted to know why she was there before sending the FBI after her. He looked up and saw Hicks and Decker watching him and knew his eyes betrayed deep thought. He quickly diverted. "How's that girl, by the way?"

Hicks watched for a moment, then asked, "The little brunette you steamrolled outside the restroom?"

"Yeah, the *little brunette* who threw a very sharp object at my face."

"Looked like she'll be fine. At least she looked that way as a couple individuals helped her out of the place."

Dax thought for a moment. The room fell silent as Decker and Hicks waited for him to say something. He tried to change the feeling hanging in the air.

"The bar there is magnificent," said Dax.

"Say again?" said Hicks.

"The bar. In the Babylon. It's gorgeous. I'm sure you know that. But that bartender, he was up to something."

Hicks and Decker exchanged glances.

"How do you mean?" asked Decker.

Dax shrugged. "He just kept looking at me like he was trying to figure out who I was."

A few more seconds of silence ticked away. They were waiting for Dax to make a move and it was making him nervous. "So, who was she?" he finally asked. "The knife thrower."

Decker watched him carefully before saying, "Thought you didn't want to know anything more about them."

"Right, forgot. I don't." Dax took a large sip of his coffee. In truth he was quite curious about a number of things, but red flags were going off in his gut. He decided to shut up and put the ball back in their court. Suddenly, he sat up, patting himself. "You said last night you found my stuff at the Sutter, right?"

Hicks spoke. "Yes. In room five-oh-nine, just like you said. Doesn't look like anything was taken. I was going to mention that last night, but you looked delirious, and never asked." He took another sip of coffee while keeping his eyes on Dax. "Parker will be here in a few minutes and give it all back. We also found your Mustang. Still parked a couple blocks from your workplace. Nothing out of the ordinary."

Dax felt a rush of relief. "No bugs, no tracking devices on it?"

Hicks' eyebrows raised. "On the car? No."

"That camera on my back, Jack told me it had GPS. So if I got kidnapped they'd be able to track me," Dax said.

"We remember you saying that." Decker said. "But it was disabled. Not broadcasting. We're going to use that to our advantage."

"How do you mean?"

"I mean, Jack Dauer, or whoever he is, doesn't know where you are right now. As well, your cell phone never left the Sutter Hotel."

"But it's on its way over here now," Dax said.

"We've completely powered it off." Hicks said.

Dax felt his pulse began to quicken. "I don't follow." He said this even though a sinking feeling told him he was. "They've got eyes everywhere," he offered.

"There may be some truth to that," said Decker. "But we're pretty sure none of them know you're here."

"Maybe they had electronic gadgets in my shoes or jacket or something," said Dax.

"We already checked," said Hicks. "They're clean. Even the belt. We're checking your pants now. We should have done that last night, but it's unlikely anything's there. Even if it was, this building blocks all radio frequencies in and out. Normally it's the shoes."

"Is that thing that was on my back still intact?"

"No, it's ruined. But we're going to find out where it was made and all that."

"Did it record or just broadcast? Jack told me it was strictly a broadcasting device."

"We don't know that yet. Why?"

Dax shrugged. "I dunno." A long pause, then he asked, "So where could I possibly be after what went down last night? Either here or the San Francisco police station."

"Exactly," said Hicks. "That's what you're going to tell them."

Now Dax's heart was starting to thud. He was tired of these fear-fueled adrenaline rushes. "*I'm* going to tell them?"

Hicks leaned forward, a serious look on his face. "Yep."

Dax shook his head. "*This* double-oh seven," he pointed at himself, "is officially retired."

A cynical smile formed on Hicks' mouth. "Not quite yet."

"Now hold on—"

"Dax," Decker interjected. "We're in the middle of a big investigation. One that's been ongoing for some time."

Dax leaned back and looked up at the ceiling, which suddenly looked lower. "I'm really not interested in your investigation."

"Maybe so, but you're now officially a *part* of the investigation," said Decker.

"How?"

Hicks leaned back. "How? Dax, you're right in the middle of this. You've met key players. You're on the inside. You worked for them. You've been closer to them in the last few days than we've been in months."

"I had no idea who I was working for, as it turns out."

"Correct. But that's not the point now," Decker said.

"You want me to go back to them, pretend I'm still in their game. Play double agent?"

"You're good, Dax," said Hicks. He picked up his coffee and took a long gulp.

"No, I'm not good," Dax said shaking his head. "Look how I screwed up last night. They'll kill me. I'll end up like Leo and Jeremy Forrester."

"You didn't really screw up, from what you told us and from what we know now," said Hicks. "There were some unexpected things that happened."

"*Unexpected?*"

"That's undercover work for you. You never know. Besides, we'll be there watching."

"Yeah? That's the kind of reassurance Jack gave me."

"Dax," said Decker. The sternness in her voice made his eyes jerk to her. "Having you show up last night like you did and the resulting revelations in this case has been a huge break. You gave us names and leads and descriptions we didn't have before."

"Okay, look. I took what I thought was a legitimate job and was deceived." Dax didn't care he was now repeating himself.

"Correct. And now we need to roll with what happened, use it to our advantage."

"*We?*"

"We need more intel, Dax," said Hicks.

"I've given you all the intel I have."

"We need more."

"Like what?" An image of Meygan Knight in her red party dress flashed through his mind again. His eyes darted to the floor.

Hicks leaned back and was watching Dax carefully. "Well for starters, you've given us great descriptions and we've got sketches now, but we'd like pictures, video, voice samples, if possible. We need to know who this Jack Dauer is and who's working with him. And more importantly, who he's working for. We also want to know who made the hit on Jack's people last night at the Sutter. Whoever they were, they were pros. And we need more about this *sah-vah-kah*, dog character too."

Dax rubbed his nose. "So what, is some war going on between these people?"

A pause, then Decker spoke. "We're still gathering details. For your part, this is an incredible opportunity that we can't pass up. And we need to move fast."

"Well, I'll pass it up."

"I don't think so," said Decker as she closed the folder and folded her hands in front of her. "We think you'll want to cooperate." Her voice was starting to take on a threatening tone, but a phony one. Dax knew well vocal tones made to intimidate, and there were plenty of actresses that could do it better than Decker. But while actors fake internal motivators, Decker was being genuinely serious.

The room fell silent for a good ten seconds. Dax considered his situation and wondered whether or not they were bluffing. Could they really make him do this? Maybe they could, and the thought scared him. He decided then and there to stoop to begging. Maybe *his* acting skills could come in handy here. He put on a calm but timid voice and spoke slowly. "Look, I'm telling you, I can't do anymore good here."

"You're wrong," said Decker, a little more gently this time. "You're in the perfect position to help. You were brought into their world by invitation and even taught some of their moves. You wore their equipment and met, face-to-face, people they associate with. Like Hicks said, you've gotten closer than our best intelligence teams have in months of work."

Dax let his eyes wander the room. Here came the moment. "And if I refuse?" he asked slowly.

Decker stared hard, then switched back to her harsh voice. "A lot happened last night, *David*. There was a lot of confusion. Might be difficult to sort out certain details. We may need to hold on to you for a while during the investigation."

Dax shook his head. "You can't do that."

"Actually, we can," Decker said.

Dax stood. "Unbelievable!"

Hicks started to stand. "Sit down, Dax."

"How long could you possibly keep me here?"

"As long as it takes," said Decker, coldness now in her voice. "Actually, most of your day will be in a cell at San Francisco County. We're a five-star hotel by comparison."

"To figure what out? Why I had to kill a man? I defended myself—that's it!" Dax knew he sounded desperate but didn't care.

Decker sighed. "You're not listening to us, Dax. We already have those details."

Dax rested his hands on the table, feeling once again, like a scared, cornered cat ready to swipe at anything.

Decker continued. "You did more than you think."

Dax pointed a finger at Decker. "This is coercion!"

"I wouldn't call it that."

"Well I would! What crime have I committed?"

"Well let's see …" Decker tapped her fingers. "You dressed up like an Eastern European fugitive gangster who apparently is supposed to be dead, at the behest of people illegally impersonating federal officers, and were hanging out at a party sponsored by international underground criminals. *Then* someone got shot by a gun you happened to have in your possession while running from the crime scene."

"When I thought I was working for the FBI!"

"No need to go over all that again."

"I'll sue. I'll get a lawyer to ream you and the whole FBI."

Decker leaned back and appeared unfazed. "The evidence would be against you if we … went in that direction. This is a federal investigation and you're still a suspect. We have every right to do anything we deem necessary."

Dax sat back down and shook his head. He wanted to cry but instead started to laugh. "I don't believe this. I thought you were the good guys."

Decker tried to soften her tone again but remained stern. "We are. And so are you. That's why you're going to help us get these bad guys."

"*Help* you," Dax said with as much sarcasm as he could muster.

"Help your country," Hicks offered.

Dax laughed sarcastically. "I've heard that one before. Pretty recently."

"And help yourself," said Decker.

Dax glared up at her. "Screw you."

Decker remained steady and unwavering. "Dax, I'm sorry. I really am. But we can't let this one pass. We need you."

Dax tapped on the table with each word. "You'd actually put my life back in danger. Screw the FBI. I'm calling a lawyer."

Decker let out a big sigh, looked at Hicks and nodded. Hicks moved his chair closer to Dax and took on the most calm and sympathetic tone his voice could convey. "Alright Dax, you got us."

Dax looked up. "Huh?"

"You're right, we can't make you. And no, we would not force you to do something dangerous. You wanna walk? Then walk."

Dax stared at Agent Tommy Hicks for a moment and then turned to look at Decker, whose eyes were on the table. "Normally it's good cop, bad cop. But what is it here – two bad cops, then suddenly two good cops?"

"Dax," Decker said, shifting to a voice of reason tone. "Understand something. Your life is already in danger. If you walked out right now, do you really think you could just return to your normal life?" She snapped her fingers on the word *return*. "Do you think these people will just walk away while a big, no, make that a *huge* loose end like you is still running around?" She paused for effect. "They've no idea what you've said or who you've said it to. They're professionals. Eliminating you would be top of their list." Another pause. "Do you understand what I'm telling you?"

Unfortunately, she had a point. Dax just stared at the blank monitor on the wall. "I was told there would be no danger. Or little chance of it anyway." He was more babbling to himself now.

"All that's in the past," said Decker. "We move forward now."

"This isn't fair," said Dax, trying to suppress a whiny tone.

"No, it isn't. But this is the hand you've been dealt, Dax," said Hicks.

"Gee, thanks, dad."

"Hey, you wanted to work for the FBI, now you really are."

Dax glared at Hicks, who put his hands up. "Okay, okay, sorry," Hicks said.

Decker stood and walked to the end of the table and sat near Dax. Her perfume hit him in a light breeze. It was pleasant but not as appeasing as Tasha's. "You were put in a terrible and dangerous situation—"

"And *somehow,* I got out of it alive." Dax wouldn't look up at her.

"You're our best option. And frankly, helping us now is your only way out. This won't end until the people involved in all this are taken out."

Dax laughed bitterly. Decker stood, glanced at Hicks, then turned and walked back to the end of the table.

There was a knock at the door and Agent Roy Parker entered. He carried a plastic bag with folded clothes Dax recognized as his own from last night. He also had a hanger with the bloody and soiled suit. It still looked somewhat elegant despite what it had been through.

Parker walked to the end of the table where Dax was and set them down. He regarded Dax for a moment, then produced a wallet which he placed next to the clothes. Tapping it lightly with a couple fingers, he said, "Looks like nothing was taken. And here," he said holding up an object, "is your phone. We've added a little something in it to make it easier for us to pinpoint you." He handed Hicks the phone, which was in two pieces along with a square-shaped battery.

Dax stared at his clothes and said nothing. Parker set the Gucci shoes on the floor. On his way to the door, he handed Hicks a folder and nodded in Dax's direction. Hicks gave him a wink and a thumbs-up.

Decker gathered her papers and stood to follow Parker out. "We'll talk again soon, Dax."

Hicks opened the folder and perused a document that was in it. Finally, he looked up and said, "Perfect. You spent the night downtown at SFPD."

Dax looked up and said dryly, "Is that so."

Hicks tapped the paper with his palm. "Yep. Says it right here, by officer Cesar Hernandez, who was running intake last night. You were brought down to the station last night under suspicious circumstances. But you were released the next morning after no evidence of any wrongdoing could be found."

"Nice. At least someone knows I'm innocent."

Hicks watched Dax for a moment, a half-smile on his lips. "There's a restroom down the hall. I need you to change back into your party suit. Then we roll."

"Where are we going?"

"To get your car."

"Thought you were going to hold me here."

"No time for that. The wheels are set in motion with the whole police station story. Here, I have something for you." Out of a pocket, he produced a blank, white business card with something scribbled on it and handed it to Dax.

Dax took the card and examined it. On it was a telephone number with several digits in front of it. "What's this?"

"A number you can call. It's unregistered, encrypted, and can't be traced."

Dax stared dumbly at the table. "They'll start triangulating my whereabouts as soon as my phone's powered on."

"Correct. We're counting on that. We'll move quickly. They won't be able to tell you were here. First, we'll go by the SFPD station downtown and wait a few minutes while we turn your phone on."

"Why?"

"Because part of your story is that the police were called to a shooting that happened at the Sutter Hotel. There, they found your clothes, wallet and cell phone and brought it to the station. They gave it all back to you upon your release. But we're hoping not to have to go that route."

"What do you mean?"

"If your personal belongings were found at the scene of a multiple murder, do you really think they'd let you out the next morning? If you were some rich guy with a fancy lawyer and no formal charges pressed yet, then maybe. Otherwise, you'd still be there getting questioned. But try to find out what Jack Dauer knows."

"What's the other story?"

"That you took them with you to the Babylon Ballroom. That you disobeyed their instructions and had them with you the whole time."

"But if they were watching my phone's signal then they'd know that wasn't true."

"We're hoping they were more focused on their own equipment they gave you."

"Hoping?"

"Dax, we have to take a few chances here. No choice."

"Easy for you to say." Dax slowly stood to stretch, feeling aches that were too much for over-the-counter drugs to cover up. "So I can't get back into my regular clothes?"

"No, not yet. You spent the night at the police station dressed in your party outfit, remember? They might be watching by the time you get back to your car. Make like anyone normally would after an ordeal like this. You go home, take a shower, relax."

Dax sighed deeply. "So, I have an arrest record now."

Hicks waved it off. "No worries. We'll take care of that after this is all over."

"*If* I do what you tell me. And if I survive."

"You'll be fine." Hicks closed the folder, picked up his coffee and stood.

Dax picked up the hanger, his clothes and wallet. "You keep giving me the same BS Jack did."

He exited the conference room and started down the hall. He would leave the blue jogging suit in the bathroom—they could keep it.

He might keep the sneakers though.

28: Counselor Kimball

They rode in silence through downtown toward Dax's work building, Hicks driving and Parker in the passenger seat. Because it was Saturday, traffic was light in the financial district as they weaved their way through the streets.

Dax stared out the window rubbing his shoulder. It was still painful but not throbbing. The suit didn't feel nice like it did last night. The smooth material, which now stank like dried blood, sweat, and gun powder, brought to mind ugly thoughts and feelings.

The events at the Babylon Ballroom raced through his mind. He could still see the face of Meygan Knight looking at him, wide-eyed and frightened. He saw the inside the bathroom—the stalls, the mirrors, the bottles of hand soap and lotion on the sink. He could hear that horrible silencer echoing off the walls. He could see the man's face twisted in pain and rage as the bullet penetrated his body.

What in God's good name were you doing there, Meygan?

Feelings of fear and guilt were creeping over Dax as the reality he'd taken another's life settled itself even deeper into his soul. He shook his head and changed his thoughts to the instructions Hicks had given him. He was to be dropped off a couple blocks away in case anyone was watching. From there he'd walk to his car, then drive home and wait. He was secretly planning to have a drink later, a big drink.

Jack would make contact soon enough and press him for details. It all hinged on the fact that the camera device had been ruined when it was smashed against the bathroom sink. After that, Jack and his crew would not have seen or heard anything else.

Dax had been puzzled why Decker and Hicks didn't seem to be concerned about what had been broadcasted out of that ballroom. Also, if the real FBI had a *presence* there, how come no one so much had made a phone call when they saw Dax was in danger? Or maybe someone had, but it all had happened so quickly. There was so much they weren't telling him, but then everyone he'd met had been acting that way from the beginning of all this.

Anyway, back to the plan. He'd tell Jack that SFPD had picked him up near the Omni Hotel and he'd spent the night in jail. Utilizing his brilliant acting skills, he'd fooled the police that he'd been nowhere near the Babylon Ballroom. Instead, he'd been attending a different meeting downstairs. He'd seen an ad in the newspaper inviting people to attend a seminar about starting a travel agent networking business. The ad in The San Francisco Chronicle, did in fact exist, as did the meeting, and had been held in a smaller conference room called the Emerald Isle located on the first floor.

When screaming and commotion were heard, Dax had run out into the lobby and was plowed over by a man with bloody clothes who'd come running down the stairs. The two hit the floor and the man, thrashing and panicking, had torn Dax's clothes and gotten blood on him. Jack wouldn't know Dax had been shot. After that, Dax had run out into the street and made it only a couple blocks when a San Francisco police cruiser saw him and made the arrest.

If Jack asked him about the gun, there was an explanation for that too. Before getting picked up by the cops, Dax had tossed it into one of the potted trees along the sidewalk.

The next morning, he had been released and no charges filed.

A story as such in a city like San Francisco may not seem all that improbable, what with the chaos and overcrowding of holding cells on a Friday night. This made for a quick turnaround of both the innocent and guilty.

If Jack pressed further, there were more details. While in the police station, Dax had neatly avoided all talk about the Sutter Hotel and everything that had happened there.

But how did you get your cell phone back? Jack would ask.

Well, obviously, Dax had disobeyed instructions and took it with him. But if Jack knew Dax's stuff had been left at the hotel, then the story was, the police had responded to a call about a shooting at the Sutter and found his belongings. When they asked him why his personal stuff was there, he would say he'd been robbed at gunpoint earlier that day. The description of the robber just might be similar to Jeremy Forrester. Having no other evidence to hold him, the police had given Dax his belongings back and told him to stay in the city.

Jack would also ask about the camera strapped to his back. Dax would tell him that the cops found it, of course. His story was that he was a spy working for another travel agency business and was there to capture info from their presentation. The device had been broken when he was slammed into by the man coming down the stairs. The cops had taken it for evidence and never gave it back, and Dax had been afraid to ask about it the next morning.

Dax breathed steadily and tried to calm himself.

Hicks pulled the car over, put it in park, and turned around. "Okay, you know where we are. One block up, take a right, two more blocks—"

"Yes, I know."

Hicks snapped the square battery back into Dax's cell phone and handed it to him. "Good luck. We'll be in contact shortly."

Dax pocketed his phone then opened the door and stepped out. "So now I'm being watched by two parties, both claiming to be the FBI, both claiming to be the *good* guys. And both screwing me."

"A lot of good is going to come of this, Dax," Hicks said.

Dax waved it off. "Or a lot of bad, to me."

He started up the street, the plastic bag in his hand. He noticed right away that the Gucci loafers didn't feel quite as comfortable. They constricted his feet a little more, and the inside bottoms of the shoes felt stiff, like he was walking on a hardwood floor.

Dax pressed forward with his eyes down. He didn't look around like before. He honestly didn't care if anyone was watching. He just wanted to get home and go to sleep, unless a bullet to his head didn't stop him first.

He listened to the traffic as he walked. It wouldn't surprise him if Jack and Michael Staggs suddenly pulled up in a car up and told him to get in. If that happened, he'd probably cuss them out right then and there. A lot of good that'd do, but he'd do it anyway.

He turned a corner and started up toward his Mustang. A couple walking by took one look, ceased chattering and gawked. Dax returned the stare for a second, smirked and continued. What a sight he must be at this time of day on a Saturday, in a bloodied suit and a messed-up face. Must have been some party.

It was good he'd not indulged in any drinks at the Babylon's bar – it was his quick thinking and ability to fight and run that had saved him. Or maybe God had played a role in it. He had prayed, after all. When was the last time he said a sincere prayer anyway? Too long to remember. He decided then and there to start praying more often, even if he wasn't sure anyone was listening.

He looked up and saw his Mustang parked where he'd left it last night, the wheels slightly turned to the curb like he always did. The navy-blue paint glistened in the sharp sunlight. Seeing it brought a moment of comfort, he wasn't sure why. Maybe it was because this was something in his life that hadn't been touched by the activities of the last few days. But then maybe it had. Maybe there was a tracking device attached to the bottom of it. Maybe there was a bomb that would blow him to smithereens as soon as he started the engine.

As Dax approached the car, he instinctively looked around and saw nothing out of the ordinary. He paused at the side of the car and shuddered. It could very well be that Jack and the gang decided Dax was now a liability. There were already dead bodies. Leo's lifeless eyes staring up at the ceiling flashed through his mind again.

On the other hand, Jack would want to know what happened. Now his thoughts drifted to a dark dungeon and him tied to a chair with a bright light in his face. The thought of the implements they'd use for torture made him physically swipe the thought away. It'd be a shame if Tasha was the torturer. No, it'd be Staggs. What a thought …

He held the keys for a moment, took a deep breath, and unlocked the door. With a dull, metallic clunk and a small creak, the door opened.

No bomb. No big boom.

He laughed to himself, but it was a feigned laugh. The fact was, that dark feeling was settling in again. If he got whacked, he'd be little more than collateral damage.

He eased himself into the driver's seat as an ache shot through his shoulder again. Slowly and painfully, he reached for the handle, then swung the heavy door shut with a loud thud. Fumbling with the keys, he managed to find the right one and eased it into the ignition. Glancing quickly in both directions for good measure, just to make sure there were no innocent bystanders in harm's way, he twisted the key. The Mustang's engine churned then roared to life and the inside of the car rumbled and vibrated. He waited a moment, listening to the powerful tremors. "Well, not today, I guess," he muttered to himself.

In a daze, Dax managed to drive himself back to his Post Street apartment. Along the way, he thought of a couple things he would have to do tomorrow. First, he was going to run by his work and grab those brass knuckles Tom Kuka had given him. While there, he'd get that Yahoo address they'd contacted him on though it was probably anonymous and untraceable.

Next, he was going to have to look for two people: Les Abraham and Meygan Knight. He wouldn't call in case someone was listening. Maybe he'd stop by the Treasure Box where Jim Kirkland might be holding last minute auditions for *Wild Hearts*.

He dropped the bag containing his street clothes just inside his apartment door. He vaguely remembered stumbling and briefly looking around. Neither seeing nor hearing anything out of the ordinary, he thought he'd used the restroom, peeled off his worn suit and then crashed on his bed. There was blackness after that and oddly enough, no dreams. At least none he remembered the next morning.

***

Across the street from Dax's apartment, a man in the back seat of a car with dark tinted windows watched as Dax stumbled through the front door.

He picked up a radio and relayed information that the subject was back at his place of residence and still dressed in the clothes he'd worn at the Omni Hotel. The boy looked terrible, injured. Were there any other instructions?

No, just keep an eye out and let us know right away if anyone else is watching or makes contact.

***

The next morning, a Ford Crown Victoria sat across the street from the Northern District San Francisco Police Station on the corner of Fillmore and Turk. This Ford was painted bright yellow and had the word YELLOW decaled on both sides and on top, advertising the city's well-known taxi service.

Inside the cab, a heavy-set man watched from the back seat, his large, round face set on the front door. He used a handkerchief to wipe a thin layer of sweat off his neck.

Yesterday afternoon, they were informed that Dax returned to his apartment close to 4:00 p.m. Their first guess as to where he'd been last night was the police station, but that had to be verified. It was too risky to go to his door as that could have been under surveillance. His phone, which was supposed to be back at the Sutter Hotel, had gone dead and untraceable, presumably found and taken by the police. By the time someone noticed it was powered back up, he was already downtown and heading back to his apartment. They had to confirm where he'd been. Things were getting out of hand.

"Wait here for a few minutes. I'll be back," the man said to the taxi driver.

"Whatever you say," the driver said. "As long as the meter's running."

The big man squeezed himself out and started lumbering across the street. In his hand was a briefcase. He wore baggy, khaki pants and a brown sport coat, hopelessly wrinkled in the back from his body's crushing weight.

He entered the lobby and looked around the large square room. Several oversized benches with no backrests were on the tiled floor, wide enough for multiple people to sit facing opposite sides. A distraught looking young woman was on a payphone against one wall, her cheeks streaked with mascara tears. Two reception windows were at the far end, one had a NEXT WINDOW sign, the other was occupied.

The man approached the window and was met by a middle-aged Black woman, busily writing on some paperwork. Her hair was cropped neatly short, leaving just a half-inch afro with a small line of gray in front across her forehead. The shiny faux gold name tag on her uniform said K. JACKSON.

"Can I help you?" she asked with polite indifference, glancing up and looking the fat man up and down.

The man set his briefcase down and produced a card from his jacket. "My name is Adam Kimball, and a client of mine was arrested on Friday evening and spent the night here." He placed the card into the small tray below the window. The card said, *Cannon Law Firm, LLC, A. Kimball, Attorney at Law.* It had an address on Folsom Street.

Officer Jackson looked at the card for a moment and then asked, "The name?"

"A Mr. David Ribeiro." He spelled out the name. "Also goes by Dax Ribeiro."

Jackson pecked a few keys on her keyboard and studied the screen. "Your client was released yesterday afternoon, Mr. Kimball. No charges were filed." She looked at him curiously, sliding the card back under the glass.

"Can you tell me who the investigating officer or detective was?"

Jackson peered again at her screen, then shook her head. "Doesn't say. Case closed before it even officially opened."

"Did anyone else come asking about him?"

"I don't have that kind of information, Mr. Kimball. Is there anything else I can help you with?"

"No, thank you," Counselor Kimball said as he turned to leave. Breathing heavily, he waddled out the front door, pulled out a cell phone and flipped it open. He dialed a number and called a man who had another business card, one that said *Agent Jack Dauer, Federal Bureau of Investigation.*

29: A Bad Performance

Jim Kirkland stood in the empty lobby leaning against the small bar counter. In his hand was tall cup of coffee he'd hardly touched. He watched the wisps of steam floating off the dark liquid, his mind pondering how he'd been put into this position.

It'd been a very odd morning. First, Aaron Tisdale had come stumbling in paler than a ghost. His clothes looked even more frumpy than usual, and he'd appeared disturbed, his face contorted in deep thought. He'd shuffled by Jim, eyes open but seeing something else. Normally the kid said hi and at least made the attempt to be pleasant. So strange was Aaron's expression that Jim didn't bother to say anything for fear of yanking the young man out of a sleepwalk or something.

Jim never really thought much of Aaron. The kid had issues and quirks and it was obvious he'd never get over them. Over the years, Jim had seen more than a few like Aaron in the theatre arena. After reaching a certain age, these types seem to make resignations of fate about themselves and the role they played in the world. In Aaron's case, he'd never shown a whole lot of self-respect or esteem. He didn't have many friends let alone a girlfriend, or boyfriend, at least none that Jim had ever seen. He seemed to gain a little more weight each year and apparently didn't care about the impressions he made with his appearance. There were some pluses though—Aaron didn't smoke or look like he ever drank or did anything illegal, to Jim's knowledge anyway. In fact, Aaron was pretty good at his job, and reliable. Jim felt sorrier for Aaron than anything else. But at times like this, when under pressures and constraints he'd rather not deal with, a more normal stage manager would be a boon to have around.

Then there was the show's newly founded co-lead, Mario Silvestri. The young hotshot had been a good forty-five minutes late this morning. Sundays were important rehearsal days as one could take advantage of all hours. Jim had already given everyone the luxury of not having to be there until 10:30. Still, Mario, in all his arrogance, had come strolling through the door as if he owned the place, no apologies. He'd walked in with that naïve smile of his, as if expecting everyone to be thrilled. In actuality, no one had paid the slightest bit of attention, or did their best to pretend not to. This seemed to irritate the kid, and he made no effort to hide that.

Cash Giles. There were so many good actors Jim had at his disposal that could play this critical role. The kid was going to downgrade the quality of the show and there wasn't a thing Jim could do about it. Except quit, of course. And he was close to doing that, again. Any more crap from this wannabe shot caller and he'd walk away. In all his years as a director and teacher, never had he worked a job where the desire to bail almost exceeded the pleasure of putting a show together. First time for everything.

Jim let out a big sigh and raised the coffee cup to his mouth. It was dry and bitter, just like his mood. He glanced at a newspaper on the table near him. The headline story was a shooting at the Omni Hotel the other night. Damn ... this city seemed to get a little worse every day. He cocked his head and read the first couple lines of the story.

His phone buzzed—Sharon Toomey.

"How are things going over there, Jim?" she asked.

Jim only feigned a chuckle.

She giggled sympathetically. "You need me for anything right now? Anyone else I need to call?"

Jim set the phone on the counter and hit the speaker button. "I need a vacation," he said, his eyes wandering outside the lobby windows as he adjusted his glasses.

"What's bothering you, Jim?"

"A lot of things. I'm tired." He took another sip of coffee.

"Well, that's understandable. Casting has been rough."

Jim tapped the counter lightly with a finger. "I don't mean that kind of tired."

Sharon's voice took on a slight edge of alarm. "Jim?"

Jim chuckled again, more sincerely. "Relax. I'm fine. And no, I don't need you today. But thanks for checking in."

A shadowed figure suddenly appeared at the door, it was Dax Ribeiro. It startled Jim so much he almost spilled his coffee.

"Okay, Jim," Sharon was saying. "You know where—"

"Gotta run, Sharon," Jim said, cutting her off and hitting the end-call button. He put the phone in his pocket and stared at Dax, his eyes widening. Dax stood for a moment in the doorway looking up the street. Jim noticed right away that Dax's hair was slightly disheveled, and his face swollen in places. Near his left eye was a dark bruise. His expression bore a combination of exhaustion and anxiety.

"Dax?" Jim asked, taking a step toward the door.

Dax breathed deeply and looked at Jim. "Hi, Jim."

"You okay?"

Dax smiled weakly and walked forward with an extended hand. "Yeah. How's it going?"

A dozen questions popped into Jim's mind as he shook hands and looked Dax up and down. Did the kid get drunk last night? Get into a fight? He waited for Dax to say something.

Dax glanced around the lobby. He looked a little nervous. "Sorry, if you're in the middle of rehearsing."

Jim watched Dax closely. "No worries. We were taking a break."

Dax looked like he was struggling for words. "How's it going? I-I mean, the show."

"Oh, okay. I've had better shows. You never know though at this stage of the game." Jim put his fingers around the coffee cup but didn't lift it. "What's up?"

Dax shrugged. "Not much. On my way by. Just stopping to say hi."

"Yeah?"

Dax nodded. After a moment he suddenly asked, "Is Les Abraham hanging around by any chance?"

"Les?" The question caught Jim by surprise. He shrugged. "No, haven't seen him today. He's been in and out though, spying on me. Why?"

At the word *spying*, Dax glanced up quickly, but then looked away and slowly sat down on one of the bar stools.

Jim watched as Dax brought a hand up to his left shoulder and massaged it. There appeared to be a small bulge under Dax's brown leather jacket that might be a bandage or wrapping.

"Dax—" Jim started to say, but Dax held up a hand and managed to smile.

"I'm alright," Dax interrupted, hearing the concern in Jim's voice. "I've had a quite a weekend though." He managed a small chuckle through his words.

Jim was relieved to hear a little pleasantry in Dax's voice. "You look like it. No trouble, I hope."

"Well, sort of."

"You want some coffee or something?"

Dax shook his head. "No, no, I'm fine."

Jim took a seat next to Dax. "Is there something I can help you with?" *What in the heck is wrong with everyone today?*

Dax was staring at the ground thoughtfully. He looked up and said, "I'm sorry. I haven't had much of a chance to think about your offer. There was ... there *is*, another job that I've been busy with."

"Acting gig?"

"Yeah." Dax sounded cynical. "*Something* like that."

Jim adjusted the frames of his glasses on his nose. He waited for Dax to continue.

"I didn't think I was going to have time to do *Wild Hearts*," Dax said.

"But?" Jim asked hopefully.

Dax looked down again in thought. "Well, I still don't think I do. And, and I know I'm crazy for it. It's gonna be a big show. I'm crazy to say no. Lots of good actors better than me would line up for a shot at it. It's just that ... uh, I don't know." Dax turned and glanced out the window to the street, his eyes scanning back and forth.

"Dax," Jim said, and waited for Dax to make eye contact. "Are you in trouble?"

Dax only chuckled bitterly.

Jim decided to prod a little. "Les got you going on something?"

"No," said Dax, but then he smirked. "Actually, you might say he *did* get me on to something. That's why I'm looking for him. I need to talk to him."

Jim's mind whirled with curiosity, but he didn't want to push. He leaned back a little and took a long sip of coffee.

"Well, of course I was hoping you were coming here today to tell me yes. But if you can't, you can't."

"Yeah, I'm sorry. I don't think I can right now."

"Alright. Seriously though, you got me worried coming in here like this."

Dax looked puzzled for a moment. "Oh, right." He shrugged in thought and touched his face. "Got into a scuffle with a couple guys. No biggie."

"Really. Where was this?" Jim asked. His eyes went up and down Dax and then stopped at his left shoulder. A trained actor was lying to a trained acting teacher and wasn't doing a very good job at it.

Dax thumbed toward the door. "Up on California the other night. Could'uv been worse. But it's all good."

Jim couldn't help himself. "What happened?"

Dax stiffened up and pursed his lips for a moment. "Oh, I looked at some guy wrong and he went nuts on me. It's okay. Probably thought I was looking at his girl or something. He was drunk."

Jim could see Dax was struggling and not able to fabricate a lot of details on the fly. He didn't want to stress the poor kid out with too many questions. Dax was a big boy and none of it was any of Jim's business anyway. Still, Jim felt a kind of fatherly concern for Dax. But how in the heck was Les involved? He continued gently. "You won though, right? What with that karate or kung fu or whatever it is you do so well?"

Dax nodded. "Kung fu, mostly. And yeah, I won, fortunately. You should see the other guy." A pause. "He's in the morgue now."

Dax said the last line so deadpan that Jim, about to take another sip of coffee, froze midway.

Dax glanced up at Jim's face and drew a quick smile. "Just kidding." Dax's eyebrows suddenly crunched up. "Hey, while I'm here, is Meygan in the show?"

"Meygan Knight?" Jim asked. He slowly shook his head. "No. She never auditioned."

Dax looked visibly disappointed. "Oh. I need to talk to her too."

"Yeah? I hear things weren't so great between the two of you during your last show."

Dax looked surprised. "You heard that?"

Jim gave a mirthless smile. "We're a tight community. You know that."

Dax nodded. After a moment, he knocked lightly on the bar table and started to get up. "I better get going. Let you get back to rehearsal."

The auditorium door suddenly burst open, and Mario Silvestri strolled into the lobby. He looked hard at Dax as if trying to remember the name and face, then at Jim.

"Just takin' a leak," Mario said. "We still rehearsing, or what?"

Jim casually adjusted his glasses and looked at Mario for a moment before saying dryly, "Yes, I'll be there in a minute."

Mario shrugged with his face and continued, locking eyes with Dax as he passed.

Jim thumbed in the direction of the restrooms and said, "You remember him from the other day?"

"Mario, yes. Playing Cash."

Jim shook his head in disgust but said nothing.

Dax turned and stared down the hall. "I don't remember seeing him in anything before."

Jim sighed and picked up his coffee. "Neither do I."

Dax regarded Jim curiously for a moment. "Okay, well, I'll see you. Thanks again, Jim. I mean it."

Dax stared hard at the ground for a moment and thought about Mario. The kid had a certain look about him, a dangerous and challenging look that Dax had become familiar with recently. No wait, it was more than that. He recognized him from somewhere.

Jim was watching Dax. "You're sure you're okay, Dax? Anything you need at all, just ask."

"I know. I appreciate it."

"If Les or Meygan come around, I'll let them know you're looking for them."

"Thanks." Dax smiled weakly and turned to leave.

Jim stood and watched Dax exit the lobby and start up the street. Dax walked slowly and in deep thought. Jim shook his head feeling completely dumbfounded by the morning's events.

The auditorium door behind him opened again and he heard Aaron Tisdale's voice, "Jim, we're all set for Scene 3B—." He stopped and his voice suddenly grew loud and anxious. "Was that Dax Ribeiro?"

Jim turned and did a double take at the look on Aaron's face peeking out from inside the darkened theatre. "Yes, it was," Jim said.

Wide-eyed, Aaron watched Dax through the lobby windows hike up the sidewalk until he was out of view.

Jim motioned toward the front door. "If you wanna talk to him, go ahead."

Aaron's eyes danced back and forth. "Th-that's okay. Not now." He disappeared back into the theatre.

Jim shook his head again, adjusted his glasses and picked up his coffee. He glanced at the paper again. The Omni Hotel was on California Street. He looked back out the windows in the direction Dax had gone. "Nah, couldn't be," he said to himself as he turned and headed back into the theatre.

***

Jack Dauer and Michael Staggs sat in a rented gray Mercury Mountaineer two blocks north of the Treasure Box Theatre. The handheld radio sat in the drink holder next to him. It chirped and a choppy voice on the other end informed him Dax had just left the theatre and was heading up the street.

Jack pulled the cigarillo out of his mouth and gave the saliva-soaked end of it a disgusted look. Hitting the window button, he tossed out what was left of it. Next to the radio was a coffee cup. Reaching down, he took a sip and then gave the cold, bitter coffee an even more disgusted look before pulling the lid off and dumping out the remainder.

He was trying to get a little conversation out of Agent Staggs and not having much luck. He picked up the radio. "Still heading this way?" There was a pause of at least ten seconds before a "not yet" reply. The man who was tailing Dax on foot, Viktor Lozovsky, was good and wouldn't be seen. He was also good at looking for signs of other activity they would need to be aware of. The man was also a pain in the ass to work with.

Jack wanted to pull his gun and shoot something right now. From the moment Dax had entered the ballroom, the whole setup – the camera, the microphone, everything – had been a failure. Someone had used a powerful radiofrequency jammer that broadcasted a constant transmission, effectively drowning out everything on both civilian and military frequency bands in the room. By the time Dax was at the bottom of the stairs, all they were seeing and hearing was static and noise. It was a move that hadn't been anticipated. They had nothing but the eyewitness account of just one of their people who had been there, and she hadn't seen much. Dax running for his life with a gun in his hand, that's about it.

They put a man on Dax's apartment shortly after midnight, but Dax didn't come home until yesterday afternoon, still dressed in the party suit, and looking terrible. He apparently went to sleep and didn't stumble out until mid-morning today.

His personal cell phone, after being mysteriously off and untraceable, had suddenly come to life. This didn't make sense. Dax had explicit instructions to leave his personal belongings at their now compromised Sutter hotel location. Did Dax take his phone with him?

The first place Dax went was the Treasure Box theatre and talked with someone for a few minutes. Lozovsky had not been able to get any pictures through the tinted and poster-ladened windows. After that, Dax stopped by his work building which was close by and was in there for no more than ten minutes or so. Then he made a quick stop at convenience store and emerged with a small paper bag.

"Any shadows on him?" Jack asked into the radio. The question had already been asked several times, but he asked again out of impatience. A pause and then another "No," followed by, "You will be the first to know."

Jack drummed his fingers and waited for more information, but none came. He cursed and tossed the radio on the seat next to him. Viktor's voice came again. "Walking up Fourth Street." Jack cursed Viktor again, and the man's mother. None of this was Viktor's fault. Jack just needed something to spew his frustration on.

Jack glanced at Staggs and squeezed the steering wheel in frustration. Staggs was particularly glum and had said almost nothing all morning. He just sat in silence staring out the window, sulky and withdrawn. But there was a reason. The tall, thin man Dax had known as "Leo" had been a good friend of Staggs, not to mention a dependable team player. Personally, Jack never really liked Leo, but did like his work, and replacing him would be difficult.

The radio chirped and Viktor's voice announced that Dax was still heading up the street and had now turned on Howard.

"We need to talk, Dax," Jack muttered to himself. The combination of events from the last couple nights weighed heavily on his mind. In addition to losing some colleagues, it was now a race. Winners would take all, losers might end up dead.

Jack stared out the window, his eyes on random people and objects but his thoughts elsewhere. For a moment, he felt a flash of pity for Dax. He realized a part of him liked Dax's innocence as well as the boy's humor. But he dismissed the feelings right away. Business was business and the stakes were high.

When all this was over, Jack was going to disappear for good. He knew just where he'd go. He'd have to start over, make new ties, settle in. Everything would be different except for one thing—he'd be financially set for life. He'd play it low-key but eat in nice restaurants. And the tobacco and booze would be first class all the way, no skimping there. Most importantly, he'd be free of responsibility. The one drawback though would be that he'd always have to do a little casual looking over his shoulder, just to make sure. A glance here, a glance there. This burden he'd have to carry the rest of his life.

The radio chirped again, jolting him out of his thoughts. "He may have a tail," Viktor's voice cracked. Jack sat up and snatched the radio. "Anyone you recognize?" Viktor had a lot of mileage on him from the old country. The man knew a lot of faces and knew where a lot of bodies were buried. Literally.

"No," came the reply.

Jack cursed and slapped the steering wheel. Agent Staggs turned and looked but said nothing.

***

Dax moved slowly up the sidewalk, his mind in a daze. He felt bad that he'd lied to Jim Kirkland, a man he both liked and respected. And Jim had known too—the look on his face said it all. Dax wasn't the greatest actor to begin with, but today he just had no energy for any kind of performance. Someday, hopefully, he'd be able to sit down with Jim, apologize, and tell him the whole story from beginning to end.

He rubbed his shoulder and continued walking. On impulse, he'd stumbled out of his apartment a couple hours ago and caught a MUNI into downtown. Besides the brief stop at the Treasure Box and a trip to his workplace to retrieve the brass knuckles, he didn't have any other particular plans and didn't feel like making any. The only thing he was obligated to do was wait for Jack to make contact.

In the paper bag Dax toted was cheap vodka – $9.99 for a 1.75-liter plastic bottle with a brand name he didn't recognize. The label had a rough, red image of the famous Saint Basil's Cathedral to make it look authentic, but the stuff was probably made in Indiana and pure crap. At 80-proof though, it would do the job. He laughed to himself that his first choice had been vodka and not something else. But rum sounded too sweet, and he never could take much whisky. He hadn't been able to drink tequila since a high school party where he'd puked afterward for about three hours straight. So he picked the least diluted stuff he could find, and this afternoon he was planning to consume, a lot.

"*Voad-ka,*" he said to himself in his best Russian accent. Funny, the word was a diminutive form of the Slavic word *voda* which simply meant water. A *yaschik vodki*, or a whole case of vodka, is what he needed right now.

Dax smiled at the thought, but the smile quickly faded. He'd earned a little binging. Or did he? A pang of guilt swept through him. He'd been through this before, trying to sooth himself with excessive hooch. It was never good, and already instilling bad habits. What made it worse is that some time ago, he began to enjoy drinking alone. It doesn't take a counseling certification to understand that substance abuse when done alone is a dangerous sign of all sorts of things. It was just you, your problems, and your destructive attempts to distract and escape. But heck, he didn't do this that often. He was in pain, both physically and emotionally, and wanted relief.

Dax stopped suddenly, almost running into a sign pole. Glancing up and around to see who'd noticed his silliness, his eyes landed on a man across the street and about twenty feet behind. For just a split second, the man's eyes had been a bit too intense, too riveted on Dax. He broke contact with Dax and reached into a pocket.

Dax paused and did a double take. The man wore a brown windbreaker and khaki slacks. He also had on what looked like a wool flannel English cap, though the weather wasn't quite cold enough for that. He was maybe in his early thirties and the lower part of his face was covered by a thin beard. The man was now strolling up the sidewalk while pulling out a package of cigarettes. He even paused and gawked into a window, a store front that displayed nothing but dry-cleaned clothes ready for pickup. Tapping the cigarettes, he pulled one out, lit it with a small disposable lighter, then continued walking.

A bad performance. If Dax was the director of this show, there'd be no callbacks for this guy.

Dax decided to stop staring and continue walking. No need to make it obvious he'd spotted a shadow. Could be one of Hicks' guys, or one of Jack's. Could be the CIA or the Russian mafia. Could be the dude that's going to whack him when the time was right. If someone wanted to kill him, they'd eventually succeed.

And then there was the question of who'd killed Jack's people at the Sutter. He almost felt sorry for the men called Jeremy Forrester and Leo, but then again, they had played a part in a huge deception that put Dax in the mess he was in now.

The enormity of his situation hit him again in the form of a knot in his stomach. On impulse, he decided he'd better eat and took a sudden sharp right into a small sandwich shop. Straight vodka on an empty stomach would make for a bad ending, worse than what he was already anticipating.

30: Make 'em Scramble

A block behind Dax, Viktor Lozovsky relayed the information
to Jack Dauer. Viktor also gave an update on the man in the
brown windbreaker who was following Dax as well, and who
apparently the boy just made. Neither of them saw Viktor, he
was too good at this. He could tail people for days or weeks
as they went about shopping, working, travelling across cities,
and they'd never have a clue. In his younger years he'd even
shadowed subjects as they travelled internationally.

Ducking into a doorway, Viktor watched the windows to
the sandwich shop with small but powerful binoculars. The
time would come soon to eliminate this little American stage
actor who had caused all this urgent trouble. At first, the
assignment appeared almost too easy, but the young man was
looking around and did spot that other fool. He displayed a
wariness and caution that most subjects did not. This made
the American more irritating than anything else. At least in
this regard, the job wasn't completely boring.

Viktor stepped outside of the doorway and glanced up the
street. The idiot in the brown jacket had walked to the end
of the block and with his back turned, was saying something
into a radio. No radio could be seen, but the body and head

movements were obvious. If the man didn't know he'd been made, he was too amateur even for this job.

***

Jack was still tapping the steering wheel with his fingers. Now they'd have to sit around for another few minutes while Dax ate something. Just as well, except he wanted a fresh coffee. He glanced at Michael Staggs who remained quiet and staring out the window.

The news about the other tail, the man in the brown jacket, wasn't good. Who was that guy, police? SFPD didn't have resources to waste.

Jack didn't want to hurt Dax but would if he had to. If the kid had gone to the police and sang, there was going to be trouble. The scary part was, they had no idea if Dax still thought they were FBI. He wanted so badly to just pull up and have two guys grab Dax and throw him into the car, but he couldn't risk who may be watching.

***

The man in the brown windbreaker knew perfectly well he'd been spotted and was cursing himself for it. The tail's name was Roland Jacoby and he'd been with the Bureau for about two years. Yesterday morning, he'd gotten a call from downtown that he was needed for a special assignment. Follow this guy, see where he goes, what he does and so on. But more importantly, see if anyone tries to make contact.

Roland had received a file on a certain David Ribeiro, aka "Dax"—five-foot-ten, 180 pounds, age twenty-five. The file came with several pictures, employment, and other stats. A local theatre actor, in pretty good physical shape, knew some martials arts. Otherwise, your average tax-paying citizen. It seemed so simple. But Roland had gotten too close and the subject had made him. Parker was going to be pissed.

"He's in a sandwich shop, Franklin, just past Geary," he was saying into his radio.

Roy Parker's voice on the other end sounded irritated. "But he saw you?"

"Yeah, pretty sure." Roland unclicked the radio and looked down the sidewalk, shaking his head.

Parker emitted a partial curse before the radio signal deadened, then came back on. "I need you wait there till we can get McKinnis on site."

"Of course, I'll wait," Roland said back into the radio, trying not to sound sarcastic. He knew Parker was going to ask so he pressed the button and quickly added, "And no, no sign of any other tail."

The radio remained silent.

***

Jack considered the risks of trying to make contact. It had to be done, and soon. The question was who and where, now that they knew for sure other parties were interested. What they did the other night had been risky and alarms all the way from here to the Land of the Rus were going off. People with resources and knowhow to make things happen were now involved.

He glanced at his watch. "I'm going to get some coffee," he said to Staggs. "Want anything?"

Staggs turned slightly and mumbled, "No."

Jack would be glad when this day was over. Stakeout was not his thing. Slipping on dark sunglasses, he stepped out onto the sidewalk. A small coffee stand was just half a block down.

He had just taken his coffee when the radio chirped. Viktor's voice quickly crackled through the small speaker, "Someone is making contact."

Jack fumbled for the radio and brought it to his ear. "What?"

Viktor spoke a little slower. "Someone is making contact. I recognize one."

"Hey buddy," a voice behind Jack said. Jack turned quickly and looked up into the stern face of a large man in a construction outfit. "You finished here?" he asked. "I'd like to get my coffee."

Eying the man, Jack stepped back while talking into the radio, "You recognize *one*? How many are there?"

A five second pause. Jack was about to yell into the radio when Viktor's voice said, "There are two. One of them I know works for Gurkovsky."

As Jack gasped, the coffee slipped out of his hand. The tall paper cup landed with a thud and splash on the sidewalk. Ignoring it, Jack turned and hurried back up the street.

"Hey!" the construction man's voice behind him boomed. "Your coffee got all over my leg! Hey!"

Jack kept walking, almost jogging while putting a hand on the handle of the semi-automatic pistol in a shoulder holster under his coat. His heart was racing, there were much bigger things to consider now. How could Gurkovsky have found Dax so quickly? There must be a small army on the streets poking around.

Jack reached the Mountaineer and leaped into the driver's seat. Staggs, still looking out the passenger window, held up his radio and said, "I heard."

Jack cursed and smacked the steering wheel again. Putting the radio to his mouth, he said into it, "What are they doing now?"

***

Viktor sighed and looked up and down the sidewalk again. He was getting annoyed at Jack. A man with Viktor's talent and experience should be respected, and Jack should wait for the applicable information he would provide.

Viktor's situation wasn't ideal. Because of the narrow street and medium-light foot-traffic, maneuvering around hadn't been easy. He already had to waste several minutes waiting for a group of individuals to pass by so he could use them as cover to move further up the street. As it was, he'd finally gotten into a position where he could see inside the little eatery where the young American was. He didn't like being this close but had little options.

Inside less than a minute of establishing his new position, which was a small table across the street and holding a newspaper, he'd made the two other individuals who appeared to be interested in the young American. With his back almost completely turned to the sandwich shop, Viktor was unnoticeable in his gray slacks and tan cashmere sport coat. Just another employee of one of the many professional outfits in the nearby vicinity working a weekend shift and taking a lunch break.

Also unnoticeable was the package of cigarettes next to him on the table, which was actually a small camera. The cigarette box was real, but inside was a PCBA board, designed to fit into any standard cigarette box. With the flap open, any onlooker would see what appeared to be four or five cigarette ends protruding from inside, with one partially extended more than the others. The extended one contained a built-in 2,000,000-pixel CMOS camera with a 65-degree angle and a lens no bigger than a pinhole, nearly invisible to the human eye. Voice activated, the camera sent a wireless signal to the specialized pair of thick sunglasses Viktor wore, the right lens of which acted as a viewing screen. It was pricey technology available only to people with deep pockets and unique connections. Viktor wished he'd had this stuff available a few years ago when he was more active.

Viktor had the camera partially zoomed in to the entrance of the sandwich shop, allowing a medium-wide view with fifteen or so feet on each side of the doorway. Although appearing to be perusing his newspaper, he was, in fact, absorbing every movement in and around the eatery. He was looking at a girl behind the counter when two men appeared in the frame. Experience made Viktor easily spot anyone who was out of place, and these two were *definitely* that. The eyes and body language gave intentions away with such ease, it would be humorous were it not for who they were. If Gurkovsky was involved, Viktor's life would be in as much danger as anyone else's if his presence were discovered.

The two men stopped outside the shop's doorway and carefully looked around, at one point their gaze resting on the back of the casually dressed man across the street reading his paper. Professionals, taking in every detail. But Viktor had not moved, not even a flinch, and their attention on him didn't last long. But the brief stare was long enough for Viktor to see and recognize at least one of them.

After the men peered into the shop, they smiled as if they'd been conversing about something, and casually entered.

Viktor zoomed the camera in as much as possible and radioed Jack. This assignment had suddenly become a lot more interesting, and dangerous.

***

Despite how lousy he felt, Dax found himself enjoying the turkey on wheat sandwich with extra mustard and onions. The Diet Coke and salt and vinegar chips were also good.

Dax was at a corner table facing the window. A little bell on the door made it easy to glance up at anyone who entered. He looked at the two men who'd just walked in but didn't think much of it. They were broad-shouldered with cropped hair and looked to be in good physical shape. Maybe they were military. They were laughing at something and paid no attention to Dax as they ambled past.

Dax took another big bite and stared out the window. No sign of that clown in the windbreaker. The street looked perfectly benign with the kind of foot traffic one would expect for a Sunday lunch hour. If it were a weekday, there'd be three times more people.

He glanced at his watch then took another bite. His body ached a little more at the thought of how Jim Kirkland had looked at him. He may never get another call from the renowned director. Then again, he may not live long enough to enjoy a part in another play anyway.

Then his thoughts drifted to Meygan Knight. If and when Decker and Hicks find out he failed to mention her, he might get into trouble. No, scratch that, he *would* get into trouble.

A cell phone behind him beeped. Someone answered and an accented voice said "*hal-ow*" into the phone. Dax heard it but thought nothing of it. Lots of people with accents in this city. A few moments of silence and then the voice was saying, *hmm-mmm* into the phone. A one-sided conversation. Dax gazed out the window but still listened. A bike rider, perhaps a courier, pulled over to the sidewalk almost directly in front of the sandwich shop and flipped off the driver of a small truck.

Dax smirked, and at that moment, he heard the voice behind him say "*da*" into the phone—the Russian word for yes. The voice had said it quietly, but Dax distinctly heard it, and it sounded genuine, with subtleties that native speakers had.

Dax paused for a moment, his pulse quickening. Keeping his head forward, he slowly wiped his mouth with the napkin and set the rest of the sandwich down. Picking up his cup, he leaned back and took a long pull on the straw. Then, all at once, he quickly swiveled around and locked eyes with the two men. Both froze for a moment and stared back with caught-red-handed expressions of surprise. Not knowing what else to do, they looked away, feigning indifference. Another poor performance.

In a split second, Dax sized them up and decided they looked dangerous, far more than the dude in the windbreaker. Casually swiveling back around, he wiped his mouth once more and stood. Without another backward glance, he strolled out the door, drink in one hand, paper bag in the other.

Dax didn't notice the older man across the street fold his paper, put a cigarette box in his pocket, stand and start walking. But he did, with a small backward glance, notice the two men emerge from the sandwich shop and begin marching up the sidewalk in his direction.

***

Roland Jacoby was two blocks up and peering around the corner when he thought he saw the subject suddenly emerge from the sandwich shop. Cursing and fumbling for his radio, he lifted it to his mouth and said, "He's on the move again."

Parker's voice crackled through the small speaker a moment later. "Try to stay out of sight. McKinnis is almost there."

Roland shook his head and muttered, "Yeah, stay out of sight. No kidding."

A moment later, Agent Jerry McKinnis arrived. The sleek and smooth engine of his Ducati 748 could be heard as it wound its way up the street perpendicular to Franklin at the corner where Jacoby was hunkering down. The red and white bike came to a stop and the heavily tinted face mask of McKinnis' helmet turned to Roland. McKinnis donned a leather rider's jacket with bright white and fluorescent green stripes, a garment that looked pretty good on his lean, six-foot-one frame.

Roland nodded his head down the street and made motions with his fingers to indicate walking. McKinnis nodded.

"How the heck is he supposed to case a person on that bike and in that getup?" Roland said to himself.

Agent Jerry McKinnis was three years Roland Jacoby's senior with the Bureau. McKinnis normally didn't tail suspects on his bike, especially in a setting like downtown on a weekend, but at the moment he had no choice. He'd been commuting to the office when he got the urgent call from Roy Parker that Roland had blown his cover early in the game.

McKinnis removed his helmet as Roland approached. "What's up?" McKinnis asked.

"Have you seen the files on this David Ribeiro guy?"

"I was briefed, yeah. Goes by the name of Dax."

"Yeah. Well, he's headed up this way now. Across the street." Roland nodded again in that direction.

"Anyone make contact with him?"

Roland shook his head. "Not that I've seen."

"How long you been on him?"

"Close to two hours. He's been wandering. Stopped by the Treasure Box theatre near O'Farrell for a while. Just sat there and talked to someone. Then stopped by his work for a few minutes. Then got something at a store he's been carrying around."

"I know the theatre. You know who Ribeiro was talking to?"

"No. Got a decent picture of him though as I walked by the window. They're looking at it now."

"Okay." McKinnis put both feet on the ground and watched the sidewalk across the street.

"How big is this case anyway?" Roland asked.

"No one knows yet. I do know they wanted more people on it but weren't able to today. They *really* wanna know if anyone makes contact."

Jacoby sighed. "Yeah, I know." He shook his head sadly. "Parker's pissed."

"No time for that now. Where did Ribeiro see you?"

"Couple blocks down. He just suddenly turned and looked at me."

McKinnis was staring across the street. "Right. Don't sweat it."

"Sure thing. Nice bike, by the way."

"I know."

Arrogant punk, Roland thought as he turned and looked back at the corner. "There he is now."

"Get behind me," McKinnis said as he slipped the helmet back on.

Roland obeyed, turned, and hunched down for good measure.

McKinnis angled the face of his helmet down while his eyes watched Dax meander up the sidewalk. The subject walked like a man who didn't have a particular destination in mind. In his hands were a drink cup and a paper bag.

McKinnis quickly scanned the individuals behind and around Dax. There was nothing out of the ordinary.

"That bag there's from the store?" McKinnis asked.

"Yeah."

The radios of both agents crackled. McKinnis turned his head, lifted his helmet shield, and pressed the button on his radio. "Yes?"

"Parker," came the voice through the speaker. "That you McKinnis?"

"Yeah. I'm on site."

"Good. The person our subject spoke to at the theatre earlier was a Jim Kirkland. He's a director over there and former teacher of our man. Nothing on him attention-worthy at the moment, but we'll run the file. Did Jacoby brief you on that?"

"Of the conversation at the theatre, yes. Subject is also carrying around a paper sack with something he picked up at a store."

"Do you know what it is?"

McKinnis looked at Roland who shrugged and shook his head.

"We don't know."

"Okay. You have all your things?"

McKinnis glanced at his saddlebags. "I do."

"Alright. Where is he now?" Parker asked.

"Heading up the street toward us."

"Anyone on his tail?"

McKinnis' eyes flicked back and forth up and down the sidewalk. "None that I see at the moment."

"Okay. Send Jacoby back. I'll be available to help in an hour or so."

McKinnis glanced at Roland who only waved and began walking away. Flipping the kill switch to Run, he depressed the clutch and hit the ignition button. The Ducati purred to life. This was going to be tricky, but he'd figure something out till more help arrived. Glancing back, he made a sharp U-turn and headed down the street to circle around the block.

***

Dax moved with deliberate casualness. He rattled the ice in his cup then brought the straw to his mouth. Stay calm. Make them wonder. If he survived all this, would he be able to live normally again? If he'd been a happier, more content person, not needy for something more, would he have said yes to Jack Dauer? Maybe. Between biology and upbringing – nature versus nurture, as it's called – did any of us really choose anything?

Dax approached the next corner then paused. The stealthy entourage behind and around him paused as well. He almost laughed at the resignation that all of this was out of his control. The sooner something happened, the better. Let's just get this over with.

He glanced down at the paper sack in his hand and sighed. The contents of the bag really weren't going to help things, but he was going to indulge anyway.

A thought stuck him. Maybe he'd throw them for a loop and hop into a cab. Make 'em scramble. Have him be the string puller for a change.

He suddenly turned left and started across the street. The whine of an engine caught his attention and he turned to see a motorcycle approaching. The biker wasn't moving fast and slowed to almost a stop as Dax crossed. Dax stared at the dark tinted helmet and then glanced down at the bike. He wasn't an expert, but that looked like a nice bike.

As Dax hit the corner, an older gentleman in a sport coat with thick, dark sunglasses strode by. Dax didn't give him another glance as he stared up the street. No taxis here. He decided to start making his way toward the water and the Embarcadero area. There would be more cabs down that way.

31: Multiple Shadows

Inside the gray Mercury Mountaineer, Jack Dauer's mind was reeling. For Gurkovsky to already be involved was unexpected. And scary. But it also meant Gurkovsky just might know where Dax had spent last night. Jack would kill to know. His radio chirped.

"Our man just turned around and is headed back toward the theatre—other side of the street now." said Viktor's voice. Through the static, the impatience in Viktor's voice could be heard. He also sounded breathy, like he was walking quickly.

Jack cursed in frustration. Since this morning when Viktor started tailing Dax from his apartment, no one had any idea where Dax was headed. Except for the brief visit to the theatre and work, the kid seemed to be wandering aimlessly. Had he gone to there just to chew the rag with some friends, or was there more? Jack had to assume Dax had been there looking for Les Abraham to ask about him and Staggs. The aging drama teacher was now a loose end.

At first it was assumed Dax was just taking advantage of a no-obligation Sunday to stroll around and kill some time. But what was troublesome was that in Viktor Lozovsky's opinion, Dax seemed to be waiting for someone to contact him. Lozovsky was an old pro and if he sensed that, it was probably true. Jack been right to lay low and see where Dax was going and who he may try to speak with.

***

At the crosswalk, Jerry McKinnis felt like he almost pulled a Roland. After waiting until Dax was almost three blocks away, he turned and casually made his way up the street. The idea was to take stock of who was around, the problem was, everyone had just taken stock of *him*. At the last minute, Ribeiro had turned unexpectedly and crossed the street right in front him, staring hard. This Dax guy was obviously wary and observing the people and things around him – thanks at least in part to Roland. Guess Ribeiro couldn't be blamed after almost getting killed the other night. Still though, McKinnis had a bad feeling. This assignment had just shot way up the level of effort scale.

Using his trained eye, McKinnis took note of both sides of the street. Experience and practice had taught him how to purposely observe people at a quick glance—estimate their size and build, clothing, anything unusual that made them stand out that he could later pull from memory. He recalled an otherwise dull lecture class at the academy where an actor in a ski mask had suddenly burst into the room. The masked man fired a couple booming blank rounds in the air making most people duck or dive. He then grabbed a purse off a nearby desk and ran from the room. As all this went down, the instructor stood calmly watching. When it was over, the class was drilled as to what they could remember about the suspect—age, gender, ethnicity, height, weight, and so on. The actor then returned to the classroom and removed the mask. Most were not even close about anything. Some could recall next to nothing. It was an effective, eye-opening exercise.

McKinnis swore under his breath. He gunned the bike and headed up the street with the intention of turning left and circling around the block again. He saw the subject turn again and start back down Franklin. Great, this guy was going in circles on a narrow street with not a lot of foot or car traffic. Hopefully Parker would be here soon.

***

Viktor Lozovsky quickly swapped the video monitor glasses with a pair of regular sunglasses. Cursing as he went, he also removed his coat, working his arms out and turning the tan sleeves inside-out. On the other side of the sleeves was an olive-green material.

The American had looked right at him as he had passed. It was just a glance, but that was enough. Normally it wouldn't make much of a difference, but this young American was different. He was looking at everyone, foot traffic and vehicles. He had stared hard at that motorcycle. He appeared as if his mind was in a mode to remember details and Viktor did not want to be remembered in any capacity. He was beginning to feel a little intrigued with this theatre actor.

With his subtly altered appearance, Viktor took a hard right and crossed the street. Taking another right, he began moving back down the sidewalk, keeping a comfortable distance and trying to gauge a good moment to utilize his binoculars. His eyes flitted back and forth behind the glasses, taking in all pedestrians and vehicles on the street.

***

Dax smiled and strolled casually. The sack in his hand was feeling heavier now and he was looking forward to consuming what was in it. Taking one last pull on the straw, he tossed what was left of the sandwich shop soda into a nearby garbage can. Straight ahead and waiting at the next curb was a yellow taxi.

His smile widened and his pace picked up. Why not? Maybe he'd take a ride down to the Piers, or maybe the North Beach area and wander around the shops.

As Dax approached corner, the cabby glanced up and made eye contact. Dax almost waved but instead raised his eyebrows and gave a nod. He wanted this to be a surprise. The driver nodded back and set down a paperback he had been reading.

Laughing could be heard from around the corner as Dax prepared to make a quick jog toward the taxi. A group of seven or eight teenagers speaking what sounded like German almost ran into Dax. Dax stopped and let them by, taking note of each one's face as they passed. One of them carried a Sony Hi8 video camera. They ignored Dax, talking and laughing loudly while getting ready to cross the street. He felt a small pull on his jacket pocket and glanced down but saw nothing. Dax watched the teens for a moment. They were young and free of worries, busy visiting a famous foreign city and having a great time. For a moment, he envied them.

Turning in the direction the group had come from, Dax saw only an older gentleman in an olive-green coat strolling down the street. No one he'd seen before.

Dax hurried to the taxi, opened the back door and hopped in. He looked at his watch and thought for a moment. It was still early. He sighed. Fine, he'd play this out a little longer.

Chinatown. He'd send them on a wild goose chase in Chinatown.

"Clay and Stockton," he said. The driver nodded and pressed a button on the digital meter. Dax sat back and didn't bother to look out the windows. He smiled and closed his eyes.

***

Viktor had seen the yellow taxi roughly the same time Dax did and anticipated the move. Cautiously stepping up the pace, he quickly narrowed the distance between him and the young American. As he did, he reached into his pocket and retrieved a small electronic gadget. This was going to be close.

He noticed the American suddenly begin to move faster. Viktor stepped up his pace, the device now in his hand and switched on. It didn't matter if anyone noticed him; he'd be someone completely different in appearance and mannerisms shortly after this anyway.

As the subject moved toward the taxi, a group of youths came around the corner, speaking rapid German. This was Viktor's chance. Moving with speed and purpose, Viktor transferred the device to his left hand. Edging just close enough, he reached out and with a small subtle wrist movement, slipped the device into the pocket of the American.

Viktor made a sharp right and began strolling down the street in the direction from which the students came. He cursed himself because his finger had almost gotten caught on the subject's pocket. Surely the boy must have felt it.

Unknown to Dax, he now carried a GPS device that could locate him anywhere in the world, as long as the tiny battery in it lasted. At just 1.9 inches long, half an inch wide and just a few millimeters thick, the gadget carried a specialized chipset that transmitted in both GPS and GSM. Using an encrypted code that only the correct devices could see, the chipset could be triangulated anywhere on the planet with an accuracy of up to nine feet. The device even conserved power by deactivating when not in motion and could hold power for up to twelve months if unmoved.

As he walked, Viktor pulled a Nokia 9000 Communicator out of his pocket. He smiled at the thought that he'd lived long enough to see this technology. Punching in a couple different passwords, a specially designed application and map flashed up on the screen. A red dot indicated it could see the device in Dax's pocket and was tracking. They could now watch the American's every move, as long as it stayed on his person. Even if the subject stopped and didn't move for a while, they'd always have the last known position. Victor put the radio to his mouth and called Jack.

***

For the 500th time that morning, Jack cursed. This time it got the attention of Staggs who was now in the passenger seat and making every attempt to ignore everything around him. Turning his head, he gave Jack a sour look.

Jack turned to Staggs. "Our boy made a run for a taxi."

Staggs shrugged.

"No worries," said Jack cranking the Mountaineer's engine to life. "Lozovsky was able to get a tracker on him."

Slamming the car's gear into drive, Jack eased onto the road while fumbling for his phone. A loud car horn made him slam the brakes. Rolling down the window, Jack leaned out and yelled several choice words until the car passed. He tossed the phone into Staggs' lap then jerked the car forward into the lane.

***

McKinnis had just turned the block and was cruising up a cross street when two different things made his heart jump. The first was an older gentleman in an olive-green sport coat. The man had been strolling quickly down the street when he turned and stared hard at McKinnis, like Ribeiro had done. The man looked away, but he'd given that classic gaze of recognition. McKinnis watched as the man continued walking without a pause.

Then things got worse.

A yellow taxi drove by. McKinnis looked in the back window and saw the subject, Dax Ribeiro, leaned back with his eyes closed. It startled McKinnis so much he almost lost control of the bike. This whole scene was getting shoddier by the minute, and he felt a tinge of guilt over acting smug to Roland.

Gunning it, McKinnis sped the Ducati to the next corner and took a fast right. He'd have to go around again and intercept the taxi to see where it was going. Mumbling a curse, he took another sharp right and gunned it again.

***

"You need to turn left," said Staggs, staring at the small screen. The tires on the Mountaineer squealed as Jack cranked the wheel hard. Several people had to jump out of the way. Ignoring them, Jack stomped on the gas pedal.

"Taxi just took a right," said Staggs.

Jack started to move over a lane. He was feeling excitement about moving again instead of sitting around waiting for news from Lozovsky. "Where do you think he's headed?" he asked, just to make conversation.

Staggs only shrugged.

The radio crackled. "Yes?" Jack said into it. The voice of Viktor Lozovsky asked if they had the signal.

"Make your way more southeast," said Staggs, eyes glued to the small flickering screen.

Jack looked over his shoulder and attempted to move lanes. A man on a ten-speed bike slowed hard and slapped the rear side window of the Mountaineer. Jack sped up faster and prepared to go left.

"They're headed toward downtown," said Staggs.

Jack thudded the steering wheel. "What are you up to, Dax?"

***

Dax was enjoying the ride. Remaining slumped in the seat, he watched people and buildings go by. "Take your time," he said to the cab driver. The cabby looked in the rearview mirror for a moment with a puzzled expression, but then shrugged.

Easing a hand into the bag, Dax found the plastic top, gripped, and twisted. With a small crack, the cap came loose. He remained gazing out the widow as he unscrewed it. Slowly pushing the paper edges down around the top of the bottle, Dax leaned left as far as he could out of the cabby's view. Then, with a quick motion, brought the bottle up and poured a mouthful of the clear liquid in. He heard several bubbles bounce their way up the neck of the cheap plastic container. The liquid felt cold on the tongue and the alcohol vapors immediately hit his nasal cavity forcing him to swallow hard. The esophageal burn was intense and Dax began coughing. He brought the paper bag back down to his lap as the cabby glanced again in the mirror.

"You okay?" the cabby asked.

Dax held up a palm. "Yeah." He cupped his mouth in the crook of his sleeve and coughed a few more times, his face turning red. He leaned back and breathed hard, feeling the heat in the skin on his face. Strong stuff. Tasted like garbage, as expected. Slowly, he brought the mouth of the bottle back up and took a smaller sip, then another. He could feel the stuff already hitting his brain.

As he went for another swig, the whir of a motor caused his eyes to shift left out the window. As he did, he froze. Was that the ... yes, the bike he saw earlier! No question—that sleek Ducati and the bright jacket.

Dax watched the bike while slowly taking another sip. It turned on to the same street as the cab and immediately fell behind a couple car lengths. He craned his head around and looked out the back window. Okay ... *another* tail on him. How many more were there? What kind of cavalcade was he leading into Chinatown?

He turned around and slumped back down again. The cheap vodka was doing its job.

***

The radio in McKinnis' helmet chirped. Roy Parker was asking for a status. "I'm on him," McKinnis said. "He jumped into a taxi and is headed toward the piers. Looks like we're going to go through Chinatown." He gave Parker the taxi's description and license number.

"Any other shadows?"

"Not sure. I did see one suspicious person who looked at me. Older guy in a sport coat."

"It's more important you don't lose him."

McKinnis frowned and shook his head. "I know, I know."

"Hicks and I are on the way."

"Thank God." McKinnis swerved his bike to avoid a jaywalker.

"Current twenty?"

"Looks like they're about to … hang on." McKinnis skillfully weaved his powerful bike around a couple cars and pedestrians. "Just made a right on Clay."

"Okay. Lemme know in about five minutes where our boy's at."

"Raga that."

McKinnis hummed along at an even pace three cars behind the yellow taxi. The smells of various foods from Chinese eateries drifted into his helmet making his stomach growl.

The taxi's brake lights came on and the vehicle pulled over to a stop. Swiveling his head, McKinnis made sure the coast was clear then moved a lane over to the left and slowed down. As he passed, he saw Dax scooting over to get out. Gunning it, McKinnis sped the bike up to the next corner, turned right, then stopped where he could see the taxi.

The right passenger door opened and Dax exited heavily. The subject took a big deliberate step forward to the front passenger window and leaned in. McKinnis hit the radio button for his helmet and gave the location.

As McKinnis watched, his finger still on the radio button, Ribeiro suddenly stood straight, turned, and looked directly at him. He stared for a moment, grinned, and gave a big wave. For his part, McKinnis almost waved back.

"Little bastard," McKinnis muttered.

He turned, kicked the bike into first and took off out of sight.

***

Dax stood with amusement after waving at the biker. He was starting to feel mighty tipsy and quickly losing ability to care about his present circumstances. He wondered at whoever was riding that nice, expensive bike with the cool jacket – why would anyone play spook in such a loud outfit? The biker watched for a couple seconds longer and then took off. Dax then turned and waved at the taxi as it pulled away. The driver paused for a moment then sped off.

Dax laughed and reached for the bottle cap. Lifting the sack to his lips, he leaned back a bit too much and stumbled backward a step.

Whoa.

He took another small gulp and realized he wasn't tasting the 80-proof liquid much now, a sign he needed to slow down. A public intoxication charge would complicate an already complicated situation. Pealing the paper back a little, he saw he'd already drunk maybe a fifth of the bottle. Been a while since he'd take this stuff straight. At least he had a full stomach from the sandwich earlier.

Glancing around awkwardly, he saw a small shop that sold pastries and coffee. An espresso might not be so bad right now. He turned and made his way to the corner where the biker had been a minute ago.

Dax leaned against the light pole, trying put as much of his weight as possible against it. He was feeling great, but at the same time found it impossible to enjoy himself. In the past when he'd binge drink, it was in a setting where he could be much more at ease—a sports bar with a couple friends, at his house with a good movie. But here, in the middle of Chinatown with God-knew-who-all chasing him around, it just didn't feel that great.

The walk sign popped on and Dax stumbled forward. The objects in front of him bobbled and his face felt numb. He could smell barbequed chicken from somewhere nearby. A short, older Chinese woman passed by in the other direction and looked up at him with wariness. Dax laughed, maybe she was spying on him too.

Almost to the other side, Dax glanced to his right. A large gray SUV was heading up Stockton. The driver appeared to be looking at him but then quickly looked away. Dax stopped at the corner and stared. There was something recognizable about the face, but it was too far away. He paused and looked around. His whole world of vision teetered and swayed.

Turning both ways, he remembered the pastry shop he'd seen and headed that way. People sort of drifted by as he walked.

He paused and looked up. A colorful sign above the door said Z&Y Bakery and a sweet, sticky smell permeated from the entrance. He stepped in and looked around. To his right was a small counter that displayed various goodies and drinks, to his left were a few tables.

Dax stepped backward out of the door and looked up the street. There was no biker, no dangerous looking thugs, no visible anyone who might be following. He stepped back into the shop and made his way to the counter. The busy and mostly Asian employees and patrons ignored him. A middle-aged Chinese woman wiping small plates glanced up then continued without a smile.

"Coffee," said Dax. His words didn't sound slurred. Good.

She eyed him for a moment and then pointed to a stack of cups at the end of the counter. Next them were several coffee urns with various labels.

"Large or small?" the woman asked.

Dax had to think about it. Best he hang here for a few. "*Lllllarge*," he finally said.

Eying him more, she said evenly, "One dollar, seventy-nine cents."

Dax pulled his wallet and fumbled out a five, slapped it on the counter and headed for the cups. The motion caused the pain in his shoulder to burn a little. He picked a cup then went for the urn labeled Brazilian Dark Roast. The hot, dark liquid foamed and steamed as it bubbled into the cup.

The woman slapped his changed on the counter with a whack a little louder than his had been. Dax looked up and smiled politely. It had been placed strategically next to a jar with a hand-written "TIPS" note taped to the side. Dax scooped up his change to pocket it, catching his balance as he leaned backward a little too far. She didn't deserve a tip.

The coffee looked and smelled good. Lifting the cup to his mouth he took a clumsy and large mouthful and instantly felt the burn. Groaning loudly, he spit half of it back into the cup and wiped his mouth with his sleeve. Finding a pile of small napkins, he grabbed several and dabbed his mouth. Feeling a stare from the corner of his eye, he turned and saw the woman behind the counter looking again, now scowling.

"I'm just gonna go sit down. That okay with you?" he said to her with a fair amount of sarcasm. She didn't respond as she set down a plate and reached for another.

Dax turned and moved slowly toward an empty table in the back corner. Making his way across the seating area, he didn't notice the gray Mercury Mountaineer SUV pull to a stop across the street.

32: Go Now!

Hicks and Parker turned onto Clay and gunned it. The easy work had already been done. Last night with a warrant from one of their many cooperative judges, plus a few taps on the computer, and everything to and from Dax's cell phone was being recorded on a digital file with his name on it. They also had a tracker on Dax's Mustang and would be watching him wherever he went. In the next day or so, hopefully Monday morning when Dax was at work, a team would apply bugs to his apartment, just in case.

But here was the hard work. Dax was on foot wandering around the city and they had to case him the old-fashioned way. The Bureau normally had more manpower for something as potentially big as this, but not lately. Between budget cuts and a flurry of high-profile cases that were stretching them thin, they were put in a very bad position this morning.

"Is this right?" Hicks asked.

"Yes, next block," Parker said.

Although they could triangulate Dax's phone fairly easily, it wasn't as precise as having eyes on him. Hicks pulled the plain, brown sedan to the side. "I'll get this side of the street, you get the other."

The two agents hopped out. Today they were wearing non-traditional clothing, Hicks in casual slacks, a polo shirt, and a tan leather jacket. Parker wore a baseball cap, dark blue jeans, and a gray windbreaker. Both men donned dark sunglasses with large lenses.

Hicks waited for a moment pretending to look at his phone while Parker jogged across the street. The two men glanced at each other then began a slow walk up the sidewalk nonchalantly peeking into windows and doorways.

Hicks didn't like it that there wasn't a lot of traffic. He stood out too much here. He just hoped if Dax spotted them, he wouldn't make it obvious.

Hicks peered into a tourist shop that sold trinkets and overpriced junk. He turned and looked at Parker across the street who made eye contact and shook his head no. Ahead was a small eatery. Hicks approached the main window and looked around the main seating area and counter.

A movement behind the window's glare caught his attention and he looked down to see Dax sitting right there at a small table next to the window. The sight startled Hicks momentarily and he readied for Dax to notice, but the boy looked distracted and tired.

Hicks turned to Parker across the street. He gave a delicate nod at the window and Parker nodded back that he understood. Hicks then continued up the sidewalk to the crosswalk.

***

Jack watched for a moment, drumming his fingers. On the second run back up the street, Staggs had seen Dax walk into the small shop. With the tracker they had found him quickly, and now the boy sat in plain view by the window. What was he doing, waiting for someone? Jack shook his head in frustration.

"Lemme just go over there and get him," Staggs said, irritation in his voice.

Jack sighed and didn't respond. There was no way they could just march over there and take Dax. With Gurkovsky's men and who knows who else lurking about, the situation was just too dangerous.

Staggs didn't appreciate partaking in chasing the young American all over the city. Jack couldn't blame him. The man just wanted to sit in his hotel room with a bottle of something strong and mourn the loss of his friend. But Jack needed him right now. He needed everyone on deck until this little crisis was over.

"I never liked that *pindos*," Staggs said with contempt to no one in particular.

Jack turned. "I know. And the kid knows that too. That's why I tried to keep you two apart."

Staggs rolled down the window and reached for a cigarette. As he turned to blow smoke out the window, he instinctively locked on two men standing in front of a jewelry store. Something about them caught his eye—the hat and sunglasses, the body language.

"Hey," Staggs said softly. Jack turned. Staggs nodded out the window and behind them. "Two guys there."

Jack leaned back and looked through the rear tinted windows.

"American," Staggs said.

Jack tapped the steering wheel anxiously. He looked again as one of the men disappeared inside the store. The other pulled a phone out of his pocket and started thumbing it.

"They watching our boy?" Jack asked.

Staggs shrugged.

"Where's Viktor?" Jack asked the anonymous people up and down the street. His radio hissed and he snatched it up. It just happened to be Viktor.

"Just exited a taxi and I'm nearby." Viktor said.

"Yes. We're across the street watching him now. In a window in a shop. Z&Y Bakery."

"I see it. What do you want me to do?"

Jack craned his head and looked toward the jewelry store. The one man was still outside, still looking at his phone. "There may be a tail over here. Near us. Same side of the street. Hat and sunglasses."

"I see him."

"Okay," Jack said into the radio while thinking up a quick plan. "You see our car?"

"Of course."

"I'm going to write a note and I need you to somehow get it to our boy. I'm going to instruct him to meet up with us a couple blocks from here and see how receptive he is to that. Give me five minutes. I'll walk to that newspaper stand a little way past the jewelry store. Meet up with me."

Jack pulled a small notepad out of his jacket pocket and clicked a pen open. He tapped the notepad in thought. A couple blocks away there was a small outdoor strip mall with restaurants and small shops; the row of vendors inside went to the other side of the block. It was terribly risky, but it just might work.

***

Dax yawned and stared lazily at the coffee. His stomach didn't feel like taking in a lot of liquid right now and besides, the caffeine wasn't exactly injecting energy into him. He looked around and had to admit he felt good though. He breathed deep and told himself he didn't have to hit the bottle every time he wanted to escape.

Impulsively, he reached for his wallet. Without thinking, he knew what his hands would automatically go for. His fingers worked their way under the leather flap behind his driver's license and out came a small picture of Sam.

Dax stared, his mouth partially open, his eyes half shut. She stared back, but this time her smile had a hint of sadness. Sam would never point a finger and judge, but if she were here, she'd gently remind him of how much she cared. Dax cringed because he knew what would come next. She'd tell him how much God cared for him. How much more God could love him than any person could, no matter what.

Dax slowly lowered the photo to the table and massaged the bridge of his nose. His eyes settled on the paper bag next to him. The bag slowly bobbed up and down in his vision. He cursed himself, grabbed the bottle, and began unscrewing the cap.

At that moment, a Chinese boy, maybe fifteen or sixteen, entered the shop. He halted, swiveled his head, and looked at Dax for a moment. The action made Dax pause.

Dax swallowed a gulp and watched as the boy went to the counter and bought a small pastry. His movements were too casual, and suggested that his glance at Dax, however brief, had not been accidental. The kid wore a short-sleeved, blue-striped T-shirt, well faded jeans, and boot style Converse shoes. After briefly chatting in Chinese with the lady behind the counter, he dropped a coin or two into the tips jar. Taking a large bite of his pastry, he turned and began casually strolling toward Dax.

Dax smiled, screwed the cap back on, then leaned back and waited. So many bad performers around here. Made sense, most people hadn't a clue how much training is needed to confidently portray other characters or motives. The boy paused near Dax's table and stared out the window. Dax almost initiated conversation just to get things going but decided to wait.

The boy took another bite, his eyes, which were contoured with black eyeliner, flitted back and forth as if scanning for something across the street. But Dax could tell the kid was sizing him up via peripheral vision. Finally, he turned and looked at Dax.

"Whazzup?" Dax asked, grinning. His words almost slurred and he wished he knew the phrase in Mandarin or Cantonese.

The boy's expression shifted to one of slight confusion, even a little nervousness. Maybe the kid thought he was being sneakier than he was. He stared at Dax while stuffing the last of the pastry in his mouth. Then, wiping his mouth with his sleeve, the other hand went for a pocket.

Dax's eyes moved with the hand. Was this kid some assassin in training sent to do him right here in this little bakery? Nothing would be a surprise. If so, he was in no condition to defend himself.

The boy's hand came back out and produced only a small, folded piece of paper. He looked Dax up and down, his eyes resting on the paper bag and then back at Dax's tired, bloodshot eyes. He tossed the note on the table.

Dax looked for a moment, then asked, "What's this?"

The kid shrugged. "How should I know? But for twenty bucks, it's yours." He then turned and strolled out. The lady behind the counter watched the boy leave, then her eyes, now filled with hostile suspicion, went back to Dax.

Dax glanced up at the woman and waved. She gave him a contemptuous glare then disappeared into an adjacent doorway. He fumbled the note open and stared at the writing. It took his eyes a moment to adjust and focus.

Dax, J.D. here. We need to talk. Careful because you're being tailed. Two blocks north of here near – Beckett St. Take a right into the Tea Leaves restaurant. Then go as quickly as you can through to the backdoor out to Pacific Ave. Look for a gray Mountaineer. Don't lose this note. Go NOW.

As Dax read, he felt his heartbeat increase. He squinted and reread the note three times so that all the words would sink in. Jack was here? Where?

He turned and gazed back and forth out the window but saw nothing that caught his attention. No suspicious characters, no gray Mountaineer, no Ducati. He studied both sides of the street then looked at the last line of the note once more.

Go NOW.

Dax sighed. He didn't feel like facing Jack, but this was exactly what Decker and Hicks wanted him to do. He had prepped a whole set of lies, but in this state of mind they might be difficult to recall. He could see Jack now, leaning forward and looking him hard in the eyes. Jack was sharp and inquisitive and had good instincts.

Dax looked out the window again. He needed Hicks here. They knew where he was anyway; they were tracking his phone. Where were they then? Should he call that number Hicks had given him?

He clumsily slapped the table in frustration. The booze was supposed to have relaxed him, but it was now having the opposite effect. Four customers in the place turned and looked.

Go NOW!

"Oh, fer cryin' out loud," Dax muttered as he pushed himself to his feet. He glanced around the room, watching it swim for a moment. The woman at the counter was back and drilling him with her eyes.

Dax considered his situation. If he didn't go, Jack may assume the worst and just have someone, maybe Staggs, pull the trigger. And like Decker had said, it wasn't as if Dax could just keep running forever. Jack and his people had easily followed him in a taxi here to Chinatown, so no matter where he went, they'd be there, if they wanted to.

Dax eased himself forward toward the door, one step at a time. The air felt cooler outside and good to his lungs. Foot and car traffic had increased a little as the mid-morning and lunch crowds started to gather.

Okay, so which way was north? He looked up the sidewalk one way, then down the other. He gritted his teeth. It was going to be nice when all this was over, assuming he was still vertical with blood pressure.

"Beckett street," he said to himself, closing his eyes and pinching the bridge of his nose. That way. Pivoting to face what had to be north, he started up the sidewalk at a leisurely gait, staring dumbly at the divider cracks in the pavement as they passed under his feet.

***

Hicks was facing the newspaper stand looking at an alluring, airbrushed model on the cover of some fashion magazine. No matter what happened, Hicks didn't want to see Dax get hurt. He'd been around enough criminals and liars in his day and believed everything Dax had said from the beginning, he just couldn't say it yet.

The radio earpiece crackled. "He's on the move," said Parker. Hicks craned his head sideways and watched as Dax glanced up and down the street. The boy looked confused. Finally, he turned and lightly stumbled, then started up the sidewalk.

Hicks tapped his radio. "What's the matter with him? He looks drunk or something."

After a moment Parker replied, "Can't tell," then added, "Gregg is almost here."

Hicks watched Dax for a moment. "Well, it would explain what's in that bag."

Hicks smiled sadly. Poor kid. Hell of a time for some Dutch Courage though. He turned and glanced down the sidewalk past the newsstand. His eyes instantly locked with an older gentleman in a short-sleeved dress shirt and a sport coat hung over one arm. There was something in his gaze that made Hicks stop. Immediately, and with not the slightest change in expression, the man casually shifted his eyes from Hicks down to a paper in his hand. But Hicks had caught it.

Hicks turned back to Dax as he stepped behind the newsstand wall. He then tapped his radio again. "Gregg, you here yet?"

"Yes, at the south corner watching our subject."

"Good, look behind me down the sidewalk, maybe sixty feet. You see a guy with white hair and a coat over one arm?"

A pause, then, "No."

"What?" Hicks turned and looked down the sidewalk. "He was just there."

"Oh wait, hang on," Gregg said. "Yeah, I see him, but he's way down the street. Moving fast."

"Can you tail him, get a better description or a picture?"

"I can try."

Hicks shook his head as he heard heavy breathing in the radio. Gregg was jogging and forgot to depress the radio button. John Gregg was a seasoned field agent, mid-fifties and close to retirement, but out of shape. Stalking suspects was something he wasn't all that keen on anymore, but today they were pathetically short of personnel. He heard Gregg curse.

"He just hopped into a taxi and bolted. Looks like he told the cabby to step on it," Gregg said.

Hicks kicked the newsstand wall. "Parker, you hear all that?"

"Yeah."

Hicks glanced around again, this time more carefully. They were not alone out here. He watched as Dax continued moving slowly but steadily up the sidewalk. "I'm assuming you didn't get the plate or ID number on the cab."

"That is correct. Went the wrong direction."

"Okay, come on back up. Take your time and take a good look around here near that pastry shop on your way by. Get descrips of anything suspicious. We're gonna role. I need Parker on the radar watching Dax's cell phone."

"Raja that."

Parker emerged from the jewelry shop and without looking in Hicks' direction, started up toward the crosswalk. Hicks waited a moment, his head down at his phone but his eyes roving back and forth from behind the sunglasses. Parker would cross the street then head back down to the car, then Hicks would follow in another minute or so. He wanted to leave now but had a feeling someone was still here.

Dax, although acting disoriented, appeared to be heading somewhere in particular this time. Someone may have just given him instructions. It was probably that character Gregg just saw bolting away in a cab.

As Hicks looked up and down both sidewalks, he took note of everything he could remember that stood out. An old pale green Ford Pinto was pulling into traffic a few feet from the pastry shop. Hicks would remember that, but it'd be useless. A man and two women who appeared to be European tourists with cameras around their necks were making their way up the sidewalk. They didn't look like anything Hicks needed to remember as well.

An engine started nearby and he turned to look. A gray Mercury Mountaineer rumbled to life and the driver turned on the signal. Hicks watched as it eased into traffic and headed in the direction Dax had gone. He saw the backs of the heads of two men. It was probably nothing as well, but Hicks watched for a moment anyway.

***

The tires on the Mountaineer squealed as Jack took a sharp right, turning heads from pedestrians. He glanced in the rearview mirror. The last thing he needed right now was unwanted attention. One more block and he'd take a left and then head to what would hopefully be a rendezvous point.

The radio chirped. Staggs picked it up. "Yes?"

"I was spotted," said Viktor in a voice that betrayed annoyance on the verge of anger.

"By who?"

"I don't know. One of the Americans."

"Where are you?" Staggs asked.

"Four blocks away and moving. I cannot continue until later. I need to redo everything."

Jack growled in frustration. Viktor would be tied up for the next hour giving himself a total makeover. He shook his head and cursed. They'd been right. Even more players in the game now. This had better work. He honked at a delivery truck slowing down to a stop in front of him.

"Let me know when you're available," Jack said quickly and tossed the radio into Staggs' lap.

Jack swerved the Mountaineer around the truck and gunned it.

"We have time," said Staggs, taking hold of the door grip.

That was true. Jack took a deep breath and eased off the gas.

Staggs sat up straighter and stared ahead. "It's coming up. Pull over to the right."

Jack looked at a service door inlaid in the dirty wall that had to be the back of the Tea Leaves restaurant. There were several doors, but this one had carved flower décor and brass handles with what appeared to be Chinese characters.

He turned off the engine, rolled down the windows and reached for his cigarettes. Staggs leaned back and began silently gazing out the window again. If Dax decided to scrap the idea of meeting him and bolted, they'd have to play cat and mouse some more and there were too many eyes on this now.

"Let me see," he said to Staggs, who handed him the small computer. Jack watched the blip on the screen as Dax moved in their direction.

33: Any Way You Can

Dax couldn't tell how long he'd been walking. The sidewalk leaned to-and-fro in a smooth motion and the urge to consume any more of the contents in the bag was quickly diminishing.

Glancing up, he saw a garbage can approaching. Or was he approaching it? Better chuck this bottle. Maneuvering toward the receptacle, he raised the lid and slid the bag under it but then paused. If this were the expensive stuff, he'd probably take the rest home. But it was only ten bucks and about to make him sick anyway. One more quick swig? Nah. He let it slide out of his hand and heard the light thud.

Wiping his hands, Dax straightened up and had to think about where he was and why he was heading up the street. A black and white police car turned in front of him and the driver studied Dax as he went by. Dax almost waved but thought the better of it.

He pushed himself forward and a few minutes later, reached his destination. The entrance to the Tea Leaves restaurant was brightly colored and decorative. Two large red pillars supported a fancy awning that looked like the top of a pagoda. On either side of each pillar hung large red globes adorned with Chinese characters in thick black slashes, mimicking old-style hanging lanterns. He stood on the sidewalk dumbly staring at the colorful display and wondered how good the chicken chow mein was here.

Inside, the restaurant was cool and dark and filled with the odors of frying and sunflower oil. A smiling hostess, a slim Chinese woman in her mid-forties and smartly dressed in a long, elegant dark blue one-piece dress interlaced with turquoise green patterns, greeted him.

"Hello, table for one?" she asked. She studied Dax's eyes for a moment and then looked up him up and down. The smile faded.

It occurred to Dax he'd not thought of how he was supposed to get to the back of the restaurant to wherever the service door was. It also occurred to him that he probably looked as lousy as he felt.

"I-I'm looking for someone," he managed to say.

The hostess' eyebrows came together suspiciously. "Who?"

Dax scanned what he could see of the inside. There were not many customers. "I'm supposed to meet someone here."

Her expression softened. "Why don't you sit down and you can wait for your … friend?" She grabbed a menu from the hostess table and began walking into the dark interior. She chose a table close the front entrance with a decorated partition that blocked the view of the street. Dax eased himself into the seat as steadily and smoothly as he could.

"What does your friend look like?"

Dax gazed up. "Oh … uh, she's five-eight, green eyes, light brown hair, slightly wavy, about down to here." He put his hand near his shoulder as he realized he was describing Meygan Knight. "You can't miss her, she's beautiful."

The hostess smiled warmly. "I'll be on the lookout." She turned to leave.

"*Xie xie ni*," Dax said with a wink.

She turned and smiled, "You're welcome."

Dax smiled to himself. Well done, you got her on your side, sort of, for now. To what advantage, who knew? But every little bit helped.

A Chinese man with a food-stained busboy's apron appeared out of nowhere, plopped an empty glass in front of Dax, and began pouring ice water. It looked delightful as it gurgled and splashed. As soon as the busboy left, Dax snatched up the glass and took a long gulp. The water was cold and tainted with a hint of lemon and orange. A moment later, the glass was empty. He paused and looked around, feeling a twang of embarrassment. But no one was paying any attention.

Dax glanced toward the door. The hostess was behind the partition wall and there were no waiters nearby—a good time to scram and go looking for that service door.

He stood up a little too quickly and was swept over with dizziness. Grabbing the back of a chair, he steadied himself and looked around. His eyes had adjusted to the dim interior and the place appeared a little brighter. He looked at the high-back booth tables and the large round ones in the center of the room.

Straight ahead toward the left corner was what looked like a hallway entrance to maybe the restrooms. He maneuvered around chairs and started that way, stumbling at first. He slowed a bit as he turned into the doorway and almost collided with someone.

A gruff voice said, "Excuse me."

Dax nodded then started down a dimly lit hallway. The left side had several doors including one that appeared to go into the kitchen, judging from the sounds and smells that came from behind a black curtain that covered the entrance. The next door down looked like the women's restroom.

Picking up the pace, Dax tried to ignore a creepy feeling that he was being pursued. He reached the end and shoulder butted against a large double-door, which bounced and cracked, but otherwise didn't move. Glancing down, he saw a bolt lock and slid it open. Clutching the knob, he squeezed and turned, but it wouldn't move and felt slippery, like a person with greasy hands had touched it last. He gripped harder and tried again to turn but to no avail.

"Hey," a voice suddenly said behind him.

Startled, Dax whirled around and saw what appeared to be another busboy who had emerged from the kitchen. He was young, early twenties, his eyes big and owlish behind thick glasses.

"What are you doing?" the busboy asked.

"I was … looking for the restroom," Dax said, as he attempted a smile which at once felt soppy.

The busboy frowned and stared for a moment, then curtly thumbed to the door to Dax's right, clearly labeled "Men."

Dax shrugged. "Oh, sorry." He pushed himself away from the back door and toward the Men's room, feeling the eyes of the busboy. He went straight to the sink and turned on the cold water. Filling two handfuls of water, he splashed his face and rubbed down his hair. It felt pretty good.

After drying off with a hand towel, he casually emerged from the restroom and looked around. No one in sight. Moving again toward the back door, this time with more resolve, he took the handle and rammed his shoulder into it. The door grunted against the frame with a loud thud but held. He took a step back and hunched down, marking the area of the door next to the knob, and then sprang forward. With knee raised high and toes pointed up, he drove his heel into just the spot he'd targeted and connected with a loud bang.

This time the door cracked open and a bar of bright daylight burst into the dim hallway. But the lock was still partially engaged. Quickly stepping back, he leaped and smashed the door again in the same place and this time it burst open. Running through, he turned and grabbed the edge of the door, swinging it closed as best he good.

A car horn honked and Dax turned to see a gray Mercury Mountaineer parked directly across the street. Two men were in the front seat and the driver looked like Jack Dauer.

Dax cursed under his breath and started across the street in a jog.

***

"Chinese restaurant?" Parker said into the radio.

Agent Tommy Hicks used a handkerchief to wipe sweat from his forehead. The brisk walk three blocks to near the front entrance of the Tea Leaves restaurant had felt a bit taxing, especially now as the temperature was beginning to warm up.

"Yeah, the Tea Leaves." Hicks said into the radio. "Went in about five minutes ago. Gee, I'm getting a little hungry myself. Where's his cell phone?"

A pause, then, "Still there." The small screen on the laptop computer in the car could sometimes be hard to read, especially while driving. Parker was doing a good job keeping track.

Hicks checked for messages on his phone. There was none. He was sorely tempted to just walk in and sit down at a table near Dax. If Dax had been instructed to meet someone there, Hicks didn't want to miss the chance to get a good look. Besides, he couldn't just stand around in front of the place.

Glancing up the sidewalk, he saw another small newsstand and decided to first walk past the restaurant entrance and have a peek inside. The radio suddenly chirped.

"He's moving, he's no longer in the restaurant," said Parker.

"What? I've been watching the front like a hawk."

"I'm telling you, he's not in that building anymore."

Hicks frantically looked up and down the street but saw nothing. "Oh no." Snatching up the radio again, he yelled, "Where are you?"

"A block away. South."

"Go around to the back of the building to, uh … wha-what street is that?"

"Pacific."

"Yeah. Go, go, *go!*" Hicks sprinted across the street barely missing a passing car and darted into the restaurant.

The startled hostess, who'd been behind her little table stand, looked up wide-eyed. Hicks raced around the partition and squinted in the dim interior but didn't see Dax.

"Can I help you?" the hostess asked.

Hicks whirled around. "Where'd that guy go that came in a few minutes ago?"

The hostess stared and looked frightened.

"Young guy. Brown jacket. Face kinda messed up. He just walked in here a couple minutes ago."

The woman shook her head. "I-I don't know. He was right there." She stepped behind a partition and pointed at a table. One of the chairs was pulled out and an empty water glass sat on the table in front of it.

"You got a back door here?" asked Hicks.

"Well, no."

"No emergency exit? Service door? Come on!"

"I ... maybe around back..." she looked over Hicks' shoulder.

Hicks turned and followed her gaze to a hallway. He ran for it, pulling on his radio. "Parker, you see anything?" A pause, no answer. "Parker!"

At the end of the hallway, Hicks saw two Asian men dressed like employees of the restaurant standing in an open doorway.

The radio chirped. "Nothing," said Parker. "But I did just see what looked like a gray SUV hitting it hard and turning the corner."

Hicks cursed and ran toward the door. *Gray SUV...* "Was it a Mercury Mountaineer?" he said into the radio.

"Could have been, yes."

"Don't lose it!"

The two men turned to look at Hicks and then scrambled out of the way as Hicks barged past at a full sprint. As he ran out into the street, he saw Parker in the Ford sedan drive by quickly and watched as it turned the corner.

"Was that you?" he heard Parker say in the radio.

"Yes, but don't stop. Don't lose that Mountaineer! I'll catch up."

***

Dax slammed into the door's armrest as the vehicle turned so quickly the right-side tires came off the ground for a moment. After bouncing back down, he fumbled for the seat belt.

"Hi Dax," came the familiar voice of Agent Jack Dauer. It sounded strained and with a touch of anger.

Dax's head bumped the window again. Objects and people on the sidewalk blurred by. He glanced up and saw Jack's eyes in the rearview mirror. "Hi." He saw Jack's right hand on the steering wheel and took note the man was wearing gloves on this mildly warm day.

"You remember Agent Staggs." Jack slowed the car down a little and kept looking back through the mirror.

Agent Michael Staggs started to turn around but stopped before making eye contact. He gave a quick nod but said nothing.

"How's it going," said Dax. The urge to puke was coming on.

"You got your cell phone on you?" Jack asked, staring again through the mirror.

Dax froze. Here it was. He tapped the pocket of his pants. "Yeah. Why?"

Staggs swiveled around and locked eyes with Dax.

"And how is it that you have it?" Jack asked.

Dax felt a cold rush go through his body. With as much sincerity as he could muster, he said, "I took with me."

Staggs continued staring for moment, then turned back around.

Jack was still watching in the mirror. "You were instructed not to take it with you. To leave everything at the hotel."

"I know. Sorry."

"Can you pass it up here?"

Dax dug into his pocket and produced the phone. With a bad feeling, he handed it up between the seats. Staggs, who was also wearing gloves, swiped the phone.

Dax watched the back of Staggs' head as the car bounced along. The man appeared to be looking down and inspecting the phone. Then all at once, Staggs rolled down the window and tossed it out with a flick of his wrist. Dax turned and watched as it bounced and rolled down the sidewalk, pieces of it flying off.

"Hey! That was my phone!"

"Sorry Dax, but we think you're being tailed," Jack said, without any apology in his voice.

Dax paused, then replied, "Really?" He knew he sounded insincere.

The car made another turn, still a little too fast. Jack was watching through the mirror. "Yeah, really." His voice had a knowing tone to it.

Staggs said something that Dax couldn't understand. Jack turned his gaze to the rearview mirror.

Turning around and looking out the back window, Dax saw only one car, a mid-sized Ford sedan.

"Where's the camera that was on your back?" Jack suddenly asked.

Dax looked up and met eyes with Jack in the mirror again. "I guess the police took it."

"The *police*?" Jack asked in mock surprise.

"Yeah. The *real* police."

"What's that supposed to mean?" Jack asked.

Staggs turned partially without looking and asked, "You *guess* the police took it?"

Dax didn't answer. The trouble he feared was already starting. Jack's eyes went back to the road and all three rode in silence for a minute.

Jack pulled over and stopped. The Ford sedan that had been following slowed too, but then sped up and drove by. Dax watched as the driver did a quick but hard glance at the occupants of the Mountaineer and then continued forward. The driver was wearing large sunglasses, but Dax could swear it was the round face of Agent Roy Parker.

"You know that guy?" Jack asked.

Dax looked up at the rearview mirror. "No." He knew he sounded phony.

"You sure?"

Dax shrugged. "Yeah."

Staggs turned around again and looked Dax hard in the eyes. His look was cold and hostile.

Jack waited a moment and then all at once gunned it while making a sharp U-turn, tires squealing. Once again, Dax was slammed into the door of the car, this time his head painfully whiplashing against the window.

"Who are you guys running from?" Dax managed to say, rubbing his head.

"I dunno. Do you?" Jack asked.

Dax shook head then leaned back to brace himself as the car straightened up and tore down the street, rocking like a small boat on choppy water.

Jack made a sharp right and hit the gas pedal even harder. A couple cars nearby honked and someone shouted. Dax heard Staggs talking quietly on a radio or a phone but couldn't understand the words. The tires squealed again as the car made another fast turn.

A sharp pain hit Dax. *Here it comes*, he thought, as he leaned forward and vomited the remaining liquid in his stomach. The pain was intense, especially after the second spasm. Choking and gasping, he remained leaning forward, spitting now to get the acidic burn out of his mouth. He shuffled his feet to avoid the expanding puddle on the floor mat.

Sitting back up, he hit the button on his door to open the window. Cool wind hit his face as he closed his eyes, feeling the blowing air and the sounds of the city outside.

After a few minutes of more wild turning, he felt the car slow down and come to a jolting stop, tires momentarily squealing.

"Let's go, Dax," he heard Jack say, doors opening.

Dax opened his eyes and saw they had stopped in what appeared to be an outdoor parking lot. He couldn't tell what street they were on.

Staggs leaned in the window and looked down on the floor. Dax shrugged. Staggs only glared back and then yanked the door open. As Dax fumbled with the seatbelt, Jack came around.

"What happened, Dax? I didn't know you get car sick."

"Long story," Dax said, releasing the latch on his belt. "Wanna hear it?"

"Later. We have lots to talk about." Jack took him by the arm. "We need to go now. Come on." As he spoke, he was quickly scanning the streets in all directions. "You have anything else on you, like another phone?"

"No," said Dax. "Wanna frisk me?"

Staggs fell behind as the three walked.

"Who's following you ... or me?" said Dax as Jack picked up the pace. They appeared to be heading to the other side of the lot.

"You tell me, Dax," Jack said over his shoulder.

"I told you, I don't know. You're the FBI, don't you?"

Jack kept walking and didn't answer. Dax suddenly felt a little more frustrated than scared. He was also feeling a little better now that he'd puked. "Jack, where were you guys? I was almost killed."

"I'll explain everything. After *you* explain everything."

Dax knew what that last comment meant. He started hitting his memory archives for details of the cover story he'd worked out with Hicks.

Jack stepped to the edge of the sidewalk and dropped what appeared to be the Mercury's keys into a storm drain.

Dax turned around and looked at Staggs, who stood silently behind his sunglasses, a grim, if any, expression on his face.

Dax felt a weariness that superseded worry. "Jack."

Jack was peering up the street but turned to look at Dax. "Where were you guys?"

Jack turned away.

"And who's this *Vassi*? You saw him through the camera, didn't you? The girl called him Vassi. His face was inches from the camera a couple times. He almost killed me." Dax turned to look at Staggs, who gave no response. He turned back to Jack. "I almost died in there."

Jack paused for a moment, as if in thought, but then sighed impatiently. "I'm sorry about that, Dax. But we were unable to assist."

"Can I ask why?"

Staggs suddenly spoke. "Not right now." His voice sounded bitter and distant.

Dax decided it was probably best to stay quiet. There was a really ugly feeling in the air. Once again, he had voluntarily walked into the hands of the bad guys, waiting for the good guys to save him. But in all probability, Parker had lost them several minutes ago.

Behind him, Staggs mumbled something Dax couldn't understand. A small squeal of tires made Dax look up the street. He watched as a blue Jeep Cherokee quickly drove up and stopped next to Jack. Dax didn't recognize the driver.

Jack opened the back door and looked at Dax. "Let's go."

Dax hesitated. "Where are we going?"

"Where we can talk. Come on, we need to hurry."

Dax took a deep breath but remained still. The behavior of both Dauer and Staggs in the last couple minutes had been unsettling. With each passing moment, he was getting more sober, and more nervous. With a finger, he rubbed the sharp edge of the small, hard protuberance in his right front pocket, confirming the brass knuckles were still there.

A heavy hand on Dax's shoulder startled him. Staggs had stepped right up behind him, one hand on Dax's shoulder, the other inside his jacket near his underarm. Dax stared at the bulge in the jacket then looked Staggs in the eyes, at least where they should be behind the sunglasses. Staggs only nodded curtly for Dax to move.

***

"You *what!*" Hicks almost screamed.

The radio went silent. Hicks would have yelled a few more things at Parker, but he was sweating and out of breath. He'd run all the way back to Clay and Stockton where they'd parked.

"Everyone's on the lookout for that Mountaineer, right? I mean *everyone.*" he managed to say into the radio.

"Every cop in SF. Nearby, anyway." Parker's voice was slathered in frustration and shame. He imagined Roland Jacoby listening and having a good laugh.

"And the cell phone?"

"Dead on the side of the road."

"Shit." Hicks slumped into the driver's seat and leaned back, breathing hard. He didn't want to call in to headquarters with this bit of news, not yet. He punched the steering wheel. A supreme opportunity had just been lost, and Dax's life could be on the line.

Find a way to call me, Dax. Any way you can.

34: Parental Mystery

Jim Kirkland sighed deeply and reached for the tumbler of scotch. He only occasionally drank the strong stuff anymore, but at the moment, needed it. The pale, amber liquid looked innocent enough as it glided around the inside of the thick glass but had a strong bite. He'd only had three sips but was already feeling it.

The small plate of appetizers in the middle of the table—baked, stuffed mushrooms—had hardly been touched. A candle deep inside a glass holder flickered slowly next to a small vase with a freshly cut rose in it. Soft music played from somewhere, and the air held a sprightly smell of frying onions and citrus fruit.

On the other side of the table sat the distinguished Rinaldo Silvestri, donning his customary dress shirt with red suspenders. He sat, though, with uncustomary silence. He couldn't remember the last time he'd felt embarrassment, but a few minutes ago, he'd asked the respected theatre director how his son Mario was doing, and everything had gone downhill since.

Rinaldo was frustrated. He knew his son was spoiled and self-indulging. And he wanted it all to come to him easily. The boy had no appreciation for hard work and little respect for others. Rinaldo, unfortunately, was partially to blame for this; he'd take some responsibility, but not all.

He'd taught his children a work ethic, hadn't he? In retrospect, he'd been away tending to business during a lot of Mario's childhood. Mario had grown up with adults that he'd quickly learned he could give orders to. It wasn't that Mario had been given everything he'd wanted. The problem was that it didn't take long for the boy to discover that he *could* have just about everything he wanted by manipulating the system.

Mario wasn't all bad; the kid had potential, but clearly things *had* come too easy for him. And now, watching Jim Kirkland, a man Rinaldo respected, he saw the mistake he'd made when he'd twisted Jim's arm over this damned theatre play.

Rinaldo also sighed and reached for his drink. The best allegedly Italian wine this place offered was a sorry excuse of something red in color, partially fermented, and with a cheesy "Merlot Italy Italian Still" label. He sipped and swallowed quickly, trying not to grimace.

He had decided to take Jim to something different, an American-Asian fusion place called "Hyun's" on the south-end of the financial district. Someone had told him the food was good and they served all kinds of fine wines. He would forget who'd said that and promptly forget this place upon exit.

Rinaldo watched as Kirkland drained the last of his scotch. "Would you like another, Mr. Kirkland?" he said, raising a finger at the waiter.

Jim held up a hand. "No, thank you. I might not be able to find my way back." He managed a smile as he said this. The booze had lightened his spirits, somewhat.

Rinaldo forced a chuckle. "I understand. Something else then?"

"I'm okay for now."

The waiter approached and stood looking at Rinaldo, knowing instinctively who the kingpin was at this particular table.

Rinaldo gestured at Jim. "Are you ready to order?"

Jim paused and realized he really wasn't hungry and would rather just end things now. *Thanks for the drink, Don Corleone, see-ya around.* He was still wondering why he'd accepted the invitation. Deep down, was he intimidated by the local heavyweight before him? Perhaps. There were many rumors about the man, the influence he had and dealings in organized crime.

Jim shrugged to himself. May as well take advantage of the situation. Glancing back at the menu, he ordered a Hawaiian chicken salad with pineapple and papaya. Rinaldo ordered seared Ahi tuna.

The waiter left and they sat in silence for a few minutes. Jim contemplated the lunch gesture. He was still reeling at the way Cheryl Bronson had sold out. He'd known Cheryl for years and she had every much a passion for theatre as he did. Had she been in the business too long? Was she privy to the power Mr. Silvestri could wield in ways Jim was not?

Surely it was more than just money. But maybe not. It struck Jim that a man like Rinaldo Silvestri had the class to pay handsomely while politely and subtly conveying consequences for not obliging him.

Jim hadn't heard that the theatre was in financial trouble or anything. Like most of the smaller venues—San Francisco's version of the "off Broadways"—there was always the challenge of selling enough tickets to keep things clean and attractive. But were they in the hole? They'd had a few good runs lately. Why would Cheryl do this?

Rinaldo was watching Jim. He didn't want to talk about his son anymore, but there appeared to be little else to converse about. He broke the uncomfortable silence. "Mr. Kirkland, you are one of the best directors in the city."

Jim looked up, eyebrows raised. "You think so?" He wanted to ask, *how many of my shows have you seen?* Instead, he asked, "Which of my shows have you liked the best?"

Rinaldo stared back for a moment, the slightest hint of a smile in his eyes. The man before him was too old to play games, which made him respect Kirkland even more. "My son is a great admirer of yours. He would have done anything to be in one of your shows."

Jim tapped a finger on his empty glass. "I had not met your son before this," he finally said. His own statement made him pause and wonder how things would have been different had he been a father. Would he go out of his way to manipulate and pull strings if his kid needed help?

Rinaldo smiled. "You're an important man. Important men are not always easy to reach."

Jim actually laughed. He was important, huh—important enough to replace if he didn't go along with bribery. "I'm easy to find, Mr. Silvestri. If anyone wanted to put me in the trunk of a car, they wouldn't have to look very far."

Rinaldo's eyebrows tightened for a moment.

Jim raised a hand. "Seriously, I've been around here for years. Anyone who knows anything about the local theatre scene would know where to find me almost any day of the week."

Rinaldo nodded then reached for his glass. He stared at it for a moment then put it back on the table. "Mario has been studying hard. That is where he met Les Abraham, your colleague."

At the mention of Les' name, Jim froze and looked up. His mind began to whirl. Did Les have anything to do with this business with Mario? He decided to take note and bring it up with Les later.

"Yes, I know, or I've been told," Jim said. "About Mario taking classes. But my point is that I've not run into Mario anywhere before this. As far as I know, he's not actually done any real theatre. Going over scenes in class is one thing, going out on stage and performing to an audience is something else. That requires a whole different kind of effort. And proving yourself."

Rinaldo nodded again, and this time picked up the glass and sipped. He swallowed and said, "He really wants to be an actor."

Jim looked at Rinaldo. "Many young people do. Attention and admiration and all that. But do you know why?"

Rinaldo looked puzzled for a moment, but then considered the deeper implication of Kirkland's question. Mario had never really spoken of why he wanted to be an actor, but clearly, the boy thought it would be fun and glamorous. Not to mention full of beautiful women. But he asked anyway, "What do you mean?"

Jim looked at his glass, then picked it up. "I think I will have one more, if you don't mind."

Rinaldo beamed a cordial smile. "Of course." He turned and waved down a waiter.

Jim weighed his words carefully. "What I mean is … I've been a teacher of theatre and drama for many years. It's not the highest paying profession around. But I do it because I love it. Always have loved it. And I get satisfaction from mentoring others who have that same passion. There's nothing like seeing a great show come together with the right cast."

The waiter came by and Rinaldo pointed at Jim's glass. Jim watched the waiter walk away for a moment, listening to the demure clink of glasses, murmuring conversations and other noises around them.

Jim continued, "I really enjoy seeing a young person pursue their passion and go for their dreams. I was once there, many years ago. I particularly like seeing those that have the guts and gumption to really put out the blood, sweat, and tears; to do what it takes to get where they want to go. Along the way they find out who they really are and what they're really good at." Jim paused and looked up at Rinaldo. "You seem to me a man who knows about that sort of thing."

Rinaldo folded his hands in front of him and his mind drifted. He had worked hard as a busboy in four different restaurants before becoming a manager. The small Italian restaurant he managed had been owned by a man with the last name of Brown who didn't speak a word of Italian. But he liked the young and hard-working Rinaldo, and so did the patrons. Business increased when Rinaldo started running things, mostly by instinct. Rinaldo sometimes worked fourteen-hour days. His young, pretty wife bustled as a waitress for some time and made great tips. They both saved every penny until he had enough for a down-payment on a lease for what would become his own place. And, as they say, the rest was history.

Rinaldo looked up with the horrifying thought that Mario would not only go nowhere in acting, he'd go nowhere in life period. "Yes, I do. I know about hard work," he said slowly.

Jim hoped he hadn't insulted the man but continued. "What I'm getting at, is that Mario was just ... *given* this. And he wasn't just given anything." He stabbed his finger on the table. "He was given an important role in a well-known and popular show. One that's been anticipated by the local theatre community. It's a privilege to get picked for such a part. The actors that are chosen for such things have the background, the foundation. They've proven themselves with the smaller parts and worked their way up."

The waiter returned and set the glass in front of Jim. He picked it up and took a long pull, knowing that it might make him start babbling, but he didn't care. This was his chance to get some things off his chest.

"And more importantly," Jim said, setting his glass back down. "The director needs to be able to choose his actors and actresses."

"Mr. Kirkland," Rinaldo started to say.

"Please," Jim said boldly. He was, after all, still upset at the man, more so now that Les Abraham might be involved. "There are parts a kid like Mario could play, or learn to play. He has a swagger and a cocky confidence about him. And he's not bad looking. There are characters he could experiment with, get some real-world experience under his belt."

"Mr. Kirkland," Rinaldo said again, this time a little firmer.

Jim paused and reached for his drink.

Rinaldo leaned forward and rested his forearms on the table. "Do you not think I know about starting from the bottom? Do you not think I *played* my smaller parts before finding myself nearer to the top?"

Jim regarded the man in front of him. The thick red suspenders looked like they'd been around awhile, but not yet worn looking. His shirt was neatly pressed and looked expensive—thick material, light blue with a white collar. Rinaldo's dense gray hair was stylishly cut and combed precisely, set firmly in place with what looked like gel. But the man's face and hands had mileage, set deeply in rugged lines. He looked healthy and squeaky clean, but also like one who'd once held tools and worked by the strength of his back.

"Yes, I do," Jim said. "This is why I don't understand why this has been handed to Mario so easily. He hasn't earned this, Mr. Silvestri."

Rinaldo signed deeply, picked up his glass and drained the last of the contents in one gulp. He then raised it and turned his head until he caught the attention of the waiter. He slowly set the glass down and then folded his fingers together on the table. "Mario has an older brother, Arturo." A smile formed on his face for a moment. "A great son. Good head on his shoulders. He will someday run the restaurants."

And run a few other things, Jim thought.

"But Mario," Rinaldo continued, his voice lowering, the smile fading. "I've spent years trying to figure out what to do with him. When someone can't do for themselves, someone else steps in. If they care. And I do care. He has dreams; he's always been a dreamer. No solid plans, no real instinct for anything, just dreams. And wild fantasies."

Rinaldo shrugged to himself while a bunch of thoughts crossed his mind. His face softened and looked sad.

Jim took a sip of his drink and watched.

Rinaldo broke out of his thoughts and looked again at Jim. "What does a man do when he loves his son and wants to help?"

The scotch was emboldening Jim even more. "You teach him to work for what he's got," he said, holding his palms out.

Rinaldo paused as his face morphed from sadness into a slight scowl. "I have dutifully taught my sons everything I know. I have told them everything I have done and where I have come from. They've seen my scars and heard my stories." He paused. "And I am at a loss as to why one son seems to understand and the other does not."

Once again, Jim was struck with the whole mysterious parental thing. While he'd had his share of "kids" over the years in the form of students and actors, many of whom he'd been a father figure to no doubt, he knew raising one, or two, from birth would be on a whole different level.

Rinaldo had asked a question.

"I'm sorry?" Jim said, the room around him looking smoother and rounder in his vision.

The slight smile had returned to Rinaldo's eyes. "I asked, will you try with my son, to help him be the best he can be?" He leaned forward. "I can make it worth it to you. If you understand."

Jim felt his face flush. "I'm not for sale like Cheryl Bronson, Mr. Silvestri. Just please give me your word you'll never do this again." Although he meant every word, he knew three decades ago he just might have taken the money. As an established man now, past middle age and having had done well in his career, he had no desire to take anything from a man like Rinaldo Silvestri.

Rinaldo stared for a moment, then said, "You have my word that I will never do this again to any performance here. Not to any director."

Jim almost chuckled; it was all so absurd. Rinaldo looked sincere, but what if Jim said no? Would this man in front of him pull strings on every show he did going forward as punishment? Would he eventually end up in that trunk of a car getting crushed in the wrecking yard? He regarded the man in front of him, the sad and tired Dr. Jekyll father, and the Mr. Hyde local mafioso who had friends in high places.

Rinaldo sat staring back, that calm waiting-for-an-answer look that said the stare wouldn't end until there was an answer.

"Yes, Mr. Silvestri," Jim said with as much sincerity as he could muster. "I will try to get Mario to play this role as best as I can. I do, after all, have selfish reasons. But I can't make a person do what he can't. I can't give a person talent, or experience he never had."

Rinaldo stared for a few moments longer nodding in understanding, then said, "Thank you."

Jim nodded and reached for his glass.

Two waiters approached and carefully set plates down. The food was artistically and colorfully arranged and smelled quite good.

Rinaldo ripped a piece of tuna off with his fork and stuck it in his mouth. He chewed while looking up in thought, then nodded. "Not bad," he said. "Too bad the wine here is garbage. I know a good Ornellaia that would go well with this."

Jim nodded and dug into his salad.

35: Plan B

All four passengers in the Jeep Cherokee, including the driver, rode in silence. This time Jack was up front riding shotgun while Dax and Staggs rode in back. Dax had a thousand questions but was now afraid to ask. Staggs in particular was making him nervous.

The tires of the car squealed a little as they rounded a corner and began heading south. A growing headache made Dax's eyes blurry and he had to squint from the bright light.

Dax heard Jack mumble something to the driver that wasn't in English, and the Jeep slowed down. Dax wasn't sure of anything he was seeing or hearing anymore.

Who are you, Jack?

Dax turned to look at Staggs who sat stoically staring ahead from behind his sunglasses, a grim look on his face, ignoring everything around him.

Dax took a deep breath and looked out the window again, trying to control his fear. He was also trying to memorize the streets to see where he was going. Recent events had shown the importance of remembering details and locations.

"Have you guys been following me all morning?" Dax asked.

"Why do you ask?" said Jack.

"Because I'm sitting in some random place in Chinatown and suddenly you're there. I botched an important job. I lost some expensive equipment. That *Vassi* guy who almost killed me probably has friends who are looking for me, right?"

"You see anyone following you?" Jack asked, turning around.

Dax paused then shrugged and said, "No, don't think so."

They drove in silence for a minute before Jack asked, "Where were you last night?"

Okay, here it goes …

"I was arrested by San Francisco PD."

"What for?"

"Are you kidding?" Dax asked incredulously.

Staggs slowly turned and stared at Dax.

"I mean, on what charge," Jack said, trying to remain patient.

"Well, I guess I was arrested because I was dressed up for a gathering nearby where someone just got shot. My clothes were torn and I had blood on me."

"And the gun?"

"What gun?"

Jack turned further and gave Dax a stare so cold it made him pause.

"I tossed it in a planter on the sidewalk. One of those big ones with the small trees."

Jack regarded Dax for a few seconds, trying to read his eyes. "Where'd they arrest you?" he finally asked.

"A couple blocks down from the Omni. Frankly, I was glad they did. I don't know who might have been chasing me."

"You see anyone chasing you?"

Dax looked up. "Yeah. Two at least."

"What did you tell the cops?"

"I told them I was at a meeting downstairs on the first floor. One of those become your own travel agent things. I told them I heard gunshots and ran for the door. On my way through the lobby, there were people running all over the place and I collided into this big guy and he and I both hit the ground."

Staggs turned his stare back out the window.

Jack continued watching Dax's eyes. "And they believed that?" he asked, a hint of mockery in his tone.

Dax shrugged. "They must have. It was incredibly busy there. At the police station, that is. All kinds of people – drunks, junkies, hookers, whoever. I was just another face in the crowd, I guess." Dax stopped and realized he needed to be careful not to add too much speculation about circumstances or other people's motives.

"Then what?" asked Jack.

"What do you mean?"

"Did anyone talk to you, ask you questions?"

"Oh yes, later. A few hours later. Some detective took me to a room. Asked me all kinds of stuff. What did I see, what did I know, and so on. I pretty much convinced him I knew nothing, saw nothing, did nothing. I was just some guy that ran for his life when he heard gun shots."

"Did they know who you were?"

Dax was ready for such gotcha questions. "Sure, I had my ID, remember? I took that stuff with me."

"Yeah. I remember," Jack said, continuing to stare hard.

"So yeah, it was good I had all that because they were able to run me through the system. No arrest records. No warrants. They apologized, took the cuffs off, and had me wait in another, nicer room until the morning staff could process me and let me go."

"And your injuries? No trip to the hospital?"

"No. Some staff nurse there came and looked at me. Nice girl named Amy. Gave me a bandage and some pain killers." Dax looked around at the buildings going by. He wasn't entirely sure where he was, but it looked like they were going north out of the financial district.

Jack turned back around. "Let's talk about your phone again, Dax."

Dax's heart started to thump in his chest.

"You say you took it with you to the Omni?"

Dax felt his face drain of blood. In his peripheral vision, he saw Staggs turn and look at him. "Yeah, I took it. I know you said not to. But I felt naked without it."

"We don't think you did, Dax." Jack's voice had taken on a smooth, emotionless tone that Dax had not yet heard up to this point.

"W-Why's that?" Dax asked, his voice starting to quiver and betray him.

Jack turned back and was staring again, his chin down and his eyes angry. "How do you think we might know this?"

"I-I don't know … you-you may have tried to check and didn't know or … made a mistake – "

"Dax, am I an idiot?"

Dax clenched his fists in frustration. He looked out the window, desperate for the improvisation skills he'd worked hard to acquire over the years, but once again, fear was blocking everything.

Jack was watching closely, a sinister smile forming on his lips. "Actually Dax, we didn't check on your phone. You almost had us."

From the corner of his eye, he saw Staggs move but it was too late. A horrific pain burst through the side of his face as a fist smashed in. Dax screamed and reeled back.

Plan B. Here we go.

"Okay, okay," Dax said through his hands. "I left it at the Sutter like you asked me to." Dax felt as if his voice were squeaking, but he had no control. "Someone at the police station came in a few hours later and told there'd been a shooting at the Sutter hotel. People were murdered. They'd found my clothing and wallet and everything there and came over when they found out I'd been arrested." He opened his eyes and saw Jack and Staggs staring at each other.

Jack's gaze shifted back to Dax. "Go on. What happened next?"

"Did you know that? Did you know some of your friends got killed?" Dax asked, feeling a building rage that was overtaking fear. First these two had deceived him and almost got him killed. Now they were upset *he* was lying?

"Just keep talking!" Staggs sneered. "What next?"

"Nothing. I told them I was calling a lawyer, that my stuff had been stolen. I gave a description of a guy that looks like Jeremy Forrester. Said he stole it. That's how it must have gotten there."

Staggs raised a fist as if to strike again. Dax cowered down and away.

"You're not being truthful," Jack said. "That makes me angry. Now, who did you talk to last night and what did you say?"

Leaning over and clutching his face, Dax used the position to slide his hand into the upper portion of his pocket and curl a couple fingers around the rings of the brass knuckles. In this position, it would be tough to pull them out, but he had to try. His youth, strength and training had saved him before, perhaps it could again.

"I'll tell you what, Agents *Jack Dauer* and *Michael Staggs* of the FBI," Dax said through his hand. "If you were the real deal, you'd know *exactly* where I was last night!"

Positioned on Staggs' left and remembering the man was left-handed, Dax knew he had to be quick. Throwing his body up as fast as it could move, he bent his arm and delivered a right elbow as hard as possible into the side of Staggs' face. Staggs grunted and fell back into the side of the door, his hand moving to cover his cheek.

"Dax!" Jack yelled. "Stop!"

Staggs leaned forward and was going for the handle of his gun just as Dax slipped the brass knuckles around his fingers. Slapping down on Staggs' wrist to keep the gun holstered, he used all his weight and whatever strength his injured, non-dominant arm could muster and delivered a crushing, brass-reinforced blow to the faux agent's face, partially hitting the man's nose and partially under his eye.

Dax felt his knuckles crack and the edge of the yellow metal dig into skin and realized he had not been able to slide them up far enough on his fingers.

"*Sukin syn!*" Staggs roared, as blood immediately began pouring from his nostrils.

Jack had removed his seat belt, produced a gun and was swinging it over the back of the seat as Dax turned. Chopping his arm leftward and oscillating his wrist in a flipping motion, a classic martial arts block, Dax made contact and Jack's arm bounced back just as the gun went off.

This was the second time Dax had been around a gun in close proximity, but this time, the weapon had no silencer to deafen the noise. The thundering concussion produced an instantaneous high-pitched hum in his ears and caused actual pain in his head. As the rear window shattered from the bullet's impact, the boom also caused the driver to flinch hard, turning the wheel so sharp, it tipped the vehicle to one side, almost rolling it.

"Dax!" he heard Jack yell. But his hands were clutching Jack's wrist, as they both tussled for the gun. Using the bouncing motion to his advantage, Dax turned the gun toward the front windshield.

"*Kozyol!*" he heard Staggs snarl and looked to see his gun half-way out of the holster. Using the leaning position he was already in, Dax pointed his toes upward and drove a heel into the already bleeding face of Staggs. The man's head snapped backward and hit the car window with such force, it produced an instant daze in his eyes.

The driver yelled and turned hard again, swerving to miss several people in a crosswalk. Dax shoved Jack's arm forward and the gun sounded again, this time causing part of the driver's neck to explode in pieces, sending blood spattering in all directions. The man slumped forward as the Jeep careened toward the curb and several parked cars.

Dax let go and ducked behind the seat just as the car smashed into the rear fender of a mid-sized pickup truck. With a huge bang and the sound of crunching metal, he felt his body get hurled forward as he twisted and turned just in time so that his back hit flat against the back of the front seats.

The horn of the Cherokee began blaring. Dax pulled himself up. The driver's partially crushed head pressed firmly on the horn button. Jack had been thrown against the windshield with such force, almost the entirety of the glass was covered in zigzagging, spiderweb-like cracks. His eyes were closed, and he was not moving, blood tickling down over the long bridge of his nose.

As the sound of people yelling grew nearer, Dax heard a groan and turned to Staggs. The man, bloodied and banged up, clutched the back of his head, and tried to sit up. His eyes remained partially closed from the pouring blood and pain. *"Ya tebya ub'yu ..."* he mumbled, fumbling around for his gun.

"Pashol nahuy!" Dax said through gritted teeth as he switched the brass knuckles from his left to right hand, this time pushing them up tight. Sitting and swiveling his body for better leverage, he wound up and delivered a blow to Staggs' face with such force, he heard something crack.

Staggs gave one last groan, then fell back unconscious, his head thudding on the window.

Dax looked out the windows and quickly took in his surroundings. Three or four people were running up the sidewalk and several more were crossing the street. He glanced down at Staggs' gun, which had fallen on the seat between them. It was tempting, but no, this time he'd leave the weapons. He'd not touched them so there'd be no prints.

Crawling across the seat, he reached for the door handle and yanked and pushed, but the door wouldn't move. He felt pain in his left hand, almost as if some bones behind his fingers had been cracked. He heard people shouting and getting closer. Forgetting the injury to his shoulder and hand, he leaned in and rammed the door, then fell back yelling in pain. The door still had not moved.

He scurried as quickly as he could over the seat into the rear cargo area just as onlookers ran up and looked into the windows. A woman screamed at the bloody sight in the front seats just as Dax got hold of the tailgate release and shoved it open.

"Are you okay?" a man said as Dax rolled out of the back of the Jeep and on to the ground. He looked up and saw a man and woman staring in wide-eyed horror.

"Yeah, but those guys," Dax said, standing up and thumbing to the inside of the car. "Tell the cops they tried to kill me."

And with that, Dax started running.

"Hey!" he heard behind him, but he didn't turn or stop. He didn't know where he was going, he just knew he had to flee.

***

The gentleman exited the lobby of the small motel on Ellis Street and looked for a taxi. Seeing none, he headed toward the entrance to the parking lot. An hour before, the same white-haired man with glasses had entered donning gray slacks and an olive cashmere sport coat. He had been unremarkable then, and was unremarkable now, except that he was a different person. His hair was a rich brown color, and he wore a shiny soft-wax leather jacket. For pants, he wore something he almost never did – dark blue designer jeans. They were uncomfortable as hell but were necessary. He wore no glasses this time. By all appearances, he was twenty years younger than the same man an hour ago.

As he headed toward the main street, he was on alert as usual. Years of training and acquired instincts taught him that at no time should a person be unaware of his surroundings. And those instincts were kicking in quickly. It wasn't that he feared the common mugger or anything like that; the weapons he carried and skills he possessed were more than adequate to deal with such things. But he did have a healthy paranoia about his counterparts – professionals in same the business he was in.

From his peripheral vision, he noticed a vehicle that had circled around a row of cars and was now approaching in his general direction. If the car stopped, it might be dropping off a passenger at the front of the motel. But it didn't, it continued at the pace one would do to calculate intercepting him at the entrance to the street.

He quickly scanned for taxis as he approached the parking lot exit. There were none. Glancing behind and seeing the stern faces behind the windshield, he knew he was in trouble. He cursed to himself. In his older age, he was getting sloppy. For the entire trip back here, he'd scanned the road behind and around relentlessly. He'd even asked the cabby to drive around several blocks first before approaching the motel. Still, he'd been followed. These were the kind of people he feared, people who were as good or even better at their job than he was.

As he hit the sidewalk that ran parallel to the motel, he did a quick glance in both directions and made a sharp turn toward the corner that had the most people. Perhaps he could create a diversion, get someone's attention, the kind of attention other criminals did not like. He cursed again. All this effort to change appearance had been for naught.

He picked up his pace and turned his head just enough to see the car exit the parking lot and then abruptly pick up speed and stop beside him with a small squeal of tires. It was too late.

The doors of the dark Laforza 4x4 SUV quickly opened and two men jumped out and stood behind him. A third man, tall and with an unmistakable scar that lined his face from temple to chin stepped in front.

"Oh no ..." Lozovsky whispered to himself. He did not know the two men behind him, but he knew the man with the scar. Rumor was that his real name was Alexander Tsepov, better known as *Sacha the Sword*. Ukrainian-Russian by birth, he started as a hitman who would become infamous for committing several high-profile murders at a relatively young age. During that time, he worked his way up to a mid-ranking member of the Crimean Salem gang but was now running certain operations for Gurkovsky. For a man of this caliber to be involved, the young American he had been following today was part of something much bigger than Jack had told him.

"Hello, Viktor," Tsepov said. "We need to talk, yes?"

36: Eavesdropping

Dax ran until his chest hurt too much to continue. He had made his way down several blocks, zigzagging instinctively in a direction he thought was toward streets he was more familiar with. But why, he didn't know. He couldn't go back to his apartment, and now covered in blood, again, and looking like a mess, *again*, he couldn't hang around anywhere either.

Exhausted and sweat soaked, he came to a halt, leaned inside a doorway and looked around. No one had followed. Turning the door handle and easing it open a couple inches, he saw he was standing in the rear entrance of what looked like a mechanic's shop. Near the door was a milk crate full of rags. Quickly reaching in, he grabbed a couple, then began walking down the sidewalk, wiping his face.

First things first – he had to get hold of some money. With cash he might be able to get a ride back to FBI headquarters, or maybe out of the city. Too many people hunting him and maybe trying to kill him. Could Jack and his people have the ability to freeze his bank account? He was going to find out.

When he got to the end of the block, he looked around. Down the street there appeared to be more buildings which meant a gas station, convenience store, or some place that hopefully had an ATM. He started down that direction in a brisk walk, almost a jog. As he went, he took off his jacket and folded it over an arm. The sweat immediately chilled him, but by now cops could be looking for someone with his description.

He came to the corner of the block and gazed across the street to what appeared to be a small café. Running across to the doorway, he stuck his head in and asked the young woman behind the counter where an ATM was. She thumbed in the direction up the sidewalk and said, "Bank."

Dax started that way, paranoid that any second, he'd hear a police horn chirp at him and a voice telling him to stop and get on the ground.

***

Aaron Tisdale sat in his red Ford Escort with the car seat leaned back as far as it could. A tad ironic, the name of the car he did this sort of thing in. He wasn't all that comfortable in this particular alley, but it would have to do. He studied the graffiti and other spray paint creations on the old wooden wall next to him. On the other side was a red brick wall.

He looked down at the back of the head of the girl whose face was in his crotch as it bobbed up and down. She had looked real persuasive a few minutes ago as she was strolling up the street, swaying her hips and showing off long legs under tight and very short shorts. Her smooth, brown skin had looked so good against the off-white color of the shorts. But now her cheap perfume, stale cigarette stench and rude attitude was starting to disgust him. From the moment he'd picked her up and she looked him up and down, he could tell she had been disgusted as well, and that bothered him.

This girl just wanted to hurry up and get it over with. She moved faster with obvious impatience, not trying to give pleasure so much as perform a physical task she clearly hated, but one that a terrible set of circumstances in life was forcing her to do.

Normally, Aaron at least wanted to make it to completion, so it was somewhat worth the time, money, and risk. Especially the money, something he didn't have a lot of. But it was reaching a point to where he was about to tell her to forget it. Just get out and go away. I'll forget you and you'll forget me.

He was getting ready to do this when all at once a figure ran across the alleyway entrance, paused, then turned and hurried across the street.

Wait, was that Dax Ribeiro?

Grabbing the seat adjustment lever, he pulled and sat up. Yes, that was Dax.

"What are you doing?" the girl asked, looking up at him.

Aaron ignored her, staring hard across the street.

"Hello?" she asked.

Aaron grabbed his pants, which were bunched down close to his knees, and raised up to pull them and his underwear back up. "We're done," he said, pushing her head away.

The girl sat up. "You see a cop or something?"

"No, just go," Aaron said, snapping his pants and tugging at his fly.

The girl looked behind them, then forward again. "Whatever," she said, opening the door. "I'll keep the change." Slamming the door shut, she strode away, not quite swaggering like she had when he first saw her.

He was relieved when she was gone. He'd have to drive around a bit with the windows down and the air blasting to get her stench out. He watched her butt for a moment as she walked away, then returned his gaze to Dax who was now at the ATM of the bank across the street. Dax looked hurried, glancing back and forth. What was he doing in this part of town acting like that? It must have something to do with what Aaron had seen the other night.

He started the engine and waited. A moment later, Dax looked up and down the street again, then hurried away. This may be the only chance Aaron had to talk to him and understand what was going on. Perhaps he didn't want to know. Dangerous people were obviously involved and this was not his thing. It was fascinating though. And besides, Dax looked like he was in trouble.

Of all the actors Aaron had worked with in recent years, Dax was definitely one of the more agreeable ones. Him and Dennis Sheridan were the two nice ones during this last show; Elizabeth Brauner was pleasant but standoffish. Sure, the Karate Kid didn't really like him any more than anyone else did, but Dax never outright disrespected or ignored him either, and that meant something.

Easing out of the alleyway, Aaron turned into the street in the direction Dax had gone. At first he didn't see him, and sped up, worried he'd lost him. But there he was, walking quickly and with purpose. Wow, he was moving fast.

***

Dax was beginning to feel cold. He was still too close to the crash scene to put his jacket back on though. He was able to get the $500 daily limit out of the ATM though and felt much better for it.

He picked up his pace. Now that he was going in a straight line, he was able to put more distance between him and the smashed-up Jeep Cherokee that had at least one dead body in it. He had no idea if Jack had survived.

A car horn behind him made him jump and whirl with a surge of adrenaline that almost made his head pop. A red Ford

Escort crept up to the curb and stopped. Dax looked around frantically but saw nothing else that alarmed him. He slowly approached as the passenger window rolled down.

Peering in, he saw the puffy and perplexed face of the stage manager, Aaron Tisdale.

They both stared at each other, not sure of what to say. Dax took another look up and down the street then leaned back in. "Aaron?"

"You okay, Dax?" Aaron asked.

Dax thought the better of wasting time standing here when he should be moving. "I'm good," he said. "Thanks for asking. See you around." And with that he started up the street again.

He heard the car's transmission click into drive and it pulled up next to him again as he walked. "Hey," Aaron said. "Who were the guys with the guns?"

Dax froze, then turned and went back to the window. "What do you know about that?" His first thought was that Aaron had witnessed the crash a few minutes ago.

"The other night, on California street," Aaron said. "I saw you. You were in this fancy suit. I stopped and was looking at the guys in the car you just got out of. One of them jumped out and came at me. Pulled a gun partway out. Scared the shit out of me."

Dax studied Aaron for a moment and saw he was clearly telling the truth. He racked his memory and had not seen Aaron and his little red car that night. But then, he had been a little preoccupied.

"You need help?" Aaron asked.

A police siren in the near distant could be heard and was getting louder. An idea suddenly hit Dax. He grabbed the door handle, hopped in, and shut the door quickly, then leaned the seat back.

Aaron stared with wide, worried eyes. "Dax, what's going on, man? Who's chasing you, those guys with the guns?"

Dax smirked bitterly. "Actually, they are. Them and a few others."

"Are you kidding?"

"Wish I was. Listen, I gotta get out of here. Can we move?"

"Are the cops after you? I don't want to get in trouble."

"You won't, trust me. You're fine."

"Are you sure? You've got blood on you or something."

Dax sat up and looked at the visor mirror. Although he'd gotten most of the blood off with the rags, there were smears around his neck and ears that had the distinct look of post injury bleeding.

"Did you kill someone?" Aaron asked, his voice taking on a frightened tone.

Dax turned to Aaron. "No. Someone tried to kill me."

Aaron's eyes got wider.

Dax continued. "What if I told you I was hired for a big acting job, undercover work?"

Aaron looked at him for a moment. "I don't know what I'd think. But that guy with the gun didn't look like any actor. He looked like he was going to kill me."

"He wasn't an actor. Look, can we just drive? I'll tell you more as we go."

Aaron hesitated, but then put the car back in drive. "Okay, where?"

Dax racked his brain for streets that were close to the Godwin Theatre, but not too close. He could trust no one at this point with any information they didn't need to know. "Can you drop me off near Turk and Webster?" he finally asked.

"Why?"

"Just do it, please? You asked me a minute ago if I needed help. I have a friend I need to see and he's near there. I'll make it up to you."

Aaron put his eyes on the road and eased out into traffic.

Dax kept looking in the rearview mirror but there appeared to be no one following. "I appreciate this, Aaron. I really do."

They drove in silence for a couple minutes, Aaron cautiously making his way through side streets while Dax remained reclined in the passenger seat.

Aaron, feeling the urge as well as the right to ask more questions, got up the nerve and asked, "What were you talking to Jim about the other day?"

"Huh?"

"I saw you in the lobby. At the Treasure Box. Talking to Jim Kirkland. Was he offering you a part in *Wild Hearts*?"

Dax chuckled. "No, nothing like that. I just wanted to talk to him."

"Is he part of all this?"

"A part of what?"

"This undercover job thing."

"Oh no, not at all. Jim's got nothing to do with it."

Another minute of silence. "You hear about that Mario guy? He got the part of Cash Giles. Word is buzzing around that Jim didn't want him. No one knows anything about him. No one even knows why he's in the show."

Dax thought for a moment. The whole Mario thing was interesting, but nothing he had the luxury of pondering on right now. "Yeah," he said, "I did hear about it. Jim told me. I don't know the guy and I don't know why Jim would pick him."

"That's the thing. Jim didn't pick him. Someone came in and made him do it. I heard the conversation."

Dax turned and looked at Aaron in genuine surprise. "You heard the conversation? For a guy that doesn't get around much, you hear a lot of things."

Aaron looked away, a bit despondent.

Dax felt bad for making the comment. "What I mean is, you seem to know a lot." He fell silent, realizing that a guy like Aaron could be silently lurking unbeknownst in a lot of places.

Aaron started to smile, appearing to be pleased with himself for having important information to share. "I didn't hear everything, just some of it. Some bigwig guy, lots of weight I guess, comes into the office with Jim and Cheryl Bronson and they have this powwow. Next thing I know, Jim is yelling. Really pissed off. Saying things like, 'That's unacceptable!'"

Dax was incredulous. "You were there? How'd you hear all this?"

Aaron shrugged. "Not really *there*, there. I was near the door."

Dax laughed. "So you had your ear pressed to the door?" He always knew Aaron was a strange guy but hearing him confess he'd been eavesdropping on a private conversation in Cheryl Bronson's office gave him a whole new insight into the character of the theatre's stage manager.

"Well, not really," Aaron stammered. "Well, kinda, yeah. But only for a minute. I was intrigued because I heard Jim getting mad."

"So, who was it? Who made Jim cast this Mario guy?"

"I'm not sure," Aaron said. "He sounded older. I heard the name Mr. Silvestri. That's all I know."

"Mr. Silvestri, huh."

Aaron slowed the car. "We're here. You want me to pull over?"

Dax eased the seat up and looked around. "Sure, this looks fine." Dax got out then leaned into the window. "Aaron, I owe you, man. Listen, I'll be okay and so will you. Those guys aren't going to come after you. Trust me, they don't care about you."

"What about you?"

"I don't know yet. But I'll see you around, okay? Take care and thanks again." And with that, Dax turned and headed up the sidewalk.

Aaron stared after him for a moment and then breathed a sigh of relief. For whatever reason, he believed Dax just now, that no one was going be after him. It was easy to believe because no one caring about him had been his life's story.

37: Tempus Fugit

Slipping back into his jacket, Dax hurried up the block and turned right in the direction of the Godwin Theatre. It was still two blocks away. He needed a place to recoup, and this was his best option. As he walked, he thought about the old unalarmed door around the back of the building Old Ben had mentioned. Dax was counting on this to be true.

The late afternoon temperature was dropping as Dax approached the old, converted building. Just a couple nights ago, people had waited in line there next to the main doors, waiting to see him play a hero named Eric.

Dax stood at the corner and looked up and down the cross streets. There was no car or foot traffic, as one would expect at this time of day. There should be no one here building props and planning the next show. That would happen in a week or two after everyone had had a break.

He walked up to the fence that shut out the small walkway leading around the back of the building. It was a standard swinging chain-link gate with a padlock. Carefully looking around, knowing full well that if anyone were watching, he'd look mighty suspicious, he put a foot into one of the fence holes and hoisted himself up. The gate was only about five feet high and in one push, he was over and on the other side.

The old alleyway was a perfect setting for scenes he'd acted in recently. Old cobblestone paved the ground, spaced with age and wear with dark moss growing between the cracks. The building side was old bricks, cracked and aged. The windows had modern security bars fastened over them. On the other side was an old wooden fence strewn with ivy growth that separated the theatre's property from the one next to it. It was a picturesque scene that only time could create.

Moving quickly, Dax made a left and continued around the back of the building while wondering how many times Old Ben had made this same walk over the years.

Across from the service entrance, a car portal gate had been installed where a little service road jutted out between adjacent buildings. This allowed large pieces of props, lights, and various tools to be brought through to the back of the stage where the crew did their magic. Dax always admired the creative minds that were able to fabricate scenes that visually took an audience to different times and places.

A light above the entrance suddenly burst on, illuminating the area in front and around the gate. It startled Dax badly and he almost yelled out in fright. He paused and listened, but there were no sounds anywhere. Just a motion detector. He looked around and strained his eyes through the dimming afternoon light but could see no buildings or houses with windows from which someone might be looking.

Continuing, Dax followed the brick wall until he came to small, square fenced-in enclosure. There was no light here and the whole section was dimmed from even moonlight by a large Ficus tree that was growing in an adjacent lot.

Dax closed his eyes for a moment and then stared hard at the wall as his vision adjusted. It was just as Old Ben had described. The little ornamental fence itself was wrought iron and much older than the main perimeter fence. The structure was cold to the touch.

Mounted to the wall inside the enclosed area was an electric box that looked modern – tall, thin, gray in color with a round plastic covered area that displayed the meter numbers. And next to the box was an old door. The wood on the door had been properly aged by both sun and the cold, salty air of the city. Undiscernible what the original color was, it now was a pale white under what looked like chipped paint that had been repeatedly layered over the years. The only thing contemporary on it was a KEEP OUT sign.

Taking hold of the gate's latch, Dax eased it up. It squeaked a little in protest but easily gave way. The gate itself opened without a sound, as if Old Ben kept a nice coat of WD-40 on the hinges.

He paused at the door and felt around for the knob. He gave it a turn and at first would not move, but then after a little more twisting, it suddenly gave way with a sound of metal and cracking wood.

No alarm. No noises of any kind.

He eased the door open and stared into a pitch-black room. Reaching around the inside edge of the doorway wall, he felt up and down for a light switch of some kind but didn't find anyway.

Taking a deep breath, he eased into the room with his hands in front. The space had an old musty smell and held an odorous combination of paint thinner, gasoline, and oil. His right hand brushed up on what felt like wooden shelving, his other hand felt nothing.

After a couple more steps, an object gently touched his forehead, startling him. Reaching up and grabbing it, it felt like a small pull chain. He gave it a yank and with a snap, two long fluorescent bulbs on the ceiling flickered and hummed to life. With the room now well-lit, he looked around. The space was fairly small, maybe eight or nine feet across and about twelve feet long. The wooden shelves to his right had an assortment of tools – handsaws, hammers, screwdrivers, and several power tools like a drill press and a miter saw. On the floor were buckets and cans of various items one would expect to find in a small maintenance shed. Against the wall were brooms, dustpans, mops, and other cleaning implements.

Turing around quickly, Dax realized that anyone outside could see him like a goldfish in a bowl. He quickly closed the door and looked around again. In the far-right corner was another small door that led somewhere into the building's main interior. Not wanting any light to seep through cracks to any outside onlookers, Dax switched the fluorescent bulbs off and made his way across.

The knob turned easily and opened into more pitch blackness, but a recognizable smell. This was the hallway that led to the makeup room. With his hands out in front again, he felt his way to the opposite wall, then turned right. He'd walked this path many times in recent years for three different plays he'd been in at this theatre and now felt a surge of confidence.

At the end of the hallway, he felt the familiar old vinyl floor of the makeup room. He paused and listened carefully. No one should be in the building, except for maybe Old Ben. But he heard nothing. He felt for the light switch and flicked it on.

Besides the floor swept clean and the garbage taken out, everything was exactly where it had been when everyone left after the final show. The row of mirrors with lights around the edges stood ready and waiting for the next set of actors. The two small tables in the middle of the room sat with a garbage can between them. He looked at the chair and mirror he'd used when he was playing Eric.

Dax made his way to the bathroom sink to give himself the equivalent of a sponge bath, wiping off as much blood, sweat, and dirt as he could. The hot water and soap felt good on his skin. The bandage on his left shoulder peeled off easily and while the wound looked ugly – red in the center, a bile yellow around it, surrounded by bruising – it did not look infected. The impact of hitting the Jeep Cherokee's car door had reignited the pain and some more analgesics from Nurse Amy would be a boon right now.

He tried to imagine being in this situation just a few nights ago, standing in nothing but his skivvies in the old but renovated bathroom under this theatre, cleansing himself of the blood of people who had died in events he had been involved with. It was inconceivable. But here he was.

He stared at his reflection in the mirror for a moment. How much had he changed in the last few days? He thought he looked a little older, rougher, not the baby face he was used to seeing.

Speaking of appearance, he had to do something before reemerging on the street. What better place to transform oneself than in a theatre makeup room? Marcy Kotowski, the faithful makeup lady, always kept an emergency stash at every venue, and Dax knew where it was.

Putting his pants back on and returning to the makeup stations, he scanned around the room. His eyes landed on a small two-door cabinet in the corner with several plastic bottles of different lotions and cleaners on top.

Inside was an assortment of various makeup implements: a small collection of makeup brushes, spirit gum, stage blood, a powder puff, hair gel and spray, and cotton swabs. She even had a couple of stick-on prosthetic bullet holes and an open wound which must have been leftovers from the Halloween cast party last year.

I already have the wounds and the blood, thank you.

Then his eyes rested on a can of "quick bleach" powder on the bottom shelf. He picked it up and glanced over the instructions. It said that if you mix the power with cream developer, you could become an instant blonde. What the heck was a cream developer? In the back behind the can were three bottles of this stuff, a 10, 20 and 30 volume. Not having a clue, he grabbed the 30-volume, the power, a bowl and brush, and returned to the bathroom.

A few minutes later, he had a bowl of what looked like something between vomit and watery caulk. Pulling on latex gloves, he put a blob on his palm. As he smeared the stuff in, he used the brush to work it in through the layers of hair down to his scalp. With his amount of hair, it didn't take long, and he could only imagine someone with thick, long hair and what a process this would be.

The bleach went to work quickly. In about twenty minutes, he could see a noticeable difference. In another ten minutes he'd do his best to wash his hair under the sink. Too bad there wasn't a shower facility down here. Just as well – he knew plenty of sex hound actors who'd play kinky games in it and then it'd have to be regularly sanitized.

About two hours after breaking and entering, Dax sat at his makeup station chewing some stale saltine crackers he'd found on the kitchenette counter. In the small refrigerator, there were a couple water bottles and some hard salami. It would have to do.

With the mirror lights, he could see how dramatic the transformation had been. The blond hair combined with the toll the last few days had taken on him made for a face he hardly recognized. The bags under his eyes were puffy and there were visible bruises and scratches he'd not known about. As well, the right side of his face was now a bit swollen. With this new appearance, he could maybe make it safely back to the FBI building. He'd have to try.

Wait … he remembered something. Digging his wallet out, he found the card Agent Tommy Hicks had given him with the phone number. He could call and wait to get picked up, and not have to risk running around the streets. Would they believe him about what happened earlier that day in the Jeep Cherokee?

In his tired and weary state though, he decided to wait until tomorrow. The thought of sitting around that conference table answering questions all night surrounded by Decker, Hicks, Parker, and the happy, smiley Michelle Milevoi was daunting.

Once more, feelings that mingled deep sadness with anxiety began to creep up. Just a few days ago, he'd been going along living a relatively quiet and some would say boring life. He didn't really like his day job and was pretty sure he'd never be a full-time, money-making actor, but it was at least a stable life. And a safe one. But in one night, it had all changed. Here he was, like a fugitive on the lam in the basement of an old theatre. Stuff like this didn't happen to guys like him.

He suddenly wanted to talk to someone, someone who had no connection to anything that had happened recently. Someone who wouldn't prejudge him about anything.

He glanced at the old landline phone that was mounted to the wall near the kitchenette entrance. The Godwin owners said they'd keep it there as long as no one made long distance calls. He stared and thought once more of Sam. It was tempting. It had been, how long? Almost two years. *Tempus fugit* … time flies. He pulled out his wallet and stared at her picture.

Slowly, he picked up his chair and moved it to the phone. He sat there for a couple minutes pondering. He knew if he overthought this, he'd chicken out. Taking the phone off the cradle, he heard the dial tone and closed his eyes. A part of him hoped he would not remember the number, but he knew he would. She had given it to him right before moving away.

What time was it over there in Idaho? Mountain Time, just an hour ahead of California. Before he knew it, his fingers moved to the number pad and started dialing. His heart began thumping as he heard the digital tones quickly re-dial at some telephone switch somewhere, and then the other line start ringing.

After three rings a woman answered that was probably Sam's mother, Karen. "Hello?"

Dax cleared his throat. "Hi." He spoke slowly. "May I speak to Sam, please?"

There was a pause on the other end, then, "Who is this, please?" The tone of the voice had all at once become knowing and leery.

"This is ..." he cleared his throat again. "This is Dax Ribeiro."

Another pause, then, "What do you want, Dax?"

Dax took a deep breath. "I just want to talk. That's all. Not for long. Please." He could faintly hear noises on the other end of people talking and laughing.

Karen took a large breath of air through her nose and start to ask, "How did you get this number ..." But her voice faded, and Dax detected a slight tremble. Was that anger? Sadness? In one of the makeup mirrors across the room, he looked at himself and wondered how someone like him could cause such pain that lingered on and on.

He heard a man's voice say, "Karen?" and then the phone muffled, as if someone were cupping their hands over it. Karen's voice sounded argumentative. Maybe he should just hang up; clearly it had been a mistake to call.

The muted discussion went on for another minute and then Karen came back on. "Just a moment," she said curtly.

There was a pause of at least a full minute and then another phone somewhere in the house clicked and a young woman's dampened voice said, "I've got it. Hang up now." After a pause, the original phone clicked as it was hung up.

He waited in silence in the cool darkness of the theatre kitchen. Was he really on the phone with Sam right now, after all this time? What was he thinking calling like this, under these crazy circumstances? And yet there was a reason. He had to hear her voice. After more silence, he realized she was waiting for him to make the first move. It was him, after all, that initiated going separate ways, and now it was him who had initiated this call.

"Sam?" he said timidly.

He could hear her breathing on the other end, but still she remained quiet.

"Sam … I'm sorry if this was a bad idea. Say the word and I'll go away." He heard her sigh.

"No, it's okay," she finally said. "You took me by surprise. You took us all by surprise. How are you?"

Dax leaned back as far as he could in the worn, faux velvet vanity chair. "I'm ah, I'm okay. How about you? How do you like Idaho?"

Dax heard rustling on the other end as if she were moving from a chair to a bed. He tried to imagine what she looked like now, how her face had changed, what her hair looked like.

"It's pretty nice," she said. "Gets cold in the winter. Gonna have to get used to the snow and ice. That's one thing I miss about the Bay Area, the weather."

"Yeah," Dax said, trying to chuckle. "It's nice for sure. That's why we pay the big bucks to live here." He hated small talk and phony awkwardness like this.

They waited for each other, then Sam asked, "Is your dad still in New Mexico?"

"Yeah, he likes it there. He's gonna die there at this point, I guess. I keep telling him I'll visit and then I don't and then more time races by. Maybe I'll be moving out there soon. I don't know. I just don't know."

"Are you still doing shows?"

"Yes. Yes. In fact, we just finished up one. You'd have liked it. Got to use my Kung Fu chops. It was fun." He laughed. "I played a hero …" His voice trailed off.

Another long pause, then she asked, "Dax, why did you suddenly call after all this time?"

"What do you mean?" Dax took a sniff and realized his eyes were starting to water. "I'm just calling to ask how you're doing. That's okay, right? That's all I'm doing."

"Sure. It's just a little strange. And you sound different."

"I'm sorry." Dax heard trembling in his own voice.

"Is something wrong?"

"No, why?"

"I know you pretty well. I know the guy behind the performance."

Dax really didn't want to talk about himself. He took a breath and straightened up. "You know what? Your voice sounds so good right now. It sounds beautiful." He wiped a tear away.

"Dax, are you in trouble?"

"Uhm," he squinted back some tears. He never could lie to her. "Kind of. Yeah. But I'll be okay."

"Financial trouble? *Girl* trouble?"

"No. Nothing like that. Look, I'm sorry I called. And I'm sorry for everything that happened. I'm not here to ask you for anything. I just wanted to talk to someone I could trust. I just, uhm …" He covered his mouth and began crying, trying desperately not to let her hear. "I'm scared, that's all," he managed to say, then cringing because he should not have said that.

Sam's voice took on a seriousness. "Scared of what? Dax, have you been drinking again? Please be honest."

He put the phone in his lap for a moment. He didn't want to open this can of worms. "Yeah. Here and there. Not that much though. I'm okay."

"You know what that does to you. I don't want you calling here on some drunken impulse."

"No, no. I swear to God, I'm not drunk. I just … I just wanted to hear your voice."

"Dax, what's going on? What are you scared of?"

"Sam, look, I'm sorry. I shouldn't have called. I'm just … I don't know. I'll hang up now."

"Dax –"

"Sam, I'm not trying anything here. I-I …"

"Dax," Sam said, picking up her voice and sounding as if she were sitting up more. She took a deep breath. "I can't believe I'm bringing this up now. But since we're talking, I need to tell you something. My parents didn't want me to. But I need to. I owe it to you."

"I'm listening."

"Dax. You were a father." Her voice gave a small quiver on the word *father*.

Dax straightened up again, wiping his face with his shirt. "What?"

"I was pregnant. That's one of the reasons my parents moved and I went with them. To start over. They knew you weren't going to be around."

"They *knew* I wasn't going to be around? How could they know that?"

"I was going to have a baby. *Our* baby." She began to weep. "I've been waiting so long to tell you." She let out a small, sad laugh.

"Sam. Why didn't you tell me?"

"Because you were gone. You were off to your acting career. In your own world. I could have tried to force you to commit financially or whatever. But I didn't want that. I didn't want a father who wasn't involved emotionally. I had my parents. They were going to take care of things."

"What are you saying? Did you have an abortion?"

"No! I would never do that. I was going to have our baby. I was going to raise him. Or her. But —"

"But what?"

She paused. "But I miscarried. It was the most horrible day of my life."

He could hear her put her hand over the phone and muffle her cries. He waited, giving her time.

"Dax?" she finally said, sniffling loudly.

"I'm still here … I don't know what to say."

"It's okay. You don't have to say anything. I just wanted you to know. You deserve to know. You're not a bad person, Dax. You just don't know that. And you don't know what you really want. You try something, it doesn't bring you the fulfillment you sought. Then you try something else. Like you tried me. You're a wandering soul. I feel for you."

Dax took a paper towel and dabbed at his eyes. "You've no idea how true that is."

"Dax. Listen to me. I'm glad you called because I've thought about you from time to time and wondered how you were. It's good to hear your voice. I don't know what trouble you're in right now. But can I pray for you?"

For a moment, Dax dropped the phone in his lap again. He didn't know how to respond. But before he knew it, he held up the phone and said, "Yes, please. Pray for me."

Sam began. "Dear Lord. I pray for my brother and friend, Dax. Please help him in this current situation, whatever it is. Guide him. Give him wisdom. Take him out of the danger he now faces. Speak to him and show him what to do. You are the creator of all, the maker of all, and the final judge of all. Assure him that you accept him exactly the way he is right now, that he doesn't have to do one single thing to earn your love. Bring Dax to where you want him to be. Protect him and be his light in the darkness. I pray all these things, in the precious name of our Lord and Savior, Jesus Christ. Amen."

A full minute of silence passed as each held the phone to their ear. Finally, Sam said, "Dax, I need to go. I want you to take care. I want to see you again, if not in this life, then the next. Get right with God and be good to yourself."

"Thank you, Sam. Thank you for being a good person. Thank you for giving a part of your life to me."

"Goodbye, Dax." The phone clicked and went dead.

Dax sat in the dark holding the phone for how long, he didn't know. Imagine that. He could have been a father, what that would have changed. He'd have had so much more to live for than his selfish little ambitions.

He looked up at the dim ceiling. "God?" he asked. He waited but heard no answer. Hanging up, he took off his jacket and made his way to the tattered old couch by the makeup room door and laid down, pulling the jacket up like a blanket. Within minutes, his thoughts started to drift, and he felt a deep sleep coming on, a fatigue-enhanced slumber of the dead. He let his mind go blank, his muscles relax and at once was mercifully asleep.

38: The Hideaway

The day was cool and breezy, the sun's light showing brightly in wavering splotches through the trees. Leaves rustled in the branches above the two boys as they prepared to hunker down in their secret hideaway.

The ground was damp and a hint of petrichor still lingered in the air from a recent light rain. Gazing into the distance, one of the boys thought the clouds seemed to rush by too quickly, as if it were a film that had been sped up. The sky's color reflected a strange hue that wavered between blue and purple.

Behind the fence of the house, a small hill with a few densely packed trees provided perfect privacy. In the spring, the area was verdant and lush, but on this crisp fall day, the colors were brown and yellow, the branches bare.

Some time ago, they discovered a cluster of old trees that had succumbed and fallen. The upturned trunks now formed a V-shape with a deep indent in the center where roots had been yanked up like stubborn fingers still clinging to fistfuls of dirt. Below this, the boys dug into the soft dirt, extracting rocks, pinecones, old roots, and whatever else they ran into, until they achieved a small cave. For weeks they dug, single-minded in purpose. The resulting enclosure was several feet long and tall enough for the two of them to sit inside with their backs upright.

They cautiously looked around then removed branches that hid the entrance. Their hands and knees pressed on soft dirt and pine needles as they eased in. The light grew dimmer as they made their way to the back. Like two small rabbits, they now huddled in their burrow, free from prying eyes or ears, alone in their own world where they made the rules.

One of the boys grinned and produced a magazine from the folds of his jacket. He was dressed in a robe-like, all red outfit. Was this boy Typhoon, his childhood friend? The features of the face were unclear. The other boy produced a flashlight and aimed it at the publication. They both ogled and held their breath.

The shiny cover displayed a woman in a way that was not appropriate for two boys of their age to be looking at. She stared at them, her heavily painted eyes piercing and seductive, her skin unnaturally smooth and perfect. She wore a bright green outfit that for some reason the boy with the flashlight knew was called a corset. The lower half of the outfit stretched around her thighs like a tight swimsuit and black laces ran down her legs. She appeared to be in the motion of unbuttoning the upper half of her outfit as one corner of her mouth started to form a mocking smirk. Her expression said, *you want to touch me, but you can't.* Above her in big, bold, all-caps letters was the word HUSTLER.

Their hearts began to race in anticipation. The woman had no name, no persona, no voice, she wasn't even real, but yet she reached out and sadistically teased. The boy in red set the magazine down and began to open the first page.

Whatever they were about to see, it was already affecting them deeply. It engaged their senses at visceral levels, both physical and emotional, sensations impossible to attain under any other circumstance. Their bodies began to tremble, their mouths went dry. With a forestalling movement, the boy continued to the next page. So thrilling, so much fun, oh yes, yes, turn the page—.

Snap!

The sound of a branch cracking from somewhere outside the burrow made the two boys gasp and freeze. They had spent many hours here and were quite familiar with the normal surrounding sounds. They knew the birds that chirped and pecked, what the occasional squirrel or other small creature sounded like as it scampered by. They knew every sound the trees made as they swayed in the breeze. But this was different.

Another snap, although a little quieter. And a little closer.

The boys had never heard a branch crack like that before. Something heavier than either of them had made it. It alarmed them. The safety of their hideout was being violated.

"Turn if off!" the boy in red whispered harshly as he quickly scooped the magazine up and stuffed it back into his jacket. The other boy cupped a hand over the flashlight's top. He fumbled for the switch with shaking hands before finally dousing the bouncing light.

Another crackle and shuffling of dirt and leaves. Whatever it was, it was getting closer.

"What do we do?" the boy with the flashlight whispered.

"I don't know. Be quiet!"

"What is it?"

"I don't *know*. Shut up!"

The next few moments were torturous. But the boys remained remarkably still, their pulses racing, their wide eyes glued to the round light at the end that made the entrance to their lair. Through it, they could only see a few trunks and branches of other trees, and a sky with bizarre colors beyond those.

The boy with the flashlight began to shudder. His feet scratched the ground as he squirmed and shifted positions.

"Will you *please be quiet!*" the other boy pleaded.

The next sound they heard was a grunt or a muffled word. It came from an adult man. The boys suppressed a startled gasp.

"Who is that?" one boy whispered.

"How should I know?"

Two more quick snaps, this time louder, and then a voice could be heard from what sounded like right above the entrance.

The boy with the flashlight began panic. "Let's leave the magazine here and go out there," he whispered frantically.

"No way. You go."

A sudden loud scraping of dirt made the boys jump. Some mud clogs and small rocks dropped past the light. The dark silhouette of a large head abruptly appeared and took up most of the space to the burrow's entry. From the head came a deep and mocking voice: "I can *heeear* you." The voice had a wicked unseen smile attached to it.

They made no move, no sound, as if there was still a chance they were undetected.

"And just what it is you're doing in there?" the voice asked. "Nothing naughty? *Hmmm?*"

The boys didn't respond. The silhouette's shape moved and twisted as the man positioned himself into more of a squat in front of the entrance. Small rocks made a grinding sound under his weight. They saw his coat flicker and then with a loud click, they were all at once bathed in the bright illuminance of a powerful flashlight.

"Ah," the voice said with a chuckle. "There you are. And I see you're up to no good." He clicked his tongue in a tsk-tsk-tsk manner.

The boy with the flashlight spoke first. "What do you want?"

For a moment there was no reply. The light jerked slightly to the boy who had spoken. The voice spoke again, but this time more harshly. "Come out! Both of you."

The flashlight clicked off and the head disappeared from the entrance. The boys hesitated, unsure of what to do.

"I would advise you to do as I say," the calm but deadly voice came again. "I won't ask again."

The boys looked at each other in the darkness, the dim light revealing the fright in each other's eyes. Slowly, the boy in red took the magazine back out and pushed it as far as he could to the back of the cave. He looked at the other boy and then began crawling slowly toward the entrance. Heart pounding furiously, the other boy reluctantly followed.

As the boys approached the opening, the large legs moved out of the way. The air seemed much colder and brighter as they emerged and got to their feet. They stood motionless and could only gawk in terror at the man in front of them.

He was twice their height and three times broader across the shoulders and wore a long wool coat atop dress pants and shoes. His large face had a thin, dark beard. Sunglasses covered his eyes with intimidating black ovals. His hands were folded casually in front as he looked down at the two scared boys.

"I know what you were doing," he said, gesturing to the entrance of the burrow.

The boys stood in silence, then one started to say, "We weren't doing—"

"Shut up!" the man thundered. His voice seemed to echo around the trees as several birds in the distance took off flapping and squawking.

The boy in red felt the strong urge to cry but held tight.

The other boy bravely spoke again. "Who are you?" His small voice shook.

The man's chin raised slightly. "What should I do with you two?" He asked the question rhetorically and with a faint smirk. He reached deeply into his jacket. His wrist jerked and they heard a faint snap, and then out came a handgun.

Both boys tried to suppress a startled scream. The boy who had brought the flashlight somehow knew the gun was a semi-automatic pistol. The gun's steel was a dark gray, almost black, the handle looked like it had been reinforced with grip tape, which also makes fingerprinting more difficult. Wait—how did he know all this?

The man stood for a moment slowly pointing the weapon back and forth between the two boys. The only sound in the air was a few birds chirping in the distance. The boy in red began to whimper as a wet, warm stain started growing near his crotch.

The man's hand reached into a coat pocket and produced a long black cylinder-shaped object that was wide on end and narrow on the other. With smooth and practiced motions, he brought the narrow end of the cylinder to the gun barrel and began twisting in a screwing motion.

A silencer! He was going to kill them.

The boys glanced at each other. The boy in red was now crying silently, tears streaming down his face.

With a final twist and a small click, the silencer was in place. The man gave it one last squeeze and then lowered at the boys.

It was now or never. From somewhere inside him an energy sprang forth, like a ball of fire that quickly grew and sent fingers of flames up to his head and down his arms and to the end of his fingers.

"NOW!" the boy screamed in the loudest and most blood curdling cry his body had ever produced.

Ducking and leaping to the left, he began running.

"Hey!" he heard the man yell.

The silencer coughed two sharp *thwacks* and he heard the other boy scream. Was Typhoon dead? He began to yell and cry while running, dodging trees and branches as he raced forward.

Two more quick coughs and the side of a tree next to him exploded, sending bits of bark and splinters flying. Another thud hit the ground next to his foot causing a splash of dirt. He could hear the sound of heavy feet thumping after him, crushing leaves and branches.

"Get back here!" the man yelled.

One more shot was fired, and he could hear the buzz and whistle as the bullet soared through the air nearby, though this time farther away. The boy's eyes were as wide as saucers, but he hardly saw anything. He was pure instinct now, a small animal on the run from a predator. Objects flew by his line of vision in a blur as he ran on.

The sounds of the pursuer began to grow distant. For whatever reason he didn't feel tired, but he was having difficulty moving his legs, as if they were stuck in mud. He strained and struggled but managed to keep moving. He could feel large beads of sweat pouring off his forehead.

All at once he came to a stop against a tree and stood panting. The full reality of everything crashed over him. His friend was dead. He almost died too. He began to cry. His light weeping quickly turned into deep sobbing.

He heard his own bawling from a distance and felt the hot moisture on his shirt and in his hair. He tried to move his legs again, but now they were incapacitated. Something was pressing on his chest making breathing difficult. He strained and thrashed until he felt the material of the jacket draped over him. It was soaking wet.

Dax awoke breathing hard and covered with sweat. He cursed, turned, and almost fell off the couch in the dark and cold makeup room below the Godwin Theatre.

He breathed deeply, rolled back, and stared at the ceiling.

***

Viktor Lozovsky sat restrained to the hard, straight-back chair. He was gasping for air, not because he was in pain, but because of exhaustion. The one thing he was grateful for was that they hadn't used crude, old-school methods like pealing his fingernails off with pliers, smashing his toes with a hammer, or hooking electrodes to sensitive parts of his body. Instead, they'd employed the more modern technique of drugs.

Although the former Red Army officer had personally witnessed it over the years, Viktor never actually participated in interrogation. He *could* kill. That was quick and generally painless. But it took a special kind of person to perform interrogation. One needed to have the psychology of a sociopath, utterly without sympathy or compassion, or least have the ability to temporarily turn off those normal human feelings.

He had watched while people had boiling water poured on them, waterboarded until literally half-drowned, had their kneecaps shattered, or had parts of their body sawed off, all while pumped full of stimulants and unable to pass out. The methods varied and depended on whether or not it the victim was to survive; sometimes a person needed to remain alive to relay a message. It also depended on the magnitude of the offence. Those that suffered more were typically involved in personal aspersions against someone in a position of power, a person who didn't like their ego bruised or authority challenged.

The people Viktor had seen suffer these fates more or less got what was coming. After all, they had chosen to get involved in things and at levels the typical person would never do. One who was stupid enough to steal from powerful drug lords or arms dealers had to understand the risks they were taking. For example, borrowing money and not repaying was considered a big offense because it implied the lender lacked judgement. Even more stupid was someone who plays double agent or goes on the witness stand and testifies against such people.

The approach they'd used on Viktor was much gentler physically, but hugely strenuous mentally. At first, he thought they were going to use the old technique of injecting him with heroin or some other addictive drug, then after a few days, when he would do just about anything for another fix, deny it until he talked. But apparently, they didn't have time for that.

Instead, they started giving him haloperidol. Viktor knew what it was immediately, he'd seen it used in military torture. The drug was an antipsychotic used for people with everything from schizophrenia to hallucinations from alcohol withdrawal. But when deliberately overdosed, it induced an intense agitated state, and made a person shake uncontrollably as if they had Parkinson's.

At first it was controllable, but after a few hours, it was becoming unbearably taxing. To fight it, the brain wants to shut down and escape. But his captors would not allow that and cooked up a batch of methamphetamine to ensure Viktor would remain fully conscious during the whole agonizing process. He had never felt the effects of the central nervous system stimulant, and in younger years, though curious, was never tempted enough to try it. In proper doses, meth was a legitimate drug used for things such as attention deficit disorder and obesity. Upon forced overdosing, his senses had immediately skyrocketed, and he felt more capable than he'd ever had. But what was also amplified were the sensations of tormenting restlessness and uncontrollable muscle spasms.

As the ghastly minutes slowly ticked by, his world became a nightmare. Since he assumed they were going to kill him anyway, he resisted as long as possible, more for a personal challenge than anything else. Frustrating and wasting their time was the only card he had left to play. He wasn't trying to protect the young American, an individual he cared nothing for. His motives went much deeper than that, a decades-old loyalty he'd sworn to his affiliations and former soldiers.

At one point, after many questions but without satisfactory answers, it was suggested by one of the interrogators to get him drunk on top of everything else. In this way, the ethanol would induce confusion and act as a "truth serum," making him unable to remember lies.

"Should we use vodka?" they had laughed but ended up using cheap American whisky. The stuff tasted like pure shit and he tried to spit it out, but it wasn't that difficult making him consume. Holding his head by the chin in a vice-like grip, then squeezing his jaw muscles until they succumbed, another would shove the neck of the bottle so far down his throat, it was impossible not to swallow. By the time the alcohol had taken full effect, combined with muscle spasms and the haloperidol-induced feelings of psychosis, his world was spinning, and he had no idea what he'd said or not.

And this is when some of the physical stuff began. They would ask a question and he would laugh or give a ridiculous answer, then feel a sharp slap to one side of his face. He would turn in the direction of the slap, only to feel another slap on the other side. Then they would sit quietly, listening to him babble, then suddenly repeat the strikes. In this way, he started becoming fearful of when the slapping would start again, or from what direction it would come. The hitting didn't hurt all that much, but the randomness was becoming terrifying. He could hear them laughing at his distress and confusion and promising it would never, *ever* stop until he either talked or stopped breathing. He held out as long as he could, trying to find comfort in the fact that he still had this one last purpose in existence.

Finally, on the verge of breaking, he asked, "What exactly did you want me to tell you again?" It was a genuine question. He had no idea how long he'd been there or what the conversation was even about anymore. He glanced down at his shirt and saw vomit but didn't remember getting sick.

The large man with the scar on his face, the one he knew as Alexander Tsepov, sat calmly in front of him. He lit a cigarette and regarded the old master spy who had devoted so many years to his craft. He looked at Viktor with the composed indifference of a killer, and yet with something else in his eyes. Perhaps he saw himself a couple decades from now, also tied to a chair and getting tortured for information by the enemies of the man he now worked for. But no time to ponder such things – business was business and they needed to hurry.

"What we've been … *talking* about," Tsepov said, "is the encrypted code you use to track the American. We know you placed something on him."

With his voice quivering from the uncontrollable shaking, Viktor smirked resentfully and said, "Ah yes, that little theatre actor. That *sukin syn* who has caused so much trouble."

Tsepov blew a large cloud of smoke out and raised his eyebrows. "If you dislike him so much, why do you help him?"

Viktor laughed and took a big, shaky breath. "Because I disklike you more."

Tsepov smiled and drew on his cigarette again. "I guess we continue then."

Viktor shook his head.

"So, you are ready to make all this discomfort come to an end, yes?"

Viktor leaned back and wearily shook his head yes.

Tsepov nodded to one of his companions and they brought Viktor's small, handheld computer to him. Holding it up, Tsepov snapped it open and pressed a key so that it lit up and asked for a security code. Extending it so that Viktor could see the keys, he waited for the old man to talk.

Viktor slowly gave him the letters and numbers and then watched, shaking and twitching, trying to control his breathing. Another man nearby jotted on a notepad. Tsepov pecked at the keys and examined the 4X6 monochrome screen, clicking through menus until he found what he was looking for. Turning it so that Viktor could see where it asked for a password, he extended it once more and waited.

Viktor closed his eyes and saw his mind swirling. Up and down and around his thoughts raced and he wasn't sure he could remember, but he would try. So miserable did he feel at this point, he didn't care about his superiors back in the Motherland and hoped the young American would die a lavish and unhurried death. Slowly, he doled out more numbers and letters, sometimes correcting himself, sometimes repeating himself, but in the end, he delivered.

A small beep could be heard from the device and Tsepov watched. He looked up, nodded at his companions, then looked at Viktor. "I have learned much from you, *Gospadin*. About your history, your techniques, your self-discipline."

Viktor only stared back, too tired to respond and unable to recall details of anything he may have said on any subject.

"One more injection, then we are finished here."

Viktor slumped, his head dropping and his life gyrating before his eyes. His saw his early years with the Red Army and then later the Special Operations Forces, where he became an expert in communications and electronics; his wife and children, the Motherland he'd never see again, all he had built, acquired, and accomplished, the ups and downs, the wins and losses, the victories and defeats, the regrets.

He raised his eyes and saw a man with a syringe approaching. "May I ask what you have there, young man?" he heard himself ask.

The man looked at Tsepov, who answered, "Potassium cyanide. You will feel nothing."

"Oh … *spacibo*," Viktor said and watched as the needle penetrated his skin. A small red blob of blood rose and swirled in the liquid before it was depressed into his body. Within an hour he would slip into a coma and have a fatal heart attack.

Tsepov stood and stared for a moment, drawing on the last of his cigarette. "Goodbye," he said, then turned to leave.

Viktor smiled then dropped his head and closed his eyes. The last sound he heard was footsteps existing and a door shutting before his thoughts closed in and everything went black.

39: Ghosts and Competitors

Dax's head hurt and his body felt like it had been pulled out from under a truck. He eased one foot to the floor and slowly sat up and looked around. Rubbing his eyes, his senses gradually returned as he took in the familiar sights and smells of the makeup room. His thoughts flooded with everything that had happened the day before. Today, he was going to call Hicks and get somewhere he might be a little safer.

He tried to eat more salami and crackers, but it was making him sick. He did manage to gulp down two bottles of water. After a quick face wash in the sink, it was time to make his next move.

He looked at the phone on the wall. The chair he'd brought over to it last night was still there. The conversation he'd had with Sam rushed back into his thoughts. What she'd told him was still overwhelming.

Standing up and taking a big breath, he walked to the phone while fishing the card out from his wallet.

He placed himself before the phone, pulled the handset off the cradle and started to dial. The line went silent for a few seconds and it appeared nothing had happened. Then all at once he heard some computer-sounding tones and a few clicks. In another few seconds, there was a digital ringing on the other end. It rang five times and then was answered.

"This is Agent Hicks, Tommy Hicks. That you, Dax?" a familiar and urgent voice said.

"Yeah," was all Dax could reply. His head still hurt and he didn't want to talk much.

"Where the hell are you?"

"I think you guys can figure that out," Dax replied.

"Come on Dax, no games. This is deadly serious."

"I've figured out the deadly part. I'm trying to understand what happens from here. And I'm honestly wondering how I'm still alive."

"Well, I'm glad you are and we're going to keep it that way. Are you in a safe place till we can get there?" He heard Hicks muffle the phone and say something quickly to someone.

Dax went on talking. "I've no idea how safe I am. I went somewhere where I figured no one would look for me, and so far I'm correct." There was more muted talking on the other end. "Hicks?"

"Yeah, I'm here, Dax."

"Did you find the crash yesterday? Jeep Cherokee. Don't know where it was exactly."

"Yes, we found it. Or SFPD did. Called us when they started looking at IDs. Two people inside. One was your friend, the guy who calls himself Jack Dauer. His credentials looked legit."

"There were three people. Dauer, a driver, and the man who calls himself Michael Staggs."

"There were only two. No Michael Staggs."

Dax cringed. "*Shit.* He must have gotten away."

"Were you in that vehicle? Last we saw, you were in a gray Mercury Mountaineer. But we found that, abandoned. It'd been stolen."

"I was. They switched cars. Put me in the Cherokee. I managed to get away. Barely."

"You're one lucky bastard, Dax. You know that?"

"Tell me about it. Is Dauer still alive?"

"Yes. He's still out but we're ID-ing him and learning everything we can right now."

"And the driver?"

"Dead. Gunshot to the neck."

The headache suddenly got worse. "I didn't shoot him, okay? It was Jack's gun. He was pointing it at me. I was pushing it away."

"We'll sort all that out, don't worry." More muffled and muted talking on the other end. "Stay put, okay? We're coming to get you."

"You know where I am now?"

"Landlines are quickly traceable. Stay where you are. Wait for us."

"I lost my cell phone. Staggs threw it out the window."

"We know. Found it on the side of the road."

"Did you guys interview Les Abraham? He's that drama teacher and theatre director I told you about, the one who hooked me up with these characters."

"Yes, I remember. We talked to him. I'll fill you in later."

"Is he innocent?"

"Abraham? We believe he didn't know who he was dealing with any more than you did. They approached him after seeing photos of a show of his at SF City College. Told him you looked like a character they needed."

"Alright. Well, who are these people, anyway? What's going on?"

"Long story. I'll get you up to speed."

"Just tell me a little now. Please."

He heard Hicks give out a big sigh and then say something unintelligible to someone, then he was back on the line. "Alright, we have a few minutes."

"I'm listening."

"The man you know as Agent Jack Dauer told you one bit of truth, that there were clientele of international arms deals at that gathering you were at."

At once, an image of Meygan Knight in that red dress popped into Dax's mind again. The fact that he hadn't told anyone about that yet was starting to weigh on him.

Hicks continued. "We managed to run down some information about this *Собака* character you were posing as. What made the difference was that you'd remembered his real name was Gavril. That's not really true, but it is in the sense that that's an alias he's used on both forged and real documents. A Mr. Gavril Novikov."

Dax tapped his head. "Yeah, yeah. *Novikov.* Couldn't remember the other night."

"He goes by other names – *Vadim Bodrov*, for example."

Disjointed memories of the fate-filled night at the Babylon Ballroom flooded Dax's mind. The name sounded familiar.

"So this guy is wanted by a lot of folks," Hicks was saying. "Interpol didn't know who he really was until recently, but he's a bit of a rock star on the international stage. Hang on."

Dax heard rustling again on the other end of the phone. He cupped the receiver and looked around the dark theatre kitchen, listening for any sounds he should be wary of. Everything was still and silent.

Hicks came back on. "So, there's been a lot of tension at the Ukraine-Russian border for several years now you may have seen in the news. They're anticipating major conflicts for a long time to come and there are players taking advantage of the bad economy and chaos from the fall of the Soviet Union, just five years ago. You've got different factions emerging, some pro-government, others anti, who want to triumph and see one side come out on top. Encouraged by the Transnistria

War, militant groups have spread across the Ukraine, and various buyers have gone on a military spending spree that has totaled billions. Almost a third of that money was funneled into inflated arms deals, apparently designed to allow supplies and corrupt officials to siphon off government funds."

"I'd no idea." Dax rubbed his eyes. He was tired but fascinated by what he was hearing. "Whose side is the U.S. on over there?"

"Well, Ukraine broke free of the Soviet Union in '91. They're the biggest country, by size, in Europe, and being that they're right between Russia and Europe, they're a strategic ally. As such, we want them to lean West in their policies and political loyalties. So we support their military and play the loving big brother on the front."

"What does Novikov have to do with any of this?"

Hicks took a big breath. "So ... investigators and auditors have discovered that much of the equipment sourced from certain international firms in the UK, France, the Netherlands, and even China was significantly overpriced, as well, not purchased or actually delivered without going through a bidding process. Only the process was rigged and made to look highly competitive and the competitors ghosts."

"Ghosts?"

"Yeah, they were fake. Well, they were real, registered companies, but not actual people with money to spend. You thought you were bidding against another buyer, like a rival military group or opposing government, but in reality, bidding against the seller. That made the competition fierce, because no one wants weapons ending up in the hands of their enemies."

"That's clever."

"Spearheading the corruption are two businessmen who acted as intermediaries in the deals. The first is a rising star in the world of arms deals and smuggling, Viktor Bout, also known as the 'Merchant of Death.' The other guy, the mysterious one everyone's been looking for is this *Dog of Saint Petersburg* character – called so allegedly because he can fetch just about anything for the right price."

"Woof, *woof.*" Dax said with bitter sarcasm, realizing another truth Jack had told him.

Hicks continued. "He's accomplished a lot for a young man. Before this, he was a pharmaceutical contractor with no previous experience in the defense sector. It's said that Novikov was the main brains behind the rigged bids by using companies under his or Bout's control to create the illusion of competition for contracts."

"No wonder people are dying. So I was a former pharmaceutical guy, huh?"

"*The Dog* was previously known as an importer of big pharma, yeah, and managed to facilitate nearly $100 million worth of contracts for the government alone. Private deals have added up to much more. Sometime during all that, it appears he got into arms trading through his connection to Bout. Probably saw the potential for a lot more money. It's said that with his background with pharma suppliers, he also became known for getting hold of illegally manufactured chemical weapons."

"Are you serious? Haven't those been banned since like World War one?"

"Yes. And using his negotiation skills, he acquired several contracts from the Ukraine government which included some of these illegal purchases tucked away in the contract language. Victor Bout is the smuggling guy, while Novikov is the guy ostensibly doing legitimate government business. They worked well together and could get almost anything anyone wanted, and then moved anywhere."

"Wow."

"In the last several years though, buyers have been catching on that the purchasing process for many of the deals had been manipulated, that the 'competitors' weren't real. Information has been sketchy because some of the companies were registered in offshore jurisdictions that enable owners to remain anonymous. Others were formed as limited liability partnerships, which are controlled by other businesses, not individuals, and are not obligated to disclose their directors or owners."

Dax snorted. "If I had had all this background, I would have behaved completely different. Not sitting around like a lost idiot sipping tonic water at the bar."

"What would you have done differently? You were bait, right?"

"I don't know."

"The bartender said you were playing it cool, that is, until the trouble started."

"The bartender? He was one of you?"

"Let's just say he's on the right side of things."

"I should have known, the way he was looking at me."

"No, you shouldn't have. That's the whole point."

"He didn't exactly do anything to help me."

"He couldn't, not his job description."

Dax rubbed his temples. "He could have at least called for help."

"For your information, all radio transmissions including cell phones were dead. Everything was being jammed. A landline would have still worked, if accessible."

Dax's eyes got wide. "Really ... so the broadcasting camera on me wasn't working?"

"No. Even military frequencies were jammed."

"Wow." Dax chuckled cynically. At least Jack's plans had been frustrated. It also explained a few things. "Okay. Back to Novikov. I was told he was dead."

"Yeah. So, here's where we start running out of facts. An addendum to one of the bigger government contracts slated to happen this month appears to facilitate a bribe slash fee, ostensibly for transportation and security costs. Looking back, it looks like the bribes started a couple years ago and has been a routine part of the process since. What happens is that it's stipulated that one of Novikov's shell companies, in this case a Paris-based one, was to receive a million-dollar fee on the deal, but the company shut down shortly before it was completed. After that, the contract was changed to say the amount of the so-called fee would be negotiated at the time of the signing. The address in Paris where the shell company was registered belonged to a company formation agent and was used by multiple companies. Among these were several firms that are part of Viktor Bout's empire, some of which is a vast money-laundering operation that benefitted elites from several European countries."

"Because *Собака* controlled this company, it went under when he was killed?"

"It was a one-man operation. With Novikov gone, no one's there to manage the paperwork and negotiations. And to make it all even more messy, his companies had ties to overlapping political groups ranging from people protesting social injustices, to supporters of a federalization of Ukraine, to pro-Russian separatists and nationalists."

"Whose side is, or *was*, Novikov on?"

"Both. All. He learned the secret of supplying all sides to prolong conflicts to make more money."

"Dang ... So who was *Vassi* then, that huge Russian brute that tried to kill me?" A thought struck Dax. "Wait, he's the one who called me *Vadim.*"

"He called you *Vadim Bodrov?*"

"No, just Vadim."

"Fortunately, hospital staff got his fingerprints before the body was whisked away. His name was Vassi Drugov. We believe he was part of one of the anti-Ukraine factions who felt they were not only being screwed by the phony biding and overpricing, but purchasing some of the same stuff going to people who are against their interests."

"No wonder he wasn't happy to see me. And the girl he was with?"

"We've no idea who she is."

"She said I was dead, or Gavril was. Looked very surprised to see me. Or him."

"They supposedly got to Novikov before he was able to get out of France to the United Arab Emirates. Car bomb outside his hotel in Marseille. And since the incident, Bout has gone into hiding. He was surreptitious to begin with, but now he's really operating from the shadows."

"So who killed *The Dog*, Vassi or the people he works for?"

"Probably, but we don't know. Whoever it was, they didn't want any more products going to the Ukraine government or pro-Ukraine groups."

"How would it help Jack and his people to draw out *Vassi?*"

"It probably wasn't Drugov they were after. It was more likely someone with ties to Bout. If they could re-establish a connection, they could continue doing business and make lots of money."

"Who killed Jack's people then?"

"Competitors. People who differ politically or want a piece of the action. Or someone who wants to assume the control that Novikov left behind. Could be anything in the chain of procurement and distribution. A lot of the money ends up in the pockets of shady business owners and corrupt government officials. Maybe you pull strings in a certain customs agency who will look the other way for you. Perhaps you know people who transport goods across borders who are willing to put some of your stuff in with theirs. Lots of people get a cut that way."

The whole thing was overwhelming. The headache was starting to throb. "One more question."

"Go ahead."

"What's with the United Arab Emirates?"

"A handful of the shell company's ownership had trails that led to a Sharjah company with two Ukrainian directors. The United Arab Emirates is a well-known tax haven and is particularly popular with arms dealers due to its relaxed financial regulations and shady aircraft registry – stuff can move through the airport in relative obscurity. It's home to a host of shell companies doing all kinds of international underhanded business. These people depend on someone like Novikov who is a proven mediatory between parties of interest and state authorities."

"But once everyone finds out Novikov is really dead, there will be no more deals to be made."

"Unless they can work directly with Bout and figure a way to continue to make Novikov's magic work."

"This is one big, tangled web of money and corruption."

"Yep, and you're a little fly caught in that web. By the way, we found that warehouse. Looks like an older place that was abandoned more than three years ago because the zoning moved, then secretly taken over by Jack Dauer and his people. They'd been there for a while, but then looks like it had been made. They moved out quickly, left a few things behind in the rush. They then went to the Sutter Hotel."

Dax closed his eyes and breathed hard. "So, what's the plan now?"

"A car will be there in another minute or two. Get ready to quickly go outside. You'll recognize at least one face. I'll see you back at headquarters."

"Okay."

"And Dax."

"Yeah?"

"Keep low and be safe. We're going to sort this all out."

Dax hung the phone back up and considered everything he'd been told. The level of deception was staggering. After this was all over, if he was still alive, he was going to reevaluate this inner need for more adventure. And hitting the sauce – that had to slow down as well. He'd already almost become a father, and if he wanted to see any kids of his grow up, he'd have to make some changes.

Carefully putting back the chair and reorganizing Marcy's supply cabinet, he took one more look around and felt a new gratitude for the old building where he got to play roles that looked dangerous, but really were not.

He grabbed his jacket and headed back down the hall to the entrance to the maintenance room where Old Ben's secret door was. He would keep Ben's secret; it might save his or someone else's life again.

He retraced his steps around to the front gate. As he walked, he felt into his jacket pockets and his hand landed on something unfamiliar. Pulling it out, the object looked like it was made of black plastic, smooth on top and numbers stamped on the back. It wasn't even two inches long and maybe half an inch wide and not very thick. It weighed almost nothing and eerily, had been in his pocket this whole time. Dax stared, wondering what it was and how it had gotten there.

A horrifying thought hit him. Someone, somewhere knew where he was. And it wasn't the good guys. If Hicks knew about this, they would have come last night.

A plain, brown Ford sedan pulled up in front of the theatre's entrance, the brakes squeaking softly as it came to a stop. Dax ducked behind some ivy growth and watched.

The person in the passenger side turned and Dax breathed a sigh of relief as he recognized the somber face of Agent Michelle Milevoi. As she opened the door, the driver got out and Dax recognized him too, the guy from yesterday in the brown windbreaker and English cap.

Grabbing hold of the openings in the fence, Dax hoisted himself over the gate and landed nimbly on the ground. As he rounded the corner, he saw Agent Milevoi and the other man cautiously approaching the front door of the theatre.

"Hey!" Dax yelled and waved. The couple spun to face him, their hands reflexively going for their waistlines. He held up both hands. "It's me, Dax Ribeiro. I know I don't look it, but it's me."

Milevoi shook her head in a rebuking manner but bore a subtle smile; perhaps she was actually glad to see him still alive. When Dax was near enough, she said, "Agent Milevoi, if you'll recall."

"I do. You got any more Tylenol? I got a splitting headache."

"Not at the moment. This is agent Roland Jacoby," she said, gesturing at the other man. Jacoby nodded.

"Saw you yesterday watching me," Dax said with a smirk.

Jacoby looked away, embarrassed. "Yeah, yeah, don't remind me. It was a bad day."

"Trust me, it was a worse day for me."

"You spent the night here?" Milevoi asked, nodding at the theatre entrance.

Dax looked at the building. "I did."

She looked him up and down and her smile broadened a little. "Nice hair."

"It's a theatre – they got appearance transforming stuff in there."

"Well let's get going, get you back to the castle."

As they started for the car, Dax reached into his pocket and produced the small, rectangular device he'd found. "I found this in my pocket. One of you put it there?"

Milevoi turned, looked, then extended her hand. Dax dropped it into her palm while Jacoby stepped up to take a look. They both stared while Milevoi turned it over a couple times. Then they both looked at each other.

"We need to go, *now*," she said.

No sooner was the word "now" uttered, when a dark Laforza SUV drove quickly up the street and came to a screeching halt behind the agent's sedan. Dax, Jacoby and Milevoi were taken by such surprise, they only stood and gaped for a moment.

The two front doors and left rear of the vehicle opened simultaneously as three men in long coats stepped out with skilled swiftness, drawing weapons.

"Run, Dax!" Milevoi yelled as she and Jacoby scrambled for their guns.

The passenger was already standing, poised, and pointing a large semi-automatic pistol. He was tall, somber expression, and bore a large, noticeable scar along the side of his face.

As deafening booms broke the calm of the morning air, Dax instinctively clutched his head and dropped. He heard Milevoi scream and looked up to see her being spun to the left, her shoulder shattered and blood pouring out. Jacoby had dropped to one knee and managed to get two shots off before his head snapped backward and the back of his skull exploded, sending bits and pieces of bone and brain matter spattering to the ground.

Milevoi started to raise her gun, but then stopped and let it slip out of her hand. Lying on the ground, she held her palms outward in surrender. Dax then saw the three men approaching, guns extended and pointed.

The large man with the scar moved with purpose and stared without expression, like the Cyberdyne Systems Model 101 Terminator from the movie. The three of them stopped and stood around Dax and Milevoi.

The man with the scar glanced at Agent Roland Jacoby and then back to Milevoi. She was wide-eyed in fear and breathing hard, but resilience and fight were in her eyes. The man raised his gun at her face.

"No, please …" she said in a quiet plead as the gun barrel detonated, leaving an instant hole in her forehead. Her muscles relaxed and her head hit the ground, her lifeless eyes staring up at the sky.

A sudden rage filled Dax, like a burst of energy that started somewhere in his gut and rose quickly to his head. Too much had happened recently. Too much stress and sorrow and pain and death. He made the decision right then and there that he no longer cared what happened. Without thinking he screamed, "You bastards!" then sprang up and shoved the big man with the scar.

The man took a small step back while the other two raised their guns at Dax. The man didn't look surprised or angry, just remained expressionless.

Dax stepped forward and took a swing, and it would have been the hardest right hook he'd ever delivered to anyone, but the man's free hand flashed up and easily caught Dax's fist in his large palm, holding it tight.

The other two moved in closer with their guns but did not fire. Clearly, they wanted him alive, or he'd be lying on the ground next to Jacoby and Milevoi.

The man with the scar looked Dax up and down, pausing on the bleached hair, until he felt Dax's muscles begin to relax, then slowly released his grip.

Wearily, Dax let his arms fall to his side in surrender.

The man turned and with a nod, indicated to Dax to get into the car. Dax complied and began walking, the men falling behind. As Dax got in and slid over, the rage he'd felt melted away and was replaced with a curious, dull, hazy feeling. He felt nothing but resignation to fate.

Dax stared out the window and tried not to think about anything as he heard the engine start and felt the car moving away. All at once, the man beside him shoved what felt like a ski mask turned backwards over his head.

Blinded to where he was going, he leaned back and tried to remain calm.

40: Gurkovsky

Les Abraham sat in his small and cluttered office at the City College of San Francisco where he'd taught three classes for almost thirty years – a beginner's acting class that most took just to fulfil their liberal arts requirements, an intermediate class for those a bit more serious, and his most popular, an acting on camera class.

It bothered him for years that the school had let Jim Kirkland and Gene Palmer run the advanced acting classes. Both of them disliked his acting on camera curriculum, which they accused of being phony and technical, especially Kirkland. And with Kirkland's clout, he'd been able to keep Les, for the most part, out of the more significant productions and away from the more talented actors that went through the program.

But with the retirement of Gene Palmer, he just might have his shot at getting the more prestigious and coveted classes and acquire the kind of students he really wanted to teach – the ones that actually wanted to pursue an acting career. He was tired of the fresh-out-of-high school goofballs who took his classes in groups of chatty friends who had no intention of becoming actors. They would giggle and mess around, laughing at the scripts or scenes, smirking while looking at each other during an exercise, not taking anything serious.

To punish the insolents, Les had an arsenal of techniques to squeeze either the actor in them out, or the student out of the class. He would choose people he knew were uncomfortable or awkward with each other and force them into scenes that involved sexual intimacy, sometimes girls with girls and boys with boys. At such times, the adolescent behavior was quickly replaced with embarrassment as they realized they either didn't have the talent or the confidence to perform such scenes.

Additionally, nervous or insecure people often stood in various poses without realizing it. Some with a hand on their hip, others in sort of a cowboy, thumbs in their pockets, standoff way. When Les saw this, he'd yell, "Why are you posing!"

"I'm not," they'd always say defensively.

"Bullshit!" Les would yell, and then demonstrate what they were doing, mocking them in front of the class.

Oh yeah, he had his ways of weeding out the kids who enjoyed the attention but would never put in the actual work it took to be an actor.

But there were a few other things on Les' mind right now. The last couple days had been crazy. First, Aaron Tisdale had come to him in almost a panic. He said he'd seen Dax Ribeiro all decked out in a luxury party outfit headed up California. Aaron had stopped and was watching Dax, waiting for an opportunity to say hi or something, but then noticed the people in the car Dax had just come from. One had looked back at Aaron, stared for a moment, then leaped out and drew a gun.

"Are you sure it was a gun?" Les had asked.

"I know what a gun looks like, Les,'" Aaron had replied. "It was real, and the dude looked serious."

"Did he point it at you?"

"No, I took off," was Aaron's reply.

"What did he look like? Anyone you recognize?"

"No, didn't get a good look. I was too scared." The poor kid really had been frightened out of his mind.

Les questioned why Aaron never called the police and he'd said because they would have drilled him on the descriptions of the car and the gunman, and he wouldn't have been able to remember anything anyway.

But it had really rattled Aaron, and now it was starting to rattle Les. Could the shooting at the Omni hotel that was all over the news have anything to do with Dax and those characters in the car? If so, then there had to be some connection with that and those two FBI agents Les had introduced to Dax, what were their names … Jack Dauer and Michael Staggs.

But then it got stranger. Shortly after that conversation with Aaron, two *different* FBI agents paid a visit. They didn't act like Dauer and Staggs. They had been much more serious, more intimidating. More what you'd expect, really. They'd asked lots of questions about Dauer and Staggs, how Les had met them, what he knew about them, why they'd been interested in Dax Ribeiro. It was all very mysterious, and unnerving.

Les told the truth, that one day here at the college, the agents had approached him and wanted to talk about actors. They were doing some undercover investigative work and looking for an actor that fit this description.

"Nothing dangerous or anything, right?" Les had asked.

"Oh no, no," they'd said. "We assure you it's all perfectly safe. He'll even have fun."

"Who's this guy here?" they'd asked, showing Les a picture from a promotion of a show the college had put on. They were pointing at Dax Ribeiro.

"Oh sure, I know him," Les smugly said, as if he had connections to talent the United States government could use.

Les had been proud of the fact that he'd helped Dax's acting career. Something like that would be a great addition to a resume. After all, the kid was pretty good, but not great. He'd probably never be a lead man in a big production. He'd forever stay a bit more on the sidelines, playing secondary characters and supporting the leads. Dax was the kind of person most people liked and wanted to see succeed because he put his heart into what he did. But one either had the talent and looks or they didn't. The kid did have some good martial arts moves though – he should capitalize on that more.

Anyway, the whole thing was very strange and he wanted to talk to Dax badly. Too bad Dax wasn't in *Wild Hearts* – he had no idea if Jim Kirkland had the kid pegged for anything. It would have been a strategic move, to the use the steam from Dax's recent appearance as a lead man. Maybe Les would stop by the Treasure Box again and see how rehearsals were going. Perhaps Dax would show up and they'd get a chance to talk.

Les gulped down the last of his cool, stale coffee and grabbed his things. The weather was going to be good today. He'd probably stop at his favorite ice cream shop later and have a Sundae.

On the way out to the parking lot, he didn't notice the white Dodge Monaco a few rows down and the two men inside that were watching. They were quite inconspicuous, after all, and no one would have given them a second glance. They both donned sunglasses and appeared to be waiting, perhaps to pick someone up. Whatever they were doing, it was no one's business anyway.

But as Les neared his car, the Monaco's engine rumbled to life, and it began slowly moving down the rows and paused at the one Les had entered. It turned in and began following as Les found his vehicle and opened the trunk.

As he was putting his things in, the white car stopped, and a man got out. General curiosity made Les turn; students approached him in the parking lot all the time to ask a question or just to chitchat.

But the man was someone Les recognized. He looked different though in casual clothing and with a shadow of unshaven hair on his chin. But when he removed the sunglasses, there was no question. Before him stood the man that had introduced himself recently as Agent Michael Staggs of the Federal Bureau of Investigation. The face, now without glasses, also bore two painful looking bruises, one below the left eye and swollen, and one on his right cheek. There was also a cold and calculated look in his eyes.

As Les watched Staggs move toward him, he knew something was wrong. There were too many related events as of late that added up to a big, disturbing mystery. Staggs did not smile or say anything, which made the situation more alarming. He was also wearing gloves and the weather was a bit too warm for that. Les backed up until the crooks of his knees were against the edge of his trunk.

When Staggs was about three steps away, he quickly reached into his coat and produced a pistol with what looked like a long, smoothly machined silencer screwed into the end of the barrel.

Les gasped in fright as Staggs leveled the end of the silencer at his face. He held up his hands and started to yell, "No!" but the word went only half spoken. The pistol coughed and Les fell backward into the trunk, his feet still on the ground.

Re-holstering the weapon, the man looked around and glanced at the driver, who nodded. Taking hold of Les' legs, he hoisted them into the truck and then shut it.

The body would not be found for almost a week, when a passing student would notice a terrible odor coming from the car and call the police.

***

Dax sat in a comfortable black, leather bariatric chair before a big mahogany desk. His head was still sweaty from the head sock someone had just yanked off.

On the other side of the desk sat a man calmly looking Dax over. Immediately, the man's very persona expressed power and one who was comfortable with authority. With just looks and nods, he could make people move and cause things to happen. It was the kind of charisma Dax wished he had on stage, but such attributes could not be taught, it was given to a person as they were formed in the womb.

The man was perhaps in his mid-fifties with a neatly trimmed beard that was just slightly shorter than the length of his full head of gray hair. The face was naturally round, his eyes large and piercing. His tailored suit looked pricey, a portrait of affluence and success. But he also exhibited something else, something that told a discerning observer that none of this had been given to him for free. He'd earned it with clever intelligence, hard work, and whatever violence had been necessary.

"My name is Gurkovsky," the man said at last. His voice was smooth and bore a distinctive Slavic accent.

Dax took a quick glance around the spacious office. There were no windows and no sound from anywhere, suggesting it was either under a building or built deep into the back of one. A private space where private conversations and arrangements were made. Behind Gurkovsky and to his right, the huge man with the conspicuous scar on his face who had murdered

Agent Milevoi in cold blood, stood watching Dax. Behind Dax, two more men sat on a small couch.

Dax sat back. So much had happened, he wasn't sure what he felt right now. He was almost too exhausted to be frightened. He decided to ask the obvious question. "Why am I still alive?"

A slight smile formed on Gukovsky's mouth. "Straight to business. I like that." He picked up a photograph on his desk and studied it for a minute, then looked at Dax. "Your hair is wrong color."

Dax looked up, even though he couldn't see his own hair. "I dyed it this morning."

"Mmm," Gurkovsky said, nodding and looking back at the photo. "The resemblance is remarkable. No wonder you were chosen."

"Yeah, my bad luck," Dax said quietly.

"There's no such thing as luck. There are opportunities to take advantage of and there are dangers that wise avoid. That is all."

Dax crossed his arms. "*Spacibo*, for your pearls, but it looks like I'm too late to be wise. I should have said *nyet* to Dauer, and that asshole Staggs."

"Mmm," Gurkovsky said, leaning back. "Jack Dauer and Michael Staggs. Those names we heard over and over."

"You know who they are? Because if you do, I'd love to know myself."

Gurkovsky smiled again and tapped the desk. "We've been tailing them for weeks, since they arrived," he said smugly. "Always one step ahead. Listening to their conversations. Keeping tabs, as you say."

"And all of you have been looking for this *Dog of Saint Petersburg*, is that right?" Dax asked.

The smile faded from Gurkovsky's lips and he glanced again at the photo on his desk. "No need to look for dead dog." He turned the photo around and slid it across to Dax.

Dax cautiously leaned forward and took the picture. At first glance, the image in the slightly blurry but otherwise high-definition color photo looked nothing like him. The man in the picture was walking away somewhere and looking behind him, the camera capturing just the moment he was facing the lens. He was about the same age and build as Dax, maybe a couple years older, but his nose was narrower and his jaw wider. Dax stared harder, and then saw it. He put his hand over the mouth and partially over the nose of the man in the photograph. There it was. With the right hair and a couple other subtle changes, including bigger jowls, he could be this guy in the photo.

"You like to be on stage, yes?" Gurkovsky asked, watching him.

Dax looked up. "I've been known to, yes."

"And what is your reward for doing this … acting? Dressing up like someone else and pretending to be someone else."

Dax shrugged. "A few do it for the money, but most of us do it for the fun, I guess."

"Mmm. But you wanted the money. You want to be big Hollywood star, like that Sylvester Stallone."

"Sure. It was fun watching him destroy the big Russian boxer, Drago. Come to think of it, this guy here kind of looks like Drago," Dax said, thumbing at the man with the scar. "He just needs the cropped blond hair."

"There, you see?" Gurkovsky said pointing at Dax. "That silly actor is Swedish, not Russian. His accent was laughable."

"It's actually a pretty well-known fact that Dolph Lundgren is Swedish."

Gurkovsky sighed and leaned back. "I know a man here in city. A well-connected man I've done business with. He has son who wants to do this ... *play acting*. I don't know what I would do if I had such son."

Dax looked away, thinking, the conversation he'd had with Aaron Tisdale flashing through his mind. "Wait, are you talking about Mario, and his dad, ah ... Mr. Silvestri?"

Gurkovsky glanced at the big man with the scar, then back at Dax. He squinted slightly at Dax and then said, "You are full of surprises, my young American pretender. What else do you know?"

"I know you want to finish a deal that went bad. A deal worth lots of money. But this *Собака* guy messed things up. His little company in France bellied up and you didn't get your fee."

Gurkovsky reached for a fancy wooden cigar box and opened it. As he took one out and retrieved a cutter, he gestured and said, "Please, continue."

"I don't know much more. International arms deals aren't my thing."

Gurkovsky put a small torch-lighter to the cigar and took a few puffs. A cloud of blue smoke formed around him before slowly rising toward a ventilation opening on the wall behind him. "I want that dirty dog's fee. Do you know anything about being salesman?" he asked, placing an ashtray in front of himself.

Dax shook his head.

"One can learn lot from salesman – of *weapons*."

"If I could make a million bucks selling AK-47s, it might tempt me to learn."

Gurkovsky waved a hand. "The AK-47 is everywhere, costs maybe seventy-five dollars to buy in bulk, then transport and sell. Most high-profile dealers don't bother with this because margins too low. In fact, some dealers use them as loss leader, giving them away like new drug pusher in town who gives out tasty samples to hook and reel their buyers in. After establishing rapport, they start making deals on more ... sophisticated weapons."

"I didn't know that," Dax said genuinely, and wondering why he was being told this.

"There many things you don't know."

"I know *The Dog of Saint Petersburg* knows Viktor Bout, the man they call the 'Merchant of Death.'"

Gurkovsky chuckled. "*The Dog of Saint Petersburg ...*" he said slowly. "Sounds much better in Russian. But yes, the arms industry benefits greatly from competitive nature of war. If your enemy has only knives, guns will serve, but when they acquire guns, you'll want tanks. And so on. *Собака* learned many tricks from Bout, but it won't last long. Bout will be caught and put away. He's too arrogant. He likes to ... how to do you say, *shoot from hips*. He's getting bolder. Taking more risks." Pointing the cigar at Dax, he added, "It won't be long."

Dax shifted in his chair. "So how does this Gavril Novikov fit into the role of international arms salesman and why is he supposed to be dead?"

Gurkovsky raised his eyebrows. "You know this name? Someone has been talking to you."

"A lot of people have been talking to me. Some to me, some to *The Dog*."

"Mmm," Gurkovsky said, tapping his cigar on the side of the ashtray. "Well, he was overly ambitious. Started making mistakes. He won't be doing that again."

"So he is dead then?"

Gurkovsky took a draw on his cigar, then said, "He might be."

Dax lowered his head, feeling resigned to fate. "So am I, I guess."

Gurkovsky snorted a small smirk. "You are correct that arms dealing is not your … *thing*. You would not last very long."

Despite everything, Dax found himself sightly intrigued with this conversation.

Gurkovsky continued, "Most think of a weapons dealer simply as someone who can sell guns and ammunition. But really, they are provisioners of war. They supply whatever you need to wage your conflict – rockets, planes, uniforms, tanks, helicopters. Hardware is purchased in one country, then transported to destination. Most dealers charter ships and planes, but select few operate their own fleets. Viktor Bout's companies run an air fleet of sixty planes."

"What did *The Dog* do to make people mad at him?"

Gurkovsky thought for a moment. "If you were selling guns, would you sell them loaded?"

"Of course not."

"Why not?"

"Because the buyer could turn around and use them to kill or rob me and take back the money."

Gurkovsky smiled. "Precisely. But in arms business, particularly when you're doing it illegally, it is opposite. No matter what kind of product you are selling, you need to ensure it has everything buyer needs to use as intended." Gurkovsky paused and took a long draw on his cigar. "Say you bought new electronic gadget, take home, find out it doesn't come with batteries. That's frustrating because you want to use right now. Or say you buy computer just to discover there's an additional memory card or accessory you need to buy and install before it will perform functions you bought it for. Now, put that into perspective of country who makes purchases to defend sovereign borders from some invading dictator. It buys millions in aircraft or a new radar system only to find that training, spare parts, and instructions needed to use them. The lesson is, even if you give something away as good will gesture, make sure it works. Your job is it sell total solution, not just single product."

Dax stared at a figurine on Gurkovsky's desk. It looked like an intricate wood carving of a bear, perhaps a black grizzly, in a sleigh being pulled by large, muscular Friesian horses. The bear's jaws were wide open, revealing a pair of sharp canines and lower teeth, roaring, or perhaps yelling orders at the horses. The detail was quite nice. He looked up at Gurkovsky. "Did Novikov sell someone bad product?"

"Mmm. When something goes wrong, seller is always at fault. The rule in our business is always under promise, then over deliver. *Собака* had bad habit of doing the other way around. If you don't deliver exactly what you said, you burn bridges. And if you're late in delivery or can't provide terms agreed upon, you will do more damage than if you just rejected order in first place. Over promising and under delivering will overshadow deal, even if product is good."

Dax felt his thoughts bouncing around. Hicks had told him Novikov was using fake bidding to overcharge, and now he's being told the man didn't deliver. No wonder he got whacked.

Dax looked up and decided to ask, "Why are you telling all this to me?"

"To prepare you, of course," Gurkovsky said.

"For?"

"To finish what you started at Omni Hotel."

A sinking feeling hit Dax and he slumped back in his chair. With his head hung, he said, "I'm not doing that again."

Gurkovsky puffed on his cigar watching Dax for a moment, then said. "I think you will."

"I'm not good at this stuff."

"You will go back to your little acting life shortly."

"I don't understand. I don't speak Russian. I know nothing about how to act or what to do in this world of weapons deals. I was only born with a look that kind of resembles this Gavril guy."

"You will have help this time."

Dax frowned in puzzlement as Gurkovsky said something Dax could not understand, then one of the men behind him stood and left the room. A minute later Dax heard a familiar voice.

"Hello, Dax."

Before he turned, he knew it was Meygan Knight.

41: The Contract

Dax shook his head in disbelief, then slowly turned around. She had the same light brown wavy hair and alluring face which, at the moment, bore no makeup, making her look different. But when she gazed at him with that intense, penetrating stare from rich, emerald-green eyes, he briefly saw himself the dashing hero again, saving her from the bad guys. Ironic how now, it might be her saving *him* from the bad guys.

Without responding, he turned back around in his chair and rubbed the bridge of his nose. At this point, there was nothing in the world that could shock or surprise him. One of the men behind him picked up a chair and set it next to Dax and Meygan sat down.

Dax turned and looked at her. She was dressed very casually in jeans and a gray, long sleeved t-shirt. She looked like she was right at home here, wherever it was, with these murderers.

Gurkovsky chuckled. "I think you two know each other, yes?"

Dax glared at Meygan for a moment and then looked away shaking his head. All this time, he'd hoped her only connection to any of this was that, like him, she had been on some assignment that night at the Babylon Ballroom. But now, anything was game.

"No hello? No formalities?" Gurkovsky said with mockery.

Dax turned to Meygan again. She stared at Gurkovsky's desk with an odd expression Dax couldn't fully discern. She didn't look happy, nor did she look despondent either. She seemed to be contemplating something. She also appeared to be waiting for Dax to pepper her with questions. But he decided he would let her talk first. After all, it looked like she was here voluntarily, while he'd been kidnapped and blindfolded after two people next to him had been shot. He leaned back and folded his hands in his lap.

Gurkovsky's eyes moved back and forth between the two of them while he tapped his cigar. Finally, he said, "You both are going to work together, so if you're at odds, I suggest you, how do you say, kiss and make up."

"My work with her ended last week," Dax said.

"One more performance to go," Gurkovsky said.

"No way. No way in hell."

"*The Dog* has one more job to do," Gurkovsky said, his voice taking on an edge. "And you're only one that can do it."

"Why?"

"This client will only sign papers and hand over fee if Mr. Novikov makes deal and signs as well."

"I have no idea how Novikov signs his name."

"We have samples. You can practice."

"Why does anyone have to sign anything anyway? It's all illegal."

"You are incorrect," Gurkovsky said, pointing his cigar again. "This is perfectly legitimate deal. And then, thanks to you, Ukrainian military will think they have few more toys to play with."

"They'll find out I'm a fake and that *The Dog* is dead."

"By the time they do, I will already have my money. Besides, you hardly have to say a word. Your pretty stage friend here will do most of talking."

"I don't understand."

Gurkovsky sighed like an impatient schoolteacher. "You were injured from assassination attempt, remember? You're lucky to be alive."

"Yes, I remember a big brute and his girlfriend in the women's bathroom at the Babylon Ballroom tried to kill me." He saw Meygan turn and was looking at him.

"Not that," Gurkovsky said. "The bomb in La Valentine Saint Menet. You've been on the run ever since. Your throat and voice injured. And you've even dyed your hair like that rock star ..." He turned to the younger man in the back of the room and gestured.

The man said, "Billy Idol."

"Billy Idol!" Gurkovsky said. "You did that so you can move about unnoticed. It's perfect."

Dax stared for a moment. "Did you plant that bomb?"

Gurkovsky looked hard at Dax, his eyes penetrating and solid as steel, then said, "Truly you are fish out of water here to ask such questions. But no, it would not have been in our interests to eliminate little *sobashka*." Then for whatever reason, he decided to add, "He was useful in many ways. He stuck his head out, allowing us to remain unnoticed. He stuck it out too far."

Dax felt a surge of panic well up in him. He leaned forward and put his arms on the desk. "You can't make me do this again. I almost got killed the first time. People are dying. I'm finished with all this."

Gurkovsky watched, stony cold and unmoved. "Mr. Novikov needs to do one last job, *then* he finished."

"He's dead! And I'm dead if I try this again."

"You were already successful in fooling them."

"Was I? I was threatened with a gun until I said who I really was. Nobody bought it."

"They will this time. And if they don't, then it will be on you."

"What will be on me?"

Gurkovsky opened a folder on his desk. He thumbed through a couple pages until he came upon one and held it up. "Let's see, who do have here?" he said, skimming the page. "A Mr. Paulo Ribeiro, who lives at 5165 Saint Francis Drive, Santa Fe, New Mexico." He set the paper down.

Dax saw Meygan look at him again while he felt the blood drain from his head.

"You know Sasha here," Gurkovsky continued, nodding at the big man with the scar. "He has been wanting to see more of States. Perhaps New Mexico will be his next stop."

Dax sprang up, slamming his fists on the desk. "You son of a bitch!" he snarled, genuinely enraged.

"Dax, no!" Meygan yelled.

Gurkovsky calmly regarded him while his men quickly surrounded Dax, strong hands clamping down on his arms.

Dax sank back into the chair, already feeling defeated. As Gurkovsky's men released their grip, he felt a gentler hand on his shoulder.

"It'll be okay, Dax," he heard Meygan say.

"Shut up. It's already not okay."

"Then let's put an end to this once and for all," Gurkovsky said, clapping his hands. "I'm making arrangement for tomorrow morning. And I'm giving you some details to look at." Gurkovsky tossed a folder at Dax, which slid to a stop at the edge of the table. He then nodded at his men.

Meygan kept her eyes on the floor as two men took Dax by the arms and stood him up. He was led down a hallway into a smaller room with a table and a couple chairs. The door shut and he could hear the click of the lock being engaged.

A couple minutes later, one of the men brought in a bottle of water and set it on the table, then without a word, turned and exited, locking the door again.

Dax stared at the folder in front of him. The totality of everything that had happened in the last few days was almost too much to think about. What started as a phony job was now a real job. Even if he pulled it off, what were the chances Gurkovsky would let him live?

He opened the folder. The words were written in English. At first glance, the language appeared to be what one might expect in a typical business contract, although he'd not personally looked at very many in his life.

Scanning down a few paragraphs, he saw, *THIS BILL OF SALE is executed on* 09/25/1996, by and between the Ministry of Defense of Ukraine (*Міністерство Оборони України*) and then a whole bunch of names, then, *authorized by the Supreme Commander-in-Chief of the Armed Forces of Ukraine, Leonid Makarovych Kravchuk to support and improve security of a UNITED NATIONS country which is an important force for political stability and economic progress in Eastern Europe.*

A few more paragraphs, then: *This sale will improve the Ukraine's defense capability to meet current and future enemy threats. The Ukraine will use the enhanced capability to strengthen its homeland defense and deter regional threats and provide direct support to coalition and security cooperation efforts.*

Skimming through, he wanted to see what this was a transaction for. Finally, he saw a paragraph: *FOR AND CONSIDERATION of a total purchase price of $450 million United States dollars,* and then a mind-boggling bulleted list that included, *one hundred ninety-five (195) AGM-114R2 Hellfire missiles with support, one hundred and fifty (150) AIM-120 Advanced Medium-Range Air-to-Air Missiles (AMRAAM),* *one (1) F-35 Joint Strike Fighter aircraft and related equipment, ten (10) Bradley IFV infantry carriers …* the list went on.

"Holy crap," Dax said putting the papers down and reaching for the water bottle. People were out there making deals like this? It was unimaginable how someone who was barely thirty could even start to get involved in stuff like this. But it did end up killing *The Dog*, didn't it? And it was going to end up killing the schmuck who was impersonating him as well.

Dax suddenly felt tired. Sliding forward, he tilted the chair back and rested his head on the backrest. As he felt himself succumb to the heaviness of sleep, he thought of how his life was already changed forever.

42: Meygan Knight

Something woke Dax up. So hard had he slept, he didn't know how long he'd been out or if he had even dreamt. Blinking, he looked around the small room and all the events of the last couple days came crashing into his mind.

A small movement caused him to turn, and there was Meygan Knight sitting quietly at the head of the small table with the folder and papers in front of her.

She glanced up. "Welcome back," she said with a small but genuine smile.

Dax slowly eased himself into a straighter position. His head hurt, his shoulder hurt, and now his back hurt. Rubbing his eyes, he asked, "Is there any aspirin or anything around here?"

"Sure," she said, getting up. She went to the door, opened it part way, and said something quietly to someone standing nearby. The language she spoke was distinctly and fluently Russian. He even recognized one of the words, *bud'te dobry*, which is how a woman would ask for something from a man.

Dax watched as she returned to the table. He even stole a quick glance up and down her trimmed body as he had so many times backstage at the Godwin Theatre, but then looked away, feeling resentment. "So, you speak Russian, huh? Or should I say, *ty govoriš' po-Russki?*" he asked.

Meygan nodded. "*Da*. And your pronunciation could use some work."

Dax shook his head. "After this, if I live, I never want to speak another word of the damn language again."

"You'll live. And it's a beautiful language," Meygan said, sitting back.

"Yeah, well, the only way I've had it spoken to me lately is in the context of people threatening to kill me."

"It's in part because you know a little, that you got into all this. I wanted to say something to you in the last show, a passing comment or something, just to see if you'd understand."

"*You?* Wanted to speak to me *casually*, outside the performance?"

Meygan cast her eyes down and away.

Dax continued. "You knew I spoke a little Russian?"

"I heard you talk about it with Glenn and Dennis. I once heard you call Dillon a *mudak*," she chuckled.

"Oh, yeah, I think I did once." Dax suddenly glared at her in contempt. "Are you the one who helped put those assholes on to me, those two fake FBI agents?"

Meygan's smile dropped. "I've no idea who they are."

"Don't you work for these people?" Dax said, gesturing around the room. "Aren't you one of them?"

"No!" she said, with hurt in her eyes. "To be honest, I don't want to be here anymore than you."

"So what then, are they threatening your family too if you don't cooperate?"

She shook her head. "No."

"And how about this *Собака* guy? Know anything about him?"

"Not before all this. Not a thing."

Dax balled up a fist and thumped it on the table. "Whatever. Does it really matter anymore? Does anything matter …"

Meygan leaned forward. "Yes, it does matter. It matters because we're going to get this done so you can get on with your life."

"I doubt they'll let me." Dax chortled bitterly. "So what's your involvement here?"

Meygan paused, her eyes shifting.

The door opened and one of Gurkovsky's men entered. He set a bottle of aspirin in front of Dax, looked at Meygan for a moment, then exited. Dax stared at the bottle, toying with a masochistic thought that he deserved everything he'd brought on himself. Grabbing the bottle, he snapped it open and poured five, then six tablets in his hand, tossed them in his mouth, then swallowed with three big gulps of water.

Meygan was watching. "Dax," she said softly. "I'm sorry for what you've been through. I'm sorry these people are making you do this. But I promise I had nothing to do with it."

Dax threw his hands up. "Then why are you here? How do you know these people? What were you doing at the Omni Hotel?" He looked hard at her.

Meygan put her hands together and rested her arms on the table. "It's kind of a long story. I've been seeing this guy for almost a year now. At first, I thought he was just another wannabe student of acting. He'd taken a few classes at City, and we ran into each other at a workshop. Although not very talented, he was nice, at first – good looking, extraordinarily confident. Even cocky. I kinda fell for him." She looked away embarrassed.

"Women always love the arrogant types," Dax said.

"Oh please."

"Nice guys do finish last."

"Whatever."

"Go on with your story," Dax said.

Meygan crossed her arms. "I didn't know much about him at first. But then I found out his dad is some big player here in the city. Owns a bunch of restaurants and involved with a lot of other businesses. Some of it legit; some of it not so much."

"International arms dealing, perhaps?"

"I don't think so. But he knows people at the Port of Oakland. He can get things through customs, have them transported. People pay him a lot of money to make sure their items get where they're supposed to."

Dax watched, using his instincts in human behavior to gauge whether she was being truthful or not. He decided she was. "So, who's this wannabe actor? Anyone I know?" he finally asked.

Meygan waved a hand. "No one you've heard of. But you may soon. His dad pulled some strings to make Jim Kirkland put him in his new show."

Dax looked at Meygan and laughed in cynical disbelief as it all became clear. Of course, the dark-haired man in the nice suit he'd seen with Meygan that night. "Are you talking about Mario? The guy who's going to play Cash Giles in *Wild Hearts?*"

Meygan looked up in genuine surprise. "You know Mario? You know about that?"

"No, met him once briefly at the theatre. Jim told me he'd casted the guy but didn't want to talk about it. But I knew I'd seen him before. He has a certain stare, like he's challenging you. He was with you that night at the Omni, wasn't he?"

Meygan nodded slowly. "That's right. That was him."

"So, what's the connection then? Is Mario an arms dealer when he's not trying to be an actor?"

"No. I'm sure it's on his list of things to try, but he's not smart enough to play in that arena. He doesn't know what he wants.

Once he finds out having a big part in a play doesn't get him respect and admiration, he'll walk away and never look back." She sighed. "Dating him has been one of those experiences that was exciting at first, but then nothing but ... many other things since."

Dax's mind drifted to the conversation he'd had with Sam just last night. She had said similar things about him, and she was right. "But you're still with him?" he asked, trying to refocus.

"Sort of, yeah."

"Sort of?"

"I'm in over my head and want to get out, kind of like you."

"So walk away. You're good at turning your back and walking away, not giving a crap. I've seen it a few times."

"Fuck you, Dax," Meygan said, bitterly. "You think girls like me have all the power. Trust me, we don't. Most of our *power* is just over those who can't compete. The rest of the time we're as helpless to manipulating forces around us as anyone else."

Dax watched her for a moment, his anger subsiding. "Let me rephrase," he said with sardonic gentleness. "Why don't you just break up with this wannabe international Mafioso?"

Meygan stared at the table, deep in thought. "It's not so easy getting away from someone like him. He's still in the early stages of making a name for himself. I've seen him rough people up, act stupid. He's got a lot to prove to everyone. I don't know what he'd do if I dropped him. He's hurt ..." She put a hand on her arm as her voice trailed off.

Dax sensed she was trying hold back tears. All at once though, she recomposed, a hardness snapping back into her eyes.

"I'm trying to do subtle things right now to get on his nerves. Get him tired of me so he'll be the one who dumps me – that would give him the sense of control he needs. But he won't while he's on this acting kick. He thinks having me around is helping that endeavor."

"I would have never pegged you as the helpless maiden in distress."

"It's not all that."

"Okay, fine. But why were you two at that social that night?"

Meygan sighed. "He's friends with some of the acquaintances and employees of these characters. The activities they're involved in immediately intrigued him. He likes to think he's connected and up there with the big shots. He hears about things like that party and gets in on it. He wanted me there to show off as his beautiful Bay Area actress star. I was just playing a part, like you."

"Well, you certainly played it. And dressed it. You were gorgeous." As soon as Dax said that he looked away, embarrassed. He glanced up to see her smiling, but with sadness in her eyes.

"I can be eye candy when I need to," she said.

Dax wanted to change the subject. "You know the FBI had people there, right? The real FBI, I mean. They probably took pictures of everyone and have already ID-ed you."

Meygan's eyes shifted in trepidation and deep thought for a second, but then she switched gears and shrugged. "There's nothing I can do about that now." She paused. "So what about you?"

Dax sensed she was feigning indifference. "What about me?"

"Why were you at that gathering dressed up and acting like an international arms dealer?"

"Long story."

"I told you mine."

Dax sighed hard and took a drink of water. "It was the second to the last night of the show. You'd already left. Les came into the makeup room and chatted it up a bit before telling me there were two people waiting in his office that wanted to talk. Dennis thought they were talent scouts. Glenn was jealous. Dillon was out of his mind."

"Who were they?"

"They introduced themselves as Agents Jack Dauer and Michael Staggs of the FBI. Had the look, the credentials, everything. Told me they needed an actor who had my looks for an undercover investigation they were involved with. Said it would be easy and there'd be no danger. And I'd get paid. I'd be fine because they'd be watching and listening and if anything happened, they'd come running to the rescue."

"How were they watching?"

"I had a tiny camera and microphone in my bowtie attached to a broadcasting device taped to my back."

Meygan was staring, thoroughly engrossed. "Wow. What exactly was your assignment?"

Dax paused, thinking about that night. Hicks had told him all radiofrequencies were jammed in the ballroom and not working, but Meygan didn't appear to know that. He decided to keep that little fact from her. "All I was told was that I was there to flush someone out. They needed to ID someone who'd had some dealings with this *Dog of Saint Petersburg* guy. They said if I went in looking and acting like this guy, I'd probably be approached. They'd get this person or persons on camera and that'd be it. They were then going get me out of there. But as you know, that's not what happened."

"Tell me."

Dax took a big breath. "I was sipping tonic water, trying to be inconspicuous, watching the bartender pretend he wasn't interested in me." He paused, almost saying he thought the bartender was with the FBI.

"The bartender?" Meygan asked.

"Yeah. It was nothing though," Dax said, waving it off. That was close. Someone could be listening, or Meygan might talk to her boyfriend and Dax didn't want to get the bartender killed.

"What happened next?"

"So first this woman approaches me. Acted very surprised to me, or who she thought I was. Said I was supposed to be dead. Then this other guy comes along, someone she called *Vassi*."

"*Vassi?* Vassi who?"

Hicks had told him the last name was Bodrov, but for some reason, Dax didn't want to divulge that either. There was something about Meygan that was making him uneasy, and he couldn't put a finger on it.

He shrugged. "Don't know. He was big and mean. Very scary. Got even scarier when he stuck a gun in my back and led me to the bathroom. There we had a fight, him threatening to kill me if I didn't tell him why I was there and who I really was."

"How about the girl's name?"

"Never heard it. But she can hurl a mean throwing knife. Tried to use my face for target practice."

"The phony FBI agents saw all this but never showed up?"

They never saw or heard anything. "All I know is that I was left high and dry – no cavalry to the rescue. I barely made it out alive. I managed to get the gun and shoot this *Vassi* guy in the back and run for my life. I've been running ever since."

"Wow."

"I do know that at some point, some of their people were killed at the Sutter Hotel where I was prepped for the job.

Probably these guys," Dax said, thumbing toward the door. He paused and noted that Meygan did not react to the comment. "That's where I was dressed up by Tasha."

"Tasha?"

"Yeah. Hot, blonde *devushka*. Disturbingly seductive. I wasn't sure if she turned me on or freaked me out. The female spider everyone wants, but if you're the one who gets her, you'll probably end up dead."

Meygan's eyes narrowed. "I see."

Dax smirked to himself for a moment thinking about Tasha's teasing little touches, then continued. "So maybe they were distracted by reports of their friends getting whacked. Or maybe they'd gotten what they wanted and no longer gave a crap about me. The real FBI has their equipment now. They picked me up that night, questioned me till early morning. Then they used me to get back in contact. I met Dauer and Staggs and was driven around while they interrogated me. Ended up pulling guns on me. I barely managed to get out of that one too. I'm no James Bond. I'm not up for this kind of thing."

Meygan took Dax's hand. "I'm glad you got away."

"So am I."

"Dax —"

"No," he interrupted, reading her mind. "I didn't tell anyone I saw you there. Believe me, they would have come to you by now. They grilled Les. Speaking of which, I still have to talk to him to get his side to all this."

"Thank you." Meygan looked down in thought. "Les might be in trouble, huh."

"The way these guys operate, I'd say so." Dax decided to change the subject again. He was also curious. "So how is it you speak Russian like you were born there?"

Meygan shifted in her chair and crossed her legs. "I'm part Russian you know."

"No, I didn't."

"My family would say they're German. But many modern Germans are part Russian, and a few other things. We're a mixed bunch."

"How's that?"

"Many Germans of eastern Europe were actually Slavs. Ancient Slavic people were converted to Christianity by Germanic missionaries, among others. Those under German control came to speak the language and identified culturally as Germans but were still Slavic genetically. We Germans have always had a wide, diverse, genetic mix, including French and Italian."

"Okay, so you're a mutt, kind of like me."

"Perhaps. But if that weren't enough, my grandmother was one of the women who was raped and impregnated by some soldier during the Red Army occupation in Berlin. They were rounded up like cattle, used as sex toys. Some raped by dozens at a time. Over a hundred thousand in Berlin alone – anyone from eight to eighty. Mostly in the Soviet occupied territories. The abortion rate soared in the post-World War two years, and there were a lot of suicides. My grandmother was one of who knows how many who conceived, giving birth to my mother. But she raised my mother as a blessed and loved child, not a curse as many were."

Dax sat back. "That's quite a family history. Mine isn't so historically significant."

"The world is a rough place. Your family may have had its share as well."

"Maybe. Brazil has a long history of slavery, racism, and violence. So, your grandmother taught your mother Russian?"

"And German. While she was still alive. Spoke them both in the house. Rarely spoke in English. She died before I was ten, but I became fascinated with both and studied on my own. Did some traveling around Europe and Russia several years ago."

"A real polyglot. I'd think you'd hate *pa-Russki* after what happened in your family."

"Most hate the Germans far more for what they did. Russia wanted revenge for all their suffering. Hitler had no mercy on them, so when they had their chance at some retribution, they showed no mercy as well. And since I've got both in me, no point in hating myself for it."

"So you sympathize, then."

"I just do my part to make the world better."

"By helping these guys?" Dax asked, waving around the room again.

She raised her chin. "By helping *you*. Ever since that night, I've been wondering when I could talk to you."

"Did Mario tell you about me?"

"No. Mario doesn't know. He's seen all my shows, of course. But he never recognized you or your name."

"So he didn't mention seeing me at the Treasure Box talking with Jim Kirkland?"

"No." Meygan leaned forward again, her hands clutched together. "Your *appearance* that night at the ballroom caused quite a stir. People started talking, saying that this *Dog of Saint Petersburg* was still alive. Others saying it was an imposter. Only I knew it was you."

"There were others that knew. But you said you didn't know anything about this *Собака* guy."

"No, I didn't then and what I know now is only what Gurkovsky told me since I got here. I asked Mario who 'that guy' was and he started asking around, but no one could tell him much. I kept it to myself about knowing you. I didn't know what they'd do."

Dax wiped his forehead with his sleeve. He had kept her secret, and she had kept his. "Well, *spaciba* for that. Because of your confidentiality, I only had about five people trying to kill me instead of ten. But that still doesn't explain why you're here now, in Gurkovsky's little hideaway."

Meygan blew out a deep breath. "One of Mario's friends who works for Gurkovsky said they knew where the imposter was and were looking for you. Mario was going on about it the other day after a couple drinks. No names or events were mentioned, but I knew he was talking about you. I went around Mario's back and contacted this employee and told him I knew who you were and if they could get to you, and not hurt you, I'd help get information."

"You believed they wouldn't hurt me?"

"Someone is going to kill you anyway, Dax. This is a way out."

Dax sighed in resignation; Special Agent in Charge, Sharon Decker had said the same thing. "So who is this employee of Gurkovsky?"

"The younger guy out there, name's Kiril. He's the one who gave you the aspirin."

"I see. So you did tell them who I was then."

"I was very vague. I said I only knew your first name and had been in a show with you and didn't know you very well."

Dax snorted. "Well, that part's kind of true, actually."

Meygan sighed and shook her head.

"So, what's going to happen when Mario finds out?"

"I don't know yet." She looked down despondently, her hands wringing.

Dax considered Meygan's situation and felt the last bit of ire he still had for her melt away. This actress who had dissed him over and over, who had shown zero interest in him as even just a human being had stuck her neck out for him. He was curious why though. It had to be more than just concern. Instinct told him to be wary. He studied her eyes while saying, "You've put yourself at terrible risk by doing this, you know."

"Yes, I know."

Dax took another long drink, then asked, "So what now?"

Meygan tapped the folder in front of her. "We prepare to do this."

"And what exactly is that?"

"We're going to finish a deal this *Собака* started with the Ukrainian government, then get on with our lives."

"Do you really think they're going to let us do that? I'm sure Mario will try to protect you, but me? I'm going to be a loose end after this. I've witnessed them murder. If Gurkovsky doesn't kill me, then the people those phony FBI agents work for will. That Staggs guy I know wanted to kill me. There's no way out."

Meygan put her hand on Dax's again. "We're going to be okay. *You're* going to be okay."

Dax looked hard at her before saying, "Why are you really doing this, Meygan?"

She studied him back for a moment then her expression went soft. "You looked so terrified that night. I couldn't believe you were there, dressed like that and then the shooting and police. I had to find out why you were there." She smiled. "You saved my life a few times, or Eric did."

Dax sensed the actress in her talking, but he played along. "When is this going to happen?"

"In a few hours. Early in the morning. The story they've been told is that *The Dog* has been hiding in this area."

"Who's they?"

"I don't know. The people representing the buyers I guess."

"What am I supposed to do when they start talking to me in Russian?"

"Most likely it will be in English. But if they start talking Russian, that's where I come in. You just touch your throat and whisper *da* or *nyet* and I'll do the rest."

For the next two hours, Dax and Meygan went over details of the contract. Among other things, it stipulated there was an extra fee for "transportation and security" that the buyers had to provide, paid in cash, for an amount that would be specified verbally, at the time. Dax was told it would be one and a half million dollars, US currency. *The Dog* had been charging these "fees" on most of his latest transactions to pay off people in charge of the aircraft, ships, and trucks that moved items around. Buyers understood that if they wanted a guarantee for their purchases, it was necessary to line a few pockets. And they trusted Gavril Novikov with all his connections to make this happen.

Dax asked the obvious question. If this transaction was legit, then why the bribes and sneaking around? Gurkovsky had told Meygan that it wasn't all what it appeared to be on paper, that there were many side deals going on and things moving around that were not supposed to be bought and sold across international lines.

So we're taking advantage of a country in the throes of political and economic turmoil? Dax had asked.

Everyone takes advantage of everyone, Meygan said. She had said this with a coldness Dax took note of.

After a couple more hours of rehearsing and going over details, one of Gurkovsky's men opened the door and said something to Meygan.

"We're getting close," she said, standing up to leave. "I'll see you in about thirty minutes."

43: All the World's a Stage

Dax was led back to Gurkovsky's office.

Gurkovsky studied Dax's face. "You don't look rested."

Dax looked around. "Not the Hilton or Marriott here."

Gurkovsky smirked. "It will go well with your story. The marks on your face, bags under your eyes, bleach top. You look like man who's had it rough lately."

"I have."

"Ms. Knight briefed you on what's going to happen, yes?"

"She did."

Gurkovsky nodded at one of his men, who walked over, pushed Dax's chin up with a finger, and started wrapping a thick gauze around Dax's neck.

"Take it easy," Dax said, the gauze feeling suffocating. Gurkovsky mumbled something and the man eased up and made it a little looser.

Gurkovsky nodded again and the man called Kiril came over with a dark green corduroy sport coat with brown patches on the elbows. After Dax put it on, Gurkovsky stood and looked Dax over.

"It's perfect," Gurkovsky said. "You're a man who wants to blend in right now. Go unnoticed. You wish to be, uh –"

"Incognito?" Dax suggested, but with a sarcasm that was lost to Gurkovsky.

"I like that, *een – koag – nee – toh.*" Gurkovsky said, nodding. "Now listen, good Russian businessman would never go to meeting without tie, so Ms. Knight is going to apologize for you. That you cannot wear one because of injuries to your neck."

Dax touched his throat and shrugged. "Okay."

"Kiril here is going to drive you both to meeting place in few minutes," he said, thumbing at the men in the room.

Gurkovsky clapped his hands rubbing them together. "Showtime, as they say in your Hollywood." He stuck a half-smoked cigar into his mouth and turned back to his desk.

"This isn't a show," Dax said with bitterness.

Gurkovsky smiled. "Of course it is. What is that saying from Shakespeare, that all the world's stage, and all of us players?"

"Yes. From *As You Like It.*"

Gurkovsky waved. "I don't care where it's from. The point is that it is true. I perform for money, you perform for fun."

"When you *perform*, the guns have real bullets and real people die." Dax said.

"Mmm," Gurkovsky said, smiling wickedly with his eyes.

Dax looked around the clandestine office space he'd never again. And he didn't want to.

Gurkovsky sat and leaned back in his chair, regarding Dax. After a minute he said, "Russians and Ukrainians do business similarly and there are some rules of conduct. No need for coaching on talking. But there are some other things you should know. First, maintain eye contact. Looking away makes you appear weak and un-trustable, or that you're not interested in long-term relationship. Next, don't stand around with your hands in your pockets, that's considered sloppy, which would be impolite." He nodded downward with his eyes.

Dax looked down and saw his hands were buried in his pockets. He pulled them out and feigned an apologetic smile.

Gurkovsky continued. "When you sit, do not sit with your legs apart or with one ankle resting upon knee, especially if it points bottom of your shoe at anyone next to you. Showing soles of your shoes is considered rude as they are dirty from dogshit you've been stepping in outside. And don't let your shoes touch seat. Oh, and it is insulting to beckon someone with index finger. I don't think you'll be doing that, but if, say, you summon Ms. Knight or anyone, turn your hand down and motion inward with all four fingers."

As Gurkovsky was talking, Dax thought about something he'd learned in England. Most Europeans count with their hands starting with the thumb, but Americans start with the index finger. This would normally not be a problem, but in England, holding up the index and middle finger together, facing backward at someone, was the equivalent of giving that person the birdie, or saying, *up your bum*, as they used to. Consequently, many Americans have gotten dirty looks at pubs when holding up their hands in this fashion while saying, "I'll take two pints, please."

Dax snapped out of his thoughts.

"It's good to know these things," Gurkovsky was saying. "You know that in election just six years ago, Ukraine declared her independence from Soviet Union? This is an important time for them. It's good to do business right."

Dax shrugged.

Gurkovsky became sterner. "I hope you are taking this seriously, American *actor*. The economy in Ukraine has been in shambles, people are in line early in morning to buy food with coupons from their work. They need to get their defenses up if they are to have any future and they don't have money to piss away. Ukraine never had its own statehood; it was always divided between different European powers. Poland was cruel and sadistic to them. That was key reason why radical Ukrainian nationalism has begun to emerge. They need this, and everything hinges on them believing that you're man who can make this happen, and quickly. Do you understand?"

The little history lesson was interesting, but the agitation in Gurkovsky's voice momentarily startled Dax. He nodded a quick yes and thought of mentioning that he'd heard things were pretty awful back in Russia too and people were lining up for toilet paper, but decided against it. He stood for a moment in awkward silence. "Anything else I should know?" he asked.

Gurkovsky locked eyes with him and said, "Just that you'd better make this happen." He pointed with his cigar at a chair against the wall. "Sit there and wait." He then nodded at one of the men and said something that sounded like a question. The man answered with a *da*, palms up and out. Gurkovsky turned back to Dax, an evil look in his eye. "Kiril here trusts that little actress *suka*. I do not."

Dax realized a part of him didn't fully trust Meygan either.

Save for a few quiet exchanges in Russian that Dax couldn't understand, there was little talking in the next ten minutes or so as Gurkovsky's men prepared what was presumably the contract and whatever else was needed and placed them in a tan, leather messenger bag on Gurkovsky's desk.

Then Meygan walked in, instantly and dynamically adding a new energy to the room. Every man turned, stopped, and stared. Her transformation was astonishing. The pretty, casual, twenty-something American actress had become a classy Russian businesswoman who could be ten years older. Her hair was combed upward around her head in an older updo style, exposing her ears and slender neck, with layers of hair artistically folding over each other and held perfectly in place by a decorative, but not gaudy hairpin. Although makeup on Russian women has a reputation for being heavy and glamorous, hers was subtler, more becoming of seasoned maturity, with eyes highlighted just enough to make one ogle and lips painted a delicate dark crimson red. She wore rectangular, black-rimmed glasses, props that added a smart, professional quality to her face. For clothing, she donned a houndstooth pantsuit with a matching blazer and straight-leg pants. Her V-neck stretch shirt teased by exposing just enough cleavage to start one's imagination going. The full package was a chic, sophisticated and instantly persuasive woman any man would gladly do business with.

She stood for a moment, her mouth straight but her eyes smirking, deciphering the thoughts of the men in the room like a skilled poker player reading the other hands. "Shall we?" she said.

Gurkovsky held up the messenger bag. "Everything is here."

Meygan walked over and retrieved it, slipping her arm into the shoulder strap. She looked at Dax, her eyes quickly scanning him from head to toe. Then, in a perfect heavy accent said, "*I am Mahreenah and I veel ah-seest you today. You oh-r ready, yes?*"

Dax could see she was already practicing her character and not just messing around. He played along by touching his throat and saying in a raspy voice, "*Da. You veel be moheye voice.*"

Gurkovsky shook his head. "Actors ... Just get job done."

Suddenly thinking of something, Dax asked Meygan, "Do you have any gum on you? Four pieces if you do, please." Meygan looked oddly at him then dug a package out of her small purse.

Everyone in the room watched silently as Dax carefully rolled the gum sticks up, two in each roll, then pushed and wedged them into the bottom of his cheeks on either side of his lower jaw. He then slowly looked around the room, taking on the expression of the man he'd seen in the photograph of the real Gavril Novikov.

"Mmm," Gurkovsky said with satisfaction. Then nodded at his men.

The man called Kiril walked up to Dax and put a blindfold on him, then took him by the arm and led him out of the room. From the sound, Dax felt he was being taken down a long hallway. The floor was covered in thin carpet and the smells consistent with an older building. He could hear Meygan's footsteps behind him. A door opened and a rush of cool air hit him. His feet felt a cement floor. After about 100 steps and several turns, he heard a car door open and felt a hand push his head down as he got in.

Dax sat as he heard the car door shut and the other door open as Meygan slid in next to him. Although she wasn't wearing perfume, he recognized the aroma from her hair and other body products from the many times he'd held and kissed her on stage.

This morning, they were going to perform together again, no doubt their last performance as a couple. But this time it was no stage.

As before, he leaned back in his seat, breathed deep, and tried to relax.

44: Air Dispersed Agents

As the car started to move, Dax felt Meygan's hand rest on his leg with a reassuring touch. On impulse, he put his hand on hers and their fingers interlocked. He was filled with both apprehension and anger. To think they'd actually threaten his father. Did they really mean it? After witnessing their murderous capabilities, he wasn't going to call their bluff.

On the assumption that someone would speak in Russian to him, he and Meygan had worked out a simple and silent way to communicate. She would rest her hand on her thigh, whichever one was closest to him, and use her fingers. If she tapped herself with just the forefinger, it meant he should reply with a Yes; if she tapped with four fingers, it meant No. If she lightly rubbed her leg with her whole hand, it meant he either didn't know the answer or didn't wish to discuss the subject. In such a case, she would do her best to answer for him.

After the car had driven a few blocks, he heard Kiril say something to Meygan. She gently removed the blindfold and patted Dax's hair back into place. Blinded by the bright light, Dax squinted and blinked, looking around.

"Hyde street?" Dax asked.

"Yes."

"Toward Russian Hill. How ironic."

All three rode in silence as the car made its way up to Bay Street, then turned left and started in the direction of the Marina District.

Dax looked at Meygan. "Marina, huh. Got a last name, Comrade *MarEEna?*"

She smiled softly, her gaze out the window in deep thought. "Not today."

Buildings and storefronts went by in a blur as Dax contemplated his situation. This might the last time he saw the city. They left the busy high-traffic streets and were now in a quieter neighborhood, somewhere close to the Presidio.

The car came to a stop in front of a modest three-story building Dax had never seen before. Cherry wood color on one side and beige white on the other, it looked like spacious apartment suites inside. Kiril said a few words to Meygan again.

Meygan turned to Dax. "We go now. Remember, you're in charge, but follow my lead." She looked steadily at him. "You okay?"

Dax took a deep breath. "Not really. Let's just do this."

"Nice touch, by the way," she said, smiling and touching his cheeks where the bulges from the gum were. "Kiril will wait here for us. I told him it will probably be between sixty and ninety minutes." She reached up and adjusted the collar on his coat, then looked him in the eye and tapping on the leather bag said, "From here on out, only speak when you *have* to." She then slowly nodded, giving him a signal Dax interpreted as there was a listening device in the bag.

Dax put his thumb and forefinger to his mouth and slid them across, making the *my-lips-are-sealed* gesture. He glanced up and saw Kiril watching intently in the rearview mirror with an almost jealous boyfriend kind of glare. Dax raised his eyebrows to ask, *what are you looking at?* then opened the door.

With her chin up, her eyes straight forward, Meygan walked with purpose to the front door of the building, Dax in tow. As they entered, Dax felt his acting instincts welling up within. He was no longer the small-time theatre actor with the little day job. He was *The Dog of Saint Petersburg*, a clever young businessman who'd successfully navigated the maze of the international arms trade. He was going in there to seal a deal and he needed an air of confidence to pull it off. He strode a little faster, matching Meygan's pace and walking with her, not behind. She glanced up and gave him a small, approving nod.

They walked up one flight of steps, then turned in the direction of the arrow pointing to 220 – 280.

"Two-forty-two," Meygan said quietly.

With his heart racing faster with each step, they approached the room's door. Meygan motioned to Dax. With as much poise as he could muster, he stepped up and knocked three times, deliberately and slowly. As he waited, something Gene Palmer told him flashed through his mind: *The next time you perform, be dangerous, be cunning, even shocking. Take a few more risks. Do exactly, precisely, what your instincts tell you to do. Hold back nothing.*

A muffled voice behind the door could be heard and a few seconds later, they heard the click of a lock and the rustling of the door chain. It opened part way and an older gentleman, perhaps in his early sixties stood in the doorway. His thick, gray eyebrows crinkled up as he looked at Dax.

Meygan took charge. Stepping up beside Dax, she said, "Hello. Please meet Mr. Novikov. We are at the right place, yes?"

Dax took note that Meygan's accent had changed and wasn't so exaggerated. She now exhibited a generic Slavic accent, one that could have been refined from traveling around many places and spending time in the U.S.

The man looked Dax up and down for a few long seconds and then opened the door wider, motioning for them to come in. They entered a hallway. To the left was a doorway that led into what looked like a nice but unused, full kitchen. The hallway opened to a spacious reclining room with a couch, loveseat and coffee table facing a large screen television entertainment center. The place was neat and tidy and looked as if it hadn't been lived in much. There was another table at the far end near the window that could comfortably seat at least six. At that table were two other men, one about the same age, late fifties to early sixties, the other younger, perhaps in his mid-thirties. They both stood as Dax and Meygan approached.

The man who had answered the door and the younger man both wore tailored Western suits – one a navy blue and the other a charcoal gray. Each had a white dress shirt and a plain black tie. Nothing fancy, but professional. The younger man's skin was darker, his hair jet black and wavy. Next to him, the third gentleman, wore a Ukrainian military uniform – dark, olive-green with wide collars and perfectly matching pants. His green tie matched a military visor cap with a shiny black brim that was hanging in the corner on a coat rack. On the breast of the coat were an assortment of medals and ribbons in various shades of red with engravings and symbols.

They came around the table and stood in front. Remembering his coaching, Dax consciously kept his chin up, his hands free, and his eyes unwavering on the three that stood before him.

Meygan stepped forward. "Good morning. I am Marina, and I am here to assist Mr. Novikov who apologizes for his appearance. He was injured in Marseille a few months ago and is having difficulties speaking."

Dax took note that Meygan pronounced *Marseille* with a perfect French accent. Did she speak that as well?

The three men's gaze mostly remained on Dax as she spoke. They were closely looking him over, from the top of his blond-bleached hair, pausing at the bruises and injuries around his face, to his feet. The younger man was eyeing Dax in a particularly skeptical way.

Dax held tight. There had been, of course, the risk that someone here would have known the real Gavril Novikov from a previous personal encounter. Thankfully, these three didn't have that dangerous, homicidal look Dax had come to recognize. They more or less had the appearance one would expect from government officials, not that Dax knew what Ukrainian officials looked like, until now anyway.

"I am Artem Evanko," the first man in the navy-blue suit said. Dax reached to shake the man's hand and took it with a firm, confident grasp.

"I am Colonel Yevhen Zlenko," the man in the military uniform said. Dax shook his hand.

The third man paused for a moment, still watching Dax carefully, then said, "And I am Nazar Ohanian." His accent was different, an odd mix of Slavic and perhaps Arminian. As Dax shook his hand, the man asked, "You have been here in San Francisco?"

Dax nodded, lightly touched his throat, and whispered, "Yes." He added a harshness to his whisper.

"For how long, may I ask?" Ohanian asked, looking hard into Dax's eyes.

Dax looked up and gave a small shrug with his mouth, then held up four fingers, using his thumb through ring fingers.

Meygan, watching, said, "He has been here about four months, in hiding. It has been very difficult for him."

Ohanian looked at his companions, his eyes betraying suspicion, then looked back at Dax. The other two men watched Ohanian, waiting for what may have been a signal of some kind.

Thinking quickly, despite the rising tension, and pulling from his arsenal of improvisation training, Dax raised his chin just a hair to exude more confidence and decided to toss in a psychological bone. He took a step forward and put a hand on Ohanian's shoulder, smiled, and then in a scratchy, breathy voice said, "I almost died. But I am here now, for you." It was a bold move, but adding an emotional element was one of the most effective tools in a salesman's kit. He was now depending on the whole presentation coming together to create a credible illusion, just like on stage.

Ohanian stared for a moment, his body relaxing as he let his guard down. He gave Dax one last lookover, turned to the other men, nodded, then walked around the table to his seat. The other two followed and Dax and Meygan sat down. Dax saw Meygan give him a glance of approval as she slid her chair in.

From the messenger bag, Meygan retrieved a pile of papers. Sifting through them, she separated out three copies of the contract and doled them out, one to each man. Keeping one copy for herself, she set what appeared to be the original before Dax. He picked it up and pretended to peruse while flipping through the first several pages.

Mr. Ohanian glanced briefly at the document in front of him, then looked up and said something to Dax. He spoke in conversational Russian and it sounded like a statement followed by a question. Maintaining steady eye contact, Dax strained with his peripheral vision and saw Meygan tapping her thigh with one finger.

"*Da*," Dax whispered, nodding. He noticed Ohanian looking at the gauze wrapping on his neck, so Dax touched it gently and smiled weakly.

Smiling, Meygan reached up and brushed the back of Dax's neck and said something he couldn't understand, but considering the vocal intonations, was probably along the lines of, *he'll be fine, he's getting better every day*.

Dax smiled back at Meygan, looking at her with sincere respect – she was good.

For the next few minutes, the men at the table carefully read each page, pausing at places and asking each other questions.

Artem Evanko was the next to speak. "What happened to …" He glanced down at the paper, then spoke slowly, struggling with his French: "Importations du nil blue?"

"Blue Nile Imports, yes," Meygan said. "This was a matter of problems with the tax auditors. It could have been cleared up, but it was easier to dissolve the company and use the more stable Stealth Trade Corp. It is listed there on page two, paragraph three, with all licensing and exporting information."

"Yes, I see it," Evanko said, looking from Meygan to Dax. "Do you guarantee this company?" he asked.

"Yes," Dax whispered.

Colonel Zlenko tapped the pages. "On page four, section fifteen, can we have some clarification?"

Dax and Meygan leaned forward, listening intently.

"Where it says, three hundred *air dispersed agents*. I want to be clear on this," said Zlenko.

Although he didn't have a clue what the man was referring to, Dax stared and nodded in total agreement. Zlenko took a small notepad and slid it across the table to Dax and made the motioning of writing on it.

Dax nodded again as if this was all expected and normal, but he could feel cold sweat starting to form on his forehead. Taking the paper, he held the pen and willed his hand not to shake. He could see Ohanian staring intently at his hands with an expression of confusion.

Dax started to write, then whispered a groan and put the pen down, holding his wrist as if he were in pain. Meygan said something in Russian that sounded like, *here, let me help*. She took the paper and wrote two words using perfect Russian Cyrillic letters: химическое ору́жие. She then handed the paper to Dax.

Dax had no idea what the words meant and had to force himself not to look like the village idiot missing from every Russian township north of Saint Petersburg. Moving quickly though, he nodded, turned the paper around, extended it, and slowly showed it to the three men. Zlenko didn't seem to fully understand, but Evanko nodded silently and patted Zlenko on the arm. Ohanian nodded in full agreement. Taking the cue from the fact that no one had verbalized anything and made no attempt to take the paper, Dax ripped it into small pieces and put it into a pile in front of him.

For the next thirty minutes, they continued perusing the contract in silence. On page eight was what looked like a bank wire form, with both English and Ukrainian. It didn't appear to be much different than any other money wire form Dax had seen before. In addition to the usual fields for account numbers and such, there were also extra ones he was unfamiliar with for things like Currency type, Bank SWIFT code, and IBAN # that "will be required for European banks beginning Jan 1, 1997." Dax studied it with interest, but pretended he was examining it for accuracy.

Evanko had another question. "This security and transportation fee?"

Dax nodded and said, "Yes."

Meygan spoke. "Per the original agreement, one point five million US dollars, cash."

Dax gulped but gave no visible reaction. Were they really going to see that kind of money in cash?

Evanko studied the paper for a moment, then looked up and said, "I believe it was for one million."

Thinking quickly, Dax leaned forward, and started to talk, beginning the sentence with, "That was before ..." he let his voice trail off as he touched his throat and coughed.

"That was over six months ago and some of the arrangements have become more, shall we say, complicated," Meygan said. "This is a cushion that is needed."

Evanko and Zlenko exchanged looks and said a few quiet words in Ukrainian.

"It will be good for future business, yes?" Meygan added. The two men looked at Ohanian and then nodded at each other. Everyone sat in silence as Evanko wrote the information on the bank wire form. Dax noticed Ohanian casting glances his way, but Dax kept is eyes on the table.

All at once Meygan said, "Excuse me for one moment." She stood and walked across the room, down the hall and into the kitchen, pressing buttons on her cell phone.

The unexpected move startled Dax and he could feel the pulse in his throat. If she didn't return soon, this would be an opportunity for him to be tested. Ohanian or Evanko could say something in Russian and see right away if Dax understood or not. From down the hall, they could hear Meygan's muffled voice. His mind reeled. He had to appear he had no problem with his assistant leaving his side. In fact, it could be assumed this was the first time *The Dog* had ever used an assistant at all. He casually glanced around.

"Gavril," he heard Ohanian say.

The man knew Gavril by his first name. His heart began to gallop.

45: Deal Done

Please speak English ... Dax thought.

Dax looked up, raising his eyebrows, acknowledging.

Ohanian started to say something in Russian, but Zlenko looked up, and seeing this, Ohanian switched to English. "Where was the attempt on your life?"

Bullet dodged.

Dax cleared his throat while his mind spun. The incident no doubt had been news in Europe and at least one of the men here had knowledge of it, probably Ohanian.

Think, Dax, think ... It was in France. What's in France? Don't panic. Where was the Notra Dame? In Paris, no, no, it wasn't in Paris. Wait. Both Hicks and now Meygan had said Marseille. Great, a place he knew almost nothing of. What should he say? Think! Every place had a main hotel, museum, and landmarks, but what's in Marseille? No idea. Wait, Gurkovsky mentioned a place earlier ... what was it. Come on, think! Ah! La Valentine Saint Menet, that was it!

Dax steadied his eyes on Ohanian, considered the pronunciation, and rasped, "Hotel. *La Valentine Saint Menet.*" He put his hands together and spread them apart quickly, making an explosion sound with a burst of air from his mouth.

The three men exchanged glances and then looked Dax over again, eyeing his injuries and the gauze around his neck. Ohanian's eyes went back up to Dax's and he said, "Thank, God."

"Yes," Dax whispered. Behind him, he heard Meygan's steps as she returned. He felt a physical sensation of relief sweep over him.

"I apologize for that interruption," she said, sitting down. "Everything is good, yes?"

Dax nodded. The three men had gone back to the contract.

After another ten minutes, Evanko finally slid the papers to Dax who pretended to give them one final look over for correctness.

As the minutes ticked by, Dax noticed that Meygan had started to glance at her watch more and even appeared to be slightly anxious, though no one else would have noticed through what had been a flawless performance.

Taking a final look at the last page, Dax set the small pile down, then steepled his fingers together and looked at Evanko. Evanko returned the look and gave a nod. Dax repeated with Colonel Zlenko who also nodded. Dax then looked at Ohanian and waited. The man tapped the papers with his pen and appeared to be stalling. Dax watched for a moment and concluded that Ohanian's uncertainty could probably be cured with one last gesture of good faith.

Snapping his pen loudly, he found the line with the name Gavril Novikov next to it, and using his practiced routine, swirled out the signature, wincing from the pain. He then turned the paper around and with a smile that mixed pleasantness with a touch of arrogance, handed it to Ohanian.

Ohanian studied the signature for a moment, rubbing the paper with his thumbs, deep in thought. After a few agonizing seconds, he lifted his gaze to Dax and said slowly, "I'm sorry. I thought you were left-handed."

Evanko and Zlenko looked up and stared at Dax, then at his hands.

Dax felt his guts go watery and his skin turn cold. Both he and Meygan were too professional to cast a glance at each other, but he did see her hand rubbing her thigh. Was that just nervousness or a signal for him to let her make a move? He waited for a moment, but she remained silent, apparently as lost for words as he was. But then he thought of something, and it brought with it a swift feeling of gratitude for the man who called himself Agent Michael Staggs and the struggle they'd had in the Jeep Cherokee. He also owed Tom Kuka a thanks for those brass knuckles. Holding up his left hand and slowly turning it, he displayed the bruising and cuts around his knuckles, and the blue, purple and red colors of injuries that spilled down the back of his hand. They did look rather painful, and even Marcy Kotowski's magic couldn't make it more realistic.

It was then Meygan stepped in. "Mr. Novikov hurt his hand, as you can see. It was hit by shrapnel. He has had to learn to do many things with his right hand." She turned and gave Dax a wicked grin and wink. "*Everything*, actually."

Dax returned a knowing smile, but then quickly went back and locked eyes with Ohanian. As he watched the wheels turning in Ohanian's head, he understood what might have just happened. Gavril Novikov could very well have been left-handed, and Dax had to hope his move worked. Or, Novikov could be right-handed and this was a test, a test he and Meygan just failed.

The seconds ticked by. Ohanian stared at Dax's hand while Dax pretended he couldn't extend his fingers all the way, slowly moving them in a wave pattern. Although there was some actual pain, he winced and feigned there was much more.

Finally, Ohanian nodded, smiling with embarrassment. "Forgive me," he said. He turned to Evanko and Zlenko and said something. He then turned to Dax and Meygan and said, "We are good to go."

"Excellent," Meygan said, with a gracious but subdued smile to display her displeasure at Ohanian's challenge.

Dax and Meygan watched in silence as all three men put their signatures on the last page of the document. Peripherally, Dax saw Meygan taking glances at her watch. Finally, the papers were handed back to Dax.

Dax carefully went through each page, nodding as if it all made perfect sense to him. He then set it down and waited.

"There is the fee now, yes? US dollars. Paid in cash," Meygan said.

Evanko and Zlenko looked at Ohanian and nodded.

"Excuse me," Ohanian said, standing, then moving around the table and going into the adjacent room. Dax turned to look through the door Ohanian walked through and saw a young man in a military uniform, fully armed, waiting patiently in a chair by the bed.

"*Spacibo*," Evanko said, smiling. Then added, "I hope you recover soon."

"*Da, spacibo*," Colonel Zlenko said, but maintaining his serious military poise.

Dax nodded with a smile, putting his hands together and giving a slight bow.

A minute later, Ohanian returned carrying a brown, leather briefcase with two faux gold combination locks, one for each latch, and set it gently in front of Dax. Ohanian then said the combination numbers in Russian to allow Dax the honor. Dax had studied Russian numbers in class a few times and did pick up the first two – *shehst* and *ahdeen* – but knew he lost the rest. Slowly, using his left thumb, he rolled the first rotating dial to the number six, then rolled the second dial to one. Abruptly, he stopped and shook his hands as if he were in pain. He looked at Meygan who took the cue as he slid the case a little more toward her. She rolled out the rest of the numbers then re-slid the case back in front of Dax.

When the case opened, Dax took a silent breath. Inside were several long, neat rows of 100-dollar bills, multiple stacks in each row. The little piles were bundled in paper wrappers with yellow writing that had the numbers "10,000" printed on them. He tried to think of how an experienced international arms dealer would respond to such a sight. He decided to take the nonchalant approach, as if this were all routine.

Picking up a stack, he thumbed through it then set it back and did the same with one other. Was there really a million and a half bucks here? Everyone in the room watched without speaking. Dax noticed Meygan watching with especially keen interest.

Finally, he shut the lid, looked at everyone and gave a big nod. Everyone stood to shake hands. Ohanian gave Dax one final look to say he still was not 100 percent convinced of everything he had just seen.

"Someone will return with the final copy after the wire transfer has been made. Before three o'clock today," Meygan said. "You will be here, yes?"

"With vodka!" Evanko said, and everyone chuckled.

With a final nod, Dax and Meygan turned to exit with Evanko following to let them out. Behind them, they heard Ohanian say something into his phone and Dax thought he heard the name "Mr. Gurkovsky."

As soon as the door shut, Meygan turned left instead of right toward the steps they had come up earlier. "*Oh my god,*" she whispered.

"*Pssst!*" Dax hissed.

She turned and motioned him to follow her.

"It's this way," Dax whispered, pointing down the hall.

Glancing at her watch, she mouthed, *follow me, NOW!*

Confused but obedient, Dax began to walk as Meygan picked up her pace.

"Kiril is going to be pissed," Dax said quietly.

"*Shhh!*" Meygan said as they approached another staircase at the end of the hall.

They quickly stepped down concrete stairs to what looked like a fire exit at the bottom.

"What did you write on the paper?" Dax whispered.

"Chemical weapons."

"Holy shit." His mind flashed to the conversation he'd had with Hicks. "Air dispersed agents," he muttered.

Meygan hit the large steel bar handle and they both stepped outside. Dax looked around while dislodging the gum from his cheeks and spitting them out. They were at the corner on the other side of the building, opposite of where Kiril was waiting.

Dax held up his hands. "Okay, *Marina*. Now what?"

Meygan set the messenger bag on the sidewalk, then motioned for Dax to follow her a few feet away and behind a large plant pot. "Here," she said, reaching for the briefcase.

Instinctively, Dax pulled back. "What are you doing?"

She looked steadily at him. "Dax, please give it to me."

"Why? What's going on?"

"Right now. They called Gurkovsky to thank him and tell him the deal is done."

"So?" Dax studied her eyes. For the first time since he'd run into her at Gurkovsky's office, she looked somewhat frightened.

Just then a yellow taxi pulled up and Meygan waved at it. She turned back to Dax, a pleading starting to sound in her voice. "Dax, I saved your life. It's time for you to do the same for me."

She had indeed saved him back there, he could not have pulled it off without her. "Meygan," he said, trying to sound like a voice of reason. "You're going to get us both killed."

"No. I'll tell Gurkovsky you had nothing to do with this. It's all on me. Go back to Kiril to show your good faith."

Dax shook his head. "They're not going to believe that."

The taxi honked.

"Dax, *please!*" Meygan said with the frightened voice of a real young woman, not an actress. "Take some of it if you want, but hurry!"

Was it her now throwing *him* a psychological bone? The money was temping for sure, but not worth it. If they found any of it on him, he'd be killed on the spot. If he took it and ran, he'd be running for the rest of his life and probably signing his father's death warrant.

"No," he said firmly. "They'll kill my dad."

"We're out of time," Meygan said, reaching into her purse. Dax watched her hand closely as it came part way out of the zippered opening, revealing the handle of a small pistol.

Dax almost laughed out loud. "You've got to be kidding. You, who were so concerned for me."

One of her eyes flooded, causing her to blink two large tears out. She held out her hand. "This is the only way I can get out. I'm sorry." Her expression then turned hard. "*Now.*"

Dax smiled mockingly at her. "No way you'd shoot me."

Her eyes flashed an icy resolve as she took the pistol further out, her body blocking the cab driver's view. In that moment, Dax saw the Meygan Knight he knew from the show, cold and detached. Only this time, she had a million and a half reasons to do something as desperate as kill someone.

Dax shrugged, shook his head, then extended his arm, handing her the briefcase. She quickly grabbed it then took several steps back.

"This isn't going to end well for you, Meygan."

"It already hasn't," she said softly. She started to turn, then paused. "You were good back there, Dax. You're better than you think. Goodbye." At that she started for the taxi.

"Meygan!" Dax called.

She took one last look, then hopped in while pulling her cell phone out. He heard her say "Go quickly please!" as the door slammed shut, and the car took off.

Dax stood in disbelief until the yellow vehicle turned a corner and disappeared. How many times had he told himself in recent days that nothing else in the world could surprise him, only to be thoroughly flabbergasted by the very next event? He leaned against the plant pot and rubbed his face, but then stopped at the thought of facing Gurkovsky. He had to do it. He had to go back. If he didn't, they'd think he conspired with Meygan. Retrieving the messenger bag, he started casually down the sidewalk around the building.

As he approached the street in front, he could see Kiril on the phone speaking with someone. Kiril stuffed the phone into his jacket then looked around frantically at the front of the building. His head swiveled to the adjacent sidewalk as his eyes locked on Dax. Swinging the car door open, he leaped out drawing a pistol and started walking quickly at Dax. Dax raised both hands as Kiril yelled something in Russian he didn't understand.

"*Chto ty skazal?*" Dax asked. "*Govorite po-angliyski?*" Kiril yelled again.

"You gonna shoot me?" Dax asked. "Go ahead."

Kiril motioned with the gun for him to move to the car.

"Oh, you want me to get in. I'd have never guessed."

"*Yeys! Gyet een!*" Kiril yelled.

"Alright," Dax said, then strode quickly to the car, Kiril pushing him from behind. He dropped heavily into the seat, the engine roared on, and the back of his head slammed into the seat rest as Kiril gunned it.

Dax watched Kiril in the rearview mirror. "I didn't take it. Your boss know that? Meygan said he knew. Or was going to."

Kiril ignored him, his eyes swirling with fear and anger.

"Where are we going?" Dax asked. Driving fast and screeching around corners, he had to brace himself from falling over. Feeling nothing left to lose, he asked, "Did Meygan sleep with you to get this gig?"

"*Zavali yebalo!*" Kiril hissed.

Dax recognized the phrase and decided to keep quiet. After a few minutes of reckless driving, he almost felt carsick. That would be something if they got pulled over. This guy with a gun who knows little English, and Dax with a contract for an international arms deal. That'd be some fun explaining to a judge.

He thought more about Meygan as the car screeched around turns and found himself getting angrier at her. If Gurkovsky didn't believe Dax had nothing to do with this, she will have killed him and maybe his father with this little stunt. She had no right to take that kind of risk.

They finally pulled into the parking lot of a small strip mall. Kiril stopped the car with a jolt in front of a drycleaners.

Dax barely had time to breathe again before the door next to him was yanked open and Kiril motioned with his head to get out. Complying, Dax was led a couple parking spaces down to a larger sedan with tinted windows. Kiril opened the back-seat door and motioned for Dax to get in.

Gurkovsky sat on the other side of the seat calmly sucking a cigar and doing a decent job faking composure. Wisps of smoke floated up and out a partially cracked window.

Dax held the messenger bag out. "Here's your contract, deal done!" he said with mocking cheerfulness.

Gurkovsky turned and gave the bag a sideways glance before grabbing it and throwing it on the floor between them. He then turned and studied Dax. "Where is she? That little bitch friend of yours."

Dax stared back, unwavering. "I have no idea. And she was never my friend." He had believed all morning he was going to die anyway and now, resolved to fate, felt no fear. It was kind of nice not to be freaked out for once.

"You must know something." Gurkovsky growled.

"She told me goodbye and got into a taxi. I had no idea she was planning this."

Gurkovsky frowned and studied Dax's eyes. "And you just let her walk with all that money? Nothing for you?"

"She pulled a gun on me. And why would I steal from a man who threatened my father?"

"Bullshit," Gurkovsky said. He stared into Dax's eyes for what seemed like an eternity. He then snatched the messenger bag off the floor, undid the straps and began rifling through it. He pulled the contract out, slapped it on the seat, then unzipped an inner pouch. He pulled out a black, rectangular device with what looked like a small antenna. He held the object up. "I heard you say, 'Kiril is going to be pissed.'"

"Yes, I said that after she took off."

Gurkovsky threw the bag back on the floor and said something to the driver, who abruptly got out and yanked open the door next to Dax. The man began to roughly frisk Dax, feeling up and down his arms, then around his back, his pockets, and down each leg. He motioned for Dax to raise himself, then reached around and took his wallet. Saying something to Gurkovsky, he handed Gurkovsky the wallet, shut the door, and returned to the driver's seat.

Dax watched as Gurkovsky opened his wallet and looked at the contents. Gurkovsky looked up in disgust.

"Drained my little bank account to get that the other day," Dax said. After a pause, he added, "She called and said I had nothing to do with it, right?"

Gurkovsky tossed the wallet at him, then eyed him. "I don't think I need to tell you what will happen if I find out you're working with that *chertovski suka*."

Dax returned the hard stare. "I told you. It's not worth my father's life, and it's not worth having to look over my shoulder for the rest of my life, expecting to see you or Mr. Scarface."

A small smile formed on Gurkovsky's mouth, but it vanished quickly. He sat back and pulled on the cigar. "She threatened to go to police and tell them everything. Do you think she would be that stupid?"

"I honestly have no idea. She did look desperate though."

Gurkovsky snorted and looked away. "She will be desperate," he muttered to himself. Then he turned to Dax. "Get out."

"You're not going to kill me?"

"You're not worth the trouble to bury you. But you will be if I ever have to deal with you again." Gurkovsky looked him with an expression of such passive rage that Dax decided to scram before the man changed his mind. Holding up one hand in surrender, he reached for the door handle. As soon as he'd gotten out and closed the door, the car backed out with a small squeal, turned, and headed out of the parking lot, Kiril following.

"You're in trouble, Kiril," Dax said quietly to the cars as they exited the parking lot. He stood on the sidewalk for a moment, then turned and noticed a reflection of himself in the tall glass window of the drycleaner shop he was standing in front of. He stared at his blond hair, the sport coat he was wearing, and thought about all that had happened recently. He didn't know if he felt like laughing, crying, or screaming.

A woman came out of the cleaners, paused, and looked him up and down for a moment, alarm spreading over her face. She turned and hurried to her car.

Dax smiled. "Thank you for the prayers, Sam."

46: After the Storm

Jim Kirkland had been rubbing the bridge of his nose all morning. With each rehearsal, things had steadily gone from bad to worse, and he decided today was the day he was going to make the decision whether or not to continue with the show.

Sharon Toomey, Jim's faithful assistant, sat next to him with a copy of the script. At first, she had thought it all was somewhat amusing, but now it was really rubbing everyone wrong, and seriously affecting morale. When no one could get answers from Jim, the cast had come to her demanding to know why this Mario guy, an arrogant jerk who couldn't act his way out of a paper bag, had been given a crucial role in the show. She had not known the answer and was dying to know herself.

"Oh my *gawd*, really?" Dillon Christie was saying on the stage. He was staring at Mario, his partner for the scene. After three rehearsals, Mario still did not know his lines and was not only fumbling but smirking and shrugging the whole thing off.

"This is ridiculous! I work with professionals," Dillon said.

Mario looked up, his face suddenly twisting in anger. "Watch your mouth, lollipop."

Dillon stepped back, wide-eyed.

Sitting in the front row, Glenn Brock was also at his wits end. Although cast in a minor role, he'd been excited to be a part of this production as it was going to get a lot of attention. It was sickening that this guy could be ruining it for everyone. The big bald man stood up as Mario took a step toward Dillon. He felt a hand on his arm and looked down at Dennis Sheridan.

"Not worth it, Glenn," Dennis said.

"My patience is at zero with this guy," Glenn said.

"All of ours is. Just be cool. Something will give soon."

Mario took another step forward and gave Dillon a shove.

Dillon looked at Jim with outstretched arms. "What the hell!" he yelled.

Glenn hopped up on the stage and started walking at Mario. "Back off dude. Right now."

Mario turned and sneered at Glenn. "No, you better back off, man. You've no idea who you're messing with."

Aaron Tisdale sat in the back row surrounded by his usual junk food wrappers and soiled napkins. He would have been amused at the whole scene, but his mind was on other things, mainly Dax Ribeiro. For the last two days he'd been calling Les Abraham because he wanted to talk more, but there was no answer. That was odd; Les always answered his phone. Besides, the man had classes to teach and had been keenly interested in how Jim's show was going. But now both Les and Dax were nowhere to be found. It all had to be intertwined somehow, but he either wasn't smart enough to connect the dots, or just didn't have enough to go on. He dipped three French fries in ketchup and stuffed them in his mouth.

"Everyone, take twenty!" Jim yelled, standing up. The decision had been made. He was going to tell the cast goodbye and good luck. In all his years of directing theatre, never had he been put in such a position, and he would never forgive Cheryl Bronson or Rinaldo Silvestri for their parts in all this.

Mario hopped off stage and began strutting up the main aisle toward the exit. Everyone stared, waiting for Jim to say something, but Jim kept his eyes forward and ignored Mario as he strode by. Aaron cautiously watched as Mario shoved the auditorium doors open and exit. He had become afraid of Mario during the last couple rehearsals and didn't want to look him in the eye.

Motioning with his hands, Jim said, "Gather around everyone. I have something I need to tell you." Slowly, and with an air of despondence, the cast and crew of *Wild Hearts* made their way to Jim.

Mario strode across the lobby to the front door, muttering curses. They had no right to speak to him that way. They wouldn't if they knew who he was. He was going to show them. He was going to show all of them. He suddenly had a brilliant idea. He would call Meygan and tell her she's in the show too. He'd have his dad make Jim give her a part, a good part. She could show him what to do and then he'd get the respect he deserved. He paused at the door, dialing her number. Her phone immediately went to voice mail, as if it had been powered off.

"It's me. Call me back, right away," he said in a commanding tone. "Bitch better say yes," he mumbled to himself. Snapping the phone shut, he shoved the front door open and walked out into the cool air of the city. Turning right, he decided to have a cigarette in the doorway next to the theatre. As he snapped open his Zippo lighter, two car doors thumped shut behind him and two men began walking toward him.

As they approached, Mario glanced up and then did a double take. These men had an appearance and presence about them that Mario was familiar enough with to make him pause.

Mario sucked on his cigarette pretending to be unconcerned as the two men walked up and stood on either side of him. He looked up and gazed into the cold eyes of a huge man with a vicious-looking scar running down the side of his face.

The car the men had come from pulled up adjacent to them along the curb. The man with the scar motioned with his head for Mario to get in. Fear suddenly seized Mario. He reached behind him where he always kept a Beretta model 81 .32 caliber pistol tucked in his belt, but he didn't get far. The man with the scar moved with lightning speed, clutching Mario's arm in a vice-like grip. Mario was led to the car, where he was roughly shoved in.

As the car began to move, Mario glanced back to see Aaron Tisdale standing in the doorway, staring in wide-eyed wonder. It was the last time Mario would see the Treasure Box theatre.

***

Dax was nearing the end of an almost eighteen-hour drive to Santa Fe. Exhausted and weary, he had not checked into any motel along the way, but rather took power naps here and there, outside a diner or at a truck stop. The seats in the small rental car were not as comfortable as his Mustang's which he really missed right now.

The trip had been pleasantly uneventful. He'd even kept the radio off, opting for the sounds of the engine, other cars blowing by, and the rumble of motorcycles.

His plan was to call Tommy Hicks as soon as he got to his father's place and tell him everything. It was good that Jack Dauer was in custody, but the man called Michael Staggs still running around was bad. Dax didn't want to have to look over his shoulder the rest of his life. Hopefully interests had shifted to more important things. After all, he was just an actor, an imposter, a nobody really. The real *Dog* was dead. Gurkovsky had said it – Dax wasn't worth the trouble to get rid of the body.

Ninety minutes later he pulled up in front of the single-family home his father had occupied for the last several years. Built in 1964, the one-story, two-bedroom, flat-roofed structure would more resemble a mobile home in the eyes of someone from California. But it was spacious and comfortable, especially for one person. Unless dad had acquired a girlfriend by now.

Nah – the only woman he ever loved was mom.

Dax got out and looked around, carefully scanning up and down the street, but saw nothing. The front yard was barren, mostly dirt but with a few flattened weeds. The tan color of the siding and dirty white trim was just as he remembered from close to eight years ago. The old Chevy pickup was still parked in the yard.

He walked up the three steps to the front door. To the left of the door was a small card table, two Adirondack chairs and an old rocking chair. A new-looking mat rested on the doorstep with a Brazilian flag and a quote underneath that Dax recognized as a Portuguese proverb: *Depois da tempestade, vem a bonança*. Dax paused and smiled, remembering. "After the storm comes the easiness," he said to himself, hoping that was true.

He knocked three times loudly, reminding him of how he'd knocked on the apartment door, Meygan beside him. He shoved the thought from his mind. After a minute, he heard some shuffling behind the door.

As the door lock rattled, a strong emotion began rising in him, starting from the gut, and working its way to his head. It was a strange combination of rage, terror, loss, loneliness and a few other unidentifiable but powerful feelings. His father had lived here alone with hardly a phone call from Dax. So much had Dax been wrapped up in his unhappy career and struggles to get more prominent acting parts, he'd neglected one of the most important parts of his life – his remaining family. And he should have made more effort to stay in touch Sam as well.

The door opened and a familiar but aged face looked at him. His father's full but short hair was now completely gray and rested on his head in natural curls and waves. His skin was darker and more cracked, no doubt from the New Mexico sun. He wore a light cotton short-sleeved shirt with the top three buttons undone, revealing curly gray chest hairs.

He looked Dax up and down, pausing on Dax's hair, and then his eyes became wide. "David?" he said in disbelief.

"Hello, *pai*," Dax said, his eyes filling with tears.

"What are you doing –" Paulo Ribeiro started to say. But his words were cut short as Dax threw his arms around his father's neck and began to cry. Standing there sobbing, soaking his father's shirt, Dax could not remember when he had cried so hard. He cried for time lost, he cried for his mother who had been taken early, he cried for the baby he almost had with Sam, and he cried for the innocent people who had died recently because of him. He even cried for his childhood friend Typhoon and wondered where he was and what he was doing.

***

It was almost three days later when Dax awoke. Glancing out the window, the sun shown in shards through small, cotton-fluffy clouds under a rich, blue sky. He stood, stretched, and went to the window. Parts of the ground around the house and between homes were graced with small trees and shrubs covered in leaves of various shades of light green, gold, orange, and red. It looked to be a beautiful but warm day.

The last forty-eight plus hours had gone by in a blur, mostly because Dax had been asleep. He remembered a couple quick meals with his dad, some light talk about recent events, a couple trips to the bathroom. The rest of the time spent was in the wonderful world of deep, dreamless sleep.

He sat at the small kitchen table sipping coffee while his father made toast, cooked eggs, and cut slices of papaya. Next to his cup was a Ryrie Study Bible he'd been thumbing through, having his dad translate the Portuguese words. That was the language he should have studied years ago, not *pa-Russki*.

He didn't know what time it was and didn't care. It was glorious being able to go whole days without a care about time. So deep was he in thought, he hardly heard the knock at the door or saw his father put down the knife and exit the kitchen, muttering something about how he couldn't remember having so many visitors in one week.

Dax heard voices at the door, and then his father call him. *Uh oh …*

As he went to the door, his father stepped aside and standing in the doorway was a man and woman. The man wore khaki pants and a green nylon jacket. On the left breast of the jacket was a silver star inside a circle displaying the words U.S. MARSHAL. The woman's outfit was nearly identical except she wore silver-gray cargo pants. Under the right side of the jackets of each of them there was a bulge, no doubt pricey pistols with high-capacity magazines. They both gave Dax big, broad smiles.

The man spoke. "Good morning, Mister, uh, ree-bee –"

"Ribeiro," Dax said, leaning against the door frame and crossing his arms.

"Yes, of course. My name is Jones," the man said. "And this is Miller," he said gesturing at the woman.

"Jones. And Miller," Dax said, looking back and forth at the two.

"We're from the US Marshals," Miller said, still wearing a big smile.

"*The*, US Marshals, huh," Dax said slowly, mimicking Jones, but neither seemed to sense that.

On cue, they produced leather-bound wallets and opened to reveal two business card-sized IDs with the Department of Justice symbol. Each card said, THIS IS TO CERTIFY THAT TYLER JONES (and AMANDA MILLER) IS REGULARLY APPOINTED AND SWORN AS A DEPUTY U.S. MARSHAL. Another card-sized ID below had a picture with some stamps and signatures.

It all looked good. Authentic. Genuine.

"Sorry to disturb," Miller said as she produced a photo from a jacket pocket and held it up. On it was the beautiful face of Meygan Knight bearing her classic softened and seductive smile. The image looked like it had been copied from a headshot Meygan had routinely distributed to various casting agencies and directors around the city.

"Do you know this woman?" Miller asked.

Dax put his chin to his chest and started laughing quietly. The two agents looked at each other.

Dax nodded to the chairs on the porch. "Please have a seat, *marshals*," Dax said. "I'll get us each a bottle of water and we can talk. Gimme a minute." He shut the door, leaving the couple standing outside.

His father was behind him. "Who are they, son?"

"I need to use your phone," Dax said. "I'll tell you everything." He went to the kitchen where a wall phone with a long curly cord hung next to the pantry, similar to the one in the Godwin Theatre's kitchen. He pulled a card from his wallet and quickly dialed a number.

A familiar voice answered. "Yes?"

"Agent Tommy Hicks," Dax said. "How are you?"

"Dax? Is that you? Where the hell are you this time? We've been worried sick!"

"Yes, it's me. Listen. I didn't kill Agent Milevoi and that other guy, what's his name …"

"Jacoby."

"Yes, him. It wasn't my fault."

"We know you didn't. But we need to talk."

"Look, you're gonna trace this call anyway, but I'm at my father's place in Santa Fe. His name is Paulo Ribeiro. I need you come down here right away."

"Dax –"

"Just get on the first plane and come here now, please. And if you have any people in this area, send them over."

"Why? What's going on?"

"Some folks who say they're with the US Marshals are here."

"*What!*"

"See you soon, Hicks." Dax hung up. Retrieving three bottles of water from the refrigerator, he started to the front door. He paused and put a hand on his father's shoulder. "It's okay, pops. Just another exciting day in the life of a professional actor."

Paulo Ribeiro watched with wonder as Dax stepped outside. As the door closed, he heard his son say in a slightly strange accent, "*So, Agents Jones and Miller. You veesh to toalk about Meez Knight, yes?*"